Brian Sigmon

ARCHIMEDES

briansigmon.com

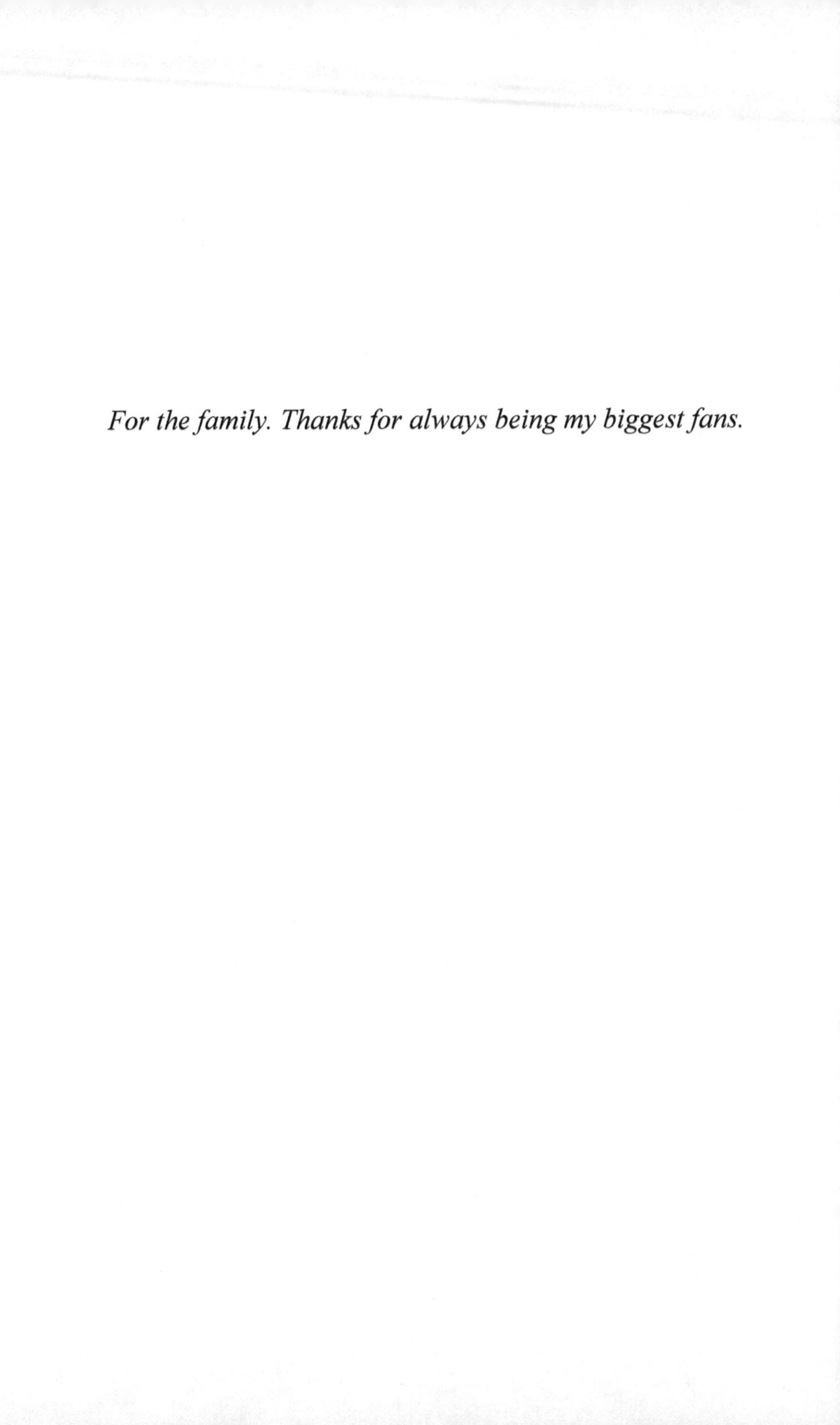

For the family. Thanks for always being my biggest fans.

Contents

Prologue

Verona reflected two cold slivers of light. The captain smiled as his ship approached the colony. Twin cylinders, the usual arrangement.

The engineers said it was about holding position. Rotation provided gravity. Two can cities, rotating opposite each other, canceled out gyroscopic effects and kept the colony pointed toward its Dyson Array. Stable orientation brought to you by the conservation of angular momentum.

That was true. O'Neill cylinders were a standard design. But the captain figured it was psychological, too, especially this far out. The setup meant you had a partner, no matter what. Hard to feel lonely when there were always two of you.

He looked at his gem and shook his head. Verona A and Verona B. They hadn't even bothered to name the cylinders. Lazy or unimaginative, or maybe just practical.

Miranda hung in the distance. There was a lot of Dorium down there on the odd, carved-up little moon. Well, enough to make a colony like Verona worthwhile anyway. It was small potatoes compared to the big operations around Neptune and Saturn's moons. But they got by out here. Nine thousand people, give or take, mining and refining and grabbing enough market share to draw attention. That's why the captain was here, after all.

"Verona's in range, sir," the first mate said.

He glanced at her. "Thank you." She was ice cold, as always. If she felt squeamish about what was about to go down, it didn't show. She'd been by his side for the better part of two decades. They'd done a lot of bad and survived worse. Still, this was a step beyond. He wouldn't blame her if she hesitated. Around the bridge, the rest of the crew was tense with anticipation.

"The gunner's awaiting your order," she said. Even her voice was cold.

"Remember, no survivors."

"Yes, sir."

The captain nodded. The first mate tapped her gem. "Fire."

There was no blaze or flash out the window, no shudder throughout the ship to let them know the weapon had fired. Just a wavy disturbance at those two slivers of light before a glowing, jagged gash appeared across Verona. Both cylinders ripped open, and damaged hull pieces turned outward like blossoming flowers. Their integrity failed as immense stress twisted the structures of steel and carbon. The openings yawned wider and the two cans flung debris into space and across the gap between them. Still they turned, their own inertia compiling the damage in a wicked feedback loop. Angular momentum giveth, and angular momentum taketh away.

Something gave out and the cylinders collapsed toward each other. Their fractured hulls slammed together at incredible velocity. The twisting impact drove the two cans apart in a violent burst, like spinning coins colliding and then flying in different directions. Liberated atmosphere swirled around the scene in a hazy spiral. Seconds later, the first of the bodies began to tumble out.

The captain set his jaw as he watched the destruction, debris and corpses drawing into a trail of death tens of kilometers long and growing. "Move us in," he told the first mate. "Keep our turrets hot, not that we need them. Remember, no comms and no survivors."

She began barking orders into her gem. No hesitation. Ice cold. Beside her, the captain narrowed his eyes. Everything was different now.

Chapter 1

Two loaders dealt with the wrecked shipping cubes. Six of the huge containers lay dented and scratched in Ligeia's loading area, their doors smashed open and contents spilled across the ground. It would take the bots a while to gather and repack everything.

Port Ligeia's acting cargo chief ignored the mess and focused on the twenty-six other loaders transferring the intact containers to the monorail cars. The stacks had dwindled, but there were still a lot left. He checked his gem for the fourth time in as many minutes.

"How much longer?" he said to his deputy.

"There's no more coming off the elevator," the younger man said. "Just these stacks. Forty-eight minutes, according to the Coordinator."

"I trust the Coordinator about as far as I can throw it right now," the chief said. "First the train's late, now this shit. They don't pay me enough to babysit rogue AIs."

"Hacked, sir," the deputy said.

"Huh?"

"The loaders were hacked, they didn't go rogue. That only happens in the movies. Now that we've rebooted the system—"

"Whatever," the chief said with a wave, then frowned as his gem buzzed with an alert. He glanced at his wrist. The message hovering above the small device flashed red, indicating an anomaly. *Cameras 22159 and 22181 obstructed.*

"Yeah, no kidding," the chief said as he tapped twice, clearing the alert.

"Another breach, sir?" the deputy asked.

"Nah, those two bots back there keep blocking the cameras, creating blind spots." He jerked his thumb over his shoulder. "What are they supposed to do? It's a big mess, all the usual protocols are out the window. Wish there was a way to mute these alerts, though. They keep pinging me every time it happens."

"Have you tried—"

"Don't worry about it, it's annoying but it's fine. Let's just get this train loaded up before we get further behind. Port authority's gonna bust my butt enough as it is. Everybody's on edge after what happened out at Miranda last month."

"Yes, sir," the deputy said.

Behind the chief's back, the two bots continued cleaning up debris. Loader 315 obstructed two more cameras, which the Coordinating AI registered and sent as an alert to the chief's gem. The bot stayed in front of the cameras for six seconds as it pushed aside a broken pallet and picked up the shrink-wrapped machines beneath. In those six seconds, a figure darted out from between two of the downed containers, lifted the top off a crate, and piled its contents into a backpack. The figure ducked back out of sight just as the bot moved and the camera's view was restored. Fifty meters away, the chief cursed and cleared the latest anomaly as he watched the other bots impatiently.

Ben Ashley sat at the controls of Loader 315, sweating in the cramped and rarely used driver's seat. He nudged the bot forward, blocking the cameras yet again, and watched on the screen as Tiro finished emptying the crate. Tiro gave the bot a quick thumbs-up, then disappeared into the shadows.

"Finally," Ben whispered. He opened his gem and tapped out a message to Jess. *Open sesame.* He smiled. He could almost hear Jess's eyes roll from here.

A moment later the bot's lower hatch opened. Ben shoved his gem in his pocket and crawled out, careful to stay on this side of the loader. There was a light hum as the hatch closed behind him, and he ran forward and joined Tiro between the containers. The bot, now remotely controlled by Jess, moved away to grab more debris.

"Nice driving," Tiro said as Ben crouched beside him. "Looked just like an AI. I don't know how you do it. Even I wasn't sure there was a person in there at the controls."

"Guess all my goofing off at Novalink paid off," Ben said. "How's our haul looking?"

Tiro grinned and gestured behind him where six large, overstuffed backpacks leaned against the side of the container.

Ben's eyes widened. "Six? How are we supposed to get that out of here?"

"Eight," Tiro corrected, pointing to two more farther down. "We'll manage, the truck's close. What, did you think we were robbing the port for a handful of boxes? There's so much good stuff in here, man. Gems, those next-gen batteries from Venus, links, wearables. That one over there is packed with nothing but chips and components for navigation AIs. That alone is well into six figures."

Ben whistled. Six figures. He'd warned Tiro about going too big, but Tiro never listened. Now, even Ben started to get greedy. Six figures was a big sum for anybody, especially a couple of kids from the colony's Third Ward. That kind of money could do a lot for them and their friends. For Simon.

Or get you all into a ton of trouble, Ben reminded himself. He had no qualms about robbing the people on the other end of this cargo shipment—most of those business owners and traders had sold out to the Interior. Titan was better off if they had to live a little leaner. Stealing from them was practically a moral imperative as far as Ben was concerned. Getting caught, on the other hand, well. He had no desire to be shipped off to a prison can, or worse.

"Let's get out of here," he said. He and Tiro heaved one pack each onto their backs. Ben winced as he tightened the straps, then slung a second over his shoulder. "These are heavy," he said. "I can get one more, but not two."

Tiro struggled to manage three packs as he bent to lift one more. He looked like he could handle the weight, but the packs were bulky and hard to maneuver. Whatever he tried, he couldn't get them to stay put. "Damn, me neither," he said, dropping the fourth pack. "Leave these two, we'll come back for them."

Ben opened his mouth to protest, then shut it. Best not to argue with Tiro right here between two containers. He'd just lose the argument anyway. "In that case, let's take two each," he said instead. "We have to come back anyway, and this way we'll move faster."

Tiro nodded, then hefted two backpacks and opened his gem. *Ready*, he typed. Jess didn't respond, but they heard a low whine as Loader 315 drove away at full speed.

Seconds later there was a crash at the far end of the containers, followed by a loud and surprisingly elegant string of curse words. Tiro and Ben grinned. That grizzled cargo chief was almost a poet.

A metallic thump sounded on the other side of the container as the bot closest to them shut down. Similar clanks and pings across the loading area told them the other bots also went off-line for the second time that night.

"Let's roll," Tiro said, and darted out from between the containers. Ben came out right behind him, and the two of them sprinted past the wrecked containers, across the short open space between them and the port wall. They ran awkwardly, each with one pack on their back and another slung over a shoulder.

"Hope those cameras are down," Ben said, his voice low.

"They'd be all over us already if they weren't," Tiro said, switching a backpack to his other shoulder.

Ben and Tiro made their way two hundred meters along the exterior wall of Port Ligeia, mostly hidden by the wall's shadow. To their right lay the loading area, where moments earlier the bots had been busy loading monorail cars with the latest shipment from the spaceport up above. Beyond the loading area, the Terminus stood huge and imposing, stretching as far as they could see above them and to either side. The elevator shaft to the spaceport proper cut a vertical path up the Terminus, vanishing toward its center somewhere overhead.

Living on Ligeia, you couldn't help being aware of the Terminus, but Ben didn't like being this close to it. He couldn't shake a feeling of limitation and confinement whenever he glanced at it. Titan was the largest of Saturn's colonies. Its two cylinders, Ligeia and Kraken, were huge by most standards. But beyond that wall lay a whole *universe*. Ben looked away. He focused his attention instead on the eastern gate of the port, where he and Tiro were headed.

At the moment the gate was smashed outward, the left one coming off its massive hinges, with a dented cargo container propping it open. Jess had done a good job earlier, and they'd gotten a decent break. That gate was the one part of Ben's plan that hinged on a bit of luck, but fortune smiled on them and here they were.

He and Tiro ran quickly, not worried about being seen. The port was designed for cameras to provide surveillance, which they could do in much lower light than human eyes. Not having lights on the wall in case the cameras went down was a clear weak point in the design, which Ben's plan had taken advantage of. Jess's hack—or rather, the security response to it—rebooted the whole system and reset all the loader bots and the Coordinating AI that observed and managed the process. It also took the cameras off-line, buying fifteen minutes of unobserved time for Ben and Tiro to escape.

So far everything had gone according to the plan Ben drew up. Hack a couple of loader bots to drive them remotely, then topple some containers and create a huge, loud mess. Using the distraction, another hacked bot grabs a shipping container and bolts for the eastern gates. Unless they were complete morons, port security would realize they'd been hacked and trigger a system reboot, to wipe and reset any other compromised loaders. Ben counted on that; he and his friends weren't after a whole container. They just needed a way in with security down. As long as the bot made it far enough to break through the eastern gate before it lost power, Tiro could get in through the breach while the cameras were off-line. When the port authorities had everything back to normal, or what they thought was normal, Tiro could load up a few bags from the spilled containers with Ben providing cover. Then create a second big, loud mess to trigger another shutdown so Tiro and Ben could escape. Simple. Easy.

Of course, it meant breaking into the port hours earlier to install their program in three of the bots. And Ben sitting inside a bot the whole time, at the mandatory but rarely used human controls, so he could reinstall Jess's code after the first security reboot. And then driving it precisely enough to fool the system into thinking an AI was in control. Not to mention delaying the monorail train the bots were loading so they'd have to stack up the containers as they came off the elevator instead of going right to the tracks. *Yeah*, Ben thought with a grin. *This was a pretty tight plan.* Now the end was in sight.

Ben and Tiro got to the breach without incident. The bot Jess had crashed earlier lay on its side in front of the ruined gate, with the container it carried extending forward and through the large, broken doors. Tiro led Ben to the opening he'd passed through earlier, still under the cover of the wall's shadows. There were no human guards in sight; despite the wreck here, the container in the gate was still sealed, and all the attention was back at the container stacks and the new mess Jess had made moments ago.

The breach was narrow. Tiro went through first, and Ben passed the four backpacks to him one at a time. Then Ben squeezed through, and he and Tiro took up the packs again and moved farther east along the wall, outside now, to where their friend Miles waited beside a nondescript personal van.

"Hell yeah, boys!" Miles said, way too loud, when he saw them walk up with two packs each. Ben winced; probably nobody could hear them out here, but you never knew.

"Shut up, you trying to tell the whole colony where we are?" Tiro said. He dropped his backpacks and leaned them against the van. "We have four more packs inside. Load these up while we go back for them."

"At least tell me what you got," Miles said, unzipping a pack and peeking in. "Holy— Are these gems?"

"Damn right. Novalink Twenties, I think," Tiro said. "I didn't get a good look."

"Whew," Miles said. "What else is in there?" He started to dig through the backpack.

Tiro snatched it from him and closed it. "Load them up. We'll sort it back at the house." Miles made a face, but didn't argue.

Ben checked his gem. Crap, the time was short. He didn't like it. "Hey man, let's leave the other bags and get out of here. We're away clean with some good stuff. Going back in is too much of a risk."

"We have enough time and it'll double our take. No way we're leaving those packs behind." Tiro started back along the wall toward the gates.

"Tiro." Ben said, grabbing his arm. "Use your head. The plan was one time in, one time out. It's gone well so far, but not perfect. We can't extend—"

"We have six minutes and I'm going back in. You want to wait out here, I'll remember it when we're sorting out shares.

Or you can stop being a punk. Your call, but make it now. We're on the clock." He jogged off toward the gates.

"Shit," Ben said. They'd been friends since they were twelve; he should have known by now not to count on Tiro backing down. He took off, caught up to Tiro outside the breach. "You know I'm not gonna let you go in alone."

Tiro smiled. "Yeah, I know. Six minutes. Let's go."

Ben followed Tiro through the breach and back along the inner wall of the port, moving rapidly now with nothing to carry. In no time they were back between the containers, strapping on the four remaining backpacks.

"Three minutes," Ben whispered. "Gotta hurry."

"Wait," Tiro hissed, grabbing Ben before he left cover. He pointed straight ahead, where a guard had walked right into their path. The guy stopped directly between them and the port wall.

"Thanks," Ben said. "I would've run right past him."

The guard held a plasma gun loosely, his gaze wandering across the yard. He looked bored, like his mind was somewhere else. Ben wished the rest of him would go somewhere else too.

"What's he doing?" Ben asked.

"Doesn't seem suspicious or anything. Just decided to stand right there, I guess. Bad luck."

Ben checked his gem again. "Two point five minutes. We gotta get rid of this guy."

Tiro dropped one of his packs and pulled out a small object. It looked like one of the Novalinks Miles was so excited about. He threw it at one of the downed containers, where it bounced off the side with a loud ping.

If the guard noticed it, he didn't care. Guy didn't even turn his head.

"Try again," Ben said.

Tiro grabbed a second Novalink and threw it harder this time. Ping! Again, nothing.

"Is this guy deaf?" Tiro said. He threw another one, which clanged off the metal loud enough that Ben worried other guards would hear it too. "Dammit, that's three good gems. More than five grand."

"We're stuck," Ben said, checking his own gem again. His heart raced as he watched the seconds tick down. Under two minutes now. He didn't like the idea of being trapped here, but he was never one to give up. They could message Jess, maybe she could hack in a different way this time. Or maybe Miles could make some noise outside, trigger another shutdown that way. Stay patient, calm. Work the problem.

"Can you do that energy power thing?" Tiro asked. "Make a noise or a light or something?"

Ben frowned. "The Aurora's a mutation, not a superpower, and no. It's risky as hell and there's nothing for me to act on. Even if there was, it would take time we don't have."

"Come on, man. What if—"

"No," Ben said. "Trust me, if I thought it would work, I would try."

"All right," Tiro said. He started to throw another gem, but Ben stopped him. "Don't waste it. We're out of time anyway. We're hidden for now, even after the system reboots. Sit tight, let's message Jess and get her and the others to work on it. They'll find us a way out."

"Screw that, we're going."

"No way, he'll see us," Ben said.

"We can take him out."

"Huh? That's not part of the plan. No violence, remember?"

"Plans change," Tiro said. "Let's go. Now."

"What are you—"

Tiro bolted out and ran straight toward the guard. Ben watched from his hiding spot, unable to move. It happened in a blur. The guard saw Tiro and reacted, too slow. Tiro closed the distance as the guy raised his gun, then swung one of the backpacks and clocked him in the head. The guard sprawled on the ground, motionless. Tiro darted past him into the shadow of the port wall.

Ben snapped out of his stupor and started to follow Tiro, then voices in the distance made him shrink back. The guard must've gotten an alert off before Tiro hit him. Three more guards skidded into view. One stooped to check on their companion, while another spoke into the gem at his shoulder and the third started looking around, blaster up and ready. None of them looked bored now.

In the distance, Ben saw a glint of light along the wall. Tiro was almost there. He checked the time. Twenty seconds left. It would be close, but Tiro might just make it. Unlike Ben. He had hesitated, and now he had nowhere to go.

He opened his gem and began typing. *I'm stuck inside the port. How fast can you work up another security shutdown?* He waited for a reply, hoping Jess or Miles or one of the others was watching.

A blur by the broken gate told Ben that Tiro was out just as the port hummed back to life. Activity was almost immediate. Most of the bots began loading the train again, while two came over near Ben and resumed cleaning up the wreckage from their earlier hack. Instinctively Ben retreated further into the shadows between his two containers. He didn't know how long it would be before a bot moved one of them or got too close. He was more worried about the guard Tiro hit. The guy was sitting up now, shaking his head as the other three spoke to him.

Ben's gem pinged with a reply from Tiro.

Abort.

Ben blinked, read the message again. *Abort.*

I'm still inside, Ben typed. His heart beat faster. *Need another security reboot.*

Negative. All hands abort.

"No no no," Ben whispered through his teeth. What was Tiro thinking?

The guard on the ground suddenly straightened, waved to the others, and pointed right in Ben's direction. The others looked at him, and he pointed again. He gestured at the port wall behind him, then back toward Ben. Two of the guards ran to the wall, blasters drawn, while the third ran straight toward Ben. Ben crouched in the shadows with nowhere to go, his heart hammering in his chest. The guy was twenty meters away now. Fifteen. Ten.

Chapter 2

Just before he got to Ben's hiding spot, the guard skidded to a stop as a loader moved between them. Ben jumped out and dove inside the nearest container while the guard's view was blocked, hoping like crazy the cameras had been blocked too. He crawled toward the back, dragging both backpacks behind him. He got behind some stray crates and small machinery, out of sight. He kept going, quiet as he could manage, all the way to the back.

Ben's hand bumped into something and he looked down. A sleek black box lay beside him, metallic and squarish, about as long and wide as Ben's forearm and half as tall. Something about it caught Ben's eye, and on a whim he pushed it forward. It wasn't heavy. For some reason, he decided to grab it—a little something extra on the off chance he made it out of here. When he got to the back wall of the container, he unzipped one of the backpacks and stuffed the box inside. It was tight, but he managed to fit it after rearranging a few smaller items.

Ben could hear the guard poking around just outside, then another guard joined him. Probably the one Tiro knocked out, unless more had come to investigate. *Please, no*, Ben thought. They said something Ben couldn't hear, their muffled voices growing louder then softer as they moved away. Ben waited for them to peek inside the container, but they never did.

OK, Ben thought. They must have concluded Tiro was alone or that anybody with Tiro escaped too. Ben was safe, for now, but those bots would clear out this container sooner rather than later. Tiro called an abort, which meant no further operations. He and Miles were gone, the others had cut communications. Ben was on his own. He cursed Tiro for leaving him, but mostly he was mad at himself. Why had he hesitated when Tiro bolted for the wall? He knew what his friend was doing, saw it happen. Yet Ben had stayed put until it was too late.

Ben shook his head. No use worrying about it now. He ran through his options instead. Option One: turn himself in. Option Two: come up with something better than Option One. He grimaced. Option Two it was.

He looked around. Some of the crates were big enough to hide in. If he could unseal one and climb inside, he could stay hidden until the train left the port. Then he could break out…

Unless the bots resealed the crate with Ben inside, or security at the next monorail stop was tight, or they decided to reroute the train through a radiation exposed area to make up time. Who knows how long he'd be in there before he got a chance to get out?

Maybe he could trigger another shutdown on his own? He still had Jess's program on his gem. If her code hadn't gotten wiped, maybe he could still access one of the bots remotely. He opened the program and tried several times but couldn't establish a link to anything. Either all the loaders were clean or Ben didn't know what he was doing.

He considered using his "power," as Tiro called it, but like he told Tiro, there was nothing for him to act on. In theory he could manipulate the loader bots or even the Coordinating AI from a distance, but he'd never tried something like that. Plus it was a huge risk. The Aurora was more curse than blessing, and failed implants were often fatal for those who had it. Turning his off on purpose was flirting with death.

Hiding in a crate left too many unknowns. Remotely connecting through Jess's software was out too. Maybe he could break into one of the bots manually? Install Jess's software from the inside, like he'd done before, then drive it with her software masking him. Get close enough to the wall where he could drop out and make a run for the breach.

The more Ben thought about it, the more he liked the idea. It would be tough. It would still require using his ability. But if he got close, he could do it fast and minimize the risk. The loader would flag an anomaly as soon as he touched it. But if he got in quick enough, the cargo chief might not follow up. The bots by the wreckage had to be sending up all kinds of alerts—camera obstructions, unexpected movement patterns—which the official so far was ignoring. There was at least a decent chance he'd ignore this one too. Ben would have to be fast.

A scraping at the container's door made Ben look up. One of the bots was at the entrance, clearing out a few of the larger pieces of machinery, evidently making room to start repacking the vessel. He'd have his chance sooner than he thought. The bot was going to come inside the container.

He waited for the loader to move away from the opening, then crawled up closer to the entrance. He ducked behind another crate as the bot came back in, deeper into the container this time. It was just three meters away now. Ben waited for it to turn.

He activated his gem and opened the Aurora program. A crude hack, but it worked. The simple controls sprang up in a holo image above the gem. Ben took a breath, touched the image, and turned off the implant.

Instantly the inside of the container grew brighter as Ben's eyes registered the energy emanating from the walls and other surfaces within them. Ben's heart rate and body temperature increased, and his hands began to shake. He closed his eyes, took a breath. Then another, steadying himself. He regained control, the rush of overstimulation giving way to heightened awareness.

Ben opened his eyes. The loader bot stood out as a bright blaze filling the space, its power source and circuitry radiating light and heat just a meter away from him. The bot turned, and Ben circled to the front of the crate, staying low. It was now or never.

Ben rushed forward, lightning quick, and put his hand against the bot's hatch. He focused himself, closed his eyes, and *reached.* A thread of energy left his hand and connected with the bot's controls. The energy guiding him, he found the bot's door and activated its lock. It clicked, and the bot stopped, but the hatch didn't open. Ben tried again, heart pounding. Nothing. Ben opened his eyes. Suddenly the bot swiveled so that its front was aimed right at Ben. The bot's hull was a smooth metal surface, but Ben couldn't shake the thought that he was staring at a dangerous animal. It seemed angry.

WAAAAAAAAA!

The bot sounded a deafening alarm that echoed in the container and nearly paralyzed Ben. A bright red light flashed on its top.

Ben didn't stop to think about the security response he'd just activated. Whatever he'd done was more than trigger an anomaly, and there was no more hiding. He grabbed one of the backpacks and ran past the bot, leaving the second bag behind.

Ben ran out of the container and past the second bot, using the gem to turn his implant back on as he tore across the cargo area. His vision returned to normal and the quiet hum in his consciousness subsided. He was dimly aware of a flurry of activity in the port. Dozens of guards and more bots seemed to converge toward him. He didn't think, just made for the broken eastern gate as fast as he could, no longer worried about getting to the cover of the wall.

Flashes of bright red lit up around him, driving him onward. He didn't know if those plasma bursts were intended to kill him, but he didn't care. It was a toss-up whether death would be better or worse than getting caught.

By some miracle, Ben made it to the gate. He glanced backward, saw at least ten guards running his way and firing. Man, they were bad shots. They were less than fifty meters away and closing fast, with at least that many more behind them. Four bots were coming on strong too.

Ben pushed his pack through the narrow opening between the wrecked container and the left gate, then squeezed in after it. He got through, turned, and jammed the pack between the container and the door's edge, wedging it in place with a hard kick. It wouldn't slow the pursuers down much, but it might buy him a minute or two. The pack's top ripped open when Ben kicked it, and the metallic black box he'd found earlier tumbled out. Ben grabbed it and ran. Might as well get away with something. He grimaced at the small victory, thinking of the two large backpacks he'd left behind.

Ben sprinted down one of the access roads leading away from the port. Ahead of him Ligeia stretched away into the distance, its skyline curving gently upward on either side. The nearest neighborhood was more than half a kilometer away, but there was a cluster of multistory offices and shops a good bit closer toward the left. Ben heard the whine of aerial drones in the air behind him and made up his mind. No way would he outrun those birds to the residential areas, but maybe he could lose them among the densely packed office buildings. Voices farther back told him the guards had gotten through his makeshift barrier at the breach and had been joined by supporting agents from elsewhere in the port.

The lead drone drew even with him as he got to the first building. Instinctively Ben stopped, just as a blast from the drone lanced the air in front of him and left a smoking pit in the building's facade. Lightning quick Ben started again, then turned and swung the box into the drone, slamming it backward. The drone was unharmed. Even the lower-end models were almost impossible to destroy, but Ben knocked it off course. By the time it recovered he'd rounded the building's corner. He sprinted along its side, then ducked into an alley between it and the next building.

Keep moving, that's the key, Ben told himself. Erratic, unpredictable, random. It was his only hope of evading the drones. Hiding out here now was useless; they had detailed maps of the area and real-time data on their side. If he stayed put, the drones or guards would find him in minutes. All he could do was stay on the move, keep increasing the physical distance and range of variables they'd have to account for. The pursuers would cast a web and draw it tighter until they had him. He had to stay ahead of that web at all costs.

Ben turned and twisted his way through the maze of alleys and streets between the buildings. The cluster of office spaces had seemed small from far away, but now that Ben was among them he saw they stretched farther into Ligeia than he'd guessed. He hadn't seen more drones yet, but they had to be close.

A low whine up ahead made Ben skid to a stop, and he backtracked toward the alley he'd just come from. As Ben emerged onto the next road, he heard two voices to his left. Ben immediately fled the other direction, taking off at a dead sprint. Chunks of debris and wisps of smoke exploded from the ground at his feet as the guards fired at him. Ben turned into another alley, desperate to get away. He could only hope there wasn't a drone waiting for him.

Halfway to the next street, Ben saw another narrow alley partially obscured by a stack of metal boxes. He turned into the opening, then stopped short, nearly falling forward. A drone floated level with his head less than ten meters away. The light on its front brightened as it found its target and prepared to fire.

Out of instinct more than anything else, Ben held the black box out in front of him in a defensive posture, just as the drone let loose a blast. Ben flinched, turning his head and closing his eyes, absently wondering if he'd feel anything when the plasma hit him.

Instead of searing pain in his chest, Ben felt heat on his face. He opened one eye to see a bright light on the other side of the box. There was a small explosion from somewhere in front of him, and the light faded. He cautiously lowered the box, then gasped as he saw the smoldering wreckage of the drone in front of him.

Ben looked around. Who shot it? He glanced down at the black box and saw a large, angry looking hole in the front where the blast had struck. Whatever was inside had been tough enough to withstand a shot of plasma. He looked around some more, wondering what could have possibly taken out the drone. He didn't see anything. Whatever it was had to be powerful, and Ben didn't want to end up on the wrong end of it.

Voices in the street behind him put any curiosity out of mind. He had to get out of here right now. Ben sprinted past the ruined drone to the end of the small alley, across a narrow street where he thankfully didn't encounter anyone, and onto a path between two more buildings. These buildings, unlike most others he'd passed, had several wide doors lining the alley on either side. He must've stumbled into a loading area or access for vendors in the first-floor shops. The doors brought him a surge of hope. If he could get inside one of the buildings, maybe he could lose the drones.

It was worth a shot. He was getting tired, and the drones would keep coming until they caught him. In the end, running all night was just as futile as hiding out here. He had to get off the street, and finding a way into a building was the only reasonable chance he had.

He tried the first door, found it locked, and moved on. The next one was locked too. He hadn't really expected them to be wide open, but he had vaguely been hoping for some good luck. Not tonight, apparently. He got about halfway down the row, trying every door, when he heard the telltale whine of another drone. He couldn't tell which direction it was coming from and it sounded far away still, but he was running out of time.

Instead of moving to the next door, which was probably locked too, Ben decided to force the lock on this one. He found the access panel and tried several basic security codes on the off chance somebody just used a factory default. Again, no such luck. This was the night everything was going to be hard. His breathing increased as he took out his gem and opened one of Jess's programs. Maybe he could hack the lock. He looked frantically from side to side as he waited for a connection. After several excruciating seconds, the screen flashed blank. He couldn't establish a link. Ben swore. Jess would have this door open in three seconds if she were here; she could probably even do it remotely if he could get in touch with her. Why, why, why had Tiro called an abort?

The drone's whine grew louder. Now Ben could tell it was coming from the street he'd just run across. It was joined by another drone, this one from the far end of the alley. Ben heard voices nearby now too, and he thought he could make out a third drone a little farther away. They were tightening the net. For the first time, he began to really think he might not make it. Maybe if he gave himself up, they would go easy on him…

No. Ben had one more play. He took a breath. He never used the Aurora twice in one day. He had a feeling this time it would hurt. He clenched his fist as he got ready for the pain, then opened the program on his gem. *You can do this*, Ben thought, steeling himself. For the second time in ten minutes, he killed his implant.

The effect was immediate. The world around him brightened again, grew more vivid. For a wondrous moment Ben could see everything. He could see *through* everything. He perceived the drones two buildings over, the lights and electricity in the structures around him and the floor beneath him, the stacked hulls of Ligeia somewhere below that. Kilometers overhead, at the spaceport proper, the massive fusion engines in the docked ships blazed like a furnace in his awareness.

The next instant the flood of energy and information assaulted Ben's mind and body. A dull pain emerged behind his eyes. It penetrated to the center of his consciousness and rattled in his skull. His heart rate soared, and a fever overtook him so quickly that he dropped his gem and the mysterious black box.

He fell to the floor, tense and groaning. A subconscious imperative urged him onward. Door. Off the street. The reason for his pain asserted itself and demanded that he respond.

Ben shut his eyes, gathered himself, and turned his cry into an outburst of energy. He pushed himself off the ground, dimly aware that his hands were glowing, and raised his palm toward the door's controls. He wanted to blast it, wanted to burst the whole door inward in a flood of rage and pain and intensity, but he held it back. He reached with the energy, gestured, touched, activated the door's lock. The door hissed open and Ben collapsed inside.

He reached back through the opening, grabbed the gem and the black box, and pulled both items inside. He slapped the door's inner controls and shut it. His fingers worked the gem, fumbling with the holographic controls as his eyes struggled to follow them. Finally he activated the right sequence and brought the implant back online.

The blinding stream of light and energy stopped as quickly as if a curtain had fallen over the world. Ben lay inside the door, shivering, his body temperature dropping and his heart rate slowing. He shuddered and felt weak. Using the Aurora twice left him more drained than he'd expected.

He heard a noise outside the door as the drones passed by. The whine of their small engines came and went without interruption, no indication that they'd stopped to investigate. Good. At least for the moment, he was safe.

After five minutes, he had recovered enough to stand. He looked around and found a small hallway that ended at a door. Ben walked through it, cautiously, but soon discovered he was alone. Whoever owed this building hadn't bothered to outfit it with security, human or otherwise. Ben found some stairs and went to the top floor, eight stories above the street. It turned out he was in an office building, and judging from the equipment, rent was pretty low. That explained the lack of security, for which Ben was grateful.

He made his way to a window, where he was able to watch the drones and human guards down below. They were still searching in earnest, but nothing about their activity indicated they knew where Ben was. It was unlikely anyone could get into a building without leaving some sort of trail or sign, so their search still focused on the streets and building exteriors. Ben grimaced. Maybe the Aurora was a superpower after all. But the dull pain remaining in his head kept him from being too happy about it.

The guards and drones gradually expanded their search, and Ben stayed put. He passed the time by watching the activity in the port and its silent sentinel, the Terminus. A large holo display near the port's entrance showed endless news programs. Ben could just make it out from his spot at the window. The talking heads and scrolling text brought little that was new or interesting, but it kept Ben from going stir-crazy.

One news segment promised the latest on the Verona investigation, but there wasn't much to report. The Dorium from the colony's refinery was missing, which was consistent with a Raptor attack gone out of hand. It would be months before investigators finished analyzing how the Dyson Array's fail-safes had malfunctioned. In the meantime, the Venus Solar Alliance was deploying ships to Miranda for security. Et cetera. All the same as yesterday and last week. It sounded to

Ben like nobody knew what happened, and nobody much cared as long as it didn't happen to them. Meanwhile VESA was capitalizing on the tragedy by moving to expand their influence. It all might as well have been scripted.

The teams searching for Ben abandoned their efforts sometime after two in the morning. Ben forced himself to wait one more hour before he deemed it safe to start making his way home. He exited the building by a different route, and cautiously made his way to the residential neighborhood nearby. He felt more confident there, despite how quiet it was, and picked up his pace. It was several kilometers to his house in the Third Ward, and he wanted to get there before dawn.

Chapter 3

Ben arrived home just as the sola was beginning to brighten. Its light cast long shadows in the direction of Port Ligeia, a clever trick of mirrors and lenses to give a realistic approximation of the sun rising and setting like on Earth. The street was quiet, old three- and four-story homes packed together in a tight row on either side, none of them with so much as a lamp on in the window. At this hour, not even the Third Ward's criminals were still out on the sidewalks.

Ben approached his house cautiously, though it appeared just as still as the street and the small patch of grass out front. Nothing looked out of the ordinary as he made his way along the crooked fence, past the holes and cracks in the paint he knew so well, to the back door that led into the kitchen. He checked over his shoulder for the hundredth time since leaving the port but saw nothing. He opened the door slowly and peeked inside; everything seemed all right. He took a breath and walked in, closed the door and leaned back against it, eyes closed. Only now did he allow himself to feel a bit of relief. He would be on edge for days, probably weeks, but there was no indication he'd been followed or that the house had been raided in his absence.

Ben set his mysterious black box on the kitchen table and made his way to the living room. The Sola's pale light shone through the front windows on the far side of the room, illuminating sheer curtains that had once been white. The room was large, but filled with an assortment of old couches and chairs that made it feel cramped. Open bottles and half-empty food containers covered the coffee table and most other flat surfaces, making the room look like a postapocalyptic cityscape from the holovids. Ben couldn't tell if the vessels were new or left over from two or three nights ago. He spotted two of Tiro's backpacks leaned against the right wall, near the front door. That was a good sign; Tiro and Miles had made it back. A third backpack lay open on the floor at Ben's feet, with some of the contents piled beside it as if it had been emptied and then hastily repacked not quite as efficiently as before.

Ben didn't spot the other three backpacks. Tiro must have them upstairs; leaving them in the van would have been uncharacteristically sloppy. Tiro was never sloppy. Ben grimaced. *Unless it's alerting guards to your presence and leaving your friend behind.* The thought reignited Ben's anger despite the hour and his fatigue after an eventful night. He retrieved the black box from the kitchen and stalked up the stairs two at a time, his footsteps heavy and resolved.

Ben ignored the doors on the second floor—the room Axel and Tory shared on the right, Dom's small room to the left, Miles's bright yellow door with the poster of a seminude model holding a blaster. All three were closed. He made straight for the second set of stairs up to the third floor, pausing at his own room long enough to toss the black box onto his bed.

Tiro's door was closed, but a thin, bright ribbon underneath it told Ben the light was on. He crossed the distance in three steps, past the open door to Jess's room. He was vaguely aware of hushed voices behind Tiro's door as he threw it open and walked in.

"You fucking left me, man. What the hell?"

Tiro and Jess turned, stared at him in a mixture of alarm and surprise.

Ben's anger wavered slightly when he registered the worry and fatigue on their faces. They'd been awake all night too.

"Ben?" Jess said when she recovered from her shock. She rose from the couch and walked to him, placed her hands on his shoulders. She looked him up and down. "You look all right. What happened?"

"I'm fine," Ben said, staring daggers at Tiro. "No thanks to you."

Tiro stood but stayed at his desk chair, hands raised in a gesture of surrender. "I know you're mad," he said, "I get it. But you're here, you made it. That's what matters. Holy shit, how'd you do it?"

"That's not what matters. What matters is you left me. You. Left. Me." Ben stepped closer, raised his voice with each syllable. "Did you think I'd take the fall?"

"Let me explain—"

"I'd go rot in prison somewhere while you got clear? Is that what you had in mind when you called a fucking *abort* with me still inside?"

"Easy, man, easy," Tiro said. "You're gonna wake the whole damn house."

"Ask how much sleep I got tonight," Ben said through clenched teeth. "I don't care who wakes up."

"We were going to get you," Jess said, her tone even. She was still standing between him and Tiro; if she hadn't been there they would have been fighting already.

"Sure."

"It's true," Tiro said. "Why do you think we're still up?" He stepped aside and gestured to his desk, where Ben noticed for the first time that Tiro's gem rested. Unidentified maps and schematics switched at three-second intervals in the air above the gem, beside a slowly scrolling column of text too small to read. "We were trying to find you."

Ben looked at the gem display, then back at Tiro. He narrowed his eyes, not sure if he believed his friend. He looked at Jess and raised an eyebrow.

"That's the real-time feed from the port's security team," Jess said. "Hacking their cameras to get visuals was too risky, but I was able to access this without detection. They're setting up a perimeter one kilometer from the Terminus. They think you're still within it based on this. That's what we thought, too, until you showed up."

"That's right," Tiro said. "We were waiting to see when they caught you, find out their next step, and boom! Hit them at a weak spot and pick you up. We couldn't really do anything until we knew where you were and what they planned."

"Yeah, imagine that," Ben said. "If only you could have picked me up while I was still in the port."

"I'm sorry, man. Here, sit down." Tiro gestured to the couch. Ben stayed put. "Will you sit down? I know you're tired."

Ben sat, still on edge. Jess sat down beside him as Tiro returned to his desk chair.

"It killed me to call that abort," Tiro said. "You have no idea. I thought you were right behind me; I was halfway to the breach when I realized you weren't there."

"Three more guards showed up just as I was about to move," Ben said.

Tiro nodded. "I looked back when I got to the breach and saw them. I was gonna go back, come up with something, but there was a guard at the van talking to Miles. He was suspicious. Miles was feeding him a bunch of bullshit, but you know Miles. He wasn't getting rid of the guy."

Ben took in the new information, said nothing as Tiro continued. "I knocked him out with my backpack, same as that first guard. But I heard him shout something into his gem just before I got him. We couldn't risk hanging around. Miles and I had to get out of there before reinforcements showed up."

Ben sat back, processing Tiro's story. It was plausible, and Tiro was right. Miles was a terrible liar. "Why kill our communications, too, though? We could have figured out a way to get me out of there. Jess could have—"

"It was too risky," Tiro said. "The whole port was alerted to something else going on. They knew our hacks were a diversion, or they were gonna realize it soon enough after they saw me and Miles. Anything we came up with to get you out, there was no way to predict how they'd respond. It was either abort right then or jeopardize all of us."

Ben looked down, took a deep breath. Clenched and unclenched his right fist. He was still mad, but he could understand the hard position Tiro had been in. Ben wasn't sure he would have made the same call, but he believed Tiro had good reasons for ending the operation.

"We started working on a way to get you out as soon as Miles and I got back," Tiro said. "We've been sitting up all night trying to find out your status."

Ben sighed and closed his eyes. "OK." He believed Tiro, he guessed, and fatigue outweighed any lingering anger he was feeling. He leaned back on the couch. "It's OK, I get it. And I'm here, like you said."

"All right. You sure? We're cool?"

"Yeah," Ben said without opening his eyes. "We're cool."

"Damn, what a night."

"Drink?" Jess asked.

"Yes," Ben said.

She reached behind Tiro's desk and pulled out his bottle of Watson Red, then grabbed three glasses from a small cabinet on the wall. She gave them each a healthy pour of the cheap scotch, and Tiro offered a toast. "To friends, felony, and narrow escapes."

The three clinked glasses and drank. Ben savored the smoky flavor, felt the warmth of it deep in his chest. Nobody would call the stuff premium, but it was theirs. Watson Red had been a part of many memories. Tonight would be one more.

"What'd you do with the bags?" Tiro asked.

Ben sat forward, looked at him with a quizzical expression.

"The two backpacks," Tiro said. "You lug them all the way here, or did you have to stash them somewhere?"

"I left them in the port," Ben said, draining his glass. "It was the only way to get away fast enough."

Tiro was silent for a moment. A cloud passed over his face—just a fraction of a second, but Ben caught the unmistakable flash of disappointment. Of anger.

Then Tiro smiled and spread his hands wide. "Hey, the important thing is, you got away." He poured a little more Watson into Ben's glass, then refilled his own. "We're all beat, but give us the short version of tonight's adventure before you head to bed."

Ben started with the short version, but it became the long version by the time he was finished. The sola was bright outside when Ben got to the end.

"Hot damn," Jess whispered. "That's incredible." Ben grinned. For her, that was practically an emotional outburst.

"No kidding," Tiro said. "So what was in the box?"

"I never did get a good look," Ben said, standing up. "We'll check it out in the morning. Well, later this morning," he added after a glance out the window. "I'm beat."

"Big night," Tiro said, standing and giving Ben a hug. "The others will be up soon I bet. I'll message everyone that you're back and resting. Take your time."

Ben walked out and Jess followed him, no doubt to get some rest of her own. She and Tiro had been up all night too.

"You know, Ben, I'm really glad you're back," Jess said as she approached her door. "Hacking back in or whatever was gonna be a shit ton of work."

"Hour at least," Ben said, "maybe two."

Jess raised an eyebrow. "Try twenty minutes. But my time's valuable."

Ben smiled and shook his head, headed for his room. "Night, Jess," he said over his shoulder.

"Ben."

He turned, saw Jess still standing beside her door, looking him in the eye. "Seriously," she said without a hint of her usual dry wit.

"I know," Ben said. "Good night."

Ben walked into his small but comfortable room, turned on the overhead light, and closed the door. As tired as he was, he couldn't resist opening the black box to find out what was inside. He'd left out the part about it—whatever it was—absorbing a plasma shot and saving his life. He wasn't sure himself what it meant, or even whether that had really happened.

Ben cleared some space on his small desk, pushing aside the drawings, puzzles, and sketch pad, and set the box in the center. He put his gaming controller and helmet on the low bookshelf beside the speakers, then turned on the lamp to give himself some extra light.

Carefully Ben opened the lid, which turned smoothly and noiselessly on its hinges. Inside the box were fifteen small spheres, arranged in three rows of five and surrounded by thick black foam. They looked identical, a dull white color, flawlessly smooth, with no markings or coloration.

Ben picked one up and held it up to the light. It was heavier than he'd expected. About four centimeters across. It was hard and dense, slightly translucent, and as he angled it he noticed a faint shimmer of color that seemed to come from deep within the sphere. No bubbles or flaws that he could make out. No apparent damage or other evidence that any of them had been struck by plasma. That was odd; a blast like that should have left some kind of mark or discoloration.

Ben checked the lid. There was a hole, just like he remembered. The blast hadn't been stopped by the lid or the layer of foam underneath. He started to turn back to the spheres, but something on the inside of the lid made him look again. He inspected the lid's bottom closely, then turned it over and looked at the top. Then back at the bottom. Ben frowned. The edges of the hole were turned ever so slightly outward, toward the top of the lid. It was as if the blast had come from *inside* the box, not outside.

Ben pictured a scenario in his head: the drone blasts the box, making a small, neat hole going in. In response, the spheres inside the box send a second blast outward, creating a larger hole turned out and obliterating the drone. Which was silly, except that *something* had destroyed the drone. But how could the spheres do that? They didn't look like any batteries he'd ever seen. What was their energy source?

Ben carefully removed the spheres one by one. He wondered vaguely if they were radioactive, but if they were then the damage was done. He'd toted them around all night with a hole in the box. He set them on his bed and pulled at the foam lining, working it gently until it came free of the box and the lid. As Ben thought, it was just foam, nothing special, no embedded wires or other surprises. It was just there to hold the spheres in place, maybe provide some cushioning. He reinserted the foam and replaced the spheres, then closed the box.

Ben was intrigued by the puzzle the box presented but knew better than to try solving it this morning. He desperately needed sleep. Ben set the box on the floor beside his bed, then stretched out on top of the covers. He kicked off his shoes, put his hands behind his head, and closed his eyes.

Sleep didn't come right away. He was too keyed up from robbing the port, escaping by the skin of his teeth, confronting Tiro, and now the mystery of the black box and its strange contents. He lay there for ten minutes, then decided it was futile. He'd been meaning to write to Simon. Now was as good a time as any.

He opened his gem and tapped out a short message.

Hey Little Brother,

I hope your second semester is off to a good start. You've been at it for a few weeks now, and I suppose midterms are around the corner already, huh? Don't sweat it. I've never met anyone smarter than you, and I know you're keeping up with everything. Mom and Dad would be proud of you. I know I am.

I have some good news. Work has been going really well lately, and I've managed to save more than I'd expected. I should be able to cover that planetary survey class you were talking about, no problem—the one with the trip down to Titan's surface. Don't hold me to it, but I'm hoping to be able to buy you your own suit and respirator before next semester starts, so you won't have to rent anything. Tuition first, as always, but things are looking better than they have in a long time.

Let's do a Starfleet night soon. I miss kicking your butt. Axel and Tory can't hang anymore. Romance does that to you, I suppose. They said to tell you hey. Tiro and the others too.

Keep up the good work. Love you, bro.

Ben

By the time Ben finished, he was fighting to keep his eyes open. Writing to Simon always put his mind at ease. He felt a little guilty lying to his brother. The truth was, he'd been laid off weeks ago as Novalink "right-sized" their mining division by reducing the number of remote operators. Simon didn't need to know about that, though. Ben was finding a way to keep the money coming; that's all that mattered.

He tapped Send and closed his gem. He hoped Simon saw the note before his first class. Harlow Academy was tough by anyone's measure. Even a kid as bright as Simon could use a bit of good news to start the day.

Ben set the gem on his nightstand, rolled onto his side, and fell asleep.

Chapter 4

Ben woke to the sound of voices downstairs, loud enough to carry all the way to the third floor. He checked his gem. No reply yet from Simon, but that was typical. It was not quite noon. He'd slept for, what, four hours? He considered going back to sleep, but the empty pang in his stomach got him up and moving. He hadn't eaten since lunch yesterday, he realized as he descended the final flight of stairs.

"Ben!" Everyone yelled in unison as he entered the living room. Ben blinked in surprise as they clapped and whooped.

"Oh wow, did you guys rehearse or something?" he said with a grin. He could smell something savory in the kitchen, and his mouth watered as he tried to place the scent.

"Tiro told us the quick version," Tory said from the couch, "but we want the full story. Tell us the tale, O great adventurer!"

"Yeah, dude, out with it!" Miles yelled, looking up from the backpack he was exploring.

"Food first, then I'll tell you everything you want to know," Ben said. "Something smells amazing."

"You're just in time, my man," Axel said, peeking around the corner from the kitchen. We're about to feast, and you're first in line."

Ben walked into the kitchen and immediately took in the spread Axel had laid out. He loaded a plate with a huge lunch of fresh bread, steak, chicken, and mixed vegetables. As he sat down he caught a piece of something dark in the vegetables, then tasted it. He turned to Tiro in surprise. "Bacon?"

Tiro smiled. "There was a small pack in one of the crates," he said. "Some restaurant is gonna be ticked when they find out it's missing."

"No kidding," Ben said, taking another bite and eating it slower this time. Huge farms on the nearby colony of Theia raised chicken and beef, but most pork came from Rhea, smaller and much farther away. Bacon was expensive. Ben's vegetables rarely tasted this good.

They ate and drank well into the afternoon. The whole house was in good spirits after last night's successful operation and the news this morning that Ben had returned home safely. He told them the story of last night, starting with Tiro hitting the guard and bolting out of the port, leaving Ben behind. He remembered more details now than he had this morning, and Jess and Tiro shook their heads as he recounted things he'd left out.

They cleaned the kitchen quickly and Tiro set everyone to work unpacking and sorting the bags from last night. The mood improved even more as the value of their haul kept climbing. Even a conservative estimate put them well above six figures already, and they'd only finished going through the first two bags.

Ben went to get a drink and found Axel and Tory in the kitchen taking a break.

"I never got a chance to ask you how it went at the station last night," Ben said. Axel and Tory had delayed the train coming into Port Ligeia—a key part of their plan, since it meant the loaders had to put the shipping containers in a holding area instead of loading the train directly from the elevator.

Tory's eyes brightened. "It was awesome," she said. "You wouldn't believe the number of people that showed up."

"I thought you weren't going to recruit anybody," Ben said, suddenly worried. Involving others increased their risk significantly.

"We didn't," Axel said. "People just came. Only a few at first, I guess they were curious. But when it became clear what we were doing, the crowd really grew. Angry, passionate. Few hundred people at least."

Tory shook her head, her short hair bobbing with the movement. "More like a thousand, maybe two."

Ben shook his head. "Wait, so what exactly did you guys do?" It had been his idea to stage a protest to delay the train, but Axel and Tory had handled the details.

"We stood on the track," Axel said.

"And?" Ben asked.

"And what? We stood on the track."

"You just stood there? The whole time?"

"Protested. We protested," Tory corrected.

"By standing on the track." Ben said.

"Yes."

"And that worked?"

"Unbelievably well," Tory said, a little too quickly and way too loud. She was short, with hair dyed pink and a round face, a look most people described as cute. Her fast, enthusiastic speech and high-energy demeanor reinforced that impression.

"That's right," Axel said. He was as tall and imposing as Tory was compact. They'd been dating for years. "It's the perfect approach. Nonviolent interruption of their basic operation. It strikes right at the heart of the problem."

"The problem?" Ben asked.

"Unequal access to goods and services." Axel said. "Oppression of the working class by people who are more loyal to the Interior than to Titan. Exploitation of the people's labor with insufficient compensation and—"

"Blah blah blah," Tory cut him off. "Rage against the machine and all that—"

"So we put a stop to it," Axel continued. "Put our bodies, *ourselves*, in harm's way until they saw we were serious—"

"Whole laundry list of demands," Tory said.

"We refused to move until they agreed to specific reforms that prioritize Titan's interests, especially the average citizen."

"Anyway, it worked. People noticed, and nobody was moving the train after the crowd got involved. Pretty good, huh?" Tory couldn't stop smiling.

Ben shook his head, incredulous. All that planning, every bit and piece fitting together perfectly, and it all hinged on two dummies standing on the monorail track for an hour hoping nobody would call their bluff. He couldn't decide which part of the whole thing was funniest.

"So how'd it end?" Ben asked.

"That's the best part," Axel said. "The director came out— guy over the whole MTA on Ligeia—and said he was willing to hear us out. We were onto something, man. He asked who we represented, wanted to hear our demands. I guess they've been having some unrest and rumors over in the Fifth Ward and farther in, toward the industrial areas. Plus all the off-world trouble with that attack or whatever it was at Miranda. He wanted to show some goodwill before the local issues turned into a whole thing closer to the port."

"The big crowd helped, I think," Tory said. "The director was definitely nervous."

"What'd you tell him?" Ben asked, wide-eyed.

Tory burst out laughing. "We ran!" she practically yelled, drawing a laugh from Axel too. "Just hauled ass out of there, got lost in the crowd and ditched our masks and amplifier."

"He was so confused," Axel said. "He yelled after us trying to get us back at first, but then noticed that the track was clear and he ordered the train to start before the rest of the crowd decided to block it again."

"We bought you ninety minutes," Tory said. "I guess that was enough."

"It was perfect," Ben said. He'd have to check the news sites later, see what the talking heads had to say about the protests. Everyone was feeling the effects of Titan's tensions with the Interior, especially the working-class citizens. Axel and Tory had picked a good angle.

"I'm telling you, we were onto something," Axel said. "I was telling Tory last night, we ignited a freaking movement. They just needed a spark."

Tory gave him a playful nudge. "Since when are you political?"

Axel shrugged. "Didn't you feel it last night?"

She thought for a moment. "Nah," she said, but Axel didn't miss the hint of mischief in her smile.

Ben left them in the kitchen, glad to see all of his friends in such good spirits. Jess was already working intently on two new, next-generation gems they'd gotten last night, programming them for who knows what. Miles was dozing on the couch in a very expensive-looking haptic bodysuit. Ben made a note to ask Tiro where he'd found that thing. He passed a table filled with more gems, AR lenses, scores of batteries, and five recreational, vacuum-rated drones. The drones reminded him of last night, and the black box with its clear, evidently plasma-proof spheres.

Ben ran upstairs, found the box right where he'd left it this morning, and came back down. He scanned the room for Dom, the youngest member of their crew and therefore the one who always got the crap jobs like cataloging the whole haul and estimated value of everything. At the moment Dom was trying to get Miles out of his bodysuit. Judging from the way it was going, Miles could sleep through the apocalypse.

"Dom," Ben said. The younger guy looked up. "Come here a second, I want to show you something."

Dom walked over, grateful for an interruption. He was fresh-faced with blond hair, tall and lean but not quite skinny. At fifteen, he still carried a hint of youthful softness. Only the long scar down the left side of his face betrayed the violence and hardship he'd known, same as the rest of them. Dom was young, but he was tough and sharp and pulled his weight as well as anyone.

"How's it going?" Ben asked.

"Pretty fast," Dom said in his drawl that pegged him as an Io native. He'd come to Ligeia when his parents took a job in Titan's surface mines. "I've got most everything accounted for already. He gestured back at Miles, still asleep. "Couple of problem pieces, you know, but I'll get it."

"You get yourself a gem and some lenses? Tiro said he was gonna be sure to hook you up."

Dom nodded. "Jess has them, she's going to set them up for me. She insisted, something about optimizing so these beautiful pieces of tech aren't wasted on a moron, you know the drill. Lovely personality. Just sunny as hell."

Ben laughed. He liked Dom.

Dom tapped the side of his head. "I'm due for a new link next year, but that gem's so good, I might need to get it sooner just to keep up."

"Nah, I bet Jess can hook it up right for you. She can work wonders, even with outdated implants," Ben said. "Listen, you want to take a break, work on something else for a minute?"

"Sure," Dom said. "What you got?"

Ben showed him the black box and the spheres inside. "Any idea what this could be?"

"Hmmm…" Dom took the box, looked at it from all angles. He shook his head.

"Can you do a Quill search? Be sure to keep it—"

"Yeah," Dom said. "I'll keep it simple, vague, nothing that will be a giveaway that we just stole something."

Dom was a sharp kid. "Good. Let me know what you find."

While the kid walked away, Ben thought back to last night inside the container. The box had been alone, hadn't it? Yes, he was sure of that. He recalled seeing only larger, unopened crates and pieces of machinery as he hid inside. It was deep in the container, too, making it unlikely that other boxes had simply fallen out while this one didn't. What would somebody be shipping all alone, in a box that fit in Ben's hands?

Power sources, maybe. Smaller versions of batteries that powered cargo loaders and other big equipment. The color was similar, but those batteries were usually cube-shaped and these spheres had no visible contacts or connections. Computer chips? Ben didn't know much about them, but that didn't seem right. And neither idea explained why there were only fifteen of the spheres in a small, lonely box. He waved his hand over one, then tapped it and swiped across it, trying to see if it would activate like a gem. He got no response.

"Hey, Jess," Ben called. "Come here a minute." If their resident tech expert didn't recognize them, maybe she could at least give him some more ideas for Dom's search.

"What's up?" she said, sounding annoyed.

"Do you recognize these? Any clue what they might be?" He showed her the spheres.

"Nope. Anything else?" She turned to get back to her new gems on the table.

"Hang on, hang on," Ben said. "I spent two hours in that cramped loader last night. You can spare three minutes away from your new toys."

She raised an eyebrow. "Tick tock."

Ben sighed, then handed her one. "Take a close look. Anything about it ring a bell?"

Jess took the sphere, held it up to the light. She hefted its weight, then attempted to look inside. The cube was milky white but slightly translucent. Ben wondered if she'd see anything in the center.

"No, I've never seen one of these before."

"So no idea at all?" Ben asked. "You don't think they could be any computer or chip of some kind? Battery?"

"Like I said…"

"OK fine," Ben said. "Then help me set up an encrypted search on the Quill. I found this in the port last night. I don't want to tip off anybody who might be snooping that we have it. Dom is looking on some vague terms, but if you can give me a secure link maybe I can try something more targeted and specific. Maybe I can at least figure out what they're made of."

"Oh, actually you don't need a search for that," Jess said, tucking a ring of hair behind her ear. "These new gems have a built-in spectrometer." She retrieved one from her table and showed him the program, suddenly almost excited. "Supposedly they're being marketed to miners and prospectors as tough, do-anything, lab-on-the-go devices." She rolled her eyes. "Dumb as hell if you ask me, but it means they're cramming a lot of cool stuff on here that I can use. Most of it will only interface directly with super expensive links, not basic implants like ours. But we can still use the features with visuals and manual controls."

Ben made a note to ask Jess what other tricks these new gems had.

"So what, it can tell you what these are made of?" he said, holding up one of the spheres. She nodded. "We'll still need to set up an encryption though, right? If this is sensitive stuff, we don't want the gem broadcasting it through the Quill."

"No Quill," Jess said, already running the program and setting up the aperture for spectral analysis. She tapped the gem. "Local database all right here. Like I said, full lab-on-the-go."

Before Ben could get another word out, Jess grabbed the sphere from him and set it on the table. "Careful," he cautioned as she pointed the aperture at it and prepared to take a reading.

Jess rolled her eyes, made a small adjustment in the floating interface above the gem, and tapped Go.

A small beam of light flashed quickly toward the sphere, establishing it as the target, followed by a wide, flat beam that scanned it from top to bottom. The beam turned off when it hit the table, and a small status bar appeared briefly on Jess's interface. Less than a second later, the result appeared.

"Uh…" Ben opened his mouth, then closed it. He suddenly felt hot.

Jess whipped around to look at him, eyes wide, then back to her screen. "Is that…"

"Yeah." Ben swallowed.

"But that can't be right. It has to be a mistake." Jess was speaking fast. "You found this in a container, didn't you? Why are they shipping it this way? Why here?"

Ben shook his head. "I don't know. You set it up right, didn't you?"

Jess glared at him. "Of course."

"Then what else could it be?"

Jess said nothing, just looked at the sphere, then the display, then back at the sphere.

"Dom, come here a minute," Ben called. Jess began whispering something unintelligible, but Ben thought he heard the words "prison" and "life" somewhere in there.

"You find out what it is?" Dom asked as he walked up.

"Go get Tiro," Ben said. "Hurry."

Dom leaned over to look at Jess's display. "What is…oh. Oh God." Without another word, he ran to find Tiro.

Ben looked at the screen again, hoping he'd read it wrong, but no. There it was. Fifteen spheres of Dorium.

They were fucked.

Chapter 5

All seven of them gathered around the table, staring at the fifteen small spheres that would likely send them to a correctional colony for a long time.

"You're sure it's Dorium?" Miles asked. He was wide awake now but still wearing the haptic suit.

"We did the analysis twice," Ben said.

"All of them?"

Tiro spoke before Jess could throw the box at Miles. "Yes, all of them. Jess ran the analysis every way we could think of."

Axel asked, "So how much is there? And how much is it—"

Tiro waved a hand and cut him off. "It's just over eight kilograms all together. At today's rates, that's about ninety-eight million ether."

Ben's breath caught just hearing the numbers again. A basic Dyson Array used five kilos (Jess had looked it up, of course.) In theory, eight was enough to power one of Titan's smaller sister colonies.

Few understood how Dorium worked, even at the top of the energy industry. But almost everyone knew how vital the mineral was thanks to the Interior's constant power grabs. Almost daily there was news of this or that skirmish over beam pathways, or a threat to a colony's Dyson Array, or the effects of the latest trade embargoes—all with tired, boilerplate explanations of the mineral's critical role in the solar system's energy infrastructure. Venus, Mars, and the many nations of

Earth wanted more raw materials, more manufacturing—more of everything—and their access to the Sun's precious energy was the leverage they used to get it. Dorium was instrumental in that pipeline, propping up each note of the web of energy beams across the solar system. As the most prominent of the Outer Colonies, Titan and its residents felt the conflict more keenly than most.

Judging by how the others shifted their weight and looked around in silence, Ben wasn't the only one who felt like he was in way over his head.

"So what do we do?" Dom finally asked.

"Sell it!" Miles said.

"Not that simple," Ben said.

"Sure it is. We just won the lottery!"

"And how are we going to sell it?" Axel asked, rolling his eyes. "Where? Who's going to buy it?"

"We shouldn't rule it out," Jess said.

"Are you all forgetting the big-ass elephant in the room?" Tory asked. Everybody stopped and looked at her.

"Verona. A month ago a whole colony was massacred. Attacked. The structure torn apart. No survivors. Maybe that part was an accident, maybe not. But they were attacked, and the only clue about who did it or why is that Verona dealt in Dorium. And their Dorium is missing."

Everyone fell silent as the gravity of Tory's words sank in.

Dom broke the silence. "Do you think it's…you know. Do you think this is from Verona?" He eyed the Dorium with something between reverence and sadness.

"I don't know," Ben said. "It's likely, though. I think we have to assume it is."

Jess said, "But nobody would think that we were involved with—"

"Why wouldn't they?" Tory said. "Dorium went missing and now some turns up here. Ben's right. This stuff is electric.

Hot. Always has been, but now more than ever. We have to ditch it. Send it far away."

"We're taking a risk already," Dom said. "We already have it. Might as well get something for our troubles."

The room erupted again as everyone tried to talk at once. Sell it. That's stupid. Toss it. Are you kidding me? Confess and return it. Do it anonymously. You can't be serious. Jet it into space. Angry. Excited. Scared out of their minds.

Dorium wasn't necessary, in theory, for collecting power from the sun or for beaming it through space. But its properties made collecting, storing, and beaming energy far more efficient and practical than alternative processes using other materials. Many experts said colonizing the outer solar system simply wouldn't have been possible without Dorium, and it undoubtedly accelerated the efforts to terraform Mars and Venus. New deposits were rare but potentially lucrative enough to draw prospectors all the way to the Kuiper Belt. Dorium was at the heart of energy production and trade within the solar system. It was the lifeline for the Colonies and a key bargaining chip—or target—for the many entities in the Interior who wanted to take advantage of the Colonies.

People killed for Dorium, made war over it. Slaughtered an entire colony for it, most recently. And Ben and his friends had accidentally stolen eight kilos.

Tiro let the argument go for a few minutes, then said "Enough." His firm voice brought quiet to the room. "We're not ditching it."

"Tiro—" Ben started.

"We're not." Tiro looked at Ben, then back at the others. "We're not ditching it. Look, we're in over our heads, but this stuff fell into our laps. Nobody ever got anywhere by running from an opportunity. We're going to sell it or trade it or something. We can't keep it long, but we're going to get *something* out of this mess."

Tiro looked around the room, watching each person for silent confirmation that they were on board. Miles smiled and whispered, "Hell yeah." The others were more subtle about it—a barely perceptible nod, a slight shift in posture. But they were all willing to go for it.

Ben thought the whole idea was crazy. They'd almost certainly get caught by the Titan police no matter how they went about it. That is, if they didn't get killed by whoever was rich and bold enough to buy underground Dorium. Or by the people who stole it from Verona in the first place. Ben should have argued the point. He should have spoken up, should have threatened to get rid of the stuff on his own if he had to.

Then again, once Tiro set his mind on something, there was no arguing with him, especially if the others were already convinced. Maybe working the problem a bit, seeing how tough it was going to be, would change their minds.

So Ben stood up, put his hands on the table, and said, "Well then. Nice speech. Let's get on with it."

Tiro clapped him on the back, a smile on his face, then he turned to the others. "We know we want to get something. Let's just figure out what and how."

With that now decided, Ben slid comfortably into his usual role as the problem solver. "All right," he said, "we're not going to get anywhere by slinging ideas around. Let's step back and think for a minute. What do we know? What do we need to find out?"

Tory went first. "We know this was in the port. Deep in a shipping container, all by itself. Right?"

Ben nodded.

"You sure there weren't any other boxes in there?" Miles asked. "You didn't miss anything?"

"As sure as I can be. I was hiding, not taking inventory. But the reason I grabbed the box in the first place was because it was so unusual. If there were others nearby, I would've noticed them."

"Can we find out the box's point of origin?" Axel asked. "I assume it didn't come directly here from Verona."

Ben shook his head. "We could, but it won't help. Those big cargo ships sling around from Neptune to Mercury on gravity assists, and containers come to them from all over. In theory we could get into the shipping records and track the container I found it in, but snooping like that might tip somebody off. And we can't narrow it down to where in its journey the box was added. It's a dead end."

"So it came from Verona—probably—but we don't know where else it was before coming here," Tiro said. "What else?"

"Why bring it here?" Dom asked. "That's what I want to know. Why Ligeia? And what does, whoever it is, want to do with it?"

"Well," Tory said, "somebody sent it here in a single box buried in a shipping container. That smells like smuggling to me."

"Me too," Jess said. Axel nodded.

"It was coming here," Dom said. "If it's smuggling, someone on Ligeia was involved."

"Not necessarily," Jess pointed out. "We don't know Ligeia was the destination."

"Could've been Kraken. The monorail goes there after passing through the industrial zone," Miles said.

"It could be intended for anywhere, doesn't even have to be Titan ultimately. Maybe it was just changing hands here, on its way to somewhere else."

Dom shook his head. "Either way, it came off the cargo ship. That means somebody on Titan was gonna have to handle it, even if they were passing it along."

Ben cleared his throat before pointing out the obvious. "Which means somebody on Titan is missing eight kilos of Dorium."

"Maybe we can sell it back to them," Miles said.

"Maybe they'll take it and kill us to keep it quiet," said Tory.

"It means we can be sure they're already looking for it," Ben said. "By now everybody in the colony knows what went down at the port last night. They'll assume their missing Dorium was stolen in the robbery, and they'll be right. So we have to keep an eye out not just for the police but for an angry smuggler too. Somebody at least tangentially involved in what happened out at Miranda."

Nobody spoke for a moment. They looked at one another in tense silence as their situation sank in once more.

"In that case, we have to move fast," Tiro said. "And act anonymously. Let's keep at it."

They stayed around the table late into the night, coming up with one idea after another, then shooting them down just as quickly. When they finally stopped, close to midnight, they had nothing to show for it.

Ben walked up the stairs and into his room, blew out a breath as he sat in his desk chair. He leaned his head back and closed his eyes, only just now feeling the weight of the day's frustration and fatigue. Hours of work, and they'd gotten nowhere. The Dorium felt radioactive, a source of slowly leaking destruction that would consume them unless they got rid of it fast. The urgency prevented him from thinking straight.

And no sleep, he reminded himself. He'd had only four hours for the past two days. Maybe things would seem clearer in the morning.

He stood and moved toward the bed, then his gem pinged. He activated it and found a short message from Simon.

You up? Got time for some Starfleet?

Ben cleared the message and got into bed. He was too tired to play right now. He'd reply in the morning. He closed his eyes and laid on his back for several minutes. Then he opened them. Crap, he couldn't resist.

He grabbed the gem and tapped out a message back to Simon. *I'm in. Let's go!*

Ben fired up his console, donned his helmet, and logged in. Within minutes he was chatting with his little brother as they joined their first match. Ben chose his usual, a sleek Wildcat fighter built for speed, while Simon opted for the slower but more armored Eagle. Both ships were outfitted with a Lightbeam. In the game it cost you some speed, but that was a small sacrifice for such a powerful weapon and almost everyone chose to use it.

Ben and Simon joined a bit late and the melee was already in progress, but they quickly found a groove. Dozens of fighters zoomed around scattered debris and inert spacecraft with the blue jewel of Neptune hanging in the distance against a background of stars. Ben whooped as he caught somebody with a perfectly timed Beam, instantly turning the ship to a trail of debris. "Did you see that? Dude was booking it out of range and I picked him off from twenty thousand klicks!"

"Can't outrun light," Simon said.

"Best weapon ever. I can't believe I resisted using it for so long."

The Starfleet series of games had a long tradition of realism. Its ships were closely related to military designs, and the controls faithfully mimicked those in standard fighter cockpits. Lightbeams were the one element in the latest release where the creators sacrificed realism for the fun factor. In reality, only the largest naval warships carried Lightbeams. They were tightly regulated by one interplanetary treaty after another, and for good reason. The weapons unleashed tremendous energy. Lightbeam ships were strategically deployed throughout the solar system to threaten and deter. Actually firing a Lightbeam was a good way to start an interplanetary war that would threaten most human life.

At first Ben had been annoyed that Starfleet included small, starfighter-sized versions of the weapons. He was a purist when it came to realistic gameplay, and avoided using Beams on principle. He changed his mind the first time he tried using one. Destroying an enemy at the speed of light, with a single shot, sure was fun.

Ben and Simon worked together, eliminating opponents and racking up kills, their conversation focused on the game and strategy. Their team won handily, and Ben finished at the top of the leaderboard with Simon in fourth.

"I got your note this morning," Simon said while they waited for the next match to start. "That's great news about work going so well."

"Thanks," Ben said. He hoped his brother wouldn't press for details. "I'm excited about it, things are looking good. Lots more hours, and they gave me a raise. The money will be nice to take some of the pressure off."

"Yeah," Simon said. "Listen, about that. I decided not to take that survey class after all."

"What? Why not? You were so excited about it last time we talked."

"I know, but there are a lot of other classes that will transfer to university. I can take those and eliminate some of the core courses, leaving myself more room to focus on planetary survey then. I don't have to take the survey class now. With the added cost…"

"Uh-uh, don't be doing that man," Ben said. "That's the class you want to take, and I want to make it happen. Other classes will transfer, maybe, but we both know this will give you some great experience and a head start at college, right?"

"Yeah, that's right I guess, but it's so much more tuition. I appreciate all you're sacrificing to keep me here at Harlow, and…"

"What are you talking about?"

"Come on, Ben. I'm not stupid. I know you're busting your butt to keep me here. You try to hide it, but you're a terrible liar.

Ben sighed. "Fine. You're right. Of course it's hard. But look: it's also worthwhile. And I wasn't kidding about the money—things aren't as tight now as they were before."

"But…"

"No buts, kid. You're taking that planetary survey class. It's gonna be great."

"OK. Are you sure?"

"Of course."

"Thanks, Ben," Simon said. "I don't know how to repay you. Someday I will."

"You repay me by studying hard, getting good grades, and making something of yourself. Looks like round two is about to start. You ready?"

"You know it," Simon said as the next match got underway. "How about saving some kills for the rest of us this time?"

"No chance," Ben said. "You get to go to Harlow. I'm gonna blast anybody I want to. Try to keep up."

He and Simon played for two more hours, chatting between matches and enjoying the chance to catch up. Ben kicked himself when he saw the clock. It was nearly three, and he was dead tired. He told Simon good night and logged off, smiling to himself as he got in bed and hit the light. He'd pay for it tomorrow morning, but even so it was good to talk with his brother and take his mind off Dorium for a while.

Minutes later, he fell asleep.

Ben woke in a sweat. The dream had been vivid, but he didn't remember it all. Something about a candle? Dorium, maybe? Yes, there was definitely Dorium. He could still see the milky, translucent sphere. He attempted to recover the details, but already they were fleeting. The more he tried to remember, the more the dream eluded him. The only part he recalled clearly was how he felt: like a child running away from home, exhilarated and free, but then suddenly lost, unmoored, lonely. Afraid.

It was still dark outside, but the sola was casting its first rays onto the street. Despite the early hour, he knew trying to sleep again was useless. Instead, Ben put on his shoes and quietly left the house.

He turned right out of their front door, careful to lock it behind him. He walked east—that is, the direction of Ligeia's spin—toward the broad park that marked the edge of his neighborhood.

After a few blocks he began to jog, the sleep falling from his body and the morning air filling his lungs. Ben always loved walking or running in the early hours; it was quiet, empty. Like he was the only person in the world.

He came to the other edge of the park and continued east, following the wide main street of the neighborhood where he and Simon had grown up. Ahead, the terrain curved gently but unmistakably upward. In the distance, barely visible, the buildings angled toward Ben. He glanced up, looking for the telltale blips of street lamps on the opposite side of the cylinder, roughly forty kilometers away. The air was clear this morning, but the early light of the sola washed out the view. To his left, the Terminus rose dark and infinite like a fortress of the gods.

Ben returned his gaze to the street, let his mind wander. Last night's dream began to come back to him, its details emerging in his mind as if from a fog.

He saw a small flame at the tip of a candle. It flew through space, connected by an unseen tether to another, identical flame, a point of light far away in the distance. The two lights moved around each other, circling forever. The first flame became restless. It sputtered and grew brighter, longed to fly farther and burn through all the universe. It yearned to be released from the force that bound it to its companion.

The small flame struggled against the invisible thread, striving to be free of its twin and the predictable course it had run for its whole life. The flame bit and tore, and finally it broke away. But the moment the connection snapped, the flame went out, and the dark lonesome candle went tumbling away, while its twin in the far distance blazed as bright as ever.

The extinguished candle morphed into a sphere of Dorium, which ignited again and began to grow. It blazed with light, brighter and brighter, until the whole of Titan was consumed. Still it expanded, until it dwarfed the great planet Jupiter. On and on it went, until it was equal to the Sun. The Dorium and the sun began to orbit each other, dancing round and round until one by one the stars burned out around them. And after an eternity, or a moment, they merged into one and poured away their light into the void.

A wave of grief and terror washed over Ben as he relived the dream, and he shivered even as he ran. But its imagery gave him an idea, a picture, and he latched onto it as an anchor, desperate to cling to it until the mystery was revealed. The part near the end, where the Dorium orbited the Sun… orbited the Sun…solar system. The next instant Ben had it—a way to get rid of the Dorium and maybe turn a profit. The idea was less world-shattering than it had seemed before he pinned it down, as so many hints of brilliance turn out to be mundane when brought into the light. But it would do. It would give them a chance.

Ben turned and ran home at an easy pace, found the rest of the house was already awake and eating breakfast. Ben filled his plate with two waffles and an apple, then sat down to eat with Tiro. "I have an idea," he said.

"Ashley coming through as always," Tiro said with a smile. "Let's hear it."

Ben described the basic plan to his friend, and they invited the others to bounce it around and flesh out some of the details. Jess confirmed that the technical parts were difficult but doable, and could be encrypted sufficiently. By midmorning they were all hard at work, with a firm direction and sense of progress that last night had lacked.

The plan was simple: someone, ideally Ben or Tiro, would pose as a midlevel research director at one of the larger system-wide conglomerates. They would sell five kilos illegally to someone off-world, and arrange Titan as a covert meeting place for the exchange. At the meeting they would offer the remaining three kilos in exchange for more cash or a trade or even as a gesture of goodwill to encourage quiet. If they did it right, nobody would ever suspect they were locals.

The first task was to find a good identity to borrow. Only a handful of people within a given company would plausibly have access to that much Dorium. Solacore, Helia, and Novalink were the most promising targets, with a handful of others as backups if all three fell through.

Jess got on the Quill and hacked the corporate database for each company to download org charts and personnel files. They concentrated on the big energy research facilities, looking for directors and others who could get their hands on that much Dorium but who might also have a good reason for stealing it and selling to the highest bidder.

Helia and Novalink didn't pan out, but they got lucky with Solacore. Peter Emerson was a materials specialist at the New Horizons, a research center on Mars owned by Solacore. He had developed a ceramic shield that would allow mining bots to operate deeper in the gas giants' atmospheres, potentially opening a new source of rare minerals that hadn't been tapped before. It was a major breakthrough that landed Emerson industry-wide recognition, not to mention a juicy promotion and a tripled research budget. Only problem was, it was the deputy specialist, John Shepard, who had designed and perfected the shield. Jess found internal emails where Shepard had claimed credit but was effectively silenced by the higher-ups because Emerson had seniority and had already gone public with his claim.

John Shepard was their guy—he was no longer in Emerson's lab but still worked at New Horizons and had access to its Dorium. He definitely fit the bill for an employee with a grudge. Plus he looked a little like Axel.

Tiro knew plenty of people in the underground on Titan, and he put the word out to find a buyer. He knew a guy who knew a guy, et cetera, and could they help point him in the right direction? Jess did something similar with her off-world contacts in the hacker community, and between the two of them they had a lot of feelers out there, both locally and through the Quill.

That was the riskiest part, Ben knew, but there was no way around it. You could never be 100 percent sure, and they covered their tracks pretty well.

Word got around fast, and a couple of days later they had their contact. Asher Garrison was a Raptor—one of the hundred-odd independent outfits who existed apart from the law and most human society. They lived on ships, not colonies or terraformed worlds, and made their way by smuggling, robbery, and anything else they could accomplish through stealth and violence.

Asher Garrison moved weapons, drugs, stolen tech, you name it. He'd started out his Raptor career as a smuggler-for-hire, but eventually got into black-market trading, purchasing illicit goods himself and selling them for a profit. Rumor had it that lately he'd been robbing cargo shuttles on their way to and from the huge trans-system carriers.

That last part made Ben nervous. "You really think we should mess with a guy like that?" he asked when they met that evening to discuss the plan.

"He's the one that kept coming up," Tiro said. Jess nodded. "I got a handful of names, but most are really big dogs we want to avoid. He's big enough to handle our situation, but not one of the huge outfits."

Ben saw that several of the others were reluctant too. "I still don't like it," he said. "What's to stop him from robbing us? Or killing us?"

"We'll take precautions. Make him come alone, we have our people keeping an eye on him. Make him show us the cash before we bring in the Dorium, all that. We got this. Trust me. Hell, trust *yourself.* This was your plan, and it's a good one. But one way or another we were gonna bump up against a guy like this. We take initiative, do it on our terms, it's gonna work."

Ben stared ahead, thinking. He just didn't feel good about this.

"Look," Tiro said, "It's this or toss the Dorium. We don't have any better ideas."

That did the trick. One by one, everybody else voted to go with the plan—they couldn't bear the thought of passing up that much cash.

"You really good with this, Axel?" Ben said quietly. "It's your face the guy's gonna see the most."

Axel smiled. "Appreciate the concern, man, but like Tiro said, we got this." Tory squeezed his arm.

Ben nodded. "All right," he said.

Chapter 6

Hundreds of ships traversed the starfield. Visible only as pinpricks of light—the nearest of them was hundreds of kilometers away—they seemed to be so many wandering stars, as the planets had appeared to Earth's first astronomers. Freight shuttles, passenger ships, and mining transports moved in all directions with no discernible pattern. The effect was mesmerizing and eerie, as if space itself were beginning to come alive. Watching it through the train's window, Ben was tense with anticipation. The upcoming meeting with Asher Garrison weighed on him, sure, but this was different, an elusive feeling he couldn't quite name. As he looked on the intricate dance, Ben couldn't shake the impression that the universe had set something in motion.

He thought again of his dream, of Dorium and the Sun, and loneliness.

"You good, man?" Axel said beside him.

"Huh? Oh, yeah," Ben said. "Just antsy, that's all. Ready to get this done."

"I know what you mean," Axel said, his hand resting lightly on the case strapped securely across his legs. Inside the case were ten spheres of Dorium, just over five kilos. Ben had the other five zipped away in his pocket, ready to bring them out when the time was right. He looked over and saw his friend's hand float upward, before Axel brought it back down to his lap with a frustrated look.

Ben chuckled. Axel was really struggling in the train's zero-gravity environment. Ben couldn't tell if it was genuine or a nice touch to sell the part. John Shepard. They'd all thought Axel looked like the Solacore researcher supposedly disgusted enough to boost some Dorium. But when he donned the expensive but ill-fitting suit and wire-frame glasses, the resemblance was uncanny. Long as he could halfway act the role of Nervous Scientist with a Terrible Secret, Axel would have anybody fooled. Looking terribly unused to zero gravity was certainly in character, Ben thought. He could almost imagine Axel tumbling helplessly across the train car if the restraints were loosened.

"Breathtaking, isn't it?" Axel said, nodding back toward the window. "All that empty space, big and wide open."

"Yeah," Ben said. "I'd forgotten. The last time I made this trip was…I guess it was five years ago, for…for my entrance exams." His voice grew quiet.

"Mmm," Axel grunted. He looked warily at Ben.

Ben noticed the glance, smiled back at Axel. "It's cool man, all that's in the past. I'm over it."

Axel gave him a look that said he wasn't buying it.

"Really, I mean it. Besides, we have other things to focus on now." He glanced meaningfully at Axel's briefcase. Axel nodded and dropped the subject.

Across the aisle, Tiro sat by himself. When the train reached Kraken, they would all head for The Occident, the upscale restaurant where they'd arranged to contact Garrison.

The train streaked along the kilometer-wide Spine. The massive span of steel and carbon linked Titan's two habitats, Ligeia and Kraken. Across from Ben there was a crisp display showing a model of Titan: two cylinders, Ligeia on the left and Kraken on the right. They were long and their ends were rounded in gentle domes, making them appear like two cigars sitting side-by-side. The Spine linked them at their tops, looking in the image like a toothpick balanced across their tips.

The diagram showed a spine at the bottom too, but most people never saw it. That one conveyed cargo between the industrial zones of Ligeia and Kraken. The one on top housed the massive spaceport with its hundreds of docks, and it carried passengers from one cylinder to the other. Whenever someone mentioned the Spine, this was the one they meant.

A large sphere in the bottom of the picture represented their namesake: Saturn's moon Titan, which the colony orbited. Ben felt a swelling of pride when he saw that. There were hundreds of colonies orbiting Saturn or one of its moons. But Titan was the first. Titan symbolized so much for so many people. Bravery, ambition, the human drive toward adventure and exploration. Life had been hard for Ben, but he was glad he lived here.

He looked back out the window, glad they'd chosen the Orion Route that traveled on the outside of the Spine rather than one of the trains in its interior. It catered to tourists and those, like Ben, for whom a trip to the other cylinder was a rare occasion. He knew it was cheesy, but he enjoyed the rare opportunity to peer at space beyond.

There was a distant thud, and the train car bounced ever so slightly. Overhead a huge ship swooped past Ben's window, low-level thrusters carrying it away from the nearby dock it had just left. When it reached the requisite ten-kilometer distance from the port, it fired the fusion engines and sped rapidly toward the expanse beyond, seeming eager to join the dance of ships in the starlight.

Ben wondered what it would be like to leave the port in one of those massive spacecraft. What would he feel? What did Titan look like from that far away?

An automated voice brought Ben out of his reverie. "Now arriving, Port Kraken. Please remain seated until transport to the surface is completed."

The train slowed, then stopped. Looking out the window, Ben could now make out the enormous dome at the end of

Kraken, gently curving toward an abrupt horizon some twenty kilometers away. He craned his neck to look backward along the rail, which stretched away down the center of a wide, empty path. His own home, Ligeia, was visible at the other end, its dome capping the cylinder proper. Hundreds of docked spacecraft flanked the rail's path on either side, like mechanical statues lining an old world road.

One by one the cars uncoupled and entered a large chamber, where they attached to a conveyor that carried them inside the cylinder. Soon their car was up. They passed through a dim corridor and then emerged near the center of Kraken's Terminus. An elevator carried them along out to the edge of the Terminus. The sensation of weight gradually returned during the car's ten-minute trip to the edge, which they soon perceived as a descent to the surface. By the time they reached the bottom, they were back at a standard one G of gravity.

The car came to a stop, and they disembarked along with the other passengers. Behind them, the car slid forward to the departure platform, where a small crowd waited their turn to board and ascend to the spaceport. Not for the first time, Ben marveled at the feat of engineering and coordination that kept the passenger cars moving steadily up and down the elevator and across the Spine.

They descended the small arrival platform into the bustling throng of people below. As the capital, Titan saw more than its share of visitors from off-world. Most of them came to Kraken, which not only housed the massive government complex but also served as a center for history, arts, and entertainment. Where Ligeia was the lifeblood of the colony's production and remote mining, Kraken was the outward-facing metropolis, the hub of connection not only with the many colonies Titan controlled but also with the rest of the solar system.

Ben, Axel, and Tiro navigated the diverse crowd and boarded a monorail car toward the habitat's center. They rode for nearly fifteen minutes. Several kilometers to the south, the capital complex was easily visible, distinguished by its dominating skyscrapers and the eight monorail lines that converged toward it.

After an uneventful ride, they got off at their stop in Hyperia, a high-end entertainment district that clearly catered to tourists with means. Windows were heavily tinted, signage was alluring but subtle, and most people walking the streets sported outfits that likely cost as much as a month's tuition for Simon. Ben felt self-conscious in his own clothing, not just because they were lower quality but because his dress marked him as a clear outsider, somebody who had stumbled into the wrong part of town. He suddenly felt exposed, as if anybody could tell that the three of them were there on illegal business.

Maybe that's why Ben began looking for signs of trouble as they walked east, toward The Occident where they'd arranged to meet Garrison. Or maybe he was just nervous about the highly illegal business that they were, in fact, there to conduct. Whatever the reason, Ben started to notice things around them.

Two tall men in police uniforms stood on the corner up ahead. Their demeanor was casual and they made no move to hinder Ben and his companions, but he could feel their eyes on him as they passed. Were they just keeping tabs on out-of-towners, or did they suspect something more about what they were up to?

That wasn't the only thing that felt out of place. One person had been several paces behind them since they left the monorail. The streets were busy and the guy could have been up to anything, but Ben would feel a lot better if he turned or stopped.

Stay calm, Ben thought. *It's just nerves. Don't let them get the best of you.* He breathed steadily. Axel and Tiro seemed at ease. Tiro especially was always aware of his surroundings; even if he was bold, things seldom took him by surprise. If he didn't smell trouble, it was probably just Ben's imagination.

A young woman crossed the street ahead of them, walking in their direction. Nothing in particular about her appearance stood out; she looked no different from the hundred other men and women that they'd been passing for the last several blocks. But something about her caught Ben's eye—maybe her posture or the way she looked ahead, seemingly more alert than most others. She wore a stylish but casual outfit: dark pants and boots with a trim jacket over a bright, orange and gray shirt. A few years older than Ben, she had dark brown hair pulled up in a tight ponytail. She walked quickly, hands in her pockets. She caught Ben's eye as they passed each other, gave him a quick smile, and kept walking.

She'd been on the train, he realized suddenly. That's what it was. He'd noticed that same ponytail exiting the monorail a few cars ahead. That meant two people following them, and they were now five blocks from the train. He glanced backward but couldn't find her amid the crowd.

"Something's off," he whispered to Tiro without looking at his friend. "I think we're being followed."

"You're just nervous. Relax," Tiro said.

"I've seen two people now. Maybe more."

"We're almost there," Tiro said under his breath. "The Occident isn't much farther. You'll feel better when we're inside."

They walked two more blocks, and Ben fought to silence the alarms going off in his head. He thought he felt eyes on him, but whenever he looked he didn't see anything definitive out of place. Yet as he let his eyes wander, scanning the crowd ahead and beside them, he began to discern a subtle pattern. Certain individuals moved in a way that looked planned, balanced. One or two could be written off as odd behavior, but four or five suddenly felt like deliberate coordination—with Ben and his friends at the center.

He made a fist, relaxed his hands. The Occident was just ahead. *Breathe, relax. Focus.* It made no sense why anyone would follow them. He was just being paranoid.

They reached the restaurant without incident, and Ben opened the door. Tiro entered first, followed by Axel. Ben gave one last scan of the street, saw nothing of interest, and walked in. The Occident was impressive. Its understated exterior belied the sophisticated, heady atmosphere inside. The space was crowded without being cramped, with high ceilings and dim, electric blue lighting arranged in intricate fractal patterns overhead. Vibrant holo displays adorned the walls, with images constantly, slowly shifting. Crisp architectural lines defined the space and created a natural flow through the room. Low music played in the background, underneath the din of a hundred private conversations. This was as good a place as any to talk, to conduct sensitive business, illegal or otherwise.

Axel walked to the host's stand, briefcase in hand, as Ben and Tiro scanned the room like practiced security personnel. "I have a reservation for Quincy," Axel told the host, following the instructions they'd been given by Garrison through the Quill.

The host smiled. "Of course. One moment please." She tapped a few commands on the holo display in front of her. "Follow me. Mr. Garrison is expecting you."

Ben and his friends exchanged a wary look, then followed the host. She led them through the restaurant, a winding course that took them to the far right corner. She opened a door that blended into the wall, which led to a private dining area that was much quieter than the main restaurant outside. Garrison must have good connections, Ben thought.

The dining area was empty, and the host led them to the other side, through another door. It opened into a long, narrow room, and Ben could hear the sounds of the kitchen to his left. He frowned as the host walked that way, but they had little choice but to follow. She stopped halfway across the room and opened another door. This time she didn't go through, but held it open for them.

"Mr. Garrison is in there?" Axel asked. The woman said nothing, just smiled and gestured for them to enter.

"Well then," Axel said nervously. "Thank you." Tiro went in, followed by Axel with Ben at the back. The door closed behind him. The low light showed them a single flight of stairs ahead, and they walked up. When they reached the top, another door stood closed before them. They looked at one another, and Tiro shrugged. Axel knocked twice.

"It's open," came a deep, rich voice from the other side. They opened the door and walked through into a wide but otherwise unremarkable hallway.

Ben blinked. He didn't know what he'd imagined. The kind of place where you'd expect to make a shady deal with a crime boss, he supposed. Dark wood panels, red carpet, plush sofas, and a massive desk, like the things you saw in the holovids. But this ninety-million-ether black-market transaction with a smuggler was evidently going to go down in a hallway. It was even well lit, with bright overhead lights and large windows on the opposite side.

Two men and a woman waited in the center of the hall. They'd been conversing among themselves but fell quiet and turned to face Tiro, Axel, and Ben as they arrived. The man in the center was tall, just shy of two meters. He looked about forty-five years old, give or take, with short brown hair. He wore casual pants and a coarse, dark brown jacket, with heavy boots. His face was weathered and rough, but handsome, darker than Ben would have expected for someone who probably spent most of his time on a spaceship. Even a quick first impression suggested charisma and authority. That had to be Garrison.

The other man and the woman were dressed similarly, and both were shorter than Garrison. The man had close blond hair and a thick, muscular chest. He seemed tense, eager, maybe a bit angry, as if he would explode on someone at the first sign of confrontation. The woman stood relaxed, her short dark hair swept back from her face, regarding Ben and his friends with a cool indifference. Ben couldn't decide which of the two was more intimidating.

"John Shepard, I take it?" the man in the center said, addressing Axel.

"Yes," Axel said, turning to face the trio in the center of the hall. "Asher Garrison?"

"Pleased to meet you," the man said. He glanced at Ben and Tiro. "I see you brought company."

Tiro took up position close to Axel on his left side, near the door. Ben walked to the opposite side by the window, turned so he was facing Axel but could also see down both sides of the hall.

Axel nodded. "For security. One can't be too careful. I see you agree."

"Indeed," Garrison said. Ben now noticed a fourth person standing several meters behind Garrison, leaned against the wall, and another man and woman at the far end of the hall with their backs to him, evidently guarding the hallway from that side. They all wore dark business suits, almost as if it were a uniform. The other end of the hall, behind Axel, took a turn about ten meters away. Ben guessed there were at least two more guarding the hallway there, out of sight. That made eight altogether, at least, and almost certainly all armed.

"Well," Garrison went on, "is that it?" He gestured to the briefcase Axel carried.

"Yes," Axel said, opening the case. "Ten spheres of Dorium, five point three three kilos total."

Garrison took the case and looked inside, then handed it to the man beside him, who began lifting out the spheres and scanning them with a gem one by one. Ben assumed the gem held a spectrometer, like Jess had used at the house. He watched impatiently as the man methodically analyzed the spheres and returned each one to the case as he finished with it. The other guy, leaning against the wall behind Garrison, craned his neck forward, clearly interested.

The man's mouth twitched in a satisfied half-smile as he read the report on the fourth sphere. He frowned as he got to the tenth. He looked intently at the readout on his gem, then glanced at Garrison and subtly shook his head.

"All right," Garrison said, closing the case with all ten spheres back inside and handing it to the woman. She held it under one arm, regarding Ben and his friends with the same casual attitude as before.

"Is there a problem?" Axel asked.

Garrison put his lips together and narrowed his eyes. "No," he said. "No, it all checks out."

Axel cleared his throat. "Excellent. And payment? We agreed on ninety million. Nine per sphere."

"Of course," Garrison said. "But first, remind me how you came by it."

Chapter 7

"What does it matter?" Axel said. "The spectrometer showed it is authentic, yes?"

"Oh yes," Garrison said. "Just like I expected, for the most part. But I like a good story. Humor me."

Axel shifted uncomfortably. "It belongs, er, belonged, to my institution, New Horizons. I took it from them."

"Why? You don't strike me as the greedy type."

"You'd be surprised," Axel said. "But also…they screwed me. Patented an invention of mine without credit, promoted my superior instead, and hung me out to dry. But why are you asking me this? Surely you dug into my background for yourself."

"I did," Garrison said with a smile. "Which is why I'm curious. You're a ceramics specialist, right? So why do you have access to Dorium?"

"It's a blanket security clearance," Axel said with a shrug. "You never know what you'll come across in the course of research."

"But wasn't it suspicious? Access is different from just taking it home. What are the security protocols, and how did you skirt them?"

Axel hesitated a moment, but only a moment. "Mr. Garrison," he said, "that's revealing too much about New Horizons. I've stolen enough from them already, and I haven't been paid for that yet." Ben was impressed. Go Axel.

Garrison smiled. "Fair enough. It's interesting, though." He paused and looked around, back down the hall toward the guards behind him.

"You see, I have a big crew," Garrison went on, "I guess you probably know I'm a Raptor, you seem like you did your homework. Well, whenever I have to visit a colony for a job, I like to leave the crew behind. Bring them to a colony, especially one like Titan, and all of a sudden they start acting like they're on leave—drinking, getting in fights, bunch of bush-league pirate shit, not like proper Raptors." He paused and gestured to his two companions. "These two are cool, but the rest, well.

"Thing is, though, I do like to be careful. I want a lot of guys on my side when I'm meeting someone. So I did what I usually do. I reached out to the local criminals, I know a few of them here on Titan. I talked to Val Minos, worked with him before. You probably don't know them, but the Minos family owns the restaurant back there. The Occident. They own this whole building, actually. Good piece of real estate. Got their hands in a little bit of everything.

"Anyway, I reached out to Val Minos, told him I needed to see about some Dorium, would they be interested in running security for me while I take care of the deal? You know what he said?"

Garrison paused and regarded Axel. "He said we're missing some Dorium. Eight kilos, just up and disappeared right here on Titan less than a week ago."

Ben didn't like where this was heading.

Axel swallowed hard. "You should tell your friend to be more careful. Eight kilos is a lot of Dorium to lose. Now, about the payment. You can transmit—"

Garrison laughed, cutting him off. "Hey, Val!" he yelled. The guy in the suit leaning against the wall stepped forward and turned to face them. "This guy says you need to be more careful!"

Shit shit shit, it was a setup. Ben's heart pounded, and he suddenly realized just how outnumbered they were. Screw the money, they had to get out of here now.

The one called Val walked over slowly, stood beside Garrison, and glared at Axel.

Garrison turned serious all of a sudden. "Let me ask you again. How exactly did you steal Dorium from New Horizons? Where'd they have it? What did you do? How did you extract it without raising suspicion?"

Axel took a step back. "Mr. Garrison, as I said before, only the Dorium is for sale. If you want proprietary information about my institute, we'll have to negotiate that separately."

"Here's what I think," Garrison said. He looked at Tiro and Ben before continuing. "I think the three of you are some shit kickers who stumbled onto a little Dorium. I don't know if you're that smart or just that lucky, but here you are. And I think you have access to three more kilos that you haven't told me about."

Ben noticed that the suits down the hall had started moving their way. Four more were coming around the corner on the other end.

"Now, Val here tells me this is his Dorium and he's very interested in getting ahold of it again. The business people or whoever he's involved with will be all over his butt if he doesn't deliver. Isn't that right, Val?"

Val stiffened at the all-too-accurate summary of his predicament but said nothing.

"And I said to him, Val, this is a good price and I've worked out buying this black-market Dorium fair and square," Garrison went on. "And you three are probably lying, but maybe Val is. But it really don't matter to me. Ninety million for five kilos. That's what I care about. So this is what I decided."

Garrison backed away and his two crew members went with him, the woman still holding the case with its ten precious spheres inside. "We're gonna keep this. All this," he said with a glance at Val, who watched him anxiously and with a hint of anger. "And I'm gonna hang onto my money for now. I'll let you and the Minos family work out who the Dorium belongs to. You settle it…however you feel like, and just let me know who to pay. You both know how to reach me."

By now, all seven suits stood around Tiro, Ben, and Axel, way too close for comfort. The one called Val looked at them with murder in his eyes. Garrison and his two mates walked out the same door that Ben and the others had come through earlier, leaving it wide open in a gesture of indifference.

"Where's the rest of it?" Val Minos said, stalking toward Axel.

"I don't know what you mean," Axel said. "I don't know what happened to your Dorium. We just arrived here today from—"

"Bullshit," Val said. "You're local boys. You smell like Ligeia. Now hand over the other five spheres, or—"

"Or what?" Tiro said. He'd been silent till now, but Ben could tell his blood was boiling. Tiro was ready to fight. Not good. Think Ben, think. It was seven against three, no way out and no way they could win a fight with these odds. Think!

Val snorted. "You three don't have a clue what you're mixed up in, do you?"

Val and the others advanced until Ben and his friends were pinned against the windows.

Ben glanced out the window, vaguely aware of movement outside that reminded him of the coordination he'd imagined earlier. He caught a glimpse of the same woman, too, the one who'd followed them from the train. What was going on now?

"Sounds to me like we're all up in some smuggler bullshit," Tiro said. "It's not our fault you can't manage to—"

The guy beside Val cuffed Tiro across the temple, cutting him off. "You stole from the Minos family," he said. "The rest of our Dorium is the difference between a quick death and a slow, painful one." He touched the blaster in a holster at his hip.

Val stepped forward and punched Tiro in the face, sending him to the ground. A second guy did the same to Axel, while a third caught Ben in the stomach, knocking the breath out of him.

Val hit Tiro a second time, then dragged him to his feet. "The Dorium," he said. "Now!" He practically lifted Tiro by the collar of his shirt.

Ben coughed as he straightened, his stomach aching. He had an idea, and they were way past Hail Mary time. "Hey, new guy!" he wheezed to nobody in particular. He saw someone stir out of the corner of his eye. He turned to the right, found his man. "Yeah, you," he said, more clearly this time. He nodded toward Val. "Does he know you're a cop?"

The guy laughed. "What?"

"It took me a minute to remember where I'd seen you," Ben said. "I'm guessing he don't know."

"Whatever," the guy said, dismissing him, but Val paused. He relaxed his grip on Tiro's shirt, turned slightly, and looked at his companion. "What does he mean?"

"What? Oh come on, don't tell me you believe this kid."

"What does he mean?" Val said, an edge to his voice.

A glance, a shift in posture—a split second of confusion and hesitation—that was the best opening Ben would get. He stiffened his hand and slammed it into Val's throat, then lowered his shoulder and knocked him into the guy beside him. He rushed across the hall toward the open door Garrison had left through.

Tiro and Axel reacted immediately, catching onto Ben's idea. They each hit a different member of the Minos gang and knocked them backward before following Ben. The sudden violence bought them precious seconds, and they crossed the five meters to the door hoping it would be enough.

Three meters to the door. One meter. Nearly there…

The world exploded. A brilliant flash blinded Ben just as he reached the door, and a concussive force slammed against his back and set off ringing in his ears. It was disorienting, and he stumbled forward and through the opening. He missed a step and fell, too long, vaguely remembering something about a set of stairs. Then his shoulder erupted with pain, and his vision went dark.

"Ben? Ben!" The voice sounded like he was under water. "Ben!"

Ben shook his head, saw a blur in front of his face that resolved into Tiro and Axel. Blood was coming from one of Tiro's ears, but otherwise they seemed normal. "Ben! Ben, are you OK?"

Ben groaned. His shoulder was on fire and his ears were ringing.

"Ben, listen to me. You gotta go!"

Ben's head cleared, and the ringing faded into a roar somewhere behind Tiro. He saw the top of the stairs, where there was smoke and flashes of light, and lots of shouting. Somehow he'd only been out for a second or two.

"What, what happened?" Ben asked.

"Not sure," Tiro said. "Felt like a concussion grenade and now the Minos guys are fighting."

"They didn't follow us?"

"No, there's a lot more voices now. It sounds like they're fighting somebody else."

Ben suddenly remembered the feeling back on the street, how he'd seen the same thing outside the window moments earlier. "Police raid," he groaned. "Told you we were being followed before. They were waiting to bust us."

Tiro nodded. "Makes sense. We got lucky. Gotta move now, though. One way or another, somebody's bound to come down those stairs."

Ben stood, wobbled, then steadied himself. "I'm OK," he said. "Let's go."

"You and Axel get back to the house," Tiro said. "Work with Jess, she'll get some new IDs into your gems. You shouldn't have trouble getting back across the Spine."

"Wait, why aren't you coming?" Ben asked.

"I'm going after Garrison," Tiro said, his voice hard.

"No way!" Ben said. "That's—"

Tiro didn't wait, he was gone before Ben could say another word.

"Come on," Axel said. "Tiro will be fine."

"Hey!" The voice came from the top of the stairs.

"Let's *go!*" Axel pulled Ben and took off down the hall back toward the restaurant.

Ben stumbled after him and regained his footing just as a blast struck the wall behind him. He didn't know if it was the Minos family or the police.

Ben and Axel flew down the hall toward The Occident. They reached the private dining room, then the main floor. Startled patrons turned and shouted as they weaved through the elegant space, knocking over servers and drinks on their dash to the front.

Axel and Ben burst through the door onto the street, startling a woman in street clothes standing outside. She recovered immediately and chased them, catching Ben from behind before he'd even gotten five steps away. She jerked him backward, nearly pulling him down.

Ben caught his balance and spun to face her, then stopped. It was the same woman he'd seen on the street earlier and then out the window, the one who'd given him a brief smile. Now her face was all business, and she was swinging a fist at Ben's head.

He blocked it, and she struck his arm with bone-jarring force. Ben stepped inside her guard and caught her with an uppercut that made his hurt shoulder roar with pain. He followed with a shove to knock her backward. She rolled with it, grabbed his hand, and pulled him off balance. They tussled briefly, then she caught him with a blow to the face and a quick kick to the ribs. He swung again at her, but she easily dodged and shoved him against the restaurant's window, then to the ground. She stood over him and brought up her gem to call for help.

Axel tackled her from behind, knocking her off of Ben and scrambling free before she could engage him too. Ben got up and they scrambled away, neither wanting any more to do with a clearly well-trained fighter.

Ben and Axel rounded the corner and started up the next street, not sure who exactly was after them or how many there were. The woman was probably the police. Were they the ones who'd chased them in the restaurant too? Or was it one of Val's guys? Ben didn't care to find out.

They sprinted up the street, made three quick turns, but they knew the police or whoever would be close behind. "In here!" Ben yelled, darting into a store front.

The store sold high-end clothing and fashion accessories, and at the moment there were no patrons inside. "Welcome to—" the lone manager said. Ben and Axel didn't wait to hear more. They ran to the back of the store, looking desperately for a supply room or whatever back entrance the store might have.

They found a door and ran through, leaving the confused store manager behind, and found themselves in a hall that looked eerily similar to the one where they'd met Asher Garrison. "What now?" Axel asked.

"There's a lot of doors here," Ben said. "If we can get through one and into some upper floors, maybe we can lose them. This building connects with at least three others, and they can't cover all the exits."

"OK," Axel said. He ran four doors down and tried it. "Locked." He tried the next one. "This one too."

Ben tried two more with the same result. "Second time in two weeks," Ben muttered.

"Huh?" Axel asked.

"Nothing," Ben said. "Let's do this one."

"But it's locked."

"Not for long," Ben said, tapping his gem. "Just sit tight."

"Ah," Axel said, suddenly understanding. He stepped back. "Good luck."

Ben opened his gem, brought up the controls for the Aurora program, and turned off his implant. Light and color became more vivid as the surge of energy flooded his consciousness, and a familiar buzzing rose behind his eyes. He fought through it, put his hand to the door's controls, and reached. Heat and energy assailed him, his focus wavered. His body temperature climbed and his breathing sped up. Nearly there. He sensed the mechanism and nudged it.

"In!" Axel said when the lock flashed green. He opened the door and stepped through just as Ben fell to his knees, tired from the run and now the intense exertion of his ability. Axel reached toward Ben to help him up.

Down the hall, the door to the clothing store opened and the woman from before stepped through. She looked the other way first. Ben shoved Axel backward and slammed the door closed, using his mind to lock it before Axel could come back through.

The woman heard the noise and ran toward Ben. He straightened, staggered to his feet. He pawed at his gem, desperate to reengage his implant. His vision narrowed, his hand slipped. The woman stopped short, seeing that he was struggling with something.

The pain grew, the urgency of his escape suddenly overshadowed by the danger of the Aurora. The energy was too much. He felt like he was going to burst. He couldn't get caught, couldn't go to prison or whatever else they had in mind for him. Something about that desperation channeled the energy coming at him, turned his Aurora into something more powerful than a clever way to open doors. A switch flipped, his vision cleared, and the energy within him surged outward. He turned it toward the woman coming at him, hit her in the chest with an impossibly quick and powerful blow.

She staggered backward, looked at him in shock. He kept after it, pressing his advantage, fueled by his ability and the incoming energy it allowed him to harness. He caught her above her eye, opening a nasty-looking cut that registered in his vision as a bright blemish. The woman responded quickly, coming back at him with a flurry of kicks and punches. Enormous quantities of energy coursed through Ben. He was burning like a torch. He moved like lightning, but the woman evaded, he couldn't hit her.

Ben's control didn't last. The surge of energy soon surpassed his ability to contain it, and he slowed. The woman stepped forward and kicked him in the stomach, knocking the breath out of him. He collapsed, gasping for air, head pounding from the rush of energy still assaulting him. The woman stepped backward, watching him with wariness and mild astonishment. She saw his gem on the floor, picked it up, and calmly examined the Aurora program. At her feet Ben fought the surge of pain. The woman reached into the gem's display and made a single swipe. Ben's implant reengaged.

The raging heat inside him subsided, the blinding light faded, his body temperature lowered. He lay there, exhausted, unable to run, barely able to breathe. The woman muttered something into her gem, then walked over to Ben. She looked into his eyes, narrowed her own as she seemed to consider what she would do. Then she reached into her pocket, pulled out a syringe, and injected its contents into Ben's arm.

Ben resisted feebly, then not at all. His world faded, and all became dark.

Chapter 8

Ben walked through a dim place in search of his friends, walls of rock on all sides like the caves on Earth he'd read about and seen in the holovids. Water surrounded him, and as he splashed through it began to rise. Faster and faster the water rose, and Ben soon found himself trapped in a small room. His friends were somewhere nearby, but he couldn't remember who they were or where. He activated his gem and tried to contact them, yelled into the darkness, but no one answered.

The water rushed in, higher than Ben's head. He swam, furiously kicking to stay on the surface as water swirled and the ceiling grew closer. Ben fought, mouth and nose above the water, terrified. The water pushed all the way to the top, overwhelmed Ben, and pulled him under. Ben sank to the bottom. He felt calm and opened his eyes. He began to walk around, and discovered he could breathe. All was still. Water engulfed him, but it was no more deadly than the air around him had been moments earlier. Ben moved through the room, felt the water slide gently past his legs and arms and face. He saw an open door that had been there all along. Still under water, Ben walked out of the room. He made his way through the cave once again in search of his friends…

Ben woke to a loud, thrashing sound. He shook his head, clearing it of the dream. What time was it? He registered the sound again. It was music. Fast-paced and percussive, with an aggressive melody and heavy vocals. *Dammit Miles, turn it down. The rest of us are trying to sleep.* Wait, why was his room so dark? Where was his window?

Ben sat up, curious and mildly alarmed. Then the fog cleared and he remembered. The events of yesterday crashed back into his consciousness like an avalanche, heavy and violent and final. He'd been caught. Arrested. Tried to run, got his ass kicked. At least he was alive. That counted for something, right? God, they'd nearly died at the hands of that Minos family. Had Axel gotten away? He hoped so. Tiro too.

Ben looked around. Faint light was coming from somewhere. After a few moments his eyes adjusted and he could make out the rest of the room. More like a cell. Roughly square, about three meters to a side, with an uncomfortably low ceiling. Other than his narrow bed, a small empty table, and an austere chair, all bolted to the floor, the place was empty. He was alone, but that didn't tell him much. If he were the cops, he'd want to keep everybody separate to question them. He had no way of knowing if Tiro and Axel had gotten caught, too, or if they'd managed to get away.

The door was completely transparent, but Ben was under no illusion that he could break it. It was surely a high-strength synthetic polymer that could withstand an explosion. The little light was coming from the hall. The music too. Ben stood and walked toward the door. He looked out, and was surprised to see a woman standing with her back against the opposite wall, eyes closed and head leaned back. She wore a dark green shirt and and black pants, respectable but comfortable, the kind of thing business folks wore if they expected to be running errands all day. A gem strapped to her wrist, the source of the music, was glowing in a rapid, rhythmic pulse as it played.

Ben tapped softly on the door. She started, opened her eyes, and regarded him as she slapped the holo and cut the music. "You're up," she said.

Ben recognized her as the street clothes officer who'd fought and apprehended him the day before. Same brown hair, now worn loose, same hard look in her eyes. He remembered those green eyes, the subtle angles of her face, the full lips pressed together tightly. It was the last thing he'd seen before she knocked him out. In her suit she looked younger than she'd appeared yesterday. She couldn't be more than a couple years older than he was.

The officer studied Ben for a moment, then frowned and tapped her gem. The door clicked as it unlocked. "I thought I'd have a little more time to myself." She opened the door and gestured for Ben to step out. "Let's go."

Ben stepped past her and noted she was shorter by a few centimeters. She was probably armed but didn't have a weapon in her hand. If he timed it right, maybe he could catch her by surprise…No. Terrible idea. His ribs still ached from that kick yesterday, and he was sure his face looked like hell. He was in no mood for round two in the middle of a hall where he didn't know which way was out.

She jutted her chin down the hall. "That way," she said. Ben walked down the dim corridor toward a door at the far end, passing several doors on either side. He wondered if they all contained cells like his, and whether Axel or Tiro might be in one of them. He hoped they'd gotten away.

Ben cleared his throat. "You always listen to that kind of music? Doesn't it hurt your head?" Nothing. He tried again. "You, uh, really worked me over yesterday. Do all cops know how to fight like that?" Silence.

They kept walking down long, close halls and through a series of open doors. They made several turns, the woman indicating where to go with clipped commands. "Left. Keep going. That way." The overhead lights were brighter after the first turn, but the halls were bare. No signs even at the larger intersections, not even room numbers on the doors they passed. Most doors were closed. Occasionally they passed an open door, and more than once the space opened up into a wide, open area with hallways leading various directions, but they saw no other people. Soon Ben was thoroughly lost.

Ben tried to make conversation again after a few minutes. If he could get her to talk, maybe he could find out what kind of trouble he was in. "Do you guys usually let prisoners wake up on their own? I figured this would be a 'you-follow-our-schedule-not-the-other-way-around' kind of place."

"You needed time to recover," she said. "My orders were to bring you as soon as you were up."

Time to recover. Orders. OK, yeah, that wasn't much to go on. He could be at the local police headquarters on Kraken, or maybe they'd turned him over to the Titan Militia. That seemed likely. Their facilities would probably be about this size; it felt too big for police.

Ben snorted to himself. This was barely more than guesswork. He'd never been inside a police office before, much less a Militia base. For all he knew, this was a spaceship…

The thought stopped him in his tracks. Narrow hall, low ceiling. His heart beat faster.

"Ow," the woman behind him said as she bumped into him. He stumbled forward. "I didn't say stop. Go on."

Ben recovered his balance and kept walking, his mind rattling off dreadful possibilities. If he was on a ship, that meant he was in big trouble. With no long-term prisons on Ligeia or Kraken, most offenders on Titan were placed under house arrest. Only the big-time convicts were sent off-colony to dedicated prison cylinders or asteroid mines. He looked around. The space was tight, efficient, like you'd expect on a ship. His cell or whatever room that was had been the same.

Surely he wasn't on a ship already, though, was he? It wouldn't make sense, he'd have to be tried first. But then again he'd committed a serious crime—stealing Dorium and associating with a Raptor and whoever the hell those Minos guys were. That might be Colony Security level crime. What was he thinking? Of course it was now, with everybody on heightened alert after Verona. He'd done the kind of crime that could get you disappeared and locked away. Without a hearing, without a trace. Shit. Why had he gone along with Tiro's plan? Why why why why?

Ben was still cursing his luck and his own poor choices when he rounded a corner and saw a closed door a few meters away. He approached the door then stopped, unsure whether he should open it. His mind swirled with possibilities, none of them good. He considered another escape attempt, then dismissed the idea immediately. Where could he run if he really was on a ship?

"It's unlocked," the officer behind him said. "Open it. Slow."

Ben slid it open and half turned as he did so, glancing backward at his guard. "Go on," she said.

On the other side of the door, the hall widened into some kind of waiting area. It was furnished with wooden tables and padded black chairs that looked expensive but not comfortable. The right wall held a single door, in the old-fashioned style that swung on hinges rather than sliding.

Ben walked in and the officer followed close behind. "In there," she said, indicating the door. "He's expecting you."

Ben turned the handle and opened the door cautiously, unsure if he should have knocked. "Come in," said a gruff voice before he'd gotten it halfway open. Ben continued, glancing back as he stepped into the room. The officer who'd escorted him didn't follow, and the door swung closed behind him. "Have a seat."

In front of Ben were two cushioned chairs facing a large, dark wooden desk. A middle-aged man sat behind it reading a document on his gem. He wore a dark brown suit, considerably more formal than what the officer outside wore. He looked more ready for a business meeting than a police interrogation or prisoner processing or whatever Ben was about to endure.

Ben glanced around the room as he sat. The office was large, sparsely decorated but well used. Lived in. To the right of the desk was a table piled with stacks of paper, loose pens, and two coffee mugs. Beyond that was a sitting area with a similarly cluttered coffee table in front of a worn sofa and loveseat. A large shelf against the far wall held books, more paper, and a vintage plasma gun and space helmet. The walls were bare except for two large maps to the left of the desk: one of the solar system, and one showing Titan's orbital colonies. Titan itself, Saturn's largest moon, sat in the center, with the colonies scattered around it like a swarm of stars. The most prominent colonies were indicated with bright red dots. Ben noted with a twinge of heartache the red star that indicated the capital colony, his home. Ligeia and Kraken. Titan. Would he ever see it again?

The man behind the desk finished reading, made a few swipes through the document hovering above his gem, then swiped down to put the device on standby.

"Ben Ashley," the man said, turning his attention toward Ben. He smoothed his jacket and leaned forward. "You sleep OK? We thought you'd be out for a bit longer."

Ben cleared his throat. "Yes. Uh, yes sir."

"Do you know where you are?"

Ben paused a moment, his throat dry, then spoke his nightmare aloud. "Prison ship?"

"Ha!" the man leaned his head back, genuinely amused. "That'd be something, wouldn't it? No, you're still on Titan. Kraken."

Relief washed over Ben, followed by confusion. "Then where am I? Which police headquarters is this?"

The man shook his head. "Good guess, but I'm not the police. It's up to you if that's a good thing or a bad thing. I'm with TI, and you're in our Bradley headquarters."

Ben made a face. "TI...Titan Intelligence?" he asked as the acronym's meaning suddenly came to him.

"That's right. I'm John Nichols, Titan Intel Special Agent in Charge. I've taken responsibility for you for the time being."

Titan Intel. Bradley. What was Ben doing in the nerve center of Kraken, in the building complex that housed the offices of the Titan federal government? Why was he speaking with a T.I. special agent?

"Pleased to meet you, sir, but I think there's been a mistake. I don't know what I'm doing here, but I—"

"You're in big trouble, Ben Ashley. You know that?" Ben fell quiet, swallowed hard. He was suddenly on the verge of tears.

"Huge trouble," Nichols went on. "Not only do you hack the cargo loaders at Port Ligeia, vandalize colony property, rob a cargo shipment, evade police, and fence stolen property all over the Third Ward…" He jabbed a finger at the desk to punctuate each violation.

"Not only do you do all that," Nichols said, his voice growing louder. "You steal and attempt to sell almost a *hundred million ether* worth of Dorium to one of the most dangerous Raptors this side of the asteroid belt, and you invite him here to our capital colony." He gritted his teeth and practically growled that last part.

"The Dorium," Ben said. "We didn't have anything to do with Verona. We only found it—"

Nichols cut him off with a wave. "I know Verona wasn't you. Hell, anybody can tell you've never been off the colony. The stuff you actually did was bad enough that I don't have to frame you for something you didn't do."

Ben opened his mouth to reply, then stopped short as Nichols's earlier words hit home. He suddenly felt like the room was spinning. *Hack the cargo loaders. Vandalize. Rob a cargo shipment. Evade police.* This wasn't just about getting caught making a black-market sale, Ben realized. Not about being a suspect in the Verona massacre. Not even about being in possession of an outrageous amount of Dorium with no good explanation. The special agent knew everything Ben and his friends had done from the night of the robbery. Everything. Ben's hands were clammy. He couldn't speak. Couldn't move.

Special Agent Nichols saw him grow pale and wide-eyed. "Oh yes," he said, his voice normal again. "Yes, we know all that. You and your friends are…pretty clever. And pretty lucky. But you'll find we're resourceful, too, here at Bradley. We are in the intelligence business, after all." He slid his gem to the center of the desk and activated it, made a motion with his finger to bring up an image. A still shot of Tiro walking down the street appeared in the air above the device. Ben recognized the place, it wasn't too far from their house. "Tiro Washburn," Nichols said.

He swiped left, and an image of Axel replaced Tiro. "Axel Martin, aka John Shepard. Good likeness for that Solacore guy, all told. Like I said, you're clever."

Another swipe brought up a short woman with golden hair. Even at a distance, her posture looked like she was annoyed with something. "Jessica Davis. She's the computer whiz, isn't she? We found a lot of nice programs on your gem. That was her doing, I guess. You two have a romantic thing going on? Or just a weird, 'it's complicated,' she's-my-friend-who's-a-girl-but-not-my-girlfriend sort of deal? Anything?"

Ben said nothing, just stared. Seeing Tiro, Axel, and Jess brought a wave of remorse, and he suddenly didn't trust himself to say anything without crying.

Nichols shrugged, then swiped again, and again, each time bringing up another of Ben's friends. "Tory Alvarez." *Swipe.* "Miles Williams." *Swipe.* "Dominic Jacobs." *Swipe.* The last swipe brought up a picture of Simon, in his Harlow Academy uniform, walking across the courtyard with some friends. "Simon Ashley." Nichols paused, stared hard at Ben, then shut the gem down. Simon's image disappeared, leaving Ben alone with the intelligence officer. "Little brother wasn't in on it, best we can tell, but you know, we have to keep tabs on him, too. Due diligence and all."

Ben's mind spun out of control as he tried to wrangle meaning from the facts in front of him, to place himself in the situation and figure out where he and his friends stood. His voice trembled as he croaked out the only question he could pin down: "How?"

"We've been keeping tabs on the Minos family. They smuggle stuff in and out of Titan, mostly too small for TI to bother with. But we got a tip about a bigger than usual deal going down linked to the port robbery a while back. We sent one of our agents to check it out. Agent Adams out there," he said with a wave at the door. "She and her team blew up the meeting and brought you in with most of the Minos guys. We hacked your gem and reconstructed everything up to that point, including your known associates. Speaking of…" He fished something out of his coat pocket and slid it across the desk. Ben's gem.

Ben reached for it, surprised. Nichols caught his hesitation. "We have to give it back. Confiscating a gem is considered unethical treatment of a prisoner. A couple centuries ago something like a gem might have been considered a tool or possession. But that device works in tandem with your link." Nichols tapped the side of his head. "That makes it really an extension of your body. Separating you from your gem is tantamount to cutting off your hand. Or so the legal arguments go. I mean sure, you're a federal security case and that's a gray area. But us keeping it is more hassle than it's worth, really. Unless you want to give it to us. Sign a thing, you know? You want to sign a thing?" Ben shook his head. "That's what I thought. It's all yours, then."

Ben took the gem and tucked it into his pocket. He'd have to check it later. They probably deleted some stuff. Gray area and all that.

"So we were being followed," Ben said. "On our way to The Occident. That was you guys?"

Special Agent Nichols raised an eyebrow. "You noticed that? I'll have to have a talk with our team, it sounds like somebody got sloppy."

"I saw…something," Ben said. "I'm still not sure what. I thought I was just being paranoid."

Nichols nodded, then rested a hand on the desk and looked hard at Ben. "Anyway, you can imagine our surprise when we found out we were dealing with a small-time, mostly unknown local crew, and that you all initiated things with Asher Garrison, not the Minos family." He shook his head. "We still aren't sure exactly how you pulled off the robbery. That was impressive."

Ben said nothing for a long moment. "Where are they?" he said finally. It came out as a whisper.

"Hmmm?" the special agent leaned forward.

"What did you do with them?"

"The Minos guys? We sent them off-world already. A little place where…well let's call it an unofficial purgatory. Off-the-books ship. We're trying to get one to flip on Val. Little shit got away, can you believe it? Anyway, the one who flips on him gets a deal, the rest—"

"I meant my friends," Ben said. "Jess and the others. Where are they? I want to talk to them."

Nichols shrugged. "Sorry, no."

"Why not?"

The special agent fixed Ben with a look that suggested he'd asked a very stupid question. "You have to know that's not how this works. Besides, we don't have all of them, not that I should be telling you that."

"I—I don't understand," Ben said, "Why not? What am I doing here? Why haven't I seen a lawyer yet?" Ben suddenly stopped. "I'm not saying another word until you bring me an attorney."

"You done?" Nichols asked calmly.

Ben responded by crossing his arms and looking coldly at the officer. At least, he hoped it was cold.

"Here's how it is," Nichols said, resting his elbows on the table. "You and your friends committed crimes. Big crimes. Crimes serious enough to take away your future and ship you out to a cold, dark prison colony with a bunch of other lowlifes. Faraway place—you wouldn't believe how big space is—and just forget about you; let you rot."

He leaned back as he continued, eyebrows raised in something that approached admiration. "But then you went and committed even bigger crimes. Huge fucking crimes. Crimes against more than just your neighborhood, or even all of Titan. Crimes that put you on the level of an interplanetary war criminal."

"That's not—"

"You stole *Dorium*, kid. A whole shitload of it. You stole a quantity that could have provided energy for a whole new colony. You disrupted interplanetary infrastructure development and tried to make yourself rich with it on the black market. After Verona you can guess how well that kind of thing goes over with security-minded people like myself." He pointed at Ben. "And if you'd been just a little bit better, had just a little bit more resources than seven amateurs and a handful of good tech, you would have pulled it off."

"Is that supposed to make me feel better?" Ben asked.

"You applied to the Academy a while back, didn't you?" Nichols said, ignoring Ben's question. "You wanted to be a Militia officer."

Ben started at the sudden change of subject and recollection of ancient history. "Yeah," he said. "That was a long time ago."

"Five years isn't that long," Nichols said. "I looked at your file last night. You got in, sent in your acceptance letter and intent to enroll. Then a week out, you deferred to the following year. When next year rolled around—"

"I withdrew my acceptance," Ben finished. "I remember. Like you said, five years isn't that long."

"Seems like you had a bright future," Nichols said. "I saw your grades and test scores. Top of your class, some of the best marks in the system. I'm talking all across Titan, not just here in the capital. And you must've been a patriot. Or at least you saw the Militia as a viable path. You believed in Titan. Wanted to make a difference, didn't you?"

"What's that got to do with anything?" Ben asked, his tone bitter. "Am I in more trouble because I was a promising student?"

"What I'm trying to figure out is how a sharp kid like you ended up robbing businesses and cargo shipments. You're on a good path, then all of a sudden you're running around with Tiro Washburn and getting yourself in trouble with the Minos family. Why'd you withdraw?"

"You read my file, you know why."

"I know what you told the Academy."

"There's nothing else to tell," Ben said. "I had to take care of my brother. Simon was my responsibility after our parents disappeared. Before they left, I promised them that I'd look after both of us. They didn't expect to die and I didn't expect it either, but a promise is a promise. I withdrew so I could go to work, get together enough money to get him into Harlow."

"You sacrificed your future for your brother's," Nichols said.

"I kept my promise to my parents."

"You said you promised to look after both of you, not just Simon. Sounds to me like you kept half your promise."

Ben shrugged off the sting of his words. "I told myself I'd go back, get Simon settled and then worry about myself. But it turns out that once you close those doors, it's pretty tough to open them again."

Nichols snorted and shook his head. "You're a smart kid. You're what, twenty-three? And got yourself a hold of some Dorium and a meeting with Asher Garrison. Seems to me that if you wanted a door opened, you could find a way in."

"Yeah, well," Ben said. "What's my past got to do with anything now?"

"More than you think," Nichols said. "You're in it deep, no question about that. But some people can swim in the deep if you give them a chance. Based on your file, I think you could be one of those people."

Ben blinked. "What's…what are you saying?"

"I'm saying I want to give you a chance. I want you to work for me. Swim in the deep."

"What? Why?"

"The short answer is you're capable, and sending you to prison would be a huge waste."

Ben's eyes narrowed as he wavered among relief, dread, and genuine confusion.

"Look," Nichols said, "You did bad things. But people like me, the line of work we do—we can always use bad. As far as I'm concerned, criminals are useless. We put them in house arrest till they're sorry or we send them off-world to remove them from society. But big-time criminals…big-time criminals aren't useless. They make stuff *happen*. Behind-the-scenes stuff, things necessary to keep a colony safe and competitive, the kind of things most normal folk don't want to know about. Intel shit. Colonies, planetary governments, trans-system companies—Titan Intel—we all use big-time criminals."

Nichols paused here and looked Ben dead in the eye. "And whoever you think you are, or were, you're a big-time criminal now. That means you can be useful, and I want to use you. I want you to work with us."

Ben actually laughed. "Be an Intel agent?"

"Not exactly, no. But you won't go to prison."

"I'm not...," Ben started, then stopped himself. "What about the police?" he asked instead.

"I haven't reported you to the capital police or Titan Militia, or anybody else, and if you agree to my terms I'll see that nobody reports it."

Nichols leaned back, knit his hands together. "So that's my offer. You go free. Well, free-ish. You'll be working for me. Indirectly, of course."

Ben was curious now. And relieved. "How do you mean?"

"From time to time, Titan Intelligence finds it necessary to partner with...let's call them independent contractors. They bring us information, goods sometimes. Sometimes we send them on errands to accomplish certain things that preclude direct TI involvement. They get their hands dirty when we can't afford to, you know what I'm saying?"

Ben nodded, wondering where the hell this was going.

"In response we pay them, sometimes directly, more often by looking the other way and keeping their records clear. Let them operate without a lot of oversight."

"Raptors," Ben said. "You're telling me you work with Raptors."

"They're not Raptors," Nichols said, a little too emphatically.

Ben chuckled. "What then, off-brand space pirates?"

Nichols ignored the sarcasm. "One of our more crucial operators lost a crew member recently. I want to send them you."

Ben coughed at the punchline. "You want me to sign on with a Rap—with a not-exactly-a-Raptor crew, secretly serving Titan Intelligence?

"None of them would say 'serve.' They have a mutually beneficial relationship with Titan Intelligence. But yes, I want you to sign on with them in exchange for your freedom."

Ben raised his eyebrows. "So you're not arresting me. You're…recruiting me? On behalf of this independent contractor?"

The corner of the special agent's mouth twitched up. "Sure, we can call it that."

"Who are they?"

"Obviously we don't want their association with TI to get out. If you accept my offer, you'll find out their identity soon enough."

"But why? Why me?"

Nichols sighed. "So many questions."

"Look, I believe you when you say I'm screwed. I don't believe you when you act like you're wiping my slate clean out of the goodness of your heart. You don't seem like the kind of guy who just hands out favors to criminals. So I need to know what's in this for you. And for them."

"My independent contractor crew is tight. Outfit like that has to be or they won't survive the kind of work they do. Their leader and I served in the Militia together. He trusts me. After that attack at Miranda, there isn't a lot of trust to go around right now. He came to me asking for a replacement crew member that he knows won't stab him in the back."

"He asked for one of your agents, didn't he?"

Nichols smiled.

"And you're sending me? They want one of your starters, and you give them—"

"The practice squad's water boy," Nichols finished. "Yeah. You're expendable. It's a hard sell, for sure. But you have some skills. I'm not screwing them."

Ben snorted. "Whatever you have to tell yourself, right?"

"I'm offering you your freedom. Are you trying to talk me out of it?"

Ben didn't respond.

"Look, all the stuff you and your friends did. You were the mastermind."

"Tiro's our leader," Ben said. "Always has been."

"I didn't say he wasn't. But you are the mastermind. It was your plan, wasn't it? You figured out how to sell the Dorium, knew how to look for a buyer on the sly and what kind of corporate schmuck to pretend to be when you reached out. You knew to offer five kilos because eight had just gone missing and you didn't want to look too suspicious."

"Yeah, but—" Ben started.

"And before that, it was your plan to break into Port Ligeia. The train, hacking the bots, one diversion after another. That was masterful. I still haven't figured out how you did all of it. That poor cargo chief." He laughed.

"But robbing the port, selling the Dorium. Those were all Tiro's ideas."

"Washburn may have made the call, decided what to do. But you're the one who figured out how. You're the one who found a way to get it done. That's what the crew needs. They have a damn good captain and a damn good first mate. They don't need a leader. What they need is somebody who can find a way to get stuff done, think fast and adjust on the fly when plans go to hell. It helps that you put up a decent fight when our agents caught you too."

"But we failed. We…I got caught."

"The plan was solid. You got caught because you were seven kids operating out of a shitty house in the Third Ward. You'll have better tech and a lot more resources with the outfit I'm sending you to."

Ben looked up at the ceiling, considering the special agent's offer. Not that he had much of a choice—it was either join up with this crew or go to prison. He didn't know anything about this crew, except that they were into some shady stuff. To put it mildly. Could he do it? Could he handle whatever ugly work was needed? Would he even survive? Would he have to sell his soul?

"You said you have some of my friends. Which ones?"

"Why would I tell you that?" Nichols asked. Ben said nothing. Nichols narrowed his eyes and let the silence grow uncomfortable, but Ben held his ground. He wasn't going to commit to anything until he learned more about his friends.

"Jacobs, Alvarez, Martin," Nichols said finally. "The others are in the wind."

Dom. Tory. Axel. Ben closed his eyes for a moment, then opened them. "Did they get a deal like this?"

"No. Just you."

"Give them one," Ben said. "Send them to the crew with me and I'll do it."

Nichols waved a hand. "Impossible."

"No it isn't."

"They have one crew spot."

"Then let them go. Release them; send them back to Ligeia."

"It doesn't work like that. Crimes were committed and somebody has to answer for them. And you aren't in a position to make demands."

"I won't leave my friends," Ben said, surprising himself at his calm conviction. "They don't go, I don't go."

"You really want to do this? I'm sure you've heard stories about how bad prison cans are. I promise you they're worse."

"That's exactly why I won't walk while my friends are being shipped off to one."

"I see." Whatever friendliness had been in Nichols's voice vanished. He tapped his gem. "Agent Adams."

The door opened and the agent from outside walked in. Clearly she'd been ordered to wait just outside.

"Take Ben Ashley back to his cell. Maybe some extra time in there will put some sense into him." Nichols looked at Ben. "My contractors dock with Titan in three days. They leave again in eight. You have until then to change your mind."

He waved impatiently toward the door, and Agent Adams took Ben out. Just before she shoved him through the door,

Ben caught a look at her face. He could have sworn he saw something bordering on sympathy as her eye caught his. Maybe it was just his imagination. They walked back to his small cell in silence. He was still wondering about it when she closed the door and walked away.

Chapter 9

Three nights in, Ben tried to escape for the first time.

The first couple of days were routine. Unpleasant, but routine. Several times a day he was put through intense questioning. Sometimes Nichols was present, more often he wasn't. Usually the sessions centered on somebody tossing around very serious, completely false accusations. New evidence came to light suggesting Ben had a connection with the Verona massacre after all. They accessed his Quill records. Did he recall communicating with a ship near Miranda on the date in question? What was the nature of that communication? One of the Minos guys said they were missing ten kilos of Dorium, not eight. Where had Ben hidden the other two? Or Ben's personal favorite: just this morning somebody claimed responsibility for the destruction of Verona, and three witnesses had Ben aboard the ship.

Ben actually laughed at that last one, which earned him a slap across the face. It was all a bunch of BS, and he saw right through it. Nichols was putting the screws to him, trying to make his predicament seem impossible and terrifying so he'd jump at the opportunity to go free. The problem was, Ben knew exactly what kind of trouble he was in. Accusing him of stealing more Dorium wasn't going to make it worse. And even Ben knew accusations about Verona wouldn't hold up under scrutiny.

Even with the questioning, Ben had ample alone time. That was part of the tactic too. Make him stew on his situation.

Wonder about Nichols's offer. Play with the possibility. Ben used the time instead to practice with the Aurora.

Titan Intel had worked his gem over. Somebody wiped several of his programs and restricted his access to the Quill. What little access he did have now was almost certainly monitored. He worried they had deleted his Aurora program, but he checked and there it was. Maybe it was too small and odd to catch, or maybe Jess had put some serious encryption on it. Whatever it was, Ben wasn't going to question a bit of good luck. He had the program, that's what mattered. That was something.

He started using it the first chance he got. He turned off his implant, watched the room grow brighter, adjusted to the light sensitivity brought on by the Aurora. It agitated his skin, raised his heart rate and body temp, caused him to lose focus. Ben stayed in it, breathed through the pain. He let the Aurora effects wash over him, made himself experience it until it became comfortable, or at least tolerable. After a while he began to experiment. He put his hand against the wall, reached out with energy, searching for the lights in his room. He nudged them, sending his own tendril of energy forth, and turned the lights off. He reached out again and brought them back on, then brighter than before, then a simple oscillation of dimming and brightening.

He did the same thing from a distance, standing in the center of the room instead of touching the wall. Then again with the lights out in the hall. Then manipulating the AI monitors, talking to them, adjusting their code so they wouldn't register that Ben was up to something. The Aurora was risky, but it gave him power that might get him and his friends out of here. He was a week away from life on a prison can, after all. If now wasn't the time for risk, what was?

The Aurora was rare, even among those who shared Ben's ancestry. Simon didn't have it. Their parents didn't either. Only Ben was blessed with the Aurora. A genetic mutation causing profound sensitivity to light. Almost always fatal unless countered with a special implant to dampen its effects. Without treatment, exposure to light caused a chain reaction in the body. High body temperature, elevated heart rate, tremors. A piercing scream in your brain that made it feel like your skull would rattle apart. Among other things. It also went the other way, allowing the subject to manipulate electromagnetic energy. If they could avoid dying, that is. That's the risk Ben embraced there in his cell in Bradley, night after night, with no other options.

By the end of the third day, Ben felt ready. He waited till night, when he hoped Bradley would be less crowded than normal. He turned off his implant, breathed through the rush of the Aurora, and walked to the door. He touched the wall, close to where the control panel was out in the hall. Monitors first. Ben found the myriad sensors that fed a steady stream of data to the AIs, and nudged them one by one. Each little thread of energy disabled a sensor and told it to relay a normal signal to the Coordinator. Nothing to see here, nothing out of the ordinary. Everything is just fine.

That done, he opened the door. He hoped he got all the sensors, or this would be a short trip. Ben hesitated, listening for some kind of alarm or any indication that he'd been detected and a team of surly Intel agents was on its way. It was quiet, so he kept going. He checked the time on his gem. He figured he had fifty minutes, maybe an hour, before the Aurora became too much for him.

Ben made his way down the corridor to the first door, stopping every twenty meters to disable any sensors that were in range. It was slow going, and along the way any number of things could go wrong. He decided to go at night, reasoning that Bradley would have a lot less foot traffic wandering the halls, but that was hardly a guarantee. He could easily miss a sensor and get himself caught, or manipulate one the wrong way and set off an alert instead of keeping things quiet. His heart beat a fast, audible rhythm in his chest as he roamed the corridors of Bradley. At each door he paused and looked for evidence that one of his friends was inside.

After a half hour with no sign of trouble, Ben grew more confident. He moved faster, checked more doors, got to know his way around the hallways. He got into a rhythm clearing the sensors. Still, there was no sign of his friends and no clear path to an exit. He rounded a corner, carefully noting which way he turned. Sweat dripped into his eyes, and he shook his head to clear them. He was getting tired. He checked the time on his gem. Coming up on forty minutes. His skin was hot to the touch, and he'd been breathing heavily for the last couple of halls. Time to head back. He took one last look at the hall ahead of him, considered the tantalizing possibility that his friends and the exit were just around the next corner. He turned and walked back toward his cell.

It took him twenty minutes to get back. He'd covered more ground that he realized, and fatigue slowed him down. He nearly fell as he got to his room and stumbled through the door. It was all he could do to lock it behind him and reset the last sensors to normal. He activated his gem and turned the implant back on. The world around him dimmed, the tingling sensation on his skin faded. Already he began to calm and cool. Ben staggered to his bed, lay down, and checked the time. He'd made it an hour and four minutes. Good to know for tomorrow night.

"Time to get up."

Ben opened his eyes. Agent Adams was standing over his bed. He squinted in confusion, recalling the last time he'd seen her. Two days ago, was it? Three?

"What?" he asked.

"Time to get up. Let's go."

"OK, just…OK. Give me a second." Ben sat up, shaking his head to clear it. He'd slept heavily and not nearly long enough after last night's escape attempt. Adams waited impatiently as he fumbled with his bed sheets and changed into fresh clothes.

"More questioning, huh?" Ben asked. "Are you participating, or just escorting me? 'Cause these little get-togethers are pretty interesting. I'd hate for you to miss out."

"Are you hungry?" she asked.

Ben blinked. "What?"

"Are you hungry? I'm hungry. Did they bring you food yet?"

"Uh, yeah. I mean no." He shook his head and started over. "Yes, I'm hungry. No, they didn't bring food."

"Come on," Adams said. "The cafeteria has breakfast."

She led him through the outer door and back into the maze of hallways he'd explored last night. This was…different. Ben kept waiting for her to turn around and slap him or jam a needle into his neck or something. Instead she walked beside him, her demeanor casual, if not quite friendly. Ben found it deeply unsettling.

"They just opened for breakfast," Adams said. "It shouldn't be too busy. We'll find a quiet spot."

After several turns, they arrived at a large, open space they'd passed through on their way to Nichols's office a few days back. Tables and chairs were arranged on one side of it, a handful of people already seated and eating. Three broad hallways led in different directions on the far side, evidently to other parts of the Intelligence complex at Bradley.

"This way," Agent Adams said. She walked toward an open door beyond the tables and chairs, and Ben followed her into the self-serving area. There was no line, and they each grabbed a tray and began to browse the selection of food. Adams chose an apple, toast, and two delicious-looking pieces of meat that Ben couldn't identify. Ben took fried potatoes, a bowl of blueberries, and some of the same meat. Whatever it was smelled of maple and smoke, and it made his mouth water.

Adams paid for their food at a small kiosk, and they chose a table in the corner of the mostly empty room.

They ate their first bites in silence, and Ben nearly forgot about his predicament as he wolfed down more than half of his meal in minutes. He was hungrier than he'd realized. God, that meat was good.

"Your cheek's looking better," Agent Adams said as she finished a bite of apple. She nodded to his jaw, which was still swollen and tender. "How are the ribs?"

Ben shifted in his chair and winced. "Still pretty sore. Do all of you fight that well?"

"What do you mean?"

"I've been in my share of street fights, and you really worked me over the day you arrested me. Is that basic intelligence training, or are you a special kind of hardass?"

She gave Ben a half-smile. "Little bit of both, I suppose. And you're not half bad yourself." She pointed to the cut above her eye. "With a little instruction and practice you could hold your own against some of our agents."

"Like you?"

"I didn't say that."

"So what's going on?" Ben asked. He gestured to Agent Adams and the table of food between them. "What is…this? Were you sent to befriend me? Some sort of good cop, bad cop kind of thing?"

She raised an eyebrow. "Busted. I'm supposed to convince you to take the deal Special Agent Nichols is offering."

"With cafeteria food. Bold choice."

Adams ignored the sarcasm. "How much did Special Agent Nichols tell you about the work we do at Titan Intel? And the outside people we sometimes have to work through? The crew Nichols wants to sign you up with."

"Not much. He said Titan Intel does the colony's dirty work, among other things—the kind of stuff most normal people prefer not to know about. The kind of thing that sometimes needs to go through outside contractors because Titan Intel can't touch it directly. He said it's the kind of thing that makes a big-time criminal like me useful."

Adams grimaced. "That sounds like him. Describing it in the worst possible way. We do important work."

"He's not wrong though, is he? About the dirty work, I mean."

"Not about that part, no," Adams said.

"But he's wrong about something?"

"Yeah." Adams picked up her piece of toast. "He's wrong about the big-time criminal thing."

"You don't work with big-time criminals?"

"We do," Agent Adams said. "But you're not one."

Absurdly, Ben was offended. "I take it you don't agree with the deal Nichols is offering me? I have to say, you are absolutely crushing this good-cop role."

"Actually, I do agree with the deal. It was my idea," she said.

"Oh," Ben blinked as he swallowed the last of his potatoes. "Why?"

She sat in silence for a long moment, looking at her plate. "Because you're twenty-three," she said finally. "Those Minos guys are bad, I've followed them for a long time now. And Garrison…" she blew out a breath. "He's a Raptor. Just him being on Titan gave me chills. The other day behind The Occident, you and your friends were the only ones in that deal we hadn't heard of before. I got curious, did my research after we brought you in. Your background was impressive. You're clearly a sharp guy, but you were in way over your head."

She paused again, then looked up at Ben. "It seems like a pity to send you to a prison colony, so I suggested to Nichols that we might find a way to work with you."

"I appreciate it, but you're wasting your time."

"It's a good crew. And they do important things on behalf of Titan. We have a lot of enemies, not just in the Interior. The jobs these guys undertake—"

"Are you going to let my friends go?"

She paused and pressed her lips into a line, annoyed at being interrupted. "That's not my call."

"Whose call is it? Nichols's? You can talk to him. You could—"

"I talked to him already. It's not going to happen." She shrugged. "Somebody has to answer for the robbery at the port. It's that simple."

"Then we have nothing to talk about. I'm not going to leave my friends."

"Their crimes aren't as bad as yours. You know that, right? They aren't looking at life on a prison can. They were accessories in the port robbery, and none of them were caught with Dorium. Ten years, that's it. Twelve for the guy who was with you when you met Garrison."

Ben shook his head.

"You're loyal. I get it. But you had three kilos of Dorium on your person when I caught you. You were on the inside at Port Ligeia. You get life. No question. How does that compare to the ten years they get? Ten years that you won't even be saving them from if you stay."

"It doesn't compare," Ben said. "All I can compare is the rest of my life knowing I turned my back on them, or knowing that I did right by them."

"You're making a mistake."

"You read my file, right? That's what you said earlier," Ben said.

Adams nodded. "I did."

"Then you know what happened to my parents. You know what Simon and I went through. Those friends helped us. All of them. Did what they could, even though it wasn't much because they were just kids too. They've been with me through it all. I can't just leave Axel and Tory and Dom in prison. Ten years, five. Doesn't matter. I don't go free unless they do."

Agent Adams sat in silence, pushing the last of her food around on her plate with her knife. "I guess I understand that," she said finally. "Not that I agree with it. It's stupid as hell if you ask me."

"Probably so," Ben said. He ate the last couple of blueberries. "So what now?"

"I take you back to your cell. Somebody comes in to question you later. Tomorrow you do it all over again without a nice breakfast. Rinse and repeat until you change your mind or it gets to be too late."

"Right. Well, thank you, Agent Adams. At least now we know where each of us stands."

"Harriet," she said.

"What?"

"Harriet. My name is Harriet. You don't need to call me Agent Adams."

"Oh. Uh, yeah. OK. Nice to meet you, Harriet. Thanks for breakfast." Ben extended a hand, but she didn't shake it. She turned and walked away, back toward the hall leading to Ben's cell.

"Come on," she called over her shoulder. "Don't make me kick your ass again."

Chapter 10

The next couple of days passed as routinely as the first. More questioning during the day with plausible-sounding threats and accusations. Escape attempts at night, always by a different route, using the Aurora to make his way discreetly around Bradley. The complex was bigger than Ben expected. Even pushing his time dangerously far, well past an hour, he found no sign of his friends or a clear way out. It took a toll on his body, made worse by a lack of sleep.

On the sixth day, Nichols brought Ben back to his office, impressing on him the urgency of his situation. "The crew I'm sending you to leaves two days from now. They can make do with a crew of eight. They won't wait around on you. I hope you've reconsidered my offer."

"Have you reconsidered your position on the status of my friends?"

"No."

"Then it looks like I'm going to prison with them."

Nichols shook his head and sent Ben away. The questioning was more focused and creative that afternoon.

Harriet visited him a couple of times too. Their exchange was friendly both times, and she didn't bring up Nichols's offer again. It felt like she was just coming by to chat, and Ben found himself warming to her. She was easy to talk to and seemed genuinely interested in him. Ben had to remind himself that she was an Intelligence agent who wanted something out of him. A handler. Of course she was being friendly and likable. He didn't intend to fall for it. He only had to hold out for another couple of days anyway. Nichols's ultimatum was almost up.

On the seventh night Ben tried one last time to escape. It was now or never. He didn't know when Nichols would put him on a shuttle to some prison can in the asteroid belt or worse, and he didn't care to find out. Tonight he had to find his friends and make it out of here.

Ben activated his gem and opened the little program. The simple, familiar controls stared at him. He closed his eyes, took a deep breath, and opened them again. He reached into the image and turned off his implant.

As always, the Aurora effect was immediate. The room brightened, Ben's heartbeat quickened, and a forceful buzz set in behind his eyes, rising like a wave that crested just short of painful. Time seemed to slow. Every sensation was richer as the ambient energy of the room, of Ligeia itself streamed into him. He shuddered through the initial rush, breathing rhythmically to gain a measure of control before reaching out to his room's AI monitors and those in the hall.

Ben left his room and closed the door behind him. He made his way down the hall quickly, turning left at the first intersection. He made several turns going as fast as he dared, relying on the memory of the past several nights to assure he was shutting down all the monitors on his way through Bradley.

In less than ten minutes Ben was in a wing of the complex he hadn't seen before. It was big, with several branching sections. There was no way to tell how many halls he'd have to cover. Past nights he'd tried to check every room. Tonight he had to cover more ground, and he focused on the doors and branches most likely to house his friends.

After half an hour, Ben cleared one wing and found himself in another. No luck so far, and he was running out of time. Even if he found them in the next ten minutes, there would still be a ways to go before they could exit the complex. And that was assuming they found it right away. He still hadn't seen much indication of an exit. His best plan was to try the stairs and hope for the best.

Ben walked up and down three halls on the wing, then turned a corner. He approached a door that looked like the entrance to another maintenance room, and almost walked right past it. A noise made him pause. He listened. There it was again. It was faint, and Ben nearly dismissed it as the whooshing of some air circulation machine. But there was an unmistakable rhythm to it, a variation of tone and pace that reminded him of human speech. Ben pressed his ear to the door and listened again.

Yes, it was people. Hushed tones, but people talking. He had a decision to make. Odds are that whoever this was, it wasn't Ben's friends. Why would the Intel guys keep Axel, Tory, and Dom together? On the other hand, Ben hadn't seen or heard anyone in the last several nights of wandering around Bradley. It was a huge gamble, but Ben was out of time for caution.

He put his palm against the door, turned off the AIs, and activated the controls. The door slid open and he stepped inside.

Something hit him on the side of the head and he stumbled forward. Another blow caught him in the stomach. Ben shook his head, trying to clear it. He saw stars. Whoever got him was strong as hell. He swung a fist blindly backward, feeling his forearm connect with something. There was a grunt of pain, so Ben swung at the same spot again. Missed this time. Somebody threw a shoulder into him. He slammed the wall hard and went down.

"Get him! Don't let him up!"

There were at least two voices and too many hands. Ben tried to assess the attack, but they came fast. He punched and kicked, landed blows as often as he missed, but the attackers landed more. Ben was pinned, surrounded. All he could do was protect his head.

He rolled to his back, fighting to keep his hands up. A strong grip forced his arms down and he felt someone over him, raising a fist.

"Whoa, stop! Look!"

"What?"

"Look."

"Shit, Ben? Ben! Ben, is that you?"

Tory. Ben opened his eyes, saw a familiar form above him.

"Yeah, it's me. Tory? Axel?"

"It's us."

"Dom too," another voice said.

The form above Ben relaxed and straightened. "I'm sorry, man. I thought you were a guard."

"I thought you were too. That's why I was beating you all up."

Axel reached down a hand and helped Ben up. "Uh-huh. Looks like you had us right where you wanted us." He smiled and drew Ben into a bear hug.

"You have no idea how good it is to see you three."

"What are you doing here?" Tory asked.

Ben shrugged. "I got arrested."

"I know that, dipshit. How'd you get in here? From what we gathered, they have you on lockdown and are leaning on you hard."

"They are."

"So what are you doing here now?"

"Escaping. Wanna come?"

Dom clapped him on the back. "My man. I said you'd find a way out, didn't I?" He slapped Tory on the shoulder. "I told you. The Aurora, right?"

Ben nodded. "I'm able to turn off AI monitors and open doors, move around this place undetected. We can get out. It has to be tonight."

"So what's been going on? What are they doing to you?"

A wave of dizziness washed over Ben. He realized he was sweating and fought the urge to sit down. "Later. Let's get out of here first. I can only use the Aurora for an hour, maybe ninety minutes, before it gets to be too much. The fever, heart rate, all that. I can feel it coming on. We have to go right now. We have maybe half an hour before…"

"Say no more," Axel said. "Go now, talk later. You know the way out?"

"I wish I did. I just know a bunch of wrong ways."

Tory shrugged. "Well that's something. Let's move."

"Lead the way," Dom said.

Ben smiled. He'd actually found them. He took a moment just to look at them, then took a deep breath. Whatever came next, he found his friends. It was going to be OK. "All right, this way." He walked into the hall.

Something tripped him right at the threshold. Ben stumbled forward and caught himself against the far wall.

"Ben!" Tory shouted. The door slid shut before she or the others could follow.

Ben regained his balance and turned around.

Agent Adams.

She was standing right in front of him, her back to the door where his friends were trapped. Ben's mind spun, trying desperately to come up with some lie about why he was here. How had she found him? Had she been waiting in the hall listening?

"No alerts have been issued," Adams said before he could speak. She held up her gem. "Some sophisticated bots monitor these halls, and they're telling the Coordinator that everything is quiet. Why?"

Ben opened his mouth, but she spoke again before he could respond.

"This door needs a security clearance to open. I know for a fact you don't have one on your gem. How'd you get in?"

"I...listen, Harriet. Agent Adams. I know it looks like I—
"

"Just stop." Adams reached behind her and placed her palm against the wall, right by the door frame. The door slid open. Tory, Axel, and Dom stood there, confused. After a moment's hesitation, they took a step toward the opening. The door slid shut.

Ben squinted. Why'd she do that? Why open the door? Did she throw something in there with his friends?

Suddenly he knew, or thought he did. His eyes went wide as he considered the possibility. The door's controls were on the other side of the frame. She hadn't used the controls.

Agent Adams saw it in Ben's face as everything clicked into place. She nodded, moving her head up and down in a barely perceptible gesture.

Ben swallowed. "Do it again," he said.

She put her hand against the wall once more, again on the side opposite the door's controls. The door opened, then closed, too fast this time for Ben's friends to react at all. Ben felt it, two tiny spikes in the energy pricking his skin and buzzing behind his eyes. Two jolts of energy that weren't supposed to be there. Agent Adams wasn't using the door's controls. She was channeling energy into the door itself with her hand. Which meant...

"You have the Aurora," Ben said.

Adams nodded slowly. She held out her hand toward him. A tiny ball of bright, blue light floated centimeters above her palm.

Ben stood transfixed. He'd never seen anything like it. This was visible energy, not like the little electronic manipulations he could do. And she had such control. He studied her face for any sign of distress, any indication the Aurora sensitivity was causing her pain. She looked calm.

She snapped her hand shut and the blue light vanished. "You were trying to escape."

"Yeah." No point denying it.

"You have the Aurora too." Adams said. "You used it to open doors and fool the AIs."

Ben nodded. His vision swam and he shuddered as a chill passed across his body. The fever was here and getting worse. "You knew, didn't you?" he said. "The day you arrested me, I was using it. You saw me, saw the program on my gem before you put me under." They stood two meters apart, guarded. Tense. Neither quite sure where this sudden revelation would lead.

"I didn't know for sure, but I suspected you had it, yes. That's why we let you have your gem back with the strange little program intact. We…I wanted to confirm what it was. To see what you'd do with it."

"You had to guess I'd try to escape."

Adams nodded. "Why do you think I'm here?"

Another wave of pain and almost-nausea coursed through Ben. He let it pass, then sighed and pulled up his gem. He turned his implant back on, letting the room dim and bringing his body much-needed relief. He relaxed, let the tension fall from his shoulders.

"You should know this was all me," Ben said. He nodded toward the door. "My friends had no idea I was coming for them. They're innocent here."

"I believe you. It doesn't change much."

"So what now?" he asked. "Are you going to report me?"

"And what, get Nichols to add some years to your life sentence?"

Ben shrugged. "I don't know. I take it you're not just going to let me and my friends escape."

"No."

"What then?"

"You're going to take the deal Nichols is offering," Adams said. "I can show you how to control the Aurora. Do more with it. Less of…that." She waved a hand at him. Ben assumed she meant how he looked pale, fatigued, and generally terrible. "I'm traveling with the crew Nichols wants you to join. If you go, I'll teach you what I know."

Ben raised an eyebrow. It was a good offer, he had to admit. He'd never met anyone else like him. The Aurora had always been a mystery, and he'd had to learn how to manipulate it by himself with a little help from his tech friend Jess and a lot of trial and error. A lot of pain and frustration. Here was a chance now to have an actual mentor, or something close to it. Maybe she knew more about the Aurora than he did. No, of course she knew more about it. And she could teach him.

"No," Ben said.

Adams closed her eyes in frustration. "Your friends."

"My friends. I'm not going to leave them. It's a good offer, but it doesn't matter. They don't go, I don't go."

"Ben, you're throwing your future away. Your life away. I don't know why you won't just—"

"This isn't about me, is it?" Ben said, suddenly understanding. "You and Nichols don't see promise or potential. You aren't looking to save a naive twenty-three-year-old from poor decisions and bad judgment. This is about the Aurora. Nichols wants somebody with that kind of power on his leash. He has you inside Titan Intel. He wants me on the outside. Doesn't he?"

Adams didn't respond, but the way her jaw twitched told Ben he was at least close.

"I was wondering why you and Nichols have been leaning on me so hard to join up with this crew he has in mind. It felt like a lot of effort on account of little old me, you know?"

"Ben—"

"Anyway, the answer is still no. I'll take my chances with prison."

"Look, forget Nichols. You're right about what he wants. But using you is not why I want you to join."

"No?"

"No. The Aurora is rare. Super rare. The ability to actually use it, even a little bit, is almost unheard of. What you have, what you can do. I have it too. I don't want it to go to waste, for me or for you. And prison would be a waste. You know it would be. You can try to convince yourself that going down with your friends is noble, but the end result is just you throwing your life away. There aren't many people like us, Ben. We need each other. And people need you. Titan needs you. That's why I've been trying to convince you."

Ben took a deep breath and looked Adams in the eye. "Harriet. You seem like a good person. You're an Intel agent and I get that you're probably very good at 'seeming' like a lot of things. But whatever. Believe it or not, I want to go with you. Hell, I want to take Nichols's deal. I'm scared to death of prison, and the idea of launching out to space with a rough crew isn't half bad anyway. But I can't leave my friends. I can't. It's not just about me. I don't expect you to get it."

"I do get it. But Nichols's hands are tied. He won't let them go."

A wild thought came to Ben. "What if they escape?"

"Huh?"

"What if Nichols and Titan Intel don't let my friends go? What if they escape on their own?"

"Titan Intel will hunt them down."

"But maybe your hands aren't tied so tightly then, you know? Titan Intel has to balance a lot of resources in the interest of colony security. Maybe if they get away, tracking them back down again isn't as high a priority as other things."

Harriet bit her lip, running the calculus in her head as she thought it over. Ben could tell the idea had some appeal, and he seized on the opening. "Escape changes the equation. They can get away. Help them. Get them out of here, and you have a deal. I'll stay, join you on this crew or whatever you want. Their freedom is all I've been after this whole time anyway."

"I can't help them escape."

"Harriet, this is—"

"I can't help them escape," she went on. "But I don't have to be here right now either. You covered your tracks pretty well with the AIs. The hunch I had…maybe I never had it."

"So you're going to…"

"I'm not going to anything," Harriet said. She turned and began walking away from the room.

"Right. Thank you for…for nothing," Ben said. He walked to the door and put his hand toward it, ready to get his friends out.

Harriet turned halfway down the hall. "Ben," she nodded toward him. "That way." Ben turned and looked behind him, the direction she'd indicated. "Your first left. Then two rights. Then another left. Just…see what's over there."

"First left. Then two rights. Then—"

"Another left. Yeah. I wasn't here."

"Thanks."

"I don't know what you're talking about."

Ben watched her walk away with something approaching gratitude. As soon as Harriet turned the corner, Ben turned off his implant and put his hand against the doorframe. The door slid open.

A fist slammed into Ben's gut, knocking the air out of him with a dramatic whoosh.

"Dammit, Axel!" Tory yelled.

"Sorry. Thought it was the Intel Agent. You all right?"

Ben nodded and tried to catch his breath. Axel stepped forward to help him up. Ben waved him off and motioned for the others to come out into the hall.

Dom looked both ways, wary. "What happened? How'd you get rid of her?"

"I made a deal."

"What kind of—"

"Doesn't matter," Ben said. "She won't give us trouble but we're not in the clear yet. We gotta move now."

"Which way?" Tory asked.

Ben nodded down the hall. "There. Follow me and stop when I stop. I have to disable the AIs so we don't get caught."

"Do what you gotta do, man. We're right behind you," Axel said.

Ben led the way, pausing every twenty meters to check for monitors and disable any he found. He moved quickly, knowing he didn't have much time before the Aurora got to be too much. Left, two rights, another left. Ten minutes after Harriet left them alone, Ben and his three friends were outside.

As soon as they were clear of the building, Ben turned his implant back on, relief washing over him. He shuddered and blinked as his body adjusted, the world growing a bit dimmer around him and the persistent itch in his brain and on his skin fading.

The streets in the Capital District were empty, but felt loud after seven days in the depths of Bradley. Street lights provided scant illumination. Distant noises of city life told them there was entertainment and transportation nearby. Harriet's directions had put them at a back exit. When Ben turned around, he saw that the door looked like the maintenance entrance for some shop whose storefront was a half block over. She'd steered them toward a semisecret exit, probably for TI agents to use on the sly.

"I know where we are," Axel said.

Dom looked around. "You do?"

"I wandered around here the day they busted up our meeting at The Occident. Police were all over the port district, so I went toward the capital. Hyperia's over that way." He pointed toward a collection of brighter lights several blocks away.

"Can you get us there?" Tory asked.

"Yeah."

"Good. I bet there's a lot of places in there with a discreet clientele. We'll find a spot, connect to the Quill, and I can get us some new IDs while we lay low."

"Good plan. Let's roll," Axel said.

Dom, Axel, and Tory took off down the street. Ben stayed by the door.

"Ben, come on!" Tory said.

Ben looked at the ground. "I, uh. I have to stay."

"What are you talking about?"

"I can't go with you."

"Shit," Dom said.

"What do you mean?" Tory looked at Dom. "What does he mean?"

"The deal he made." Dom raised an eyebrow at Ben. "Right?"

Tory looked back at Ben. "You agreed to stay so we could escape?"

"Something like that."

"Uh-uh. No way," Axel said. "We're not about to let you stay here and get shipped off to God knows where. You're coming with us."

"I can't. It's Titan Intel. They'll find us again. Easily. But if I stay, I can convince them not to look for you."

"We can't let you go off to some prison can, Ben. We'll—"

"I'm not going to a prison colony. At least, I don't think I am. The Titan Intel guy wants me to work with them. He has…something in mind."

"What?"

Ben shook his head. "It's better if you don't know. I'm not sure, but you personally knowing what somebody inside TI is up to can't be a good arrangement. The less you know, the better. But trust me, it's not prison and I'm going to be OK. He's been leaning on me to join them, and I've been refusing unless he sets you free too. I think with you escaping, he'll finally accept my terms."

"How do you know?"

Ben shrugged. "I don't. I think he'll go for it, and I have some leverage if he doesn't. But still, it's better if you all lay low for a while."

Tory said, "I don't like this. How do you know what they're going to do once you're back in?"

"I just know this is my best shot of keeping all of us out of prison."

Ben's friends looked at one another. They hesitated, but he could see in their posture that he'd convinced them. None of this was ideal. But he was accomplishing the main thing: getting them out and making sure they stayed that way.

Tory stepped forward and hugged him. She squeezed him tight, pressed her face against his chest. Axel came next, wrapping them both in his long arms. He leaned down, whispered in Ben's ear, "Take care of yourself, you hear? We won't forget this."

Dom was last, completing the circle. They stayed there for a long moment, none wanting to be the first to let go. Finally Dom, then Axel, released him.

"You'll stay in touch?" Tory said, still holding Ben.

He nodded. "When I can. Better not do it right away, but the heat will die down after a while and I'll be able to reach out."

Tory wiped the corner of her eye as she stepped back. "Good."

"Go find Tiro and Jess and Miles," Ben said. "They must be in the wind pretty good to have not gotten caught, but I'm betting you'll track them down. Or the other way around. Be sure they know TI is planning to stay away, but don't push your luck."

The three of them nodded. Ben opened the door and took one step inside.

"You sure you got this, man?" Dom said.

Ben gave them a half smile and shrugged. "No." He turned and walked back into Bradley.

Chapter 11

"So. You've changed your mind." Special Agent Nichols leaned back in his chair, regarding Ben with the confidence and calm of a guy who'd known all along this is what would happen.

"I guess so," Ben said.

"It took long enough. The crew of the *Rock Badger* ships out first thing tomorrow. You almost missed your ride."

Ben raised an eyebrow. "*Rock Badger*?"

"Nice little ship. Captained by one Jason Lawrence, former commander in the Titan Militia. I can tell you these things now that you're on board. See how that works?"

"Yes."

"What changed your mind, not that I'm upset about it?"

"My friends escaped last night."

Ben watched the special agent for any reaction, but if the news surprised him he didn't show it.

"So your condition's been met by default, is that it?"

"You could say that."

Nichols stared at the wall for a moment, seeming to consider something. "Look you're not stupid, so I won't insult you by not shooting straight. We found your friends once. We'll do it again. You deserve to know that much."

"No you won't."

"I admire your confidence in your companions. But we're Titan Intelligence."

"You never did find Tiro and Jess and Miles, so there's reason to doubt the extent of your resources. But that's not why you won't recapture the others."

"No?"

"No. The reason you won't find my friends again is because you aren't going to look for them. Consider it the foundation of trust our working relationship is built on from here on out."

Nichols smiled, trying to make light of Ben's words, but it didn't reach his eyes. He was miffed. "You're trying to tell me you'll join the crew of the *Rock Badger*, but you'll cause problems if I go after your friends. That about right?" Ben nodded. "I'm very tight with Jason Lawrence. His crew is exceptionally talented at what they do, including dealing with petty thieves like yourself. You try to make trouble, cause any problems at all for them or for Titan Intelligence, it's going to end badly for you."

"Last week I was a big-time criminal. Now I'm a petty thief. Make up your mind, Special Agent Nichols. But before you do that, ask yourself how exactly my friends escaped last night. And how I knew about it this morning. I can be dangerous for you."

"We have this whole complex monitored and you've been kept in the most secure part of it. Our AIs have registered no alerts or anomalies. You expect me to believe you broke your friends out? And then what, came back to your cell just for laughs?"

Ben leaned forward, projecting as much confidence as he could muster. "I expect you to believe I masterminded a robbery of Port Ligeia. Even you don't know everything about how we got in and out. I expect you to know I'm gifted with the Aurora, and that it probably has something to do with my friends leaving last night. I expect you to believe that maybe, just maybe, there's some gaps in your knowledge that I've been able to exploit. And I expect you to believe there's a possibility I could do it again if I were so inclined."

Nichols said nothing, but his jaw twitched when Ben mentioned the Aurora.

Ben changed gears, softened his approach. "My friends going free isn't all bad for you, you know. It gives you leverage over me. If I get out of line, try to make trouble for my new crew or for you, you'll be able to threaten my friends. You should appreciate by now how much they mean to me."

"I'm listening," Nichols said.

"You need somebody to pin the port robbery on. Pin it on me. Say you had me, but I escaped. I'm dangerous, elusive. It'll help my reputation out there, where you said yourself big-time criminals are useful." Ben pointed at the map of the solar system on Nichols's wall.

"It only works if it's true. You'll have to back it up."

Ben shrugged and smiled. "I did rob the port. And I busted out three people last night instead of just myself. What exactly are you worried about?"

Nichols chewed his lip and looked up at the ceiling. Then he laughed. "I like this. You're a real little bastard, you know that? I can deal with the political bureaucratic shit if it makes you an easier sell to Jason Lawrence. You're going to fit right in with his crew."

"So we have a deal?" Ben asked.

"We have a deal. Your friends don't have to worry about anything from me."

Harriet met Ben in the cafeteria. Some agent had escorted Ben there from the special agent's office and told him to wait. He'd been waiting for twenty minutes and was wondering if he'd been forgotten when she approached him.

"How'd it go?" she asked.

"You're looking at the newest member of Jason Lawrence's crew. Assuming they accept me. From what Nichols said, there might have to be some convincing."

"More than a little. But Nichols is good at that. What about your friends?"

"They're taken care of," Ben said.

"I'm glad."

"Thank you. For…you know. For last night."

"I went to bed early last night. I have no idea what you're talking about."

Ben gave her a half smile and nodded.

"How are you feeling about your decision?" Harriet asked.

He thought for a minute. "OK," he answered finally. "I miss my friends already, and my little brother. God, I don't know what Simon will think. Axel and the others will look after him, though. It's just hard in the meantime, you know?"

"I do," Harriet said. "It can't be easy. "You ever fly in space before?"

"No," Ben said. "Seen it before, from the Orion line across the Spine. That part is exciting. I've never left Titan. I've only even been to Kraken a handful of times. I've lived my whole life here, most of it over on Ligeia, and wondered what it would be like to go somewhere else. Everybody has dreams as a kid, but I never thought I'd have a realistic chance to go into space."

"Space travel will be cool for about two days. Then it gets pretty boring."

"Boring?" Ben asked. "How can you say that? It's space."

Harriet shrugged. "It gets old fast, especially after we get away from Saturn. Space is mostly big and empty, and after the initial rush it's a whole lot of nothing for weeks on end."

"No way," Ben said.

"You'll see." Harriet's gem pinged and she pulled up the display. "Looks like it's time to meet your new friends. Let's go say hello to the crew of the *Rock Badger*."

Harriet led him to a lift and they ascended eight floors, presumably to a different section of the Bradley Complex. They exited onto a floor with ample signage and plenty of people hurrying off to some business or other. All in all, a much more professional vibe than the secrecy and emptiness of the lower level where Ben spent the last week. As they made their way down the hall, Ben noted people in Militia uniforms and slick suits, busy administrators swiping and tapping away on their gems, and the occasional lab coat. Evidently this was the section of Bradley where people came from all across Titan to make the show run smoothly and securely.

After several minutes of walking and more turns than Ben could recall, they arrived at a door. Harriet opened it and motioned for Ben to enter. She followed right behind him.

The room was small, close but not cramped, with a single round table in the center and chairs lining two of the walls. Five others were already there.

There was an athletic-looking woman near the front of the room, about the same age as Harriet, talking with a tall, bald man with dark skin, who looked to be in his forties. From his trim uniform and confident demeanor, Ben guessed that guy was the captain, Jason Lawrence.

Two other men were looking at a gem display together, though Ben couldn't tell what the image was. The larger of the two had long brown hair pulled up in a bun, with a clean-shaven face. He had his sleeves rolled up, and Ben noted a tattoo running up his right forearm. The other one, operating the gem, was considerably shorter. He seemed to carry himself well and had bright red hair and a full beard.

Harriet walked over to the fifth person and greeted him. He was young, not much past thirty, with a tan complexion, short dark hair, and darker eyes. About Ben's height, he wore the kind of casual, durable uniform that marked him as a spacer fresh off his ship.

"This is Eric Wong," Harriet said. "He's the medical officer on the *Rock Badger*."

Eric extended his hand. "Nice to meet you. You can call me Eric. I guess you're the new guy?"

"That's right," Ben said. "I'm Ben Ashley. Good to meet you."

Eric turned to Harriet. "I hear you're joining us too for the next little bit. Is that just to keep an eye on this guy, or does Nichols have something else in mind?"

"You know John. He always has something else in mind. Doesn't mean I know what it is."

Eric smiled and turned back to Ben. "Must be something. It sounds like you don't need much looking after. I talked to John yesterday. He told me a little bit about your background." He gestured around the room. "These guys are gonna give you a hard time, but you'll be OK."

"What exactly did Nichols tell you?" Ben asked. He wondered just how much Wong and the rest of the crew knew about the circumstances of his recruitment.

"He told me you're a thief who got caught red-handed with Dorium, and now you're up to your ears in shit," Eric said. "Said it's join up with our crew or go to prison. He also said you're a smart dude and a real good thief, even though you managed to get yourself arrested. Exactly the kind of lowlife the *Rock Badger* needs. Does that about sum it up?"

Ben's mouth twitched into a lopsided smile. "Yeah. I don't know about the 'good thief' part, but the rest of it's about right."

"Ah, don't sell yourself short man," Eric said. "We do a lot for Titan Intel and Nichols isn't one to mess around. He wouldn't send you with us if he didn't think you were good."

"Good and expendable, you mean."

"Yeah, probably that too," Eric said with a smile. "Promise I won't use you as a human shield unless it gets real bad, though."

"Deal," Ben said. He already liked Eric Wong.

"Captain Lawrence will do proper introductions in a minute," Eric said. He pointed to the two guys looking at the gem. "The tall guy is Mike Hamilton. The one with the beard is Aaron McCall. They keep an eye on the ship, engines, and everything else."

He nodded toward the other pair. "That's Captain Jason Lawrence, our fearless leader for the last thirteen years and counting. That's Allison Jones beside him. She's our pilot, best I've ever seen. Whatever you do, don't call her Allison. It's just Jones."

"Uh, OK," Ben said. "Thanks." As he spoke, the door opened and three others entered. There was a tall, blonde woman followed by a broad-chested man with a shaved head and a goatee and behind him a younger-looking man with brown hair and piercing blue eyes.

"Remind me again why we're having another fucking meeting?" the big guy was asking in a loud voice. "Last I checked we're still on leave till tomorrow morning."

"What about them?" Ben said. "Who are those three?"

Before Eric could answer, Captain Lawrence spoke in a loud, clear voice. "Right on time, that makes all of us. Let's get started. And Levi, consider this meeting a way of making sure you show up at least half sober and un-hungover tomorrow morning."

The big guy snorted and grinned.

They gathered around the center table. The room's mood was relaxed but attentive. Everyone clearly respected and listened to Captain Lawrence. He carried a natural authority that grounded the others and gave a sense of certainty, if not quite comfort. Ben could see why he was in charge.

"As our gunner so gracefully reminded us, leave officially ends tomorrow morning at eight o'clock local time. We'll meet at Port Kraken. McCall has our elevator terminal and credentials; he'll send the details to your gems. You know the drill, whatever you don't bring gets left behind."

"Anything special we need to bring along?" Eric asked.

The captain nodded. "That's part of why I asked you here. Our next contract is a salvage operation. It's big and we won't have a lot of time. We need extra EVA suits—one spare per person—and a lot of spare oxygen canisters. I don't want us spending a lot of time reloading or repairing things."

"What kind of salvage operation has a tight window?" the one called Mike asked. "Are we racing another crew or something?"

"Not exactly," the captain said. "We'll get to the specifics after we launch. In the meantime, I need you and Levi to go with McCall to pick up the materials and send them up to the *Badger*. Soon as we're done here. "

Mike and the other big guy both nodded. "Done."

"The other reason I called us together is that we have two new additions to the crew. The first is someone you know." He paused and nodded at Harriet. "Harriet Adams, glad you'll be joining us again."

"Thanks for letting me tag along."

"Are we just giving you a ride somewhere, or are you finally joining us for good this time?" the pilot, Jones, asked.

"Somewhere in the middle," Harriet said. "My employer has some business along the routes you'll be taking. He's asked me to accompany you for the next several months. Tag along with you and help out where I can, in exchange for your transportation and supplies."

Eric snorted. "And whatever good intel we can get our hands on, right? 'My employer has some business.' Do we really have to pretend like we don't know you're an Intelligence agent?"

"I can neither confirm nor deny…" Harriet smiled.

"One of these days we'll pry you away from TI permanently," Captain Lawrence said. "In the meantime we'll take you as often as we can get you. Welcome aboard."

Nods and murmurs of greeting around the room told Ben this wasn't the first or even fifth time Harriet had flown with the *Rock Badger*. She clearly got along well with all of them.

"The other new addition is permanent. This is Ben Ashley," the captain gestured to Ben. "He's young, a small-time player. But he's shown flashes of big-time skills. And more importantly, my TI contacts tell me we can trust him."

Ben suddenly became aware of all eyes in the room on him, and he felt his cheeks begin to burn. "Uh, hey everybody," he said. "I'm Ben Ashley."

A bout of silence stretched on as the room wondered whether Ben had anymore to say.

"What are you, fifteen?" the big guy, Levi, said from the corner.

"I'm twenty-three," Ben said. Levi snorted.

"Where'd you go to school?" the one called Mike asked.

"I never went to university, if that's what you're asking," Ben said. "I've been working for Novalink, operating their mining bots on Titan."

Another painful stretch of silence. Finally the woman named Jones asked, "What kind of training have you had? How much experience on ships like the *Rock Badger*?"

Ben shifted his weight from one foot to another. "I've never been on a ship before."

A murmur spread across the room. Clearly this wasn't good news. "So Captain Lawrence approached an old friend about a new crew member. Somebody we can trust. Somebody with the skill set to pull his weight or at least not break the ship. And this old friend sends him…you." The tall blond woman didn't sound especially mad, just inconvenienced. Ben wondered if he should count that as a win.

"I don't have time for this," Levi said. "And neither do you. We've been getting by one hand short for a year now. We can make that permanent for all I care. Little extra work don't bother me. Babysitting and hand-holding a surprise newbie is only going to set us back even more. Send him to training. Hell, send him to college."

Ben could feel his face getting warmer, and he hoped it wasn't bright red. This wasn't going well, not that he blamed any of them for their reaction to him being here. He wanted to speak up and defend himself, but what could he say? He was seriously underqualified to be on this crew—on any crew—and he wasn't any more thrilled about being here than these folks were about having him.

"Send him to a gym," someone else said. Ben couldn't place the voice. "Can he at least hold his own in a fight? Does he have any kind of shooting or close-quarters experience? At all?"

"He fought me," Harriet said before Ben could answer. "And he gave me this." She pointed to the faded scar by her eye, which Ben had given her the day they met. "I wasn't messing around either. He's tougher than he looks."

The unknown voice grunted, and a few others around the room raised their eyebrows. Holding his own against Agent Adams apparently brought him up a few notches in their eyes. Ben looked across at Harriet and mouthed a silent "Thanks."

"Are you guys done yet?" Lawrence asked.

"No," said the taller blonde woman. "I'm not. You're asking us to add a new crew member that none of us know, not even you. Somebody who was evidently recruited outside normal channels. By TI supposedly. We're supposed to just take your contact's word for it that he can hang, when we see no evidence of that for ourselves. You mentioned trust when you first started talking about using your contact. We all need to trust one another. Somebody owes us an explanation for why he's here."

"No apologies necessary, Krista," Lawrence said. "I'd be worried if you weren't concerned. That goes for all of you." He walked over casually and stood beside Ben.

"This isn't up for discussion. He's joining our crew. I spoke with my contact about this kid. I brought up all the concerns you've mentioned, and several more of my own. This is what he told me: Ben Ashley is here because he was caught selling five kilos of Dorium to Asher Garrison and the Minos family." That part clearly got people's attention. The room shifted in a way that was at once imperceptible and unmistakable.

"He had another three kilos on his person. I'm sure you all know how hot Dorium is right now after what happened out at Miranda last month. He's not linked to that, but moving Dorium around shows he can hang. He robbed Port Ligeia and got away clean. Ashley has been at the center of some big-time moves here on Titan. He's a criminal. He's young. But he's a player. Forget his background or his lack of experience. He stumbled his way into a fortune that you've all dreamed about. Yes, it was an accident that he wound up with Dorium. And yes, he lost it. But it wasn't an accident that he successfully robbed the port, and it wasn't an accident that he hooked up with Asher Garrison. He's a thief, a planner, a problem-solver, and he didn't get his ass *completely* kicked by Adams when they went at it the day he was arrested. He'll be an asset to this crew. That's why he's here."

The room was quiet, but the silence felt less hostile than before. Maybe they still didn't want Ben here, but at least now they appreciated the reasons behind it. That was something, at least.

Once again, Ben appreciated Captain Lawrence's leadership. He had no doubt that Nichols had to sell it hard to the captain to let Ben join his crew. He could just about imagine Lawrence raising every objection, yelling, cursing his old friend for screwing him over when he came to him with a genuine need. But once the decision was made, Lawrence was all-in. He showed his crew no sign of weakness or wavering. This is how it was, and Ben was going to be an asset as a crew member. Hell, even Ben found his confidence in himself growing.

"All right," Captain Lawrence said finally. "We still have a lot of preparations to make and a long trip ahead of us. You're still on leave for another eighteen hours. I don't want to keep you. You're all dismissed."

Chapter 12

Ben stared up at the Terminus. To his right the massive elevator bank stretched up, up, fading to a point several kilometers overhead. In the distance, to either side, more elevators angled up toward the same point. Ten of them in all, though Ben could only see five, spaced evenly around the Terminus, all converging toward the spaceport like spokes of a giant wheel. The spaceport proper ran along the Spine. The *Rock Badger* was docked somewhere up there between Ligeia and Kraken.

A hand clapped him heavily on the back. "Let's go, Noob!" Eric said as he passed. Ben looked back down and saw the others, making their way toward the elevators. He adjusted his backpack and took off after them, every now and then risking another glance up. He knew it pegged him as the greenhorn—space travel was routine for everyone else—but he didn't care. He'd spent his whole life in the shadow of that wall and its twin on Ligeia, and now for the first time he was going beyond them. Not just traveling on the Spine. Really leaving it behind. This was freaking *cool*. For a second he almost forgot the arrest and everything that brought him here. He almost forgot how much he already missed his friends.

Ben carried a single backpack with a few changes of clothes and a beat-up space helmet TI had given him. He wore a suit that looked at least vaguely like the ones the rest of the crew had on. Harriet told him a few spares had already been loaded onto the *Rock Badger*, along with the extra EVA suits, canisters, and other cargo Lawrence requested yesterday. Ben felt a twinge of longing for his room back in the Third Ward, and wondered vaguely what would happen to his gaming setup, drawings, and random other things he'd collected over the past ten years. The thought brought his friends back to the forefront of his mind. Would he ever see them again?

Ben caught up to the rest of the crew just as they reached the elevator cars. This whole bank serviced the dock points out along the Spine. Two cars were ready and waiting to take them directly to the *Rock Badger*. Security AIs quickly verified their gems and allowed them aboard.

The crew split up, five to a car. Ben followed Eric aboard the left car and chose a seat beside him. He secured his backpack in the straps at his feet, then buckled himself in. Aaron McCall entered next, wearing dark sunglasses that seemed chosen specifically to complement his beard. After him came the tall blonde woman who'd introduced herself earlier as Krista Barnes, the comms officer. She'd been a bit formal and distant, but Ben gathered that was just her way. She reminded him a little bit of Jess when you caught her in a certain mood.

Ben felt a fresh pang when he thought about Jess, and wondered briefly what she and Tiro and Miles were up to. Had Axel and the others tracked them down? Would Special Agent Nichols really keep his end of the deal Ben had made? He missed all his friends, and the realization suddenly hit him that he might well never see them again. He looked out the window, feeling as if an important thread of his life had been severed. He was undoubtedly on a different path now from Tiro and the others. He'd be lucky if he ever saw them again.

"Get up."

Ben turned back, saw Mike standing in front of him. No, not Mike, the other big guy, who'd come in behind Krista at yesterday's briefing. The gunner, Levi.

"I said get up. You're in my chair," the guy said, looking down at Ben.

"Come on, Levi," Aaron said. "There's one right here."

"You know I like the window."

Krista rolled her eyes. "Jesus, Mosley, it's time to go."

"Then tell the crook here to get up. New guy doesn't get the window seat."

"Mosley," Eric started, but Ben interrupted.

"It's all right," he said. "I don't mind. Give me a sec."

Ben unstrapped himself and released his backpack, got up, and walked to the other side of the car. He sat down between Krista and Aaron and secured himself and his pack once more.

"Happy now?" Eric asked Mosley.

"Screw you. And yes," Mosley said. He leaned his head against the wall and closed his eyes.

Eric sighed, then shook his head and chuckled.

Well, at least Ben had the guy's whole name now. Levi Mosley. Occupation: huge asshole. *Pleased to meet you*, Ben thought.

"Don't mind him," Aaron said. "He's like that with everybody." Ben just nodded.

The elevator doors slid shut, and a low tone signaled their departure. The car jolted, and they began ascending at a quick but comfortable speed. They rode in silence. Ben felt lighter as they ascended, the gravity from rotation diminishing as they neared the center of the Terminus. By the time they passed into the Spine, the safety webbing was the only thing holding Ben in his chair. Twenty minutes after they left the surface, the car slid to a stop at the *Rock Badger*'s dock point.

Ben unstrapped himself and adjusted to the feeling of weightlessness. He watched the others exit the car, taking note of their movements. He did his best to imitate them, keeping one hand on the seats to keep himself moving generally in the right direction. After some trial and error, he managed to exit the car.

The inside of the dock point was a broad, tall room, roughly cylindrical, with the elevator car on one side. Opposite the car was an airlock that led to the ship. On either side of the airlock, two wide sections of the wall displayed the *Rock Badger* and local space beyond it, effectively acting as windows.

The ship dominated the view. From here only a huge, curving section of hull was visible. A narrow panel to the right of the airlock showed a diagram of the ship, with a readout below it displaying air pressure, fuel levels, total mass, and hull configuration, among other things. The airlock was narrow, creating a slight bottleneck. Ben examined the diagram of the *Badger* as the others boarded ahead of him.

The ship was a thick torus, with the bridge protruding from its center as a semispherical bulge and the massive fusion engine extending out the opposite side of the ring. It looked vaguely like a puffy model of Saturn, as if someone had inflated the rings until they swelled and touched the planet, then set the whole thing on top of an upside-down bowl. Judging from the diagram, the crew spent most of their time in the torus, which held three decks and rotated to provide gravity when the ship wasn't under thrust. The display said the *Rock Badger*'s engines could make ten Gs of thrust, though Ben guessed the real number was probably higher. The design was more than a century old, but the ship had been kept up nicely and surely contained top-of-the-line engines and a nice complement of weapons, scopes, and comms, legal and otherwise.

Harriet tapped Ben on the arm. He looked up and saw they were the last to go in. She smiled, waved at him to follow, and ducked through the entrance. Ben took one last look around at his home colony, breathed his last bit of recycled Titan air, and entered through the airlock right behind her.

He passed through a narrow tunnel about ten meters long, then through another airlock, and he was in the ship. Harriet waited for him on the other side of a large room, where there was a ladder and another door.

"Come on," Harriet said. "Quarters are up here. I'll show you where you go."

Ben floated across, feeling somewhat nauseated in the absence of gravity, but he made it to her and she helped him through. They entered a room nearly identical to the first, except this one had furniture stuck to one wall and cabinets beneath him. Ben frowned at the incongruity, then it clicked. Under spin or thrust, the wall with the furniture would be the floor.

Harriet guided him through two more doors, then they were at his room. Well, *room* was generous. It was really more of a hole—tall enough to stand in but too narrow to hold much more than a bed and a storage locker.

Harriet motioned toward the bed. "Put your backpack in the locker and be sure it's latched good. Then lie on the bed and strap in. We'll be under thrust soon and you'll be able to get around easier."

Ben did as she said, and Harriet left. He swallowed hard, suddenly aware of the enormity of what he was doing. He was leaving Titan behind, maybe for good. He was on a ship that was about to carry him…where, exactly? He didn't know, and the thought made him breathe faster and brought a smile to his face at the same time. A wave of claustrophobia rose in his chest, and Ben quickly suppressed it. What else did he expect a long-distance spaceship to be like?

Ten minutes later Ben's gem blinked. Departure in sixty seconds. A holographic timer began counting down. Thirty seconds. Fifteen. Ten. Nine. Eight.

When the countdown reached zero, Ben felt a tiny shudder as the *Rock Badger* released from its dock point. He closed his eyes and imagined it drifting away from Titan, shoved by a mechanical arm that was retracting back toward the Spine. He imagined the trail of propellant extending behind the ship as its microthrusters carried it to the requisite two-klick fusion threshold.

Several minutes later, Ben's gem flashed again. They were approaching the fusion barrier. Prepare for thrust.

That was all the warning he got. Ben's stomach suddenly lurched, then settled as the ship accelerated with the standard one G of thrust. Normal gravity suddenly returned, pressing Ben down comfortably against his bunk. Seconds later their gems flashed with the all-clear, and Ben unstrapped himself and got up from his bed. He peeked out from his room and saw Harriet, who was evidently in the berth right next door. A line of similar doors extended beyond hers. It was a safe bet that as the new guy, Ben's room was farthest from the galley and toilets and anything else that might be useful to have close by.

Ben didn't have any assigned work as they departed. Christian Wenner, the first mate—the young-looking guy with brown hair and blue eyes—had simply told him to stay out of the way and don't break anything. Ben wandered this level of the ship, which he thought must be the center deck. Eventually he came to a common area with efficient furniture and a gaming table by the far side. He stopped short when he saw the view that dominated the room—a large window or rather the large wall made to look like a window, which really displayed a view of space from the ship's exterior cameras.

He approached the wall and peered out, getting his bearings as he realized he was looking back toward Titan as the ship flew away. The illusion was perfect. Ben felt almost as if he could reach through and touch the vacuum beyond. He watched in fascination as his home colony receded into the distance, the twins Ligeia and Kraken slowly rotating in opposite directions. Beyond it lay the grand moon Titan, a hazy orange ball in a spectacular field of stars. To Ben's right, farther still, loomed Saturn and its famous rings.

Ben's breath caught as he took it all in. He'd seen plenty of pictures of Saturn and its moons, seen holovids from the terrestrial worlds of the Interior, but nothing could have prepared him for this. His whole life, everything he knew, hung there precarious against an infinite universe.

He'd always thought of his world as a big place. Limited, sure, but spacious. Vast. Titan was, after all, the third-largest colony in the solar system. But seeing it out here, so small, he suddenly grasped how *confined* his existence had been. People eked out their entire lives, birth to death, on one or the other of those rotating cylinders. Wherever he was going now, it was entire worlds beyond what he'd known before. The view became an image of the restlessness he'd always felt, the vague but persistent notion that there was something more calling to him. Ben suddenly realized he couldn't go back. This moment, this understanding of limitation and thrill of breaking beyond it, however brief and dangerous, could never be undone.

Two hours later they were comfortably underway, the ship still thrusting at the standard one G as they would be for the next couple of days. Captain Lawrence called the crew together in a spacious conference room on the third deck—that is, the one closest to the center. Krista stood by a console on the far side of the room. She was on watch and routed all visuals, sensors, and other information up here. In the short time he'd been on board, Ben had come to appreciate the design of the *Rock Badger*'s controls, or at least what he saw of them. Each room held two or three multifunctional consoles that could be quickly configured for any task, from engine diagnostics to piloting the ship to firing weapons to playing games on the Quill. It was convenient and practical, and it likely brought valuable flexibility and redundancy during an emergency.

"I bet you'd all like to know where we're heading, wouldn't you?" Captain Lawrence asked.

Everyone nodded, and Ben's ears perked up. Lawrence had said yesterday that this was a salvage operation but had been very close to the vest with where exactly the op was taking place.

Levi nodded to the display by Krista. "Sun to our backs. Looks like we're headed Out."

"That's right. We've set course for Uranus."

Mike made a face. "What are we salvaging way out there, cap? Research vessel? No way it's a military ship, and most everything else past Neptune is big cargo. Somebody get lost?"

The captain shook his head. "Not a ship. Something else."

"What kind of something else?"

Lawrence paused and looked around, making sure everybody was paying attention. "A colony. A whole colony. Well, it used to be a whole colony. We're going to Verona."

The room fell silent as everyone took in the captain's words.

Ben's mind raced. Had he heard that right? Were they really going to Verona, the colony that someone had attacked and destroyed? The event that had Titan and the rest of the outer colonies on edge and had VESA moving in ships and expanding their reach? Without thinking, he turned to Harriet. "Did you know about this?"

Everyone looked at him, then at Harriet. Ben immediately kicked himself for speaking up. *New guy, keep your mouth shut.* "Sorry," he said. "It just took me by surprise. I thought that—"

"Did you?" Mike asked. He was talking to Harriet. "This has Titan Intel all over it. Did you know? Is that why you're here?"

"Yes." She answered like she'd been expecting the questions. "TI pulled some major strings to get you in. You get whatever salvage you can recover. We get whatever information you can recover. I'm here to help with the second part."

"You're going to help with the first part, too, you know," Christian said. "We don't do free rides."

"Have I ever not pulled my weight?"

"You all knew I was meeting with John Nichols," Captain Lawrence said. "A contract for Titan Intelligence is no surprise. It's also no surprise that TI has an interest in the events out at Miranda. This is what they pay us for. And this time they're paying very well."

"What do they hope to learn?" Krista asked. The captain looked at Harriet and raised his eyebrows.

"The official story on Verona is that it suffered a Raptor attack. They fought back instead of rolling over, and it got ugly. Something went wrong and the whole colony was destroyed."

"But TI doesn't buy the official story," Lawrence said.

"No. And we aren't the only ones. There's a lot that doesn't add up. No Raptors have claimed responsibility for the attack, for one, and it's highly suspicious that there are no survivors out of a population of nine thousand. And it's awfully convenient that VESA is moving in and making a big fuss. They're "offering assistance" to eight independent colonies around Uranus and Neptune, which amounts to them assuming military control in the interest of security."

"So Venus is treating this like an opportunity to expand its territory and influence among the Outer Colonies," Mike said.

"And selling more Dorium," Jones added. "Verona mined and refined it, and they had a handful of reliable clients out here from what I understand. There aren't a lot of providers putting it out in small cuts, but that was their specialty. Their sudden absence creates a vacuum in the market. It's a small vacuum, but Venus is positioned to fill it."

"So you think VESA is behind it? Some kind of false flag attack?" Christian asked.

Harriet shrugged. "That's what we want to find out."

"It's enough of a possibility that Titan Intelligence is willing to invest considerable resources in sending us out there to snoop around," Captain Lawrence said. "VESA has control of the local space around Miranda, and they have salvage operations locked down pretty tight. I don't know what Nichols had to do to get us the right credentials, but I gather it was a lot."

"He's spent years cultivating sources in the Venus government and VESA's chain of command. He's putting it all at risk to get us in," Harriet said.

"So we'll look around, talk to some people while we're there, and feed whatever info we get back to Titan Intelligence. What about the salvage itself?" Eric held up his gem, with a document hovering above it. "The Quill says VESA and their contractors swooped into Verona almost immediately after the attack. It's been more than a month, and that'll be six weeks by the time we get there. Will there be anything left?"

The captain nodded. "That's a fair question. Obviously we won't know until we arrive, but it's my understanding that the focus so far has been on containing orbital debris and tracking down the Dorium Verona had on board. There should be enough small cargo left to make it more than worth our while."

"And Titan Intel is paying a fee on top of that, as well as all operating expenses," Harriet said.

"Well then, Verona it is," said Christian. It was the first mate's subtle way of telling them to stop asking questions. They had their assignment, now was the time to get it done.

"We'll be there in six days," the captain said. "Use the time to get in character as a roughneck salvage crew that's used to dealing with shady operations. That shouldn't be too hard for any of you. Barnes will get us in touch with the people in charge around Miranda so they know we're coming and we know what to expect. We'll come up with a game plan once we've gotten word from them."

Chapter 13

Harriet finished with Ben's gem and handed it back to him. "Here."

"Thanks. How do I access it?"

"Same as the old program. I just replaced it with this new one."

"You're sure I don't need a new link?"

"No. Yours is older but Aaron said it's in good shape. This should interface with it just fine."

Ben activated his device and went to the usual spot. The icon for his old Aurora program was gone. In its place was a new one, which looked like a stylized star going supernova.

"Comforting image," Ben said. "Am I going to go off like a dying star?"

"Consider it a good reminder. There's power in the Aurora, and danger. This new program lets you tap into more of both."

"So how does it work?" Ben asked. He and Harriet stood alone in a small studio on the *Rock Badger*'s first deck. Krista and Eric used the space for meditation, and Harriet said she used it some for solo workouts. It was one of the few places on board where she and Ben could have some privacy as she kept her promise to teach him about the Aurora.

"Your old program was a simple on/off toggle. But it only engaged with a single section of your link. That represents about five percent of your regulator's output. You could turn that on or off with the Aurora program. The rest was guarded by fail-safe after fail-safe to keep anything from going wrong and killing you outright. This new program overrides all those fail-safes and gives you control over the full regulator."

"So it takes away the safety nets and increases my Aurora sensitivity by a factor of twenty. That seems…dangerous."

"Highly. The strings aren't totally cut, though. There are similar stopgaps in the program. So the safety is still there, just not in the regulator itself. In time you'll be able to condition yourself to endure more, take your regulator down to 85 or even 80 percent."

"So I can control it and remove the fail-safes to lower the threshold for myself, but it won't happen by accident."

"Exactly." She motioned for Ben to open the program, which brought up a number and a sliding scale beside it. "The controls are simple. Right now it shows one hundred, meaning your implant is at full effect. It's suppressing 100 percent of the Aurora. You can turn it back by moving the slider down, or you can set it at a specific percentage by inputting the number directly. At the moment, 90 percent is the lowest it will let you go."

Ben reached into the holo image above his gem. He touched his finger to the slider and moved it down until the number showed 95.

"Stop there," Harriet said. "It's pretty close to what you've done before. We'll start with that and work our way down."

Already the room was growing brighter and Ben felt his heartbeat speeding up. His hand began to sweat. Ben breathed through the effects, adjusting to them, trying to maintain a sense of control and calm.

"That's it, good. Breathe through it. Feel the energy coming to you." Harriet encouraged him and waited patiently.

Ben gestured to her gem. "What about your implant? Do you need to turn yours down?"

"No," Harriet said. "Mine's all set. It protects me at 80 percent."

Ben started at that number. "Wait, all the time?"

"Yeah," Harriet said. "It lets me tap into the Aurora without having to stop and adjust anything first."

"But what about the pain, fevers, heart rate, everything?" Ben asked.

"You learn to channel it, direct it, let it move through you rather than trying to hold it in."

"All the time, you're just walking around doing that constantly? Even in your sleep?"

Harriet shrugged. "You get used to it."

"Damn," Ben said. She really was superhuman. "Where'd you learn how to do it?"

"Long story," Harriet said. "But the short version is that I had a great teacher who worked with me when I was a kid."

"OK," Ben said. He made a note to ask her about it again later. He kept breathing.

"I'm assuming you know how the Aurora works," Harriet said.

"Only a little. It enables our bodies to process and retain Dorium, right?"

"That's right," Harriet said. "There are trace amounts of it throughout our environment—too small to mine or filter out in any way. We ingest and inhale it constantly. But Dorium is completely nontoxic to most humans, just passes right through without reacting. Study after study has shown no negative health effects for most people. One in ninety million or so have the Aurora, which causes cells to store Dorium and exchange energy with the mineral."

"Lucky us," Ben said.

"If you don't get the mutation fixed genetically in utero, it creates a debilitating and deadly sensitivity to light—visible, infrared, microwave, everything in the range that energizes Dorium. Our nervous system gets overstimulated, our muscles go into hyperdrive, and our body temperature climbs as our cells take in energy. It kills you in minutes unless you have a regulator in your Link."

Harriet stepped back from Ben and stood facing him. "Mimic my movements."

She spread both arms wide, then brought them together in front of her chest. She then stretched them vertically, one hand toward the ceiling and one toward the floor, then brought them back together at her center.

"The regulator is not the only way to control that excess energy." She kept moving as she talked, moving her arms in an intricate sequence that always returned them to the center of her body. Ben followed her motions with his own. "You can train your body and mind to do it too. Move the energy around within yourself. You already know how to do that, it's how you manipulate electronics and AIs. We're just doing more of that, to give you greater control and ability to work with more energy."

Ben continued following Harriet's motions and instructions through a series of arm and then leg movements, followed by stretches and basic strikes. After a few minutes he settled into a rhythm, moving with purpose and precision, letting muscle memory take over.

"Concentrate on your breathing," Harriet said between motions. "Exhale on the strikes, gather yourself as you inhale. Bring it back to the center every time. You don't need a deep breath, quicker ones work just as well."

Ben did as she said, striking from a tight, focused center. He concentrated on returning to it each time, which prevented him from overextending himself. The Aurora hummed in his mind and body, but the movements and breathing brought control and endurance.

"Your breath is heat," Harriet said. She led him through a series of rapid combinations. *Punch-punch-kick. Block-punch-duck-punch. Step-kick-punch-punch.* "Feel that heat in your core. Feel it go out as you strike, feel it come back as you re-center."

Ben tried to picture himself breathing hot air, but it didn't seem to help. He lost focus and tried to recover quickly even as he continued to follow Harriet's motions.

Harriet tried a different tactic. "Your core, your center," she said between strikes. "Think of it as…a furnace. A fire, glowing embers, burning deep and hot. Your center, that's the heat source. Breath fuels the fire, makes it burn brighter, hotter."

Ben imagined a fire inside himself, his breath stoking the flame. Was he growing warmer or was it just his imagination?

Punch-punch-kick. Block-punch-block-step-kick. Energy into each movement, returning to the center. A flash of…something in his mind. Energy extending with his arm in a punch.

His concentration wavered again and he lost balance, stumbling forward as he pictured his energy out in front of him.

"That's OK," Harriet said. "Start again."

Round and round they went for the next half hour, Harriet the patient teacher and Ben the clumsy pupil. She tried different ways of describing the energy and its flow: he was a furnace, a laser, a mirror, a monorail track, a room full of warm air. It all nearly worked, but each time Ben felt something stir within him, sensed a hint of the energy's movement, he faltered. His awareness of it was overstimulated, to say nothing of control. It was like trying to see through a blinding, hot curtain.

When Harriet called a halt, Ben was sweating.

"Let's dial my implant back up a bit," Ben said. "Maybe I'll be able to concentrate better at 98."

She shook her head. "You have to learn control, and the first step is honing your senses, adapting to the energy coming. Don't worry, we'll keep at it."

Ben took a breath and nodded, and turned his implant back up to 100. The effects subsided and his perception of the world returned to normal.

Harriet glanced at her gem as they left the studio. "You hungry?"

"Extremely."

"Come on. It's early for dinner but tonight's Jones's night to cook. She always sets out a little something on the early side." They made way for a ladder and began ascending toward the galley.

"So why'd you decide to hack your regulator," Harriet asked. "Why develop the Aurora program?"

"I didn't do it, my friend Jess made the program." Ben shrugged. "It was unintentional at first. My regulator malfunctioned when I was ten. I got really sick, and it took the doctors a while to figure out what was wrong. The excess energy built up over time, not all at once."

"Yeah, that can happen," Harriet said. "It's tough to diagnose, I hear."

Ben nodded. "One day when it was really bad, I couldn't leave my room. I'd get tired really easily, but I was bored to tears. I was pretending…something. I don't remember what, but I was some kind of hero. I made a motion with my hand and put some intention into it. Just a kid playing, you know? But it turned my gaming console on. I thought it was a coincidence at first, and I ignored it. But then I did it again, and it happened again. I was freaked out, but also curious. Over the next few days I experimented, found out I could control it a little bit. I could turn my console off and on, lights, that kind of thing. It eased some of the boredom. And it made me feel better, you know? Like a hero. Here I was a kid with this strange illness, and being able to do that made me feel clever and strong instead of weak." He snorted and waved vaguely at her hands, hanging by her side. "You know what I mean, you have it too."

"Yeah, Ben, I do know," Harriet said, her voice softer than usual.

"Anyway, after a couple of weeks the doctors diagnosed what was wrong and they fixed my implant. I was excited to feel better, but then I couldn't do the trick with electronics anymore. It drove me crazy, I was so disappointed. But then I put two and two together and figured it must be something about the regulator malfunctioning that let me do it. I talked to my friend Jess, who was already really good with coding, and we worked on a way to turn the implant off when I wanted to."

Harriet raised her eyebrows. "That was dangerous."

"We were kids, we didn't know anything about danger. And I trusted Jess. Still do."

"It's a clever program," Harriet said.

"Jess is good. Really good."

"OK, another question. Why didn't your parents get you the genetic fix?" Harriet asked.

"There were complications with my mom's pregnancy and they kept having to delay the procedure. When the doctors finally got her stabilized, it was too late for the genetic fix. Altering my genes to correct the mutation would have been too risky, so they had to do the regulator implant as soon as I was born."

"Bad luck," Harriet said.

"Extremely," Ben said. "What about you?"

"Ask me some other time," Harriet said. She didn't elaborate, and Ben didn't press the issue. He, more than anyone, knew how sensitive the topic of the Aurora could be.

The next several days passed in a blur of activity. Krista got in touch with the VESA security forces around Miranda and received confirmation that the *Rock Badger* was clear to approach. She also received an encrypted model of the debris field around the small moon, complete with detailed descriptions of each piece's mass, volume, orbital trajectory, structural and chemical composition, and, where applicable, estimated contents. She, Captain Lawrence, Christian, and Harriet spent hours going over the data and coming up with a plan for gathering material and intel at Verona.

Much of Ben's time focused on increasing his skills and ability to contribute as a crew member. Aaron McCall, the quartermaster, showed him where the basic tools and supplies were located throughout the ship. McCall and Mike, the engineer, gave him a tutorial on fusion engines in general and the *Rock Badger*'s torch in particular. He got a crash course in the engine room and just how much of a problem it was if various pieces of equipment broke. Krista walked him through the various sensors and how to read each display. Jones showed him the pilot's controls and told him not to touch a damn thing.

There was also ample training on skills Ben hoped he wouldn't need, such as shooting and hand-to-hand combat. Mike worked daily with him on martial arts, teaching him basic grappling techniques, strikes, and counters and doing his best to drill them into his muscle memory. "Remedial lessons," Mike called their sessions, but he was good-natured about it. Mike was a good fighter and an even better teacher. Even in five days Ben felt like he was learning a lot. The first mate, Christian, tried to teach Ben how to shoot, a skill Ben struggled to master.

After wrapping up the latest training session with Mike, Ben left the gym feeling good. The *Rock Badger* was due to arrive at Miranda early the next morning, and he was pleased with the progress he'd made so far. Not exactly a one-of-us member of the crew yet, but he felt like less of an outsider than he did when they first left Titan.

He was headed off to take a shower when he passed by the studio where Harriet had been teaching him how to use the Aurora. Movement inside the room caught his eye. Ben peeked in and saw Harriet preparing to spar with somebody.

Wait, no, there were four of them. Harriet, Levi, Eric, and Mike. Mike must have come here straight from his session with Ben.

Ben decided to stay and watch. Apparently this was going to be a two-on-two match, to practice fighting alongside a partner. Maybe Ben could learn a little something.

The session began, and the four fighters began to circle one another. It all looked wrong. It took him a second to realize what it was. Harriet was moving on her own, and the other three with patterns of coordination. Harriet was taking on the others all by herself.

Mike and Levi were large men, and Eric was clearly strong and well trained, but Harriet held her own. She kept moving, struck when she could, and generally kept her distance from the bigger attackers. Ben was impressed. He knew she was a wicked fighter—his ribs were still sore from their first encounter—but these were three expert opponents. She was lightning quick and they couldn't touch her. Two minutes in, her attackers still didn't have the upper hand, and they seemed frustrated by her constant evasion.

Suddenly, if by an unseen cue, the three men rushed her at once, each from a different direction. Harriet moved toward Mike and caught him with a swift punch to the stomach, following it with an elbow to the back of his head that brought him to his knees. She dodged a punch from Eric, pivoted toward him and landed a flurry of strikes to his head and midsection before Levi grabbed her from behind. He lifted her easily and slammed her to the ground on her stomach, then moved on top of her to pin her as she tried to struggle free. He leaned forward, using his body and one arm to hold her down. He hit her twice with his free hand, then used it to push her neck toward the floor, while Eric, now recovered, stood over her and began kicking her in the ribs.

It all struck Ben as excessively violent, especially considering how outmatched Harriet was. He considered intervening before she got hurt. Before he could make a move, Levi shifted on top of Harriet, then moved up. At first Ben thought he was getting up and the fight was over, but the guy was still struggling and fighting. Ben realized that Harriet was *lifting* him, pushing herself off the floor and rising to her knees even as he fought to keep her pinned. Mike moved behind her to help his companion force her back down, while Eric stayed in front of her and delivered a powerful kick toward her stomach.

She caught his foot and twisted violently, knocking him off balancing and sending him toward the floor clutching his knee. She elbowed Levi once, twice, loosening his grip. She reached backward, grabbed his head and, still on her knees, pulled forward and flipped him over her body and onto his back. She brought a fist down onto his chest, knocking the wind out of him, then rose to her feet and turned to face Mike before he could grab her.

Mike grimaced as he faced her, knowing he would have no help from the others. He charged with a roar, lowered his shoulder as he closed the distance with incredible speed. Harriet crouched, took two steps forward to meet him head-on, and thrust both her hands forward to grab his shirt. She turned, moving out of his way and allowing his momentum to carry him past her.

The move Mike taught Ben was to shove or trip the attacker, send him tumbling to the floor. But Harriet did it differently. She picked the big man up off the ground and literally threw him three meters, where he landed with a heavy thud next to the wall.

Harriet stood in a fighting stance, glared at the three attackers in turn to see if they would come at her again. They lifted their hands to signal they were done. The fight was over.

Ben couldn't believe his eyes. Skill in combat was one thing. It could be learned, practiced, and it could allow you to fight off opponents who were bigger and stronger. Speed was a powerful weapon. But what he'd seen from Harriet wasn't just flawless technique or quickness. It was raw power, strength that was borderline superhuman.

Ben ducked away before Harriet, Eric, or one of the others caught him watching. He spent the rest of the day distracted, trying to make sense of what he'd seen.

Chapter 14

The next day the *Rock Badger* approached Miranda. They were hailed immediately by a VESA corvette whose comms officer meant business.

"This sector is restricted. Miranda and its local space are under the control of the Venus Solar Alliance. Transmit ship ID and security clearance or reverse course. You have thirty seconds to comply or you will be fired upon."

"Jesus," Eric said. "Who pissed in this guy's breakfast?"

Ben exchanged a glance with the others gathered in the common area. Captain Lawrence, Jones, and Krista were on the bridge. The rest of them had all been ordered to strap in here in case things went to hell and they had to thrust away in a hurry.

Krista's voice sounded from the console. "Copy, VESA corvette. This is the *Rock Badger*. I believe you've been expecting us. Transmitting ID and security clearance now."

Endless seconds passed in silence. If the others were as worried as Ben, they didn't show it. Finally the VESA ship replied, "Security clearance verified. Welcome to Miranda, *Rock Badger*. Proceed to Verona A at the coordinates you're about to receive. Our officer there will meet and escort you through the areas authorized for salvage."

"Escort?" Mike whispered.

Harriet shrugged. "I'm not surprised. We'll adjust."

The *Badger* lurched and slowed as Jones altered their course. Miranda grew larger in the big window wall. A thin line bisected the moon at a shallow diagonal. At least twenty bright dots moved slowly in the vicinity. Ben wondered how many were military vessels and how many were there for salvage.

"Verona A wasn't our top priority," Harriet went on, "But it was high on the list and we have a couple of days. We'll make it work."

"Think we can get any good intel out of this escort?" Ben asked.

"We'll see. He may just be a glorified babysitter."

As they neared Miranda, the line across it resolved into a trail of debris. Most of the colony's remains would circle the moon for decades, their orbits slowly decaying until gravity finally brought them down. The largest sections were visible directly, shadows and sharp contrasts giving them an aura of foreboding. The rest appeared as glints of scattered light, like silver dust someone sprinkled to commemorate the dead.

"Is that A or B?" Eric asked, pointing at the display. Ben followed his finger and saw a large structure coming into view at the edge of the moon.

Christian checked the console. "B. Verona A is on the far side, a couple thousand klicks past B."

In minutes, the remnants of Verona B were fully visible. Not even an eighth as big as Ligeia, the structure was still massive. Its general shape remained, but the top third of the cylinder was almost completely detached. Twisted at the edges, it tilted up at a steep angle and spun faster than the rest, connected to it only by a few thick, stubborn girders.

Part of the lower cylinder was shredded, torn to pieces by whatever had caused this disaster. The opposite side was mostly intact, but its rotation brought into view a broad gash, nearly vertical, that tapered to a point just before it reached the bottom. The edges were turned outward, as if the whole colony had expanded from within and burst at an irregular seam.

"Where the atmosphere vented," Christian said, his voice somber as it broke the silence. He pointed to the gash on the window wall. "Something caused a breach, and the air rushing out into the vacuum widened it."

"Aren't there multiple hulls?" Ben asked. "Ligeia and Kraken each have—"

"Six," Christian said. "And electromagnetic fail-safes to help with containment in a highly unlikely breach of every one. Verona only had four, but that's plenty for such a small colony. Something hit them hard, too hard even for the many backup systems to stop the catastrophe."

"The Dyson Array?" Eric asked.

Christian nodded. "Maybe. Hard to imagine plasma cannons doing that. It would take more firepower than the ten largest Raptor outfits could put together, combined."

"What do you mean?" Ben asked. "Dyson Arrays supply energy. How could one of them do…that?" He gestured toward the cold, lonely ruins of Verona B that were now drifting to their rear.

"Dyson Arrays channel huge quantities of energy. They collect it from the sun and beam it where it needs to go through a series of relays. The efficiency is nearly perfect, thanks to Dorium, which stores it and sends it along in a hypernarrow beam. We take it for granted, but the whole process requires the highest levels of precision and coordination through the Quill. Any deviation or disruption is adjusted immediately, or the relay is shut down. If not, the results would be catastrophic. Instead of supplying power, the beam of energy would cut apart the receiver."

"Or the colony," Ben said, understanding. "You think that's what happened here? Some part of the coordination failed and the beam got off the receiver but didn't stop?"

"That's the rumor," Christian said. "The Raptors who attacked caused a malfunction."

"If there were Raptors at all," Mike said.

"Seems unlikely," Ben said, mostly to himself. "Anything with that much sensitivity has to have all sorts of countermeasures and redundancy built in to avoid that very thing."

"I agree with you," Harriet said, "which is why we're here. The whole thing is more plausible if the malfunction was deliberate."

"Or something else entirely," Christian said.

Ben shuddered at the thought of a Raptor crew turning a colony's own Dyson Array against it. The idea was terrifying. If a Raptor outfit, hell if anybody, had that kind of ability, nobody out here was safe. He didn't think it was very likely. Probably even less likely than an accident, despite Harriet's assessment. But accidentally or intentionally, *something* had split Verona B open like ripe fruit and left its discarded husk in a tumbling orbit.

Aaron hadn't said anything since the wreckage came into view. He took slow, careful steps toward the window wall and peered at the remains of Verona B. He moved closer until his nose was centimeters from the display, mouth turned down and eyes narrowed in concentration.

"What is it?" Mike asked.

Aaron remained silent and still, except for his eyes darting between the gash in the cylinder and its severed top.

"Aaron?"

Aaron shook his head, stepped back, and turned toward Mike. "Nothing. It's nothing. I thought I saw…I don't know what. It's hard to tell from way out here. Maybe we'll get a closer look later."

"We will," Harriet said.

"There's A." Christian pointed to the edge of Miranda, where a dark shape was peeking around the moon. Around it were two long, thin, slightly curving pieces of debris—what was left of Verona's Spine linking the two cities. The B city grew slowly and moved out from behind Miranda as the *Rock Badger* circled toward it.

"Damn," Eric whispered.

One of Ben's favorite foods was canned biscuits. They had been around forever, even on Earth before colonization started. One producer boasted that their recipes and techniques were eight hundred years old. The biscuits came in a tube that hadn't changed much since way back then. You still opened them the same way: peel away the layer of paper, press a spoon or your finger against the spiral seam, and pop it open around that seam.

The ruins of Verona A reminded Ben of a biscuit can. It had been twisted apart then wrenched into a rough L shape, as if some celestial being had popped it open, dug out the inside, then crumpled it up and tossed it into orbit. The city's interior buildings and streets were clearly visible. Many of them were smashed or just gone, replaced by holes that went right through to the other side. The hull edges exposed to space were oddly clean, unlike Verona B's ugly, irregular gash. The damage here looked like the city had been cut apart instead of blown open from within. The stars shining around and through Verona's remnants, with Miranda hanging below and to the left, made the scene look more like a sculpture installation than the site of a massacre.

Verona A was rotating, and after a few minutes its spin brought into view a spaceship perched on its hull. A military vessel, from the look of it, built for carrying cargo but still armored and lightly armed. The ship looked tiny, stuck there on the side of the dead city, but as they neared, Ben realized it was at least ten times the size of the *Badger*.

A woman's voice came through the console. "*Rock Badger*, this is Captain Alice Redding of the *Chestnut*. Your course looks nominal. Proceed to docking coordinates, zero out velocity, and prepare to be boarded. We'll inspect your ship and cargo, and if all is in order we'll provide you with an escort to assist with your salvage efforts."

"Copy that, *Chestnut*," Captain Lawrence said. "See you shortly."

It took twenty minutes to navigate to the dock point and a half hour after that to link up the two ships. When airlocks were attached and seals tight, the *Chestnut*'s captain came over with twelve VESA troops and two officers. Levi and Mike bristled at the sight of the VESA personnel, and Jones radiated tension. Krista kept her cool, but a subtle shift of her demeanor suggested an uneasy alertness. Nobody was happy to have them on board.

Captain Lawrence, Jones, and Krista had joined the others in the common area, and he greeted the VESA captain there. "Captain Jason Lawrence. Welcome aboard the *Rock Badger*."

"Captain Alice Redding." She extended her hand and Captain Lawrence shook it, but there was no warmth in the greeting. "My men will inspect your ship. Standard procedure, given the sensitive nature of the salvage site. Anything unusual we should know about?"

Lawrence shook his head. "We have some weapons on board, in the hold. All legal cargo and properly registered. That's about the only thing worth mentioning."

"Thank you." She turned to her troops, gave a few curt orders, and watched them leave the common area, half headed right and half to the left. Ben had no doubt they'd go through every last corner of the *Badger*.

Captain Redding asked a litany of questions while her troops conducted the inspection, benign topics interspersed with more serious queries about the *Badger*'s origin, destination after Verona, and past salvage operations. Clearly she was an experienced interrogator. Ben wondered about her background.

"This doesn't look like a typical salvage ship," she said at one point.

"It isn't," Captain Lawrence replied. "We do a little of everything. Salvage, cargo hauling, passenger transport, you name it. Whatever it takes to get by. Most of our salvage jobs are smaller stuff, the kind of things that aren't worth the effort for bigger operations. Personal tech, smaller bots, furniture— the stuff you overlook if you're after raw materials and fusion components. It isn't much, but it adds up for a crew like ours."

"I see."

The two officers with Captain Redding didn't say anything, just observed and took the occasional note on their gems. Eventually the troops returned, reported to the captain, and went back over to the *Chestnut*.

"Well, Captain Lawrence, your ship is clean, and I'm satisfied that you and your crew are legitimately here for salvage. The best entrance to Verona A, or what's left of it, is on the *Chestnut*. We have a permanent dock you can use. Get your people in extravehicular activity gear and come over in twenty minutes. I'll have an escort waiting for you." She shook his hand once more and left.

"All right, people. You heard Captain Redding," Lawrence said. "EVA gear. Twenty minutes. I don't like her or VESA any more than the rest of you, but we're on their turf and what they say goes. I want to make the most of our time here. Everyone understand?" They nodded. "Good. Now, EVA suits. Let's go explore Verona."

Ben floated in a tunnel, struggling to stay still. He thought his first experience in extended zero G would be cool, fun, like you were flying. It mostly involved having way less control than he was used to, apologizing to people he bumped into, and feeling vaguely nauseated. He and the others, all except Harriet and Jones, were in a broad service corridor on the northern end of Verona A. He hit his head on the ceiling, watched his bag tumble out of reach (Krista helpfully caught it), and somehow managed to turn himself sideways—all before turning the first corner. All in all, a fantastic start.

Everyone else was fifty meters ahead. "Hurry up, Ashley, we ain't got all day!" Levi said over the comm. Armin Braun's cackling laugh in response made Ben grimace. Their escort was, in fact, a glorified babysitter. Ben wondered where VESA dug up the old spacer. Whoever assigned Braun to the new private salvage crew was either a genius or had a sick sense of humor.

Ben finally reached one of the side walls and was able to turn himself right side up. He aimed for the corner and pushed off with his feet.

Too fast! Ben flew across the space toward a wall where the hallway turned. He turned his head at the last second, taking the impact on his right shoulder. A hand caught him before could bounce away, guided him to a handhold, and held him in place until Ben could grab on.

Finally still, Ben noted his surroundings. Another long corridor stretched ahead, with dozens of doors lining the walls. The tunnel was dotted with pipes or other odd protrusions at roughly two-meter intervals, and each of Ben's companions was holding onto one.

At the front of the line, Braun stood out in his bright yellow EVA suit. He pointed down the corridor. "Just up there is a double cargo door leading out of the hull stack. Go through there; it'll put you on the floor of the city proper. I'm gonna check on something. I'll circle around and meet you there."

"How far? What's it look like?" Lawrence asked.

That abrasive laugh again. "It's blown to hell, man; you can't miss it."

The crew ahead of Ben took off down the corridor.

"Here you go," Krista said, handing Ben his pack. "Thanks." He awkwardly strapped it back on while maintaining his grasp on the handhold. The nausea wasn't going away, but at least it hadn't gotten worse.

Krista jetted away, and Ben watched her technique: pull with your hands to get started, kick off the same handhold with your feet, coast down the corridor to grab another hold several meters down. Repeat in a nice, fluid motion.

Ben tried it. He was by no means graceful, but it was easier than it looked. He found he could manage OK and avoid falling behind. After a few catches and kicks, his nausea grew stronger. He had to stop halfway down the corridor and close his eyes to avoid vomiting.

Krista noted his pause and said something to Aaron. He turned and kicked back toward Ben. "Hey man, all good?" he asked. Ben looked at him. "Ah," Aaron said. Even through the helmet Ben must have looked pale. He pointed down the length of the corridor, where the others were going ahead. "It helps to think of that way as down. Or up. Pick one and stick with it."

Ben looked toward the others and registered what Aaron said. He suddenly saw the corridor as a giant hole they were all falling down. A simple reorientation, but it did help. "All good?" Aaron asked again. Ben nodded. "Good," he said. "Let's go. Only eighty meters left."

Ben took off again, his nausea back at a manageable level. He was falling down, down, down, using his feet and hands to guide him on the descent between handholds. "Thanks," he said to Aaron, who responded with a thumbs-up.

They caught up with the others at the double door Braun mentioned. Ben caught his breath when he looked out at the colony's interior.

Most of the buildings were loose piles of rubble, held together by some accident of friction and tension. Some remained attached to what was once the ground. The majority were hovering and turning freely above the surface, up to several kilometers. A floating city of chaos and ruin. Past them was the field of stars and a view of Miranda, a spectacular, sobering reminder that what ultimately killed this place was exposure to the infinite, empty void. Directly overhead the hull twisted up and away like a crumpled scroll. A winding serpent of steel and carbon seemed to writhe in the foreground. It took Ben a moment to realize it was a monorail line.

A heavy hand clapped him on the back, making him jump. He waved his arms wildly trying to regain balance before whoever it was grabbed hold and set him against something solid.

"Look out, boy!" Braun's voice rang out, followed by that laugh. "You'll be part of the scenery if you ain't careful." He gestured up toward the endless spread of debris hanging in the emptiness and addressed the whole crew. "Not much worth getting up there. Big ships gonna corral it anyway, sort it out in some G. What you want is in the odd building still stuck to the floor, or else in the floor itself, between the hulls. Come on, I took inventory. Well, my bots did. I'll show you can-dwellers around."

They followed Braun a half kilometer to a building that was almost entirely intact. On the way, Captain Lawrence took the precaution of tethering the crew together so nobody would drift away and be unable to get back. Ben knew he was benefiting most from the decision, and he was grateful for it.

Braun led them inside the building, which was part of Verona's government center—their equivalent to the Bradley compex on Titan. It was sunk down into the hull structure and therefore bound to the surface more securely than most buildings, which explained why it was comparatively unscathed. Well, that and dumb luck.

Captain Lawrence divided them into teams of three and they split up to explore the building. Small stuff would go in their packs while bigger equipment would be flagged for later retrieval. Ben, Aaron, and Braun started on the sixth floor. They did pretty good, Ben thought, though he didn't have much basis for comparison. Between them they found dozens of power supplies and scores of high-end surveillance sensors.

On the eleventh floor they discovered a storage area filled with used gems, some of them the latest generation, more batteries, and the projectors and controls for holo tables. There was plenty of furniture too. They loaded up what they could, flagged the rest, and moved on.

On the next floor Ben opened a supply closet. Something fell forward and bumped against his chest. Ben pushed it aside and drifted back to get a good look at whatever it was.

He screamed. It was a body. Bluish skin covered in crystals of ice, short hair frozen in a chaotic swirl. Eyes and mouth were half opened, giving the face a look of fearful resignation. It was hard to tell if the person was a man or a woman, or how old they were. They wore a business suit. Ben guessed maybe they worked here and took cover in the closet when the world started falling apart around them. He didn't see any obvious wounds, and the closet was intact. Chills ran over Ben's skin as he realized the likeliest event was the person simply running out of air.

Ben closed his eyes, forced himself to breathe deeply. He wanted desperately to purge the image of lonely death from his mind.

"Hey man, you all right?" Braun stood beside him, seeing the body and instantly registering what was wrong. No grating laugh this time. Ben nodded and looked around. Aaron had been heading toward a different room on this floor, leaving Ben and Braun alone.

"We found a few like this," Braun went on. "Most of them look like they hid, like this one. Think they're taking shelter, then the air runs out fast. Others stayed around by accident, the body out in the open and just got caught on something—arm, pant leg, even hair on a couple of them. It's a hell of a thing, always a surprise when you see one."

Ben nodded, not trusting himself to say anything. "First time seeing a vacuum kill?" Braun asked. Ben nodded again. "First body?" Another nod. "No way, really? Ah shit man, you must really be new. They picked a hell of a place to start you out. Come on, stick with me. No more closets for you."

Ben went with Braun, suddenly grateful for the older guy's irreverent, nonchalant manner. They worked through two more rooms without finding much. "How you doing now? Better?" Braun asked.

"Yeah," Ben said. "Bit better now. Thanks." He didn't want to say a whole lot. There was always a possibility that Braun was more than a babysitter, a VESA agent who would try to draw out information from the crew. Ben thought it unlikely, but he wasn't going to take any chances.

"Let's hope you don't start with the dreams."

"Dreams?"

"Yeah. Guy who was out here a couple weeks ago saw two or three bodies. He freaked out, man, started talking about what they looked like tumbling from the cylinders in a spray of atmosphere. Hundreds of bodies, he said, big, little, men, women, dogs. Dude was talking crazy. My buddy asked him what the hell he was going on about, and he got a glassy, far-off look in his eye. Said it was dreams. He was dreaming every night about the event that killed all these people and created this mess of ruin and bodies."

"You believe him?" Ben asked.

"Oh hell yes," Braun said. "Something big and bad like that leaves a mark on the universe. If you're a sensitive person, spiritually I mean, you'll feel it. It bubbles up into your consciousness, man."

Ben just nodded, his mind turning. He wondered if this was something useful, a piece of intel they might act on. Maybe just a guy talking crazy about another guy talking crazy, but maybe something more. He filed it away to ask the others about later.

The rest of the EVA was uneventful. Captain Lawrence kept them out for a full twelve hours, then they returned to the *Badger*. They'd gotten a decent haul of small goods and flagged a lot more larger items for follow-up. Ben hoped they'd gotten some good information, too, but right now he didn't care about hearing it. He was just grateful to be back in some normal G.

Chapter 15

"Learn anything?" Captain Lawrence asked Harriet. He tore off a bit of bread and motioned for Levi to slide the jam over.

"Not really, no. Nothing immediately useful, anyway. We're the eighth private crew to come through here, smallest by far. The first couple arrived within days of the attack, I guess they were close by and VESA wanted to get them working quickly. That's in addition to the military salvage operation, which has been ongoing since they arrived."

While the others conducted the EVA, Harriet met with Captain Redding on the *Chestnut* to feel her out—under the guise of learning what was available for exploration and helping plan their efforts. Ben liked the thought of her turning the interrogation tables around. Something told Ben Harriet was good at gathering info on the sly.

"So these VESA ships aren't just here for security," Lawrence said. "They're actively searching the site, too, in addition to the private crews they're letting in."

"Looks that way."

"Think they're after anything specific?"

"Hard to say. Maybe just hoping to track down all the Dorium they can get their hands on—mining it was Verona's bread and butter, and they kept a lot up here on the colony. Or maybe they just want to control the whole narrative and a salvage front gives them good cover to have their hands everywhere."

The captain nodded. "Anybody else? Learn anything useful?" They were all eating in the common area, where they could speak freely.

"There were no storage drives," Aaron said. "We were in their government center, and I didn't see a single one. Any of the rest of you spot them?"

The others shook their heads.

"That's what I thought. I'll bet you anything VESA's already made a pass and rounded them all up. Anything that might have memory of the day of the attack. We'll keep our eyes open, there and the big communications center on the south end. The Spine too, if they let us out there. But I'm betting we won't find anything."

"OK. What else?"

"I see no evidence of plasma," Levi said. "The damage is all mass impact, local fires. Again, we'll keep looking, but it doesn't look like standard Raptor cannons are what pierced the colony."

"I saw the same thing on the outside," Jones said. "I couldn't scope much of Verona A, maybe 20 percent of the outer hull from here, but there was nothing consistent with a plasma attack. That's telling."

Lawrence looked up, thinking, then nodded. "Right. So a mystery attack, and VESA wants to control the narrative. It's looking more and more like some sort of false flag. We'll see what more we can find tomorrow. Anything else?"

Ben hesitated. Braun's mention of the dreams suddenly seemed silly. He weighed whether to say anything, then decided he'd better err on the side of looking stupid. "Maybe," he said.

The others turned to him, and his mouth went dry. "I don't know," he said. He cleared his throat. "It's probably nothing, but that guy Braun mentioned somebody who was here a couple of weeks ago. I guess the guy talked about having dreams of the dead, the people who died here. He described what it looked like when they flew out of Verona during the attack."

The captain raised his eyebrows, and the others took in the information silently. Finally Harriet asked, "Did Braun say anything else?"

"He said the guy was spiritually sensitive. Like he was hearing ghosts or something."

Levi snorted, and a couple of others rolled their eyes. Captain Lawrence leaned back, ready to dismiss the idea as a bunch of superstitious nonsense not worth their time. Only Harriet pressed Ben further.

"And do you believe that?" she asked.

"No. There's no evidence for it, and people will make up just about anything to try to make sense of something like this, especially if they're close to it."

"So why are you telling us about it?" Harriet asked.

"Because…" Ben started, then stopped. Hesitated again, then decided why not. "Because what if the guy was a witness?"

"How do you mean?" Lawrence asked.

"I mean, what if he was part of the attack, or even saw it from far off or something? What if he saw the attack go down, and it haunted him? Or what if he was one of the attackers, and got to feeling guilty? What if he came back here to try to make peace or just to see it out of morbid curiosity? You know, returning to the scene of the crime, that kind of thing."

"That's a lot of what-ifs," the captain said.

"And then what, he started having dreams?" Mike asked.

"No, not dreams. Memories. He remembered the event, and it upset him, and then all of a sudden he's talking about it and people are overhearing. And he makes up the dream thing as a cover, to hide the fact that he was here when it happened."

Captain Lawrence looked at Harriet, a silent question in his eyes. "It's possible," she said. "And we can corroborate it with that time frame. I can get a list of the other private crews that have been out here, and we can look up their prior crew manifests to find out if any new members joined since the Verona attack."

"You think it's a promising lead?" asked the captain.

"Yeah," she said. "Yeah, I do. I'll run it up to Nichols and get some of our assets on it back home, asking around on the Quill. Krista, Aaron, think one of you could get into the *Chestnut*'s records and find out who those private salvage crews were?"

"Definitely," Aaron said. "We used to hack them all the time back in my Militia days. Shouldn't be a problem now either."

"Excellent," Lawrence said. "Good work, Ashley. That goes for all of you." He checked the time on his gem. "We'll break for six hours, then another EVA. I suggest you all get some sleep between now and then. Tomorrow's going to be another long day."

They spent two more full days at Verona A, with Braun shadowing them and showing them the most likely place to find useful goods. They stayed away from the residential areas, for which Ben was grateful. He didn't think he could stomach seeing abandoned homes, blown-out living rooms and empty beds, to say nothing of the pictures and mementos that witnessed to real, full human lives. The office buildings and warehouses they explored were bad enough. Hokie posters. Favorite coffee mugs. Spare clothes. Empty liquor bottles. Toys. Humans had a way of personalizing their spaces in a thousand small ways most never noticed. Nothing was sterile, everything was touched somehow by the beauty of human life.

Ben felt like a voyeur and thief going through it all, but what else was there to do? This stuff would be claimed by someone if the *Rock Badger*'s crew didn't retrieve it— probably by VESA or someone else from the Interior. Or it would orbit for years, then plummet to Miranda, the valuable items and memories lost forever for all practical purposes. Ben told himself that their presence here was ultimately for the good—the salvage operation was a necessary cover for the information retrieval that would hopefully allow Titan Intel or someone to piece together who did this terrible thing and bring them to justice. Or at the very least prevent it from happening again to another colony.

The *Badger*'s crew worked long hours. Harriet and Aaron spent most of their time poring over the *Chestnut*'s records. Aaron had gotten them access to the vessel's files, and they were able to identify the eight others ships who'd been there conducting salvage operations. Harriet sent it to Nichols to see if Titan Intelligence could dig up any info on their crews and origin points. In the meantime, she and Krista did the same here, trying to narrow down possibilities and give TI some more specific leads.

Jones stayed with the ship. Twice a day she would undock from the *Chestnut* and take the *Badger* across the orbital debris, recording as much as she could with the ship's scopes.

The rest of the crew did twelve-hour EVAs followed by eight-hour breaks. During their downtime, when Ben wasn't sleeping or eating, Harriet taught him to use the Aurora. They finished up an intense session tonight, and Ben grabbed a quick shower. He hustled into the galley, hoping there was still some food to be found. Harriet and Jones sat at a small table. Eric and Levi were over in the corner, intent on a couple of consoles.

"Cutting it close," Jones said.

"Lost track of time," Ben called over his shoulder as he filled his water bottle. He grabbed a prepackaged meal without looking too closely at its contents. It was all a variation on the same thing anyway: some kind of grain, vegetable, and protein in each pack. He was too hungry to care too much about the specifics.

"You're welcome to join us," Harriet said. "But we'll leave you alone if you want quiet."

"No, some conversation would be good," Ben said as he sat down beside her. "Those EVAs are lonely, even though you're not the only one out there."

"Talk over the comm isn't the same, is it?" Harriet said. "Especially when the escort's right there and you have to be careful what you say."

Ben nodded, his mouth full. Chicken in a sweet sauce, with broccoli and rice. Not fine dining, but he'd had worse.

Jones turned back to Harriet. "So have you and Barnes turned up anything on the prior salvage crews?"

Harriet shook her head. "So far, no, but it takes time. Krista's narrowed it down a lot already. I always forget how intense she is, her depth of insight."

"That's her time with the Militia. Urgency and persistence, man, that's what they're about."

Ben swallowed and took a drink. "I didn't know Krista was in the Militia."

"Six years," Harriet said. "Comms officer, like she is on the *Badger*. Her ship spent a lot of that time keeping tabs on the Raptors, helping bring down some of the larger operations. She was in some tough engagements. She's been with your crew for what, eight years now?"

"Nine," said Jones. "Twice as long as me."

"What'd you do before?" Ben asked.

"Militia, same as Barnes, but we didn't know each other. I served five years, joined up as a pilot right out of college."

"She was cleared for space flight in under a year," Harriet said.

"Is that fast?" Ben asked.

"Crazy fast," Harriet said. "It takes most people three."

"So you're the shit," Ben said, turning to Jones. She shrugged and smiled. "What made you decide to join the Militia?" he asked.

"Career day at Harlow Academy," Jones said. "Sophomore year of high school. At least a hundred booths with various company and industry reps. Long lines for the best internships, you know. It all seemed so boring, a huge waste of time. But I went up one aisle, and there was this recruiter for the Militia standing at an empty booth. I walked over, mostly to get away from the crowd, and we got to talking." She smiled and shook her head at the memory. "I left thinking spaceflight is what I was born to do. A few weeks later I took their assessment exam and placed high enough for the upper tier flight school. I've been hooked ever since. When my tour was up I had enough of military life, but I still wanted to fly. Luckily Captain Lawrence was looking for a new pilot, and he appreciated my Militia record. "

"Harlow Academy, you said? My kid brother is at Harlow. Just started his sophomore year. It's a great school."

"Yeah, it is," Jones said. "They really set you up well for work or college, wherever you decide to go. Teach you a ton, and give you great connections. I didn't know you had a brother."

"Yeah, his name is Simon. Good kid, super smart, responsible."

"Is he on a scholarship? How's he paying for the Academy?" Jones asked. Harriet gave her a look. "Sorry, just curious," Jones said, looking away. "I didn't mean to pry."

"No, it's cool," Ben said. "Petty criminal in the Third Ward isn't exactly on brand for Harlow, I suppose."

Harriet elbowed him. "Petty criminals steal gems and things. You stole Dorium. You're practically a kingpin."

Ben smiled back at her and rolled his eyes. "Whatever." He turned back to Jones and said, "It's just me and Simon. Our parents died nine years ago. They left us some money to live on—not much, but we were able to stretch it and get by for a while. But Simon was having a hard time. He's so smart, and our situation wasn't great. I was about to enter Titan Militia, the Academy, actually, but I couldn't just leave him alone. So I had him apply to Harlow, he got in, and I used the rest of our savings for his first year's tuition."

"Both your parents died at the same time?" Jones asked.

"They were off Titan, on a trip. There was an accident," Ben said. He swallowed. "It's a long story. I'll tell you about it some other time."

Jones glanced at Harriet, but didn't press. "Whatever it was, it had to be hard on you two."

"It was," Ben said, looking down at the table. "I ended up having to withdraw from the Academy myself, get a job to keep paying his tuition. It's been a struggle but somehow I always scraped enough together to keep him in for another semester."

"The Militia Academy?" Jones asked. "You went to the Academy?"

Ben shook his head. "I was accepted, but never enrolled. Family had to come first." He looked down at his plate.

"Damn," Jones said. "Sorry. I didn't know."

"It's OK," Ben said. "I made my decision. I knew what I was giving up."

Harriet reached out and touched his hand. "Your brother's lucky. I hope he knows that."

Ben smiled. "Ha, I remind him every chance I get. I didn't really think too hard about it, honestly. It's a sacrifice, I know, but what else was I going to do? There was no future for either of us there. At least now he has one."

"So do you," Jones said. "It takes a special person to put someone else first like that, even family. And to stick with it and keep at it year after year. People like that rise to the top eventually. You're already contributing here, you know."

"Damn it!" Eric yelled from the corner. Ben turned toward them in alarm, worried about what the ship's sensors had picked up. Harriet just leaned sideways and calmly asked, "You guys playing that game again?"

"I'm playing," Levi said. "He's losing."

"Shut up. Let's go again," Eric said.

"Another fifty, or you wanna just go for fun this time?"

"Fifty," Eric said.

Levi shrugged. "I won't talk you out of it."

"What are they playing?" Ben asked Harriet.

"Spaceflight sim. It's called—"

"Solar Run," Levi said, eyes darting back and forth across his screen. "The controls are realistic, same as actual space nav systems."

"You'll have to ask Jones if that's true," Harriet said. "There's a racing feature that a few of the crew like to play."

"No way, really?" Ben left his food half-eaten and got up. He walked over and peered over Eric's shoulder. He was flying somewhere above a planet, Venus maybe, dodging orbital buoys on a roughly defined course. The heads-up display was a little different, but from what Ben could tell, the controls and sensors were nearly identical to the Starfleet games he loved to play with Simon. Ben cracked a smile. He had no idea the *Rock Badger* had programs like this.

Eric lost again, slammed his palm against the console, and pulled out his gem. He transferred fifty ether to a smug Levi, who also stood up.

"Can I play?" Ben asked.

Levi snorted. "You can play Eric. I don't have time for noobs."

"I can hang. I'm pretty good at Starfleet."

"Uh-uh."

Ben turned to Eric. "What do you think?"

"Hell no. I hate this damn game."

"Come on, Levi. One match."

"Sorry, kid. I only play for money. Put up a hundred ether and we can talk."

Ben's heart sank. That was a lot of money. He checked his account on his gem, saw he had enough funds in there to cover it. Barely. "OK," he said finally.

Levi raised his eyebrows and smirked. "I like Miranda. Something about this place has people lining up to give me money." He sat back down.

Ben sat at Eric's console and worked through the steps of choosing a ship. He glanced up at Eric. "Any advice?"

"Stay away from the Blades." Eric pointed to a sleek, nimble-looking design. "That whole class. Their speed is tempting but it's a lot to handle." He pointed to another set of ships. "I like the freighters. They have a good balance of acceleration and control."

Ben nodded and chose a flat, wide ship with a solid speed rating. He swiped through a handful of cheat sheets showing the controls. "Ready."

"Finally," Levi said. "You want to pick the course?"

"You go ahead. I don't know them."

Levi chose a map above Neptune's moon Triton. Ben's console screen filled with a view of the moon, its three colonies hanging like gems in the space above it. A series of buoys stretched away in front of them, leading to the left side of Triton and disappearing behind it.

The screen flashed a countdown from three, and the race began. Levi's ship, a boxy-looking light passenger vessel, shot ahead at full thrust. Ben grimaced as he fired his own ship's thrusters. The speed was more than he expected, but not too bad. Ben pulled his ship around turns and twists in the course, slowing at one point to avoid a science station passing right through the space ahead of him. Levi was still far ahead of him, but Ben pushed the thrust as high as it would go. His display told him he was making up some of the distance.

At one point the course split. One path was obviously shorter, and Ben chose it. He immediately saw the trade-off. It was littered with space junk, the wreckage of long-dead ships and decommissioned satellites, and the occasional orbital construction module. Ben had to drop his speed to avoid it, but after a few seconds he found his groove. He punched the thrust back to full and flew fast and hard, darting in and out of gaps and passing within meters of debris. Levi had chosen the longer route, and when the paths reconnected Ben was right on his tail. The finish was up ahead. Ben willed his ship to go faster, suddenly feeling its sluggishness, but its engines were maxed out. Levi apparently had some juice left. His ship accelerated, increased the gap, and crossed the finish eight seconds ahead of Ben.

Levi extended a hand toward Ben and made a gimme gesture. "Pay up. One hundred."

"Let's go again. Double or nothing."

"Come on, kid, pay up."

"Double or nothing. I want to go one more time."

"Ben," Harriet said.

Levi glanced back at her and Jones. "You guys see I'm not pushing him, right? This is his idea."

Harriet just nodded. She didn't like watching Ben throw his ether away, but what could she do about it?

"I just don't want you to give me shit for cleaning him out."

"Ben," she said again.

"It's my money," he replied.

She frowned and shrugged. "It's your money."

Ben went with the same ship the second time, but now he knew the course better and could anticipate the turns. He was able to burn full thrust from the outset.

He won easily.

"Yeah!" He pumped his fist, happy with the result but more pumped by the simple thrill of racing.

"Impressive," Jones said. "You've raced before."

"Not on this sim, but yeah," Ben started to stand up, but Levi put a heavy hand on his shoulder. "One more," the big guy said. "Five hundred."

"Come on, Mosley, leave it alone," Eric said.

"One more. Five hundred."

"I'm going to quit while I'm ahead," Ben said. "Or, you know, not behind."

"Chicken shit," Levi said.

Ben expected some ribbing, but something about the way Levi said it made him mad. He sat back down. "All right. Five hundred."

Ben was about to select the freighter again, but saw Levi choosing a different ship. He grimaced. It was a hustle, he saw, too late to back out. Levi had held back in the first two races, using a slower ship to set Ben up. Now he was going to blow Ben away. Well, Ben could be fast too. He switched his ship to one of Blades Eric had warned him about, hoping he wasn't making a mistake. He signaled his readiness to Levi, who nodded back with a smirk on his face.

There was another countdown from three, and the race started. Levi rocketed ahead. He picked a good line and held it through the first few turns, giving himself a solid lead from the start. Ben's eyes narrowed. He pushed the Blade's thrust up high and allowed the anger to bring him focus.

The turns and dives in the course flew toward him in a blur. He barely had time to react before the next maneuver was on him. He was flying on a razor's edge. The slightest mistake would take him too wide and off his line, if he didn't crash outright. But he'd already made up half the gap and was closing the rest fast.

Levi got to the split first and chose the longer route. Ben went the shorter, debris-filled path again. He eased his thrust back, full throttle wasn't possible here, but he took it faster than before. He swung too wide past an old space telescope and had to pull back hard to avoid a satellite, which cost him time. Still, he ran the rest clean and came out of the split nearly even with Levi. They made the last turn, and Ben punched the thrust. Levi accelerated, too, but the Blade was built for speed. Ben drew even and passed Levi just before the finish.

Ben leaned his head back and screamed, slapping the console.

Levi swore. If the others hadn't been watching, Ben figured he might've tried to intimidate Ben and get out of paying. As it was, the bigger guy had little choice but to settle up.

Levi transferred the five hundred ether to Ben, glared at him for a few tense seconds, then stalked out in silence. Harriet looked at Ben when he was gone, eyebrows raised.

"All right then," Jones said. "I'm officially impressed. Tell you what. Next time we get a free minute, come find me. I'll hook up one of the control consoles as a better sim and teach you a little something. We'll see how you really are flying."

"Really?" Ben asked.

Jones shrugged. "Sure. Why not? If you like flying, that is."

"I love it."

"Well there we go. We could use another pilot. Mike's my backup, and I've seen him fly. You're all in trouble if something happens to me."

"Thanks," Ben said. Jones nodded and clapped him on the shoulder as she left the galley.

Ben and Harriet were left alone. "Levi was trying to hustle you."

"I know."

"Were you hustling him?"

"No," Ben said. "I just like to fly."

Chapter 16

The crew got a break the next day while Jones flew several orbits around Miranda, giving the sensors a chance to scope out the largest remaining sections of the wrecked colony. They found nothing of consequence, which was unexpected. That left the main cylinder of Verona B as the last thing to explore. The *Chestnut* escorted them over and docked with the ruined city first, then Jones brought in the *Rock Badger*.

"Verona B is tightly restricted," Captain Redding told them as they readied for their EVA. "It contained the main facility for processing raw Dorium, and we're still dealing with radiation leaks. In addition to Armin Braun, I'm assigning four VESA troops to stay with you and monitor the site. They can safely evacuate you if anything goes wrong."

"That won't be necessary," Captain Lawrence said. "My crew is used to operating in dangerous conditions, and we have our own procedures for—"

"It's my place to decide what's necessary, not yours," Redding said. "If you don't like it, you don't have to visit Verona B."

"Of course," Captain Lawrence said with an easy smile. "The additional escort is appreciated. We just didn't want you to overburden yourselves on our account."

They worked all day, moving from one collection of buildings to the next, gathering materials and flagging others. After three days of EVAs, Ben had improved at maneuvering in zero G. He kept up easily with the others. On the inside, what they could see of Verona B looked much like the other cylinder. Destroyed buildings hovering, slowly tumbling in loose piles of rubble, with the occasional structure oddly intact. Overhead the jagged breach in the colony's hull was visible, stars shining through it to remind them that the city was mostly still enclosed. They returned to the *Badger* after twelve hours with little materials recovered and even less useful information on what happened.

"This escort is bullshit," Mike said when they were all back in the *Badger*'s common room. "We aren't anywhere near the Dorium processing facility. I got zero radiation readings out there."

"Yeah," Eric said. "Me too. This feels like a guided tour. It would look suspicious if they didn't let us see any of Verona B, so they're leading us through a handful of vetted sites."

"Which means there's something here they don't want us to see," Harriet said.

"We have to lose that escort," Eric said.

"Let's come up with a plan." The captain paused and thought for a moment. "Whatever it is they don't want us to find, it has to be pretty visible. Spread out across a wide area maybe, or just really obvious when you're looking at it. Otherwise they could have restricted a much tighter area, or they would have dealt with it already."

"That makes sense," Harriet said. "They're keeping us from most of the colony, so most of the colony must be problematic. Jones, did you get some good visuals and other readings on Verona B?"

Jones nodded.

"Did VESA restrict you at all, raise any objections?"

"No. And they had to know what I was doing. You don't just do seven or eight flybys for no reason."

"Which means whatever it is, it's on the inside of the colony. Maybe in the hull, more likely on the surface of the interior," Lawrence said. "OK, let's review all the visuals

Jones got. Prioritize the ones that look to the interior. We'll decide what the most promising areas are and come up with a plan for getting a closer look."

Four hours later, they had made little headway. Ben was hungry and tired and sick of examining Verona B from yet another angle. The images were beginning to swim together, and Ben struggled to keep his eyes open. He could tell from the tension among the others that they were feeling it too. They were working hard and making no progress. Frustration was growing. One by one the others had gone off on their own to work or to rest. Harriet and Ben were left alone in the ship's common area.

"Let's take a break," Harriet said.

Ben looked up from his console. "What did you have in mind?"

"The Aurora. What do you say?"

"I would say I'm tired, but at this point I'd welcome a punch to the face if it got me out of reviewing these images for a half hour. Let's go."

They made their way down to the studio and Harriet walked him through some warm-up movements. Then she had him take his regulator down to 93 percent. The energy began to thrash him immediately. Ben was more tired than usual after four days of EVAs and several hours looking at images. He could feel his heart rate spiking even after a few minutes.

"Concentrate," Harriet said. "Breathe."

Ben did as she said, closed his eyes. He breathed in, then out. He felt himself grow calmer, then more aware. The hum of energy pulsed through his mind and body as his vision brightened and his skin became warmer. In. Out. Ben concentrated on the energy he felt, focusing on the heat and life contained in it. He could feel it, could almost see it. The water he'd drunk earlier, flowing through his veins as part of his blood. The food he'd eaten, moving through him in tiny packets of energy and nutrients. The air brushing his hands, his face. The warmth of the room. The feel of the overhead light on his face. Breathing in. Out. In. Out.

He perceived it more keenly tonight than he ever had. Maybe it was the heightened emotion of being surrounded by so much death, or maybe it was just the fact that his regulator was lower than usual. Whatever it was had Ben's body and consciousness thrumming, like he was resonating with the universe itself.

In. Out. In. Out. Seeing himself in the flow of energy, with his next inhale Ben drew his own energy inward, down, down to the center, then sent it back out. Blue light leapt into his right hand, tighter and brighter than ever, a piercing intensity instead of the diffuse glow he'd been able to muster before.

"Good," Harriet said. "Keep going. Control it."

Ben moved his hand back and forth, the light moving with it in perfect control. He withdrew the energy, sent it to his left hand as Harriet had showed him. Then both hands at once. The day's tiredness and sadness were gone. Ben felt alive. Powerful. He pulled the energy in again, took up a fighting stance, and this time punched the air as he sent the energy toward his hand.

He felt it more than saw it. His hand moved lightning fast, extending into the punch, and a wave of…something leapt from his fist and crackled against the wall. A brief flash lit the room. Ben looked at the wall and saw a black mark where the wave had struck.

Harriet stood there, too, wide-eyed. Whatever it was had just missed her. She turned and looked toward the wall behind her, then smiled.

Ben walked over and looked closer, ran his hand over the spot. There was a shallow divot where part of the wall had crushed inward.

What did I just do? he thought. He looked at Harriet, who just nodded. "Again," she said. Ben closed his eyes and concentrated once more. It came easier, faster this time like it always did when he did something new a second time. He drew energy in, then back out fast, with a punch. Crack! Another mark on the wall. Another punch. Thud! One more divot, broader and deeper this time. With a little practice he could direct all the energy where he wanted, sending to a point on the wall or keeping it right at the tip of his hand. He could feel the power in each strike.

On a whim he dropped his implant down to 90 percent. Harriet stepped forward, reached out a hand, but held back. She let him go.

The energy flowing into Ben increased, came in a torrent that threatened to overwhelm him in a flood of light and heat. Ben opened himself to it, let the energy pour in, concentrated on harnessing it within himself. Down, down to the center. He couldn't explain what was happening, exactly, couldn't tell what someone would have seen standing there in the room beside him. But he felt the energy come in, felt it move toward his center, the energy of the *Rock Badger* itself, and the *Chestnut*, too, diverting just a bit more of their flow to him in this moment.

Ben felt it well up inside him. Too much. He struggled against the onslaught and began to shake, his heart burning. He was going to burst, or combust, or disappear in a nuclear flare. He panicked for a moment, then stopped trying to hold it. He let the energy move through him instead, flowing in and back out like a current of water or electricity. The energy coming in replenished what flowed out, and he held just a little. His own energy swelled, swirled. He pulled it down, toward the center, spinning, then…out.

Instinctively Ben punched as he released the room's energy back out of himself. A bright flash and loud rushing sound assaulted his senses, then a shattering crash. The whole room rattled, and just as rapidly went quiet. Ben snapped his eyes open, came out of the trance. His hands still contained a faint glow, his right arm still extended. Past his fist was the wall, the whole thing now dented and crumpled, the center glowing a deep red. Ben's mouth dropped open as he realized the force he'd unleashed.

He opened his gem and took the implant back to 100. The room dimmed, and everything returned to normal except for the damaged wall. Ben recovered his breath, allowed his heartrate to slow. "Was that…normal?" he asked.

Harriet threw her head back and laughed. "Normal? Nothing about the Aurora is normal."

Ben smiled, then started laughing too. "Somebody's gonna be pissed about that," he said, nodding at the wall.

"Yeah. The captain, Jones, Krista. Take your pick."

"You used the Aurora in the gym the other day, didn't you?" Ben asked. "Against Mike and the others."

"You saw that?"

Ben nodded. "I caught the beginning of it after my workout with Mike. Your strength and speed were incredible. Just raw power. That was the Aurora, right?"

"What, you don't think a woman can do that on her own?"

"Sling a dude effortlessly across the room? Nobody can do that."

Harriet smiled. "Yeah, that was the Aurora. When you harness the energy, you can augment your own physical capabilities. That's part of what I'm teaching you. It will become second nature with practice."

Ben gestured toward the crumpled wall, which was still glowing. "Have you ever done that?"

"That? No, I've never done that. Similar things, yeah. Just with more precision, less…wild smash."

"I'm still just learning," Ben said.

"That's the scary part," Harriet said, turning serious again. "You can wield a lot of power with the Aurora. It can be destructive if you aren't in full control."

Something clicked in Ben's mind. He looked at the wall, then back at Harriet. "A lot of power. Destruction…" His eyes went wide. "Let's go back. Now."

"What?" Harriet asked.

"Come on," he said, already sprinting out of the room. "I think I know what we're missing."

Harriet caught up to him at the lift. Ben was shifting his weight impatiently while he waited "Come on, come on!"

"What is it, Ben?" The lift arrived and Ben punched the button for Deck 2.

"We've been focusing on stuff inside Verona B, trying to look through the breaches to get a glimpse of what VESA is trying to hide. But what if they're trying to hide the breach itself?"

"But they're not hiding the breach," Harriet said. "How could they? It's huge."

"They can't hide it, but they don't want us getting a good close look."

The lift stopped at Deck 2 and they ran back to the common room. Most of the others were still there. Ben got to his console and started pulling up images.

"Here."

Ben zoomed in on a crisp image of the main breach, running north to south along most of Verona B. "Look how the hull is bent. The cut is clean, it pierced right through. But there's been melting at the edges, see how they turn in?"

Harriet peered closer. "Yeah. What do you make of it?"

"I don't know yet. But something tells me this is the part we need to pay attention to. If we can—"

"Oh my God," said a voice behind them.

Ben turned and saw Aaron looking over his shoulder. "What?"

"It was a Lightbeam."

"Lightbeam?"

Aaron nodded. "Sure looks like it. God, I can't believe I missed it before. I saw a Beam strike back in my Titan Militia days. I served on the *Honeyfire*. It was a test ship, designed to experiment with all kinds of new armor and weaponry. We tested a prototype Lightbeam for a while, and I was part of a team that assessed the results." He paused and pointed to the screen. "It looked just like that. How did I not see it?"

"We were looking at the wrong thing, focused on the inside of the colony because that's what VESA seemed to be hiding. It was the breach they didn't want us to get a good look at. But they didn't count on us having far better sensors than your average salvage ship, or Jones being able to line up good close visuals."

"When we first saw Verona B on the way in, something about it caught my eye. I couldn't put my finger on it, but something about the scene looked familiar. This is what it was. Somebody hit Verona with a damn Lightbeam."

"Why didn't we see it at A?" Harriet asked.

"Too much secondary damage. The colony was torn apart, battered by wreckage from B and twisted open by its own inertia. Any evidence of the Lightbeam was covered right up by further destruction."

"OK but wait," Mike said. Ben turned and saw that everyone else had joined the conversation. Only Jones, Christian, and Levi were missing.

"Lightbeams use Dorium. They're basically like mini Dyson Arrays, right?" Mike went on. "Couldn't this corroborate the official story, that Verona's Array malfunctioned and the beam hit the colony?"

"I wondered about that, but the angle looks all wrong," Ben said.

Aaron agreed. "That's right. A beam from the Dyson Array would've started at a shallow angle from the end of the colony. This was in the middle and it cut right through, a perpendicular shot. Whoever fired the Lightbeam hit the colony broadside."

The crew took in Aaron's news in silence. Ben swallowed hard as he thought through the implications. Despite the games he liked to play with his brother, Ben knew that Lightbeams were only possible on the biggest capital ships of planetary and colonial fleets. This pretty definitively ruled out a Raptor attack, and pretty clearly implicated a major military entity as the one responsible.

"If this is true, it screams false flag," Krista said. "And the only people who make sense as the ones behind it are VESA."

Captain Lawrence cleared his throat. "I agree. But it's not just that."

"What else is it?" Ben asked.

"Lightbeams are regulated," Harriet said. "Interplanetary treaties limit each entity's ability to create and deploy these weapons on their ships. Titan Intel, as you might guess, keeps tabs on all VESA's Beam-equipped vessels. And none of them were unaccounted for when Verona was destroyed."

"So you're saying—"

"I'm saying if it was VESA, they did it with a Lightbeam ship that we don't know about. They built and deployed one in secret, almost certainly in major violation of several treaties, and used it to destroy an entire colony."

"And if it's that big, Verona is just the tip of the iceberg," Lawrence said. "A VESA ship with Lightbeam operating undetected out here among the Colonies? It's a threat to Titan. It's a threat to everybody."

Harriet got on the Quill and filled in Nichols. "I agree with your assessment," he said after she finished. "This is huge and it points to something bigger still that VESA is up to. How the hell did they build this right under our noses? And what's their end game? Verona is small potatoes, all things considered. Even the things it opened up for VESA out here are incremental progress, not a major move that justifies such a risk."

"Maybe it was a test," Lawrence said. "Push against the limits of the treaty. Deploy a Lightbeam and see what the interplanetary response is."

"Except they're going to all kinds of lengths to hide the fact that it was a Lightbeam, and they're continuing to point the finger at Raptors," Nichols said.

"And taking out a whole colony of mostly civilians isn't exactly putting your toe over the line. It's sprinting past the line and not looking back," Harriet said.

There was a pause, so long that Ben and the others began to wonder if the Quill linkup had failed. Finally Nichols spoke again. "We need more intel."

"I agree, sir, but it's unlikely we'll get much out here," Harriet said. "We'll stay longer if you think it's worthwhile, but it feels like we've run this well dry."

"That's not what I had in mind. Remember that potential witness you dug up? Turns out there might be something to it."

"Really?"

"Yeah. One of the salvage ships took on a new crew member shortly before running out to Miranda. That one called the *Bright Claw*. Their point of origin was Io. One of our agents got into the docking records there. Crew of fifty-eight arrived, fifty-nine departed. The timing works out too. A guy could've been at Verona during the attack, then gotten to Io before linking up with the *Bright Claw* and heading back. Barely, but it's within our window."

"That's a lot of circumstantial evidence," Harriet said.

"We don't have much else."

"Why do I get the feeling that you're about to send us after the *Bright Claw*?" Lawrence asked.

"You're half right. I don't have agents or other assets close enough to track this lead down quickly. It has to be you. But our guy's not with the *Bright Claw* anymore."

"No?"

"No. Your crew's going to like this part." Nichols paused for effect. "He's on the *Tethys*."

Chapter 17

The *Tethys* was a passenger liner designed for pleasure.

Launched more than a century ago, it never docked anywhere. The huge vessel flew endlessly through space at more than seven hundred kilometers per second, traversing the solar system from Venus to Neptune twice a year. Private ships came and went. Shuttles visited it regularly to transport cargo, passengers, and new fuel for the massive fusion drives. All the big cruisers were like independent colonies in that respect, much smaller than orbital habitats but no less self-contained. The *Tethys* was the largest and most luxurious by far.

"You are clear for approach to Dock Point 61. Transmitting coordinates. Over." The pilot's console flashed green, and an image appeared on it as the traffic controller finished speaking. Jones looked it over and gave the captain a nod. Lawrence glanced at Krista, who acknowledged receipt.

"Copy, *Tethys*, coordinates received. Approaching Dock Point 61. Over."

"You're up, Ashley," Jones said. "Take us in."

Ben sat at the pilot's console and reviewed the data. True to her word, Jones had been training Ben on a space flight simulator. She'd even let him take the helm on an asteroid flyby, to give him a feel for the *Rock Badger*. Now she was trusting him to dock the ship. Ben swallowed and wiped his forehead. He'd run the sim a few times and Jones assured him that the AIs on the *Tethys* wouldn't let him mess it up, but he had to admit he was nervous.

Ben knew the pilot console well by now. A large screen showed a view in front of the ship, surrounded by various indicators in a heads-up display. One joystick controlled thrust in six directions, and a second controlled attitude. Other functions were activated by directly touching the display. The screen offered a wide field of vision, and could be switched to bring up various other views around the ship, up to six at a time. The main view had an overlay showing relative position and velocity along the x, y, and z axes, as well as attitude orientation and angular velocities. A display at the bottom right showed current thrust, available fuel, and fuel consumption rate. The bottom left was a map of local space with major bodies and other craft in the area. Past and future trajectories for all bodies, including the *Rock Badger*, could be toggled on or off.

Ben centered the view on the *Tethys*. It was strange to see what appeared to be a small colony all alone here in space. The huge liner looked like a miniature version of Ligeia. The *Tethys* was a single rotating cylinder, not two in opposite rotation like Ben's home colony. As with most colonies, rotation provided standard gravity of one G aboard the cruiser. The dock points were along one end of the cylinder, opposite the fusion engines.

Ben increased the *Rock Badger*'s thrust, comparing his position and velocity with the *Tethys*. Huge numbers along the x, y, and z axes wavered up and down. The display said they'd intercept the *Tethys* in four minutes.

Ben double tapped the screen and opened the navigational settings. He located Dock Point 61 and set that as his origin. The velocity and attitude readouts all changed in response. Now navigation was as simple as orienting the ship perpendicular with the dock point, then zeroing out the x, y, and z positions. Ben concentrated, making small, efficient adjustments. In just under four minutes, the *Rock Badger* was at rest relative to the *Tethys*, sitting stationary at Dock Point 61. The console flashed green.

"Nicely done," Jones said.

Captain Lawrence nodded at him. "Excellent."

Ben got up, pleased with himself, and retrieved his bag from his bunk room. He made his way to the airlock, taking it slow. They had to spin down the *Rock Badger*'s hab ring before approaching the *Tethys*, meaning the whole ship was now a zero G environment. Ben recalled the intense EVAs back at Verona and quietly shuddered. He was glad that was behind them.

The others were already waiting by the airlock when he arrived. There were lots of smiles and chitchat. The crew was visibly excited about visiting the *Tethys*, though they all understood they weren't on leave.

While they waited for the linkup to complete, Ben's thoughts turned to Tiro and Jess and his other friends back home. He wondered what they would think about the *Tethys*. Two months ago he never imagined any of this. Now he'd been cast into this incredible new world that reached across space. Once again the tiny spinning cylinders orbiting the giant moon Titan seemed confined, limited. So did his former life, he realized with a twinge of guilt. Petty crime, even something huge like robbing Port Ligeia, felt suddenly miniscule.

He'd grown oddly comfortable with the *Rock Badger*'s crew, despite the danger and pressure of their circumstances so far. It was not in a million years the role he would have chosen for himself, but being newest crew member of the *Badger* was a role he found he was willing to play. It was also a role for which he had some talent. He missed all his friends back home, and his brother, but he wasn't sure he would want to go back even if it were possible.

"Nice job back there."

Harriet's words snapped Ben out of his reverie. He smiled at her. "Thanks. Jones is a good teacher."

"You're a good pilot. You didn't crash us into a casino or anything."

"Yeah, well. I'll see what I can do on our way out." Harriet laughed. Ben enjoyed their back-and-forth. They'd grown close since leaving Titan.

The linkup with Dock Point 61 completed, and moments later they exited the ship. An elevator car, similar to the ones on Titan, took them out to the interior edge of the cylinder—the floor of the *Tethys*.

On the way here, Ben had read up on the *Tethys*. It was named after a river in a popular sci-fi story from more than a millennium ago. The River Tethys was an artificial, multiplanetary waterway, connecting hundreds of worlds by portals. You'd float for a while on one planet, pass through a portal, and suddenly find yourself on another planet in another star system. In the story, the River Tethys symbolized both humanity's reach and its excess. Cruising the river's length, you would leap across lightyears and encounter the entire span of human culture. It was a grand tourist attraction.

The crew exited the elevator banks and found themselves in a large, crowded area with directions to rooms and various amenities interspersed with advertisements. Evidently the elevators dropped newcomers right into the middle of the action.

When the crew exited the elevator, Ben decided the name *Tethys* was fitting. The scene was huge, crowded, and representative of every form of humanity imaginable. The atmosphere was festive and alluring, with several restaurants and entertainment venues easily visible just from where they stood. Signs were prominent in eight different languages, and a scan of the area just ahead revealed architecture in several different styles. The floor stretched on and on ahead of them and curved up on both sides—a microcosm of the human world stretching across the solar system. It promised an entire ship full of luxury and unforgettable experiences. Eric clapped Ben on the shoulder. "This is gonna be fun."

There would be no full-day EVAs here. Being a luxury passenger liner, the *Tethys* held restaurants and bars galore and hundreds of options for entertainment and relaxation. And while the *Rock Badger*'s crew was there to find a single witness to the solar system's greatest crime, accomplishing that meant not drawing too much attention to themselves. They had to be discreet, which meant they had to look like passengers there for pleasure as well as business.

Titan Intel had managed to turn up a name for their person of interest: Liam Higgins. Best they could tell, he had arrived on the *Bright Claw* a few weeks ago and remained on the *Tethys* when the salvage ship departed. As soon as the *Rock Badger*'s crew got settled into their rooms, they started asking around.

Harriet started with some of the Tethys crew members and service staff—the thousands of semipermanent residents who knew every inch of the ship. She established an easy rapport with a few of them, and in less than an hour had herself invited out for drinks once the shift was over.

Captain Lawrence did the same, drawing on his own Intel background. He gravitated naturally toward other ship captains, as if they recognized one another by a sixth sense, and worked that connection whenever possible.

Krista and Aaron holed up in their hotel room and started pushing on the tech side. They wanted to access the *Tethys* databases to try to narrow down their search for Mr. Higgins. Ben and the others spread throughout the ship, talking to people and asking simple questions.

Where are you from? Oh, I have a cousin who spent some time there. Liam Higgins. You probably didn't know him, it's a big place and it's been a few years since he left.

Oh you're in the salvage business? Us too. Man, it's been slim lately. I guess there's a few people having some luck, but I haven't met any of them. Have you?

That Verona business is just awful. No survivors, can you believe that? Actually a friend of mine told me there were a couple of survivors, people who saw what happened...

The first few days, they turned up nothing. Even Krista and Aaron hadn't made any headway—they were in the *Tethys* records, but no mention of Liam Higgins. Maybe he changed his name, or maybe he'd just cleared the records. If the guy was here, he clearly wasn't interested in being found.

Ben teamed up with Eric, and they stuck mostly to the lower end bars, restaurants, and casinos. The two of them caught a couple of the latest holovids at the theater, following a lead from Harriet that maybe their guy was a regular there. Another lead suggested the guy liked a particular pool bar, so they went swimming and had some frozen drinks. Both times they struck out.

On their third day, Eric suggested they check out the Time Museum. They weren't following a specific lead, but Eric figured the Time Museum attracted a different sort of crowd than pool bars and holovid theaters. Maybe it would help to widen the net a bit. Ben couldn't argue with that logic, so off they went.

Time Museums were fairly common across the Outer Colonies, but there wasn't one on Titan so this was Ben's first time visiting one. The museum was a powerful virtual reality generator that could host various programs, most of which were realistic re-creations of specific locations at various points in the past. Today's exhibit was Old Kingdom Egypt, on Earth, during the construction of the smallest of the Giza pyramids in the twenty-sixth century BC.

Ben marveled at the rich detail of the museum's scenes. From the slight shift of sand under his feet as he walked, to the heat of the room and dry desert breeze, to the exertion he felt as he climbed the pyramid's stairs, it really felt like he was in Giza. He watched as thousands of virtual slaves struggled to move huge stones into place, each person individualized and incredibly lifelike. Ben and Eric were able to see the two larger pyramids already completed, a spectacular view, while observing the construction methods and intense labor as the third was being built. Their virtual tour guide, Horemsaf, was a high-ranking official overseeing part of the construction. He took the time to explain the innovative construction methods that allowed such colossal structures to be built as well as the Egyptian religious beliefs that undergirded them. The visit turned up no leads on Liam Higgins, but Ben didn't mind. For more than three hours he marveled at the site, as much at the views of Earth with its vast open spaces as at ancient Egypt itself.

Afterward they met up with Harriet, Jones, and Christian for dinner. The restaurant, Café Europa, boasted selections from "the rich culinary traditions of the outer solar system's early settlers with a spark of exotic life"—the last part a nod to the microbial life forms that had been discovered deep in Europa's oceans. Christian had made a reservation and they were seated quickly.

"Having any luck?" Harriet asked.

"No," said Eric. "You?"

She shook her head. "We'll get there though." She wore sleek denim pants, a dark tank top, and a neatly cut red jacket, her hair in wavy brown curls down to her shoulders. Stylish and casual, she fit right in with the restaurant's other patrons. It was a side of Harriet Ben hadn't seen before, and he wondered how much of it was her and how much was a persona adopted to help her get information from people.

They ordered drinks. Ben got something called a Vintage Rocket Fuel, a strong and bitter whiskey drink with a hint of spice. "Whew," he said after taking a sip. "Gonna have to take it easy on that one."

"Hey, all this is on TI's dime," Jones said. "Drink up."

Harriet gave her a mock glare, and Jones just shrugged.

"So we decided to try a different venue today," Eric said. "The Time Museum. A little off the beaten path and more cultured than most of the *Tethys*."

"Smart," Christian said. "Rub elbows with a different circle. Krista and I have made a lot of rounds with the high rollers, the chandelier and dinner jacket crowd. And you all have made a good dent in the more popular venues. Stuff like the Time Museum falls in between. We shouldn't overlook it."

Eric shrugged. "Well, it didn't work. Place was dead, and the handful of people we talked to didn't know anything about anything."

"Doesn't make it a bad idea, though. There's a lot of similar places. The theater and orchestra, and the zero G park for adventurous fitness types."

"None of that feels like his style," Harriet said. She waved a hand when Christian started to protest. "We should look, I'm not saying that. But all the places we're not finding him…it sort of builds a weird antiprofile after a while."

"How do you mean?" Ben asked.

"We haven't heard a peep about our guy. Even the few hits we got about the *Bright Claw* haven't led to him, even second or third hand. That means he's lying low and he probably changed his name. He's making few contacts, avoiding habits or patterns. He's probably spending a lot of time alone, maybe even just holed up in his hotel for much of the time."

"You think he knows we're after him?" Eric said.

Harriet thought for a minute. "No. No, I don't. He had to be lying low before we got here, otherwise we would have heard something."

Jones raised her eyebrows. "If that's the case, there must be somebody else looking for him too."

"Which means he knows something dangerous. Which means we're on the right track with this guy," Christian said.

Harriet sighed. "Or the intel was wrong and we're chasing the wind."

"Could be that," Ben said.

Christian raised his glass toward Harriet. "Even so, if you're on the hunt I wouldn't bet on the wind."

The others raised their glasses and drank with a smile, but the mood wasn't festive. They should have turned something up by now. Every day they spent on the *Tethys* with nothing to show for it increased the odds that there was simply nothing to find. It meant they were wasting their time here, and more importantly, it meant that Titan Intel was totally in the dark about whatever VESA was up to.

Their food came and went, followed by more drinks. Ben didn't know if the cuisine really was authentic to early outer solar system settlements—he suspected the chef had taken liberties—but it was delicious. They'd just ordered dessert when Harriet's gem buzzed. She checked the message. "Krista and Aaron found another lead."

"Promising?" Ben asked.

"No more than the others. But no less, either."

"They're working late," Christian said. "Do we need to go?"

Harriet shook her head. "Captain Lawrence and Mike are on it, they were just letting me know. I guess there's been a few charges at a dive bar to the south, near the engines. They're going to go stake it out."

Ben looked around and chuckled. "I have a hard time picturing a dive bar anywhere on this ship."

"You'd be surprised," Harriet said. "The crew and other permanent residents have their own needs, and that includes cheap drinks."

The desserts arrived and Jones checked her gem. "Speaking of drinks, I know it's late, but I need to blow off some steam. Anybody up for another round somewhere else?"

"Hell yes," Harriet said. The others chuckled. She looked around and shrugged. "What? This has been frustrating. Blowing off a little steam sounds fantastic."

"I'm in too," Ben said. The others agreed.

They finished dessert and went to a bar called the *Tethys*, an upscale place near their hotel that was named for the ship itself. The place was popular, judging from the crowd inside, but it was spacious enough. There were three floors, each with its own full bar. The servers and bartenders were impeccably dressed, friendly, and thoroughly professional. The atmosphere reminded Ben vaguely of The Occident, where he'd met Asher Garrison what felt like a lifetime ago. It was simple, artfully adorned without being ostentatious, with low lighting and a tasteful mix of background music representing several different cultures across the Colonies and the Interior.

They found a semiprivate spot with a table on the third floor. The five of them talked and laughed over two rounds of drinks and ordered more food. The place's resemblance to The Occident threw Ben off, and he found himself thinking about his friends and Asher Garrison. Was the Raptor mixed up in this somehow? He had no idea, but something about it kept bugging him. His mind wandered and he was quieter than normal, which prompted the others to try to cheer him up.

Harriet, especially, seemed to want him to relax. She asked him about his favorite music, and what hobbies he'd had back on Titan. They talked about what each of them did when they had a bad day, and who they admired, and whether they could ever stomach living somewhere in the Interior. It worked, Ben really did begin to relax. He put the thoughts of Asher Garrison out of his mind. He started to wonder if Harriet was just a good Intel agent adept at drawing people out or if there was some kind of spark happening between them.

She seemed to relax herself, the frustration she expressed earlier melting away. She smiled and more than once insisted that Ben try some of her drink. As the bar grew more crowded, she leaned toward him close so they could hear each other. All five of the *Badger*'s crew members were talking, laughing together, having a great time. But it seemed to Ben that, more and more, he and Harriet were having their own private interaction that the others weren't a part of.

Normally Ben would have enjoyed this. He and Harriet had become good friends, and she was attractive. Now there was that electric feeling of possibility between them, the potential that it might turn into something more than friendship. But they had a job to do and were part of the same crew for the foreseeable future. He really didn't want to get it wrong and mess all that up. Ben wasn't sure if he could trust his feelings or his read of the situation, and he struggled to sort it all out.

"Hey," Harriet said, playfully nudging his shoulder. "What's going on? You look lost all of a sudden."

"Nothing," Ben cleared his throat, smiled. "It's fine. Just been a long few days, that's all. I'm frustrated we haven't found out more, like you. And that Time Museum really took it out of me. They make it so that you're really walking around in that desertlike environment."

"I know what you mean," Harriet said. She finished her drink and looked at him, making eye contact that lasted just a little too long to be incidental. "You ready to get out of here?"

Ben looked at the others, who had just ordered another round and were all laughing together at a joke Eric just told. "I think we're still going strong," he said.

"I meant just the two of us. Could be fun." The corners of her mouth turned up. Even Ben couldn't miss what she meant.

"I, um…" Ben stammered, buying time to think. "Sure," he said finally, smiling for good measure. God, he felt goofy.

Harriet got up, whispered something to Jones, who glanced at Ben and smiled. Eric and Christian noticed too. Eric assured Ben that he'd take care of their tab.

Harriet grabbed Ben's hand as they exited the bar, then leaned her body close to his. He caught the scent of perfume as she did so, deep and sweet. "This way," she said, "Our hotel isn't too far from here." The air was cool, breezy, and the ambient lights throughout the *Tethys* were dimmed, giving the perfect illusion of a perfect night. Ben went with her, saying nothing, enjoying the feel of her hand in his.

His gem buzzed as they began to walk, but Ben ignored it. He was too focused on the moment. He was attracted to Harriet, that was painfully obvious to him now. He glanced over at her, and she returned the look with a bright smile. Ben's heart beat faster and he wondered briefly if he'd dropped his implant and activated the Aurora. But no, it was just Harriet. Her smile. Her hair. Everything. He'd never met anyone as strong as her, and that attracted him as much as the rest.

The hotel had a courtyard surrounded by dense hedges. They went through the gate, pausing briefly for the attendant to scan Harriet's gem and verify she had a room. They walked past a fountain, through an open area dotted with small trees.

Ben's gem buzzed again, and he thought he heard Harriet's chime too. But her room was right there, and whoever it was could wait.

Harriet's place was on the first floor and opened right out onto the courtyard. They were leaning together, arms around each other's waists by the time they got to her door. Harriet pulled away, smiled nervously at Ben as she put her gem to the door scanner and waited for it to unlock. Ben smiled nervously back. She tucked a strand of hair behind her ear and looked away as the door slid open.

They walked inside. Before the door was closed Harriet pulled Ben toward her and kissed him. He kissed her back, a deep kiss, wrapped his arms around her. It was exhilarating and comfortable and suddenly nothing else mattered.

Ben's gem buzzed again, then again, then a continuous buzz that broke the spell with its persistence. He felt Harriet's gem doing the same at her wrist. She pulled away from him and looked at it, annoyed, then her eyes went wide.

Ben took a step back. "What? What is it?"

"We found him."

"Who?"

"Higgins. We have Liam Higgins."

Chapter 18

The place really was a dive bar.

Harriet and Ben had run two kilometers to the address Krista sent them. A subtle change happened as they neared the southern end of the *Tethys*. The streets, buildings, and signage became just a touch less polished than the rest of the cruiser. Subtle cues—stray bits of clutter, boxes stacked beside doors—made it look comfortable. Lived in. This was where a lot of the crew stayed, and the local bar looked and smelled like regular, messy, everyday life. The cloth awnings were intact but faded. A window sign advertised cheap drink specials, and the tables outside had weathered tops and wobbly legs. A dive bar if Ben had ever seen one.

Everyone but Krista and the captain were waiting outside when he and Harriet arrived. "Captain Lawrence is inside, keeping tabs on the target," Christian said. "There's only one other entrance, at the back. Barnes is covering that. Our guy's in there alone, drinking himself silly."

"How'd you find him?" Harriet asked, her voice low.

"He made a mistake," Aaron said. "Paid last night's bar tab with his gem. The transaction came through the ship's records this morning. I guess he's been paying with cash or running everything through his room, which is all kinds of laundered. He went above and beyond to cover his tracks and lie low."

"We got lucky," said Harriet.

Aaron nodded once. "Yeah. We never would've found him. But he got sloppy last night. Once we had his gem, we were able to track some of his movements inside the *Tethys*. Found a hotel we're pretty sure is his, and this bar where he paid last night. Mike struck out at the hotel, but Lawrence set up early here and talked to a couple of the staff. Higgins came in an hour ago and started drinking hard."

"The captain said to let you call the play," Mike said, looking at Harriet. "There's three staff and twenty patrons inside. Some pedestrian traffic out here but it's pretty light at this hour."

"OK," Harriet said. "Not great, but we don't know where his hotel is or what kind of setup he has there, and moving him gives him a chance to run. What's the space like inside?"

"There's two rooms—the main one with the bar and some gaming tables, and another one, about the same size, full of four tops and a small stage. Patrons are spread out but most are on the bar side," Aaron said.

"Kitchen?" Harriet asked.

"On the bar side at the very back. It has an exit around back, that's where Krista is right now. Our guy's on the bar side, easy to spot in a corner, drinking alone. Lawrence has eyes on him."

"All right, we'll do it here. Mike and Ben, go in and clear out the second room. Get everybody into the bar area and keep them there. Get physical if you have to. Levi, Christian, you two are at the main door. Nobody leaves, understand? Make this look like a mob matter—Higgins is in debt, we're coming to collect. Don't say much. If you have to, make it a big enough deal that everybody stays out of our way, small enough that nobody even thinks to link it with Verona. Jones, Eric, clear the kitchen. Bring the staff out to the bar area, everybody where we can see them. Aaron, go around to the back door with Krista. Nobody comes in or out until we're done. Are we all clear?"

They nodded. "Aaron, go on around back and buzz me when you're in position." Aaron left while Harriet gave some final hasty instructions to the others. "We're going in fast. Don't make a lot of noise. Quiet intimidation, not shock and awe." A minute later her gem buzzed. "Go!"

Harriet led the way and walked straight for Higgins. She caught the captain's eye and nodded for him to join her. He stood up and walked beside her, reading the play and trusting her instincts. Ben followed Mike into the other room. Two tables were occupied, both near the stage. Mike walked up to each and said something to the occupants. One table cleared out immediately, leaving unfinished drinks and food behind as they walked toward the bar. A guy at the second table protested, but Mike put a heavy hand on his shoulder and squeezed hard. "We have business in here. I promise you don't want to be a part of it," he said in a low voice. The man read the danger in Mike's eyes and backed down, leading his companions to the other room.

Ben and Mike scanned the area by the stage to be sure they hadn't missed anyone, then stood in the entrance, facing the bar. Ben copied Mike's stance, spreading his feet and crossing his arms, playing the part of a nasty bouncer who wasn't about to let anybody through. Levi and Christian were already positioned by the main entrance, and Jones was ushering the last of the servers out of the kitchen where Eric stood guard.

In the corner Harriet was saying something to Higgins. The guy's clothes were wrinkled, as if he'd been wearing the same thing for several days. It was too far for Ben to get a good look at his face. Something Harriet said must have appealed to the guy, because he got up and walked with her toward Ben and Mike. The captain followed a few steps behind, ready in case Higgins tried to bolt.

Ben stepped aside to let them through. He got a good look now at their target. A young guy, maybe five or six years older than Ben. He wore a tough, defiant expression on his face, but there was a touch of resignation in his eyes too. He'd expected someone to come for him eventually. Surely not Titan Intel, though. So who?

Harriet and the captain sat down with Higgins at a table, close enough for Ben to overhear the conversation.

"You were at Verona," Harriet said.

Liam's face darkened and he narrowed his eyes, shifting his attention from Harriet to Lawrence. "Are you here to kill me?"

"We're here to talk to you."

"Ha, what could we possibly talk about? You know everything. You were as good as there."

"Where?"

"*There*. You saw what we did. Saw it with your own eyes, same as me. Maybe on vids, but what's the difference? Why are you pretending you didn't see it? God, I wish I could pretend."

"Are you talking about your dreams?" Harriet asked.

"Dreams? Yeah, I'm talking about my dreams. That's all I have is dreams. Nightmares. Bumps in the night. Searing light. Bodies. Metal splitting open and spewing into the void."

Harriet exchanged a look with Lawrence, tried a different tack.

"What happened at Verona?"

"Why are you asking me? You've seen the vids. You've seen the reports. The official ones, and the unofficial ones. The ones with my witness statements, that you've sealed up."

Harriet shifted gears here, trying to cut through some of the confusion. "Right. We're considering releasing those statements, putting the unofficial story out there too. We just want to clear up a couple of questions about what you said. Can you give us the basics again?"

The guy laughed now, long and wheezing, tired, less vigorous than Braun's had been on those EVA walks but hardly less abrasive. "You're going to put the real story out there? Just tell everybody, just like that? Either you're lying or VESA found themselves in a river of shit. So which is it, huh? You can tell me that, can't you? Give me a good laugh before you kill me."

"We're not here to kill you, Liam."

"If you know that name, we both know I'm not walking away from here."

"We just want to talk. About what you saw, out there at Verona, when the colony was destroyed."

Higgins slammed his fist on the table loud enough to make Ben jump. "You *know*! You saw it, same as me. You weren't there, but you watched on the vids. Real time, the captain told us all about how he was piping the whole thing through the Quill. You know what we did. Why are you asking me to relive it? I can't…" his voice caught in a horrible choking sound. He sniffled, and the next words came out softer, desperate. "I can't see it again. Don't…don't make me. The bodies. The damn bodies. Just kill me, will you?"

"We didn't see any holovids," Harriet said. Her voice was even, measured, patiently trying to find a thread to pull.

Another bitter laugh. "VESA's got a hell of a red tape situation, then. Left hand doesn't know what the right hand is doing, eh? You expect me to believe that shit?"

"You seem convinced that we're here to kill you. Who do you think we are, Liam? Who wants you dead?"

"You VESA agents really think I'm an idiot, don't you? The captain told me you'd be coming. I knew he was right, and I didn't care. I still don't care. Do whatever you want, it's not going to change anything."

"We're not—"

"He told me you'd be coming, understand? This isn't a surprise. When he tried to talk me into staying, he said it'd be just like this. He said you would…well, not exactly like this. Not…" A pause. He looked around, seeming confused at where he was and who was sitting across from him. "He said you wouldn't even bother talking. Just bam! Right in the head. And I don't see any reason why he would get that part wrong. So who are you assholes? You're not with VESA, are you?"

"No."

"Who?"

"Why don't you let us ask the questions," Lawrence said, speaking for the first time. "It won't take long, and we'll let you get back to your…whatever. We can maybe even help keep VESA off your trail, if that's what you want."

"They won't find me."

"You said yourself they'd be coming."

He waved a hand. "I was just talking scared. I took precautions. Nobody knows I'm here."

"How do you think we found you?" Harriet asked.

Another long pause. "Who are you?"

"What happened at Verona? What did you see? What did you do?"

"Who are you?"

"An interested party, that's all you need to know. With resources. What happened at Verona? Why did VESA attack the colony?"

That damn laugh again. Ben winced while the guy wheezed away. "VESA. VESA. You don't know shit, do you?"

Harriet was more forceful now, her voice firm and clear. "We know plenty. Now you tell us more. Why did VESA use a Lightbeam? When did they build it? How did they move it out here without our knowledge? Why did they use it to attack Verona?"

Higgins eyed Harriet for several moments with something between admiration and pity. "You have no idea, do you? What this is about, how far it goes. 'Without our knowledge,' you said. You must be in intelligence, then. Who? Europa? Neptune? Titan? Doesn't matter, I don't guess. Not much 'intelligence' in your intelligence, I'm afraid." He gave a short chuckle at his joke.

"Why did VESA stage a false flag attack? Why use a Lightbeam? How did they get it out here?"

Another pause while the guy regarded Harriet and Captain Lawrence. He had an appraising look in his eye, as if trying to gauge how much they really knew versus how much he had to tell them.

"False flag. A secret Lightbeam," Higgins said. He wiggled his fingers and inflected his voice in mock suspense. "Cloak and dagger, VESA making moves in the big, open dark. It's spooky, isn't it? Ha. You're only seeing the tip of the iceberg. Hell, you aren't even looking at the right iceberg. Heavy Dorium, Earth to… to… to everywhere. Archimedes is a hell of a lot scarier than you know. Bodies tumbling out, spinning like little wheels. You're looking for ghosts and don't even see the boogeyman in your backyard."

"Slow down with the mixed metaphors, chief," Lawrence said. "What's Archimedes?"

"Death," Higgins said. "It's death. Simple. Dorium. Heavy Dorium wherever it needs to go. We unleashed hell on Verona. So many bodies. Archimedes." A pause, and when he spoke again his voice was lower. Ben had to strain to catch it all. "The small bodies were the worst, you know. There were more of them than I thought there would be." A sob escaped his lips, followed by more. The poor guy's breath came in ragged bursts as he relived what he saw of Verona's destruction, or maybe his own role in making it happen.

Harriet waited several minutes until the crying eased up. "We can help you. We want to help you. VESA might come, but we're not VESA." She leaned in low, whispered, "We're with Titan Intelligence. If you know much about VESA, you know we have resources too. We can help you steer clear of them, understand? But you have to help us. Come with us. Tell us what happened. Who attacked Verona? What's Archimedes? We need more."

"It's too late to do anything about it now."

"Let us be the judge of that. Tell us about Archimedes."

There was a crash by the bar. Harriet and the captain looked up, and Ben whipped his head around toward the main room. A window was broken, and a second one shattered while Ben watched. "Look out!" he shouted.

A sharp hissing sounded behind him less than a second later. Ben turned toward it, somehow already knowing what he'd see. Higgins was dead, face down against the table, a pool of red spreading slowly beneath him. Harriet and the captain were backing away, each holding a small blaster and looking toward the windows by the stage.

Something flashed in the window to the far right, just for a moment. "There!" Ben shouted. The window had a small, neat hole cut into it where someone could have stuck the barrel of a blaster through. Whoever killed Higgins must still be out there.

Harriet and the captain ran toward the front door of the bar. Without thinking, Ben sprinted toward the window. He grabbed a chair and tossed it ahead of him, shattering the glass. He jumped through after it, only when he was in the air realizing how stupid and dangerous it was.

He managed to avoid a shard of glass through his neck, just tore his pants and got a cut on his bare arm. As soon as he hit the ground outside, a blast struck right beside his head and sent up a shower of hot pavement. Ben rolled twice, a second shot hitting right where he would have been if he'd stopped at one. He scrambled to his feet, scanning for something to hide behind. A flash of light ahead showed him where the shooter was. A flurry of shots sounded to Ben's right, and he turned in alarm to see Harriet firing away. "Idiot!" she yelled. "Get down!" The guy returned fire at the new threat, then took off running toward the busy center of the *Tethys*.

More shots sounded behind him, and Ben turned to see Harriet firing at a new threat—probably whoever had busted the windows and distracted them all inside the bar. Ben weighed his options, decided Harriet could hold her own, and ran after the shooter. He activated his gem and sent the others his real-time location so they could track him.

Ben closed the gap on the guy as they entered a more crowded area. The shooter looked back a couple of times and saw Ben on his tail, but he didn't fire. Evidently he didn't want to risk the attention of shots fired in a crowd. Ben kept chasing, picking up ground gradually and hoping his legs would outlast the other guy. He noticed after a few moments they were in a familiar part of the *Tethys*, where Ben had visited earlier today. Up ahead was the entrance to the Time Museum, which was still open. The guy sprinted through the doors. Crap.

Ben was only twenty meters behind him, but he stopped at the entrance. The Time Museum wasn't big, but the layout was complicated, made more so by the VR projections that made up most of the interior. There had to be emergency exits, too, and there was no way for Ben to know about them, much less cover them all.

An idea came to him. Ben activated the Aurora program and took his implant down to 96 percent. Maybe he could sense the guy's blaster inside the Time Museum and track him that way. He breathed through the first onrush of energy, which he quickly got used to. The sessions with Harriet were paying off, and 96 wasn't bad anymore. Ben paid attention to the amplified light coming to him, the way it looked and felt. He looked for something out of the ordinary, any excess energy that moved in a way that was unexpected inside the Time Museum. There was nothing. Either the gun gave off too little energy or the ambient power of the Museum itself was too much.

Ben hesitated. The smart thing would be to wait here. The rest of the *Rock Badger*'s crew wouldn't be too far behind.

They could search the inside together and have a better shot at covering all possible exits. On the other hand, it wouldn't take long for the shooter to make his way to an exit if he knew the space well. Ben made up his mind and plunged into the Time Museum.

He waved his gem toward the kiosk where you purchased tickets. Thankfully it remembered him from earlier and quickly authorized a second admission. He strode through the lobby and into the Ancient Egypt exhibit. He was near the beginning, in an underground chamber that wound through a couple of turns before opening onto the desert above. Ben walked cautiously through the space, painfully aware of how alone he was. If there were any other people in the museum, they were in a different section of the exhibit.

Had the guy come this way? If he did, did he press on, or had he waited for Ben? Ben tried to put himself in the man's shoes as he looked around. If Ben were the one being chased, and he had a gun, what would he do? Running would be safer, Ben thought. On the other hand, if you took out the person looking for you, then you could get away without any worries. Or maybe you wanted to know who they were, and what they had learned from Higgins, the guy you just killed before he could say more. Yeah, Ben thought as he rounded a corner and saw light up ahead. This guy would probably try an ambush.

Ben stopped. He didn't like it. There were too many unknowns. He decided to go back out and wait for Harriet and the others.

"Don't move." Ben stopped short as the muzzle of a blaster pressed into his back. "Who are you? Turn around. Slow. Tell me who you are and who you're with."

Damn it. Ambush. Ben hated being right.

Chapter 19

Ben turned and got a look at the guy pointing a blaster at his chest. A tall, heavyset man who looked solid as a rock and carried himself well. His face and general posture seemed tightly wound, like he was ready to burst into violence at the first hint of a reason. His hair was cropped close. Ben had the vague idea that he'd seen the man somewhere before.

The man's eyes narrowed. "You. What the hell are you doing here? How'd you get mixed up in this?"

Suddenly it clicked. This guy had been with Asher Garrison back on Titan. Ben remembered thinking how dangerous the guy looked then, and still looked now. Garrison had handed him the Dorium he took from Ben and Axel and Tiro. But why was he here? What connection did this guy have to Liam Higgins, or to VESA and the events out at Verona?

"Answer me. Who are you with, and what are you doing on the *Tethys*?"

"I'm here for the casinos. You?"

"Why were you talking to Liam Higgins?"

Ben remembered he still had the Aurora activated, with his implant down at 96 percent. Not that it would be much use against a blaster at point-blank range.

"He was telling us about Archimedes," Ben said. "Spilled all the beans. You want to give me your version, so I can see if he was lying?"

"Shut up. Give me your gem."

"Why?" Ben asked.

"Cause I'll shoot you if you don't, that's why." Ben handed it over. "I want to be sure you're not telling your friends where we are right now." The guy opened Ben's gem and saw the Aurora program. "What the hell is this?"

It came to Ben in a flicker of awareness. He didn't understand it, at least not fully. But through the Aurora Ben perceived a subtle shift in the man's energy, a split-second de-centering that left him off balance. It felt like the guy's attention was moving one direction and his energy another.

Ben swung his fist into the opening it left, and was astonished to see the blaster fly out of the man's hand. He struck again and landed a blow right on the man's chin. The bigger guy staggered backward, shook his head once, and came back hard.

The man rushed forward and threw a hard punch aimed right for Ben's temple. Ben ducked under it and to the side, threw a punch of his own, but the bigger man adjusted and blocked. He turned forward his opposite hand, catching Ben full in his chest. Ben stumbled backward, the wind knocked out of him, and recovered just in time to see the man coming again. This time he feinted, then shot forward, low. He took Ben to the ground in a textbook tackle.

Ben kicked his legs free and rolled away. As he scrambled upright he paid attention to the Aurora. He breathed in. Then out. Then in, gauging his opponent's intent. For a brief moment he felt the flow of energy, not at the forefront of his mind as he'd always sensed it with Harriet, but in the background, a quiet hum. The furnace, a little pool of heat inside him, always present, always smoldering at his center if he had the presence to feel it. Ben fought to keep his attention there, maintaining awareness of the furnace while he focused on his opponent and the fight. It was hard but possible. With each breath he drew the energy in, down, down to the center, slow and steady.

The man came again, threw a jab at Ben's face. Ben blocked and ducked inside his guard, then punched toward his gut. As he did, Ben felt the flow reverse, sensed a little energy move from his center out toward his fist without conscious effort. The man grunted as Ben connected, the blow catching him by surprise, landing harder and faster than either of them expected.

The contact brought Ben fully back to the moment, and he lost his sense of the fire. Ben stepped aside, allowed his momentum to carry him past his opponent and out of reach. He paused, breathed, pulled the energy back in, trying to recover his awareness.

The man struck again, jabbing high and following with a hard hook to Ben's body. Ben saw the blows coming, not just as flying fists or a body's movement this time, but as currents of energy, another little furnace sending its heat toward him in two consecutive arcs.

Ben blocked the jab, and without thinking he accepted the flow, allowed the energy to travel down to his own center. It felt like pain, and fuel. His awareness oscillated between his opponent and the constant presence and movement of the furnace—between the big man's intentions and the energy of the moment. His grasp of the fire, tenuous as it was, gave Ben an advantage. Ben could control its movement, direct in or out or around it with subtle gestures of will.

He caught a hooking punch, moved his own body with the current and sidestepped, adding his own energy to the flow. He used the man's momentum against him, throwing the larger opponent several feet where he landed with a thud.

Ben allowed himself to smile. This guy was huge, strong, fast, skilled. But when you got down to it, he was a ball of energy lashing out. So was Ben. Clashing energies, nothing more, and Ben's training gave him the advantage.

With a roar, the guy rushed at Ben, stopping just short of a tackle, his charge meant to throw Ben off balance. Ben didn't fall for it. He held his ground, pivoted his body forward and caught the man with a punch to the nose. He followed it with a quick left-handed hook, but the opponent recovered fast. His nose was bleeding but if it hurt, he didn't let it show. He slapped away Ben's second strike and whipped a lightning-fast kick right to Ben's upper thigh.

Ben winced as the kick connected. It fell heavy on his thigh muscles and bruised the bone beneath. The pain broke his concentration and the furnace faded from his senses while his opponent slid forward and caught him with an elbow to the chin.

Ben's head snapped backward and he saw stars. The guy closed in again, spinning Ben around and catching him in a choke hold from behind. Ben twisted and struggled, but the more he fought, the tighter the guy held him. Ben felt something warm, wet on his shoulder, and realized that the man's nose was dripping blood. That was something, at least. Not that a moral victory right here would do him or his crew any good.

Ben's strength was fading. Thrashing accomplished little. The furnace entered his awareness as his vision narrowed. Ben focused on the slow burn of the energy around him, felt it grow hotter as it gathered and turned.

In an instant Ben saw a weakness, felt the balance of the man's energy shifted too far to the left. He rolled his body that way, sudden and strong, casting his own energy the same direction. The guy lost his footing and the two of them tumbled to the ground together. Ben landed on top. The man tried to carry on the momentum, to flip them over and regain leverage, but Ben read the energy and shot his elbow into the guy's ribs. The bigger man lost his grip, and Ben broke free.

He twisted to his feet and rushed back toward his opponent just as a shot rang out. Ben stopped short as a red spot blossomed on the man's chest. The guy looked down, eyes wide with pain, then another shot hit him in the forehead and he fell over. He didn't move again.

Ben looked around, ready to fight yet another mysterious shooter, but saw Harriet standing there with a blaster in her hands. "You OK?" she asked.

Ben nodded and took a deep breath. "Yeah. What took you so long?"

"You're sure it was him?" Mike asked.

Ben nodded and fought to keep his eyes open. It was late, and the whole crew was crowded into the captain's hotel room. "Yeah, it was the same guy," Ben said. "I wouldn't forget him, and he recognized me."

"So Asher Garrison's man shows up on the *Tethys* and shoots Liam Higgins. What's the connection?" Lawrence asked.

"Gun for hire?" Eric said.

Ben shrugged. "Maybe. But that feels a bit beneath Garrison. And the guy's a trusted crew member, Garrison told me himself back on Titan."

"You think Garrison is part of this, then? Linked to VESA and Verona somehow?"

"Yeah. But I don't know what."

The captain turned to Harriet. "What about the other two, his helpers?"

Harriet shrugged. "That's a dead end. They got away and I didn't see either of them well. I just know there were two of them, and I'm not a hundred percent on that. Maybe they're locals, *Tethys* crew that Garrison's guy paid to help him out with a hit. Or maybe they're Raptors, too, and they know Higgins told us things."

"Which means the target's on our backs next," Levi said.

"If they're with Garrison," said the captain. "Either way, our time on the *Tethys* is short after tonight. Krista and Aaron altered our records in the ship's databases, but there are two dead bodies and a lot of witnesses. We're getting back up to the *Rock Badger* and departing first thing tomorrow."

"I'm just glad we're not dealing with Garrison's whole crew," Krista said.

"How do you know we won't be?" Ben asked.

"Raptor ships are huge, and you can't hide guns like the ones they're armed with. They wouldn't dock with the *Tethys*, and if they did, we'd know it."

Ben nodded. That made sense. "So Garrison sent one or a few guys to keep tabs on Higgins. On behalf of VESA, I guess?"

"Looks that way," Lawrence said. "But it still doesn't tell us what the connection is, exactly. Let's leave that for now and go over the rest one more time."

"Archimedes. Earth. Dorium," Harriet said, counting each bit of information on her fingers. "Those are the three things we got from Higgins. And the connection with Asher Garrison makes one more." She raised one more finger and nodded toward Ben.

"Earth's probably just a figure of speech," Christian said. "Earth to everywhere, that's what he said, right?" The captain nodded. "So that just means the whole solar system."

"Any idea about Archimedes?" Lawrence asked.

"Nothing conclusive," Harriet said. "Archimedes was a mathematician and inventor more than three millennia ago. I looked him up on my gem. It's said that he used focused sunlight to burn attacking ships during a siege of his home city, Syracuse. A big parabolic mirror, or maybe soldiers holding a lot of smaller ones."

Lawrence raised his eyebrows. "Big mirror to focus sunlight and burn things? Sounds vaguely like a Lightbeam."

Harriet nodded. "Yeah. An ancient heat ray. Anyway, that's the best I've found. It could be a code word for the Lightbeam, or maybe the name of VESA's operation when they destroyed Verona. I'll give the name to Nichols so he can follow up, but not much else we can do with it right now."

"How about the Dorium?" Ben asked. "The guy said it was heavy. Anybody else think that was odd? Maybe he means there's a lot of it? Or his guilt?"

Harriet shook her head. "That one's actually easy. Heavy Dorium is slang for enriched Dorium. It's what powers Lightbeams."

"Enriched?"

"That means it's been energized. Dorium is like a battery, the best battery known to humankind. I don't know the science behind it, but a specific reaction—called the Astruc Reaction—opens the Dorium and causes it to absorb energy. Think of it as charging the battery. Enriched Dorium is stuff that's already gone through that reaction. It's a fully charged battery."

"Sounds similar to how Dyson Arrays work," Ben said.

"It's the same principle. Dyson Stations and Relays have onboard Astruc reactors, effectively enriching the Dorium in place. That's not practical for military ships, which move around. Beam ships carry a supply of heavy Dorium to deliver the energy that's required for those weapons."

"Heavy Dorium doesn't tell us much, if that's all he meant," Jones said. "It just confirms that VESA used a Lightbeam at Verona, which we already knew. Archimedes too. It all points back to a Lightbeam, but doesn't give us anything beyond that."

"Yeah, another dead end." Harriet clinched both fists. "Higgins was so close to telling us more."

"No surprise they killed him," Lawrence said. "He knew more than he was letting on. I think he was on whatever VESA Lightbeam ship attacked the colony."

Krista nodded. "I think so too. The way he talked. 'What we did.' And how much it bothered him. That wasn't just witnessing something bad. It was guilt."

"Where does the heavy Dorium come from?" Ben asked. "They don't take it from a Dyson Station, presumably."

Aaron shook his head. "There's a handful of big reactors inside Mercury's orbit. Titan has one. Each one with its own official story. Collector for decommissioned Dyson Array, things like that. But nobody in Intel believes that."

"Yeah, OK," Ben said. "That's what I thought. And I'm guessing Titan Intel has an eye on VESA's known reactors. Has their output changed in the last couple of years?"

Harriet raised her eyebrows. "No. No, they haven't. I think I see where you're going with this. If VESA has been building a Lightbeam ship in secret, its heavy Dorium had to come from somewhere. We've seen no evidence of it based on their reactors. So where did it come from?"

"Another Beam ship? One we knew about?" Mike asked.

"Nah," Aaron said. "At least not directly. Titan Intel and everybody else watches those things like hawks, and VESA knows it. They wouldn't risk transport from one of them out to a secret location."

"So they route them," Mike said. "Use private sector couriers or at least vessels disguised to look like it. Or maybe—"

"Raptors," Ben said. "Damn, they're using Raptors. That's Asher Garrison's connection. He's moving the heavy Dorium for VESA."

"You're onto something, but Raptors operate way out among the colonies," Krista said. "Their presence in the Interior would attract attention, even if they attempted to disguise themselves."

"So the Raptors help, but they're not the only ones," Lawrence said. "Maybe they handle the last leg, get it to VESA's Lightbeam ship. How does it get to them? What's the first leg?"

They sat in silence for several long moments, thinking. It felt like they were at a dead end. "Earth," Harriet said finally.

"'From Earth to everywhere' is what Higgins said. 'Heavy Dorium from Earth to everywhere.'"

Lawrence grunted his agreement. "It makes a lot of sense. Go through another planet in the Interior. Mars is its own entity, that makes it hard. But Earth is fragmented, it could go through any of the old nations. And Venus does a lot of business with Earth, so there's opportunity."

"I'd bet anything that if the enriched Dorium doesn't originate on Earth, it passes through there," Harriet said.

"It's more promising than anything else," Christian said.

"Next stop, Earth?" Eric asked.

The captain nodded. "Next stop, Earth."

Chapter 20

Ben stood in front of the window wall, trying to make out the *Tethys*. The *Rock Badger* had left its dock point two hours ago and already it was just another star. He sighed. Harriet was right: space was boring. Yes, it was life-altering, world-shattering, horizon-expanding. All that and then some. You peered into the void, and it changed you. A breathtaking, once-in-a-lifetime encounter. It turned your world upside down and more. But you couldn't very well have these internal revolutions every single day, could you?

When he first left Titan, Ben had returned to the window wall every chance he got. But now, on his third voyage into the great beyond, the view that had so starkly depicted the insignificance of human life and struggle was gone. In its place was the endless *there*-ness of vacuum and impossibly distant stars. Space just sort of existed, unchanging and forever the same every bit as much as you were irrevocably transformed by the sight of it.

"Told ya," Harriet said behind him.

Ben turned. "Told me what?"

"Told you it was boring. Space, I mean. You just decided it was boring, right?"

"No it's not! How can you say that? It totally sets in relief everything about who we are and what we do. It's incredible, it's, it's… Yeah, all right. It's boring. Boring as hell. Why is that?"

Harriet laughed. "Even you can only wax philosophical for so long, right?"

"I suppose so."

"How's the leg?" she asked.

"Better today," Ben said. He shifted his weight, feeling it as he spoke. It was still a little sore. That guy had caught him with a vicious kick in the Time Museum last night.

"Your cheek looks like hell too."

"Yeah, I have a mirror, but thanks for reminding me. Next time show with a blaster a few minutes sooner."

"What are you talking about? You had him right where you wanted him," Harriet said with a smile. "I only shot him because you were taking too long."

"At least I didn't let him get away," Ben said.

"Touché."

They stood there and looked at the view of space until the silence grew uncomfortable.

"Hey, about last night," Ben started, but Harriet cut him off.

"I didn't just come here to kid you about space. The captain wanted to see you."

"Oh. What about?"

"He didn't say, just asked me to come find you. I don't think you're in trouble, if that's what you're worried about."

"Well, I wasn't but I kind of am now that you mentioned it."

She chuckled. "Relax, Ashley, it's nothing serious."

"Harriet, last night after dinner—"

"It was crazy, right? I mean, we finally found Higgins."

"Harriet." Ben turned toward her, a serious expression on his face. "I meant before Higgins. You and me. Last night."

She closed her eyes for just a second, and took a breath. "I know what you meant. Last night was… I don't know. It was a lot of things. I was frustrated we weren't finding Higgins, and… It's a lot to sort out. And right now we have to stay focused on this VESA thing. I like you, Ben. A lot. But what happened last night, it shouldn't happen again. There's too much at stake right now to work on…whatever that was."

Ben looked away. What she said was all true, but he was disappointed. Hurt. He liked Harriet, and a big part of him had hoped last night was the beginning of something between them. "Yeah," he said. "I hear you. And, I don't know, I was going to say something similar."

"You were?"

"Yeah." He tried to make it sound convincing. "I faced death last night. So did you. And call me crazy, but something tells me it won't be the last time. You and me, if there's anything there, it can wait. We have other things to worry about."

Harriet nodded. "Good. You're right. I'm glad we talked about it."

"Me too," Ben said. "I'd better go see what the captain wanted." He turned and walked away. He told himself it was the right decision, even if he couldn't help thinking about the walk to Harriet's place last night.

Ben found Captain Lawrence in his private office. "Have a seat. Water?" the captain asked. Ben glanced at the pitcher of water on the table between them. He shook his head, and Lawrence poured some for himself.

"You did well docking us with the *Tethys* the other day," Lawrence said. "Jones says you've been doing well in the sim too. Said you applied to the Militia several years ago, intending to be a pilot. That true?"

"Yes, it is."

"You still want to fly? More than just on the sims, I mean?"

"I guess. I don't know. I haven't given it much thought, really. The Militia door closed when I declined my acceptance. Now I'm part of your crew. I get to fly plenty that way."

"But you like the helm, don't you?"

Ben smiled. "Yes, sir."

"Jones told me you're good. Really good, and getting better."

"Thank you, sir. Jones is kind. She's a good teacher and clearly a fantastic pilot."

"You have no idea," Lawrence said. "I hope you don't have to find out firsthand, but she's unmatched as a combat pilot."

"I don't doubt it," Ben said.

"I'm going to put you in the regular pilot's rotation, to get you some more experience flying the ship. We were thinking of you to help out with engineering, but Hamilton and McCall seem to have a good handle on that. Mike's an OK pilot, but he's no Jones. You aren't either, but I think you'll do better in the pilot's chair than the engine room."

"Thank you, sir." Ben couldn't hide the smile on his face. "I won't let you down. Obviously I want to contribute anyway I can, but I like the idea of working as a pilot." Ben started to get up.

"Not yet," Lawrence said. "That's not why I called you in here. Not the only reason, I mean."

"Oh, OK. Sorry," Ben said as he sat back down.

"What can you tell me about Asher Garrison?"

Ben blinked, then launched into what he'd read in some of the Titan Intel reports. "He leads a large and growing band of Raptors. As a group, Raptors are hard to pin down, Garrison more so than most. In the past three years he's been tied to attacks spanning from Jupiter's orbit as far out as Uranus. Mostly cargo heading for the colonies, a few passenger ships. Last year he started hitting military vessels, and that kind of activity has been increasing. Most of his crew is—."

"I know all that," the captain said, holding up a hand. "I've read the TI reports on him, his background and latest movements, including his recent appearance on Titan."

"Oh. Then…what do you want to know?"

"You met him," Lawrence said. It wasn't a question. "What's your impression of him? As a leader. As a man."

Ben thought back to that day behind The Occident. He hadn't thought about it much since they left Titan. He drew his arms closer together, suddenly cold as he recalled the day his whole world shattered.

"I didn't interact with him much. We exchanged a few messages to set up the deal, then he was in and out pretty quick on the day we actually met."

"But you do have an impression?"

Ben nodded. "Tall, not exactly imposing but a big presence. Perceptive. Practical. And he was…" Ben paused, trying to find the right word. "He was…in charge."

Captain Lawrence raised an eyebrow. "Authoritative. Commanding."

"Charismatic," Ben said. "He didn't have to command, exactly. People deferred to him as if it was the most natural thing in the world. He just talked about what he wanted and expected it to happen, you know?"

Lawrence nodded once. "Anything else?"

"He was sort of gruff. Talked like he was uneducated, which is silly because I know he went to the best schools on Io. Krista told me about his connections with the Remington family. But it's like he decided he's above all that elite school stuff."

"But intelligent?"

"Oh yes," Ben said. "He saw right through my friends and me. We had no chance, sir."

"How likely do you think it is that he knows we were on the *Tethys*?"

Ben thought about it. Actually, he'd been thinking about it since last night. He didn't have a good answer. "It's hard to say. It depends on how well connected he is, and a lot depends on whether the other two attackers last night were local people or more of Garrison's crew. Even if they weren't, he knows his guy hasn't contacted him and it won't take long for him to work out that something happened. If he has informants on the *Tethys*, it's a pretty good bet that he'll connect the dots to us eventually."

"I think so too," the captain said. "That's why I'm asking you about him. It takes a lot of cunning and connections to make it as a Raptor, and a good bit more on top of that to cut a profitable deal with VESA, I'd imagine. We shouldn't underestimate Asher Garrison's resources or his ambition."

Ben swallowed, remembering the Raptor's piercing eyes as the captain spoke.

"Whatever his connection is with all this, I'd be surprised if we don't run into Asher Garrison on Earth."

They ran into him before Earth.

Ben was at the helm, with Jones by his side guiding him through a close flyby of a twelve-kilometer asteroid. They'd nearly cleared the asteroid belt, and the lack of space rocks so far had surprised Ben. He'd expected the belt to be a densely packed cluster of rocky planetesimals, but so far the few visible asteroids had shown up only as points of light, marginally brighter than the stars behind them. This was the first one they'd seen up close, though even now "up close" was relative. They were passing within ten kilometers of the jagged, irregular oval so Jones could show Ben how the asteroid's gravity influenced the ship.

"You see that?" Jones said, indicating the slow drift of the numbers describing the *Rock Badger*'s trajectory. "There's nothing to register the movement against the starfield, but if there was another ship or object in the foreground, we'd be able to see the lateral motion."

"Yeah," Ben said. "It's subtle, but definitely there. Easier to see if you look right at the asteroid."

"Right. But as we move away from the asteroid, it still exerts an influence. It's why you have to pay attention to the numbers, not just your visuals, even in combat. Especially in combat. Space is big, and our perception evolved in far smaller environments. Your eyes can lie to you very easily out here."

The asteroid had just drifted out of the forward view when Krista spoke up from the comm station. "Captain, we have a contact. Unidentified. Distance twenty thousand one hundred kilometers."

"Show me. How'd they get so close?"

Krista tapped her console, and the small bridge's holo table sprang to life with a three-dimensional plot of local space hovering above it. A blue dot in the center indicated the *Rock Badger*, and a red dot near the periphery showed the new contact behind them and to the right.

"There's another midsized asteroid in their vicinity," Krista said. A small white dot appeared in the display, slightly overlapping the red dot. "Best guess is they were behind it. This is our closest approach to that asteroid."

"And not registered on the Quill?" Lawrence asked. Krista shook her head. "So they meant to come on us suddenly," he said.

"Do you think it's a military patrol?" Krista asked.

"They're unidentified. My money's on Raptors," Lawrence said. He glanced at Ben, who had an uneasy feeling that the captain had a specific outfit in mind. "How soon will they intercept?"

"Just over six hours if they maintain their current trajectory," Krista said. She tapped the console again and the current headings of both ships appeared in the holo display, the blue and red lines converging toward an unseen point. She zoomed the image out and showed the intersection far ahead of the *Rock Badger*.

Ben watched in morbid fascination, suddenly aware that he was sitting at the helm. He got up so Jones could take her chair back. Whatever was going on, they didn't need the new guy at the ship's controls.

Just as Ben stood, the comm audio sounded two brief clicks, followed by a faint tone. Then a rich, slightly accented voice began to speak. "Greetings, *Rock Badger*. This is the *Blue Fin*. Over."

Ben's heart sank. He knew that voice.

"Greetings, *Blue Fin*. This is communications officer Dana Michaels," said Krista, using the cover name she'd given herself. Any records the *Blue Fin* had would show the *Rock Badger* as a tour vessel captained by a veteran guide named Moro Paulus, on their way to Earth for an extended stay. "Our sensors indicate that you are on an intercept course. Your flight path is not registered on the Quantum Line. Please alter your trajectory or provide a flight plan showing your path's priority."

"Yeah, that intercept course is on purpose," came the reply. "I'm gonna need to talk to your captain."

Captain Lawrence stepped forward. "*Blue Fin*, this is captain Moro Paulus of the *Rock Badger*. We are a registered passenger vessel with a priority four flight plan. Alter your course or confirm higher priority through the Quill. Over."

"Captain Paulus, this is Asher Garrison, captain of the *Blue Fin*. There's no point beating around the bush so I'll just come right out and say it. I've got a ship full of Raptors here and we aim to board you. Maintain your current velocity and prepare for docking in six hours."

"I don't think so," Lawrence said. "I've just sent a distress signal reporting our location and yours. The TSG will be all over you."

"Now what kind of Raptor would I be if I was worried about the Trans-System Guard?" Garrison said moments later. "I pay good money to know their patrol routes and even better money to make sure they miss Quill signals at convenient times."

"You're bluffing," said Lawrence.

"You willing to risk your passengers' lives on that?" Garrison said. "Here's the deal. We want money, equipment, all the fancy entertainment and tech you have on board. I'm sure a nice tour like you has a pretty good setup. Of course we'll help ourselves to a bunch of your food and booze. Hell, all of your booze, might as well be up front about that. But we aren't out to hurt anybody. We're Raptors, not murderers. I mean, we don't like to be murderers. Have it in us, you know, but we don't enjoy it. Most of us, that is. Anyway, we're not planning to hurt your passengers and crew, long as you play fair and do what we say. We'll shake everybody down pretty good, free them of the burden of worldly possessions like jewelry and tech. But then we'll be on our way."

He paused for effect. "Unless, that is, you decide to put up a fight. Fighting gets our anger up, you see, and like the shrinks say, it's just not healthy to keep that anger bottled up inside. So we have to express it, take it out on something. That'd be you and the crew, passengers, pretty much everybody. You'd get to be an object lesson for the next ship we visit, so they take us a little more seriously." Another pause. "Anyway, think it over. We'll assume you're following instructions and getting the dock points ready for us, 'cause you seem like a smart guy. If things turn out differently, well…see you in six hours either way."

Chapter 21

Ben finished packing the last container in the common room and strapped it down. He stood up, wiped the sweat from his forehead, and checked the time. He and the crew had spent the past two hours prepping the ship to engage the *Blue Fin*. They stored and secured every piece of equipment and loose item, down to the contents of the refrigerator in the galley, so nothing would fly around during the intense evasive maneuvers they would soon endure.

With everything secure, Ben, Eric, and Christian locked off and depressurized the lower two decks of the hab ring to give extra protection in case of a hull breach. Everyone occupied only the third deck, closest to the center of the torus. Harriet and Krista checked and rechecked the emergency oxygen containers in each room, while Mike and Aaron brought the fusion engine up to full power. An hour ago the *Blue Fin* had begun to thrust, moving up their estimated intercept time.

Ben donned a spacesuit, snapped his helmet secure, and checked the seals and backup oxygen. With luck he wouldn't need it—the suit would draw its air supply from the ship as long as it held atmosphere—but things could change quickly in combat.

Eric double-checked Ben's suit, verified it was on properly, and they reported to the bridge with all the others.

"Nothing has changed since our earlier briefing," Captain Lawrence said when everyone was there. The bridge was cramped with all ten of them gathered there around the holo table, and they had to leave the bridge's door open.

"The *Blue Fin* is thrusting. It's a large and heavily armed vessel, and faster than ours. We can't outgun them. Our best bet is to run, but we have to be smart about it."

The captain tapped the holo and brought up a visual image of the ship obtained via long-range cameras. It was wide and flat, a single triangular shape in the center with a flat saucer above it and another below—hab rings, if Ben had to guess. Dark circles near the pointed tip of the central delta were the main twin cannons. Plasma accelerators, Lawrence explained, as if it made a difference. Those dark openings were death, plain and simple. Smaller, similar openings flanked them, extending toward the outer edges of the delta on either side, and Ben saw small semispherical bulges on the top and bottom, in the center of the saucers. "Turrets," Lawrence said, "at least four total."

Heavily armed, indeed.

"Our plan is to thrust just before they reach weapons range," the captain explained. He changed the display to show the trajectories of the two ships with a new, dotted line branching off from the *Rock Badger*'s.

"Why wait so long, sir?" Krista asked.

"We're fast, but the *Blue Fin* is a Raptor vessel. We can't match their engines. If we start now it's a fair race, and we will lose a fair race." He indicated the dotted line. "But we don't have to run a fair race. This vector will take full advantage of their inertia and put the most distance between us and them quickly. They'll have to burn hard to course correct, which will deplete their fusion drives and tip the advantage to us on speed."

"Thank you, sir," Krista said.

"We expect engagement within the next hour. Sooner if Garrison increases thrust, which is likely." The captain paused and looked at the others. "This attack isn't random. It confirms

Garrison's involvement with VESA. Odds are good he knows we're linked with Titan Intel too. Garrison has been a factor in this game already. He's smart and connected enough to know what's going on, and he's ambitious enough to take bold action. We need to find out what that is eventually, but right now we just need to get away from him. We can't get caught. We run, and if it comes down to it, we fight. We can't get caught."

Lawrence looked around the room again, making eye contact with each person. Ben couldn't say why, but he felt reassured by the simple gesture. "All right. Get to your stations and get set up. We have a little time, but not much, and it's going to go fast once they start to thrust. Stay sharp. Dismissed."

"Weapons range in four minutes."

"Copy that, Barnes," Captain Lawrence said. "Jones, stand by to thrust on my mark." His voice was calm, betraying no hint of anxiety.

"Copy, sir," Jones said.

"*Blue Fin* is holding course, maintaining thrust of one point one G," came Krista's voice.

Ben listened to them through his headset as he watched the display. Directly in front was a window wall showing space in front of the ship. There wasn't much to see now, but when the evasive maneuvers began he would be grateful for a clear view of space ahead. On the right, a holo displayed the relative positions of the *Rock Badger* and the *Blue Fin*, with faint trails behind and ahead of each ship indicating their past and future trajectories. Beneath the image was a rough schematic of each ship, which would show heat signatures, hull integrity, and estimated engine strength. An ever-changing set of numbers displayed velocities, accelerations, and other data about both vessels.

"Weapons, bring blasters online, full power," Captain Lawrence said. He sat in the bridge, together with Jones at the helm and Christian controlling the guns in case it got ugly. Everyone else was stationed in reinforced rooms on Deck 3 of the hab ring, which had ceased rotating in preparation for the upcoming engagement. Now back in zero G, everyone was strapped in tight against a wall, with their backs to the rear of the ship.

"Copy, sir," said Christian. Though they planned to run, it was better to have the blasters powered up and ready just in case.

Krista and Levi were in one room, keeping tabs on the *Blue Fin* and any incoming fire.

Ben sat between Harriet and Eric in a separate section of the hab ring, strapped tightly against the wall. Their role was damage control. They would monitor overall hull, life support, and power systems status, doing what they could to reroute power or undertake repairs in the event of damage. They could repair a lot remotely if need be, rerouting power to backup systems or finding workarounds with the *Rock Badger*'s built-in redundancy and flexibility. Mike and Aaron were located in a different, similarly reinforced room, where they kept an eye on weapons and the engine.

As he waited, Ben marveled again at the clever design of the *Rock Badger*. Each room on Deck 3 held multiple control consoles, which could be programmed to control any or all of the ship's functions. Ben sat in front of one such console, while Eric and Harriet beside him each had their own. With a simple command they could obtain the ability to repair engines, fire weapons, even fly the ship—useful capabilities in a battle. Ben took small comfort in the idea that, if a lance of plasma obliterated his room, the others could go on more or less fine without him.

Ben opened a private line to Harriet. He winced as loud, aggressive music assaulted ears. "Damn!" he shouted.

Harriet turned the noise down. "What's up?"

"How do you listen to that stuff," Ben asked.

"My music? It gets my blood pumping. Helps me stay calm and focused. You should try it."

"I don't know about calm," Ben said, taking note of his racing pulse and throbbing ears. "Anyway, have you been in a situation like this before?"

"A few times," Harriet said. "Nervous?"

"Extremely."

"That's good. You should be nervous. It'll go away when we get into it. Once it starts, you're just focused on the moment, trying to do whatever you have to do to survive and win."

Ben swallowed. "Thanks. That's oddly comforting. I think."

"You're welcome." Harriet cranked the music back up and Ben killed the line to spare his ears.

"*Blue Fin* holding thrust. Weapons range in one minute," Krista said.

"Copy," said Captain Lawrence. " Jones, prepare to burn two point two G, on my mark. Three, two, —"

"*Blue Fin* thrusting one point eight G!" said Krista.

"—one, mark!"

Jones fired the engines. Ben was crushed back against the wall as the *Rock Badger* accelerated. He felt briefly nauseated until he reoriented his perspective. He thought of himself lying on the floor, looking up at the ceiling so that the *Rock Badger* was accelerating upward, not forward. That helped, but more than two G of thrust was an odd sensation, making his whole body twice as heavy as normal.

On the display, the blip representing the *Rock Badger* sped up, a small change at first that grew steadily under constant acceleration. In seconds their velocity surpassed that of the *Blue Fin*, and the distance between the two dots on the screen slowly began to increase.

"*Blue Fin*'s guns are hot," said Krista.

The comm crackled and a new voice cut in. "Now, Captain…Paulus, was it? Do you really think running is a good idea?"

"Did you really think we'd just roll over and let you board?" Captain Lawrence replied.

"I suppose not," Garrison said. "Guess you all have some surprises on that ship of yours. Odd for a passenger vessel."

"Only one way to find out."

"You know what? Let's quit pretending. I know who you are, and you know that I know. Can we cut the crap, Jason Lawrence?"

"I didn't like Moro Paulus anyway," Lawrence said. Ben thought he heard a hint of a smile in the captain's voice. If Garrison threw him off by mentioning his real name, his reaction didn't show it. "I suppose you aren't after our high-end electronics and other valuables, are you?"

"Not especially. We just want you out of the way. I should say, our benefactors really want you out of the way. It's not personal, you know. Now, we won't say no to your booze, but I'm guessing it's a dry ship."

"Gotta keep our heads on straight." Lawrence said.

"Ah, dammit. Well, we'll just have to make do with ten valuable hostages. I bet Titan Intel will pretend they don't know you but will secretly pay a nice ransom if we use the right motivations."

"We don't intend to get caught, Garrison. I've whipped better people than you."

"Careful, captain. We might have some tricks up our sleeve too. And with you running, it makes me wonder if maybe your surprises aren't all that special."

"I might say the same thing about you talking instead of shooting."

Garrison snorted. "Last chance, Jason. Cut that burn and let us board, and we'll treat you nice. Make us work for it and, well, let's just say my guys might have to take out their frustration a little bit before we hand you over to our benefactors. What do you say? We gonna do this the easy way or the hard way?"

Captain Lawrence cut the transmission without responding.

"Pew pew, motherfucker," Eric whispered. Ben glanced beside him and cracked a smile. Eric always had a way to lighten the mood.

The window wall suddenly flashed white, then faded to crimson. "What was that?" Ben asked.

Harriet gasped.

"Warning shot," Eric said, no longer joking. He pointed at the wall, which continued to fade, showing a brighter red line streaking down the center.

Ben blinked. "But they aren't in ra——"

"Shot fired, *Blue Fin* is in range!" Krista called through the comm. "Repeat, *Blue Fin* is in range."

"Evasive action, Jones," Captain Lawrence barked. "Burn us at two point eight."

Ben sank back against the wall as the G increased, and the ship began to spin and tip with rapid, random changes of direction.

"We underestimated their firing range," Harriet said to Ben over a private channel, her voice oddly clear despite the jarring of the ship.

Ben glanced over at her, straining to speak under the high G. "That can't be good."

"No. Means they have military-grade cannons, current gen, not the older tech that dominates the black market."

"Guessing that's unlikely, or the captain would have expected it."

"Raptors historically rely on speed, stealth, and surprise. They never go gun-for-gun with navy vessels. I don't know of a single outfit that uses long-range weapons like this."

Ben took in the new info. "Shit. However they got them, it means we can't assume anything. It's likely nasty guns aren't the only advanced tech they have."

"Yeah," Harriet said, her voice tight.

The ship jolted to the left, then farther up and to the right. The screen in front of Ben flashed as plasma shot past the *Rock Badger*. Jones was flying semiauto, a combination of AI navigation and human intervention. She laid in a general course and basic parameters, in this case evasive action, and the nav bot identified the threat and handled the steering. Jones took over at random intervals, injecting a human element that increased randomness and made the maneuvers nearly impossible for the enemy's targeting AIs to predict. It was working so far.

"New weapons range established, confidence 60 percent," Krista said. "Estimate six minutes to new range limit."

The starfield out the window wall spun clockwise, then scrolled past in a blur, then spun back the other way as the *Rock Badger* tore a random course through space. After three weeks of stationary views, the visible motion was jarring. Red streaks lanced across the scene, now and then flashing brighter when the enemy fire passed too close for comfort. Ben watched the endlessly changing numbers on the display, trying to make sense of them and find some indication of distance or velocity.

A loud crash and screech broke his concentration as the *Rock Badger* lurched sideways, throwing Ben against his harness with a violence that cared little for human comfort. The next instant their thrust cut out and the ship entered a wobbling lateral spin. An alarm blared through the room, drowning out the voice screaming over his comm.

"——ained, repeat, damage sustained. Outer hull breach, ring over forty!" Ben recognized the voice as Eric's, and he glanced over to see both his companions working frantically at their consoles.

Another boom rocked the ship, sending Ben crashing once again against his harness. The *Rock Badger*'s spin intensified and shifted closer to vertical. "Plasma fire sustained, ring over sixty," Harriet shouted. "Hull—hull intact, no breach. Electrical systems off-line, rerouting power through Deck 2."

The engine engaged and thrust forward at almost a full G, the ship still in a spin, which sent them into a long, erratic spiral. It was disorienting and Ben nearly got sick, but he supposed that was better than sitting still and getting hammered by plasma.

A third blast knocked them sideways, giving rise to another alarm. "Breach at ring two fifty," Harriet said. "Crew quarters sealed, damage contained. Power systems nominal."

Jones recovered control and brought them out of the spin. She kicked the thrust back to three G and resumed her evasive flying as more plasma fire pierced the starfield.

"Damage report," Captain Lawrence said.

"Weapons nominal," said Levi.

"Engines nominal," Mike called.

"Outer hull breaches at forty and two fifty," said Harriet. "Rooms sealed. Decks 2 and 3 secure," Harriet said.

"Power restored in ring quadrant three. No power loss, all systems functional," Eric said.

Ben checked the display as Harriet and Eric called out the damage. The schematic of the *Rock Badger* showed red along the outer hull of the hab ring at two places, one in the top right quadrant—forty degrees if the top of the ring was zero—and one in the lower left at two hundred fifty degrees.

"*Blue Fin* gained on us," said Levi. "Estimated time to range limit, seven point five minutes."

"Increase thrust to three point three," Captain Lawrence said.

"Copy, sir." Jones hit the engine, and Ben pressed backward, grateful for the ample cushioning between him and the wall.

The *Rock Badger* pitched left and up, briefly eased up on the thrust, then tipped down and shot forward in a tight roll. Two blasts from the *Blue Fin* missed wildly, but the next three tracked closer.

"How are they targeting so closely?" Harriet said. "They must be using some sort of enhanced algorithm."

Ben winced as he watched the flashes outside the window wall. Harriet was right, those blasts were close and getting more precise. The evasive maneuvers weren't enough. It was only a matter of time before they got hit again.

Ben's hands twitched, and he noticed that he'd been making subconscious steering motions. He'd never piloted an actual ship before, but he'd raced plenty of loaders and played more than his share of holo games, including the simulations Jones had shown him. He felt like they should be making more frequent maneuvers, smaller, tighter motions, wasting less time and fuel on big swings back and forth. *Keep moving forward, get out of range*, screamed a voice in his head. *Evade, dodge, go go go!*

Adrenaline built within him. He itched to get ahold of the controls. The plasma was fired from a great distance. Many small maneuvers were better than fewer large ones. *Twist, turn, back, faster! Go!* Every missed opportunity to change directions, each time they oversteered or held too long on a course, Ben felt a pang of anxiety. It began to gnaw at him, and he forced himself to calm down. Jones was a seasoned pilot, and the nav bot was state of the art. He breathed deep and told himself to trust Jones and the AI.

They entered a wide, arcing trajectory, engine burning a lot of G along a vector that was too consistent. Something felt off. *Turn, turn, turn*, Ben hissed through his teeth. Too long, too predictable. Boom! A frightening impact flipped the *Rock Badger* end over end.

"——ffline, repeat, nav bot is off-line!"

"Ring breach at ninety!"

"Deck 2 breached and venting."

"Engines nominal."

Ben listened through the damage reports, alarms, and his own stomach registering a sickening spin. He landed on the obvious conclusion: they were fucked.

Two more blasts landed in quick succession, slamming Ben forward against his restraints. A loud screech sounded in his comm, then abruptly cut off.

"Ring Deck 2 breached at ninety, two fifty," Eric said.

Jones righted the ship and burned the engine once more, somehow bringing the *Rock Badger* back under control as the others called out damage. Had Ben heard right that they'd lost the nav bot? Was she flying solo right now?

"Weapons intact, power source compromised. Rerouting power," came Levi's voice.

"Ring Deck 3 breached and venting at…" Harriet's voice began, then caught. "Deck 3 breached at one eighty."

Ben checked the schematic. One eighty was the crew lounge…where Mike and Aaron were stationed.

"Engine status report," Captain Lawrence called. No response.

"Engine status report," Lawrence said again. "Hamilton, McCall, do you copy?"

Finally Eric said, "Engines nominal, Captain."

"Copy that, Wong. We need to check on Hamilton and McCall. Can you get to the crew lounge at one eighty?"

"Yes, sir," Eric said. "On my way." He unstrapped and crawled his way along the floor, maintaining a firm grasp on every handhold. He nearly lost his grip as Jones pulled the ship through an aggressive turn, but he miraculously held on by one hand, his feet dangling toward the center of the room, until the *Rock Badger* leveled out. He moved quickly across the room after that then disappeared through the portal to the next room and closed the hatch behind him.

"Mosley, you're monitoring engines till McCall and Hamilton are back online. Wenner, you're on weapons alone," Captain Lawrence said.

Levi and Christian acknowledged the instructions.

"Time to weapons range limit: nine minutes," Krista said. They were farther away than before; the *Blue Fin* was closing in.

The *Rock Badger* continued to flip, turn, and weave, its movements more crisp and direct than before. Jones was good, Ben thought, but he remembered the feeling just before the last shot caught them. He had to do something, otherwise they were toast. The *Blue Fin* was gaining too much ground, inflicting too much damage. All it took was one more mistake, and if they were flying without the nav bot…

He activated his console for the first time, inputting the command to access the *Rock Badger*'s root systems. He found the navigation directory and began to search.

"What are you doing?" Harriet asked on the private channel.

"Jones said we lost the nav bot," Ben said. "I'm gonna try to get it back online."

"You can do that?" she asked, her tone doubtful.

"Gotta try," Ben said, "We won't last long flying unassisted. My friend Jess could program anything. She taught me a few tricks."

"Don't underestimate Jones," Harriet said. "But yeah, better try. Good luck."

Ben grunted his thanks, then began to explore the ship's systems.

"That's weird," he said to himself.

"What's weird?" Harriet said. Ben forgot he still had their private comm open.

"The nav bot," Ben said. "It's still functioning, still has power. It's just…yeah, here. Look." He pointed to the screen on his console. Harriet leaned over to see, moving slowly against the jarring turns and high G. Ben's finger hovered over scrolling lines of code, beside a set of green indicators showing all was operational. "See? It's running fine, but it's disconnected from the ship's controls." He scrolled higher up, pointed to a command line. "It looks like the disconnect instruction came from the bridge."

"Must be an accident," Harriet said. "We got hit pretty hard. Good work. Can you restore the connection from here?"

"Hang on," Ben said. He'd noticed a sort of rhythm in the code, nothing concrete, just a nagging sense of repetition that he couldn't specify. He entered a few commands to disconnect his console from the ship's controls, then linked the nav bot with the console's display. He could model on his screen the instructions the nav bot was sending the ship.

Ben's eyes went wide. The evasive action instruction generated a two-dimensional, regular, zig-zagging path through space. Easily predicted, with zero randomness factored in. No wonder they'd been getting lit up. Jones must have found the problem and disconnected it, giving herself full control rather than fighting the AI.

Ben showed the discovery to Harriet. "Holy shit," she said. "Do you think it got damaged in one of those hits?"

Ben thought back over their flight. "No," he said. He told her how something had felt off from almost the beginning.

"So what? Did they hack us?"

The realization hit Ben like a steel beam. "Yeah," he said, his voice tight. "Yeah, I think they did." The Raptors had their number. He scrolled up through the nav bot's code, not quite sure what he was looking for. After a few moments he found it: eight lines that stood out from the code above and below. He scanned the lines. Ben wasn't proficient at coding, but knew enough to recognize the basics of what the hacker accomplished. The lines were complex, elegant, and struck him as oddly familiar. He got a sinking feeling in his stomach. "Shit, this guy's good," he said.

Just then, Eric's voice came through over the comm. "Captain, I've reached the crew lounge." His voice wavered. "McCall and Hamilton are gone, sir."

A long silence followed his words. "Repeat, Dr. Wong," Captain Lawrence said.

"I said they're gone, sir. Mike and Aaron are dead. The hull breach is huge and goes right through Decks 1 and 2. Aaron's body is still strapped in. His suit's charred, looks like the outside of the blast caught him. Mike's not here, but I found faceplate fragments and shreds of a space suit caught between 1 and 2. I—I think he got spaced."

Harriet gasped, and Ben felt a pang in his gut. Just like that. Gone.

"Copy, Wong. Secure McCall's body and seal off the room. Return to your position."

"Yes, sir."

Chapter 22

Krista got a sensor reading on Mike's space suit and confirmed that he was dead, his body floating somewhere several hundred kilometers behind them. His suit had lost air pressure and his helmet was open, all consistent with what Eric had reported.

Eric soon returned, fighting the ship's acceleration as he crawled to his seat beside Ben. His movements were blunt, angry, and Ben thought he saw a tear on his cheek through his faceplate. Ben put a hand on Eric's shoulder as he sat. He couldn't find any words to say, just gave a squeeze. Eric stiffened at the gesture, then patted Ben's hand in gratitude. "In position, sir," he reported as he strapped in.

The *Rock Badger* lurched and spun, and Ben wondered if they'd been hit again. Then they leveled out and turned sharply. Just Jones, flying aggressively and keeping the plasma off their hull. She was having an easier time of it without the nav bot's interference.

"Copy," the captain said. "Wong, you're back on systems and hull. Mosley, stay on engine monitoring and repair. Adams, you're on engines too. We have to keep moving. Ashley, get access to hull and engines on your console. Switch between hull and systems and engines—help Adams or Wong, whoever needs it."

"Yes, sir," they all said.

"Barnes, how close are we to weapons range?"

"Estimated time to range limit eight point five minutes," Krista said.

"Not their range. Ours. How far are we from being able to hit back?" the captain asked.

Ben started. Was Captain Lawrence really thinking of engaging the Raptors?

"Four minutes out, sir, but we can get there in two if we turn and burn back toward them."

"Copy," he said. "Jones, turn us around on my mark. We're gonna take the fight to them, deal some damage of our own."

"Sir," Ben blurted.

"Ashley. Go ahead."

Ben reported what he'd found about the nav bot, how they'd been hacked. The captain took it all in. "Jones?" he asked when Ben finished.

"The nav bot was screwy. I disengaged it." Jones spoke tersely, all her focus on piloting the ship, but that was enough for the captain. "Ashley, can you remove the bad code and get the nav bot back?"

"Negative, sir. We can remove the code but they're probably broadcasting it continuously. They'll just reestablish access and we'll be right back where we were."

"Can you block them?"

"Negative. This hacker can code circles around me."

"What about Mc———" the captain fell silent as he remembered Aaron was dead. "OK," he said after a beat. "Jones, we need you to engage the enemy, go on the offensive. You up for it without the nav bot?"

"Yes, sir," she said. The hardness in her voice dared the captain or anybody to suggest otherwise.

"Prepare to engage," Lawrence said to everyone. "Wenner, weapons hot. Get ready to light them up. Jones, turn and burn three point eight when you're clear."

Jones ducked the *Badger* through several more turns then dialed back the thrust as she entered a twisting loop. "Turning!" she yelled, then cut the thrust altogether. In an instant she turned directly toward the *Blue Fin* and reengaged the engine, pinning the *Rock Badger*'s passengers back as she burned almost four G.

Ben looked out the window wall, then immediately wished he hadn't. Plasma fire lit up the view, emanating from a single point somewhere far ahead. How the hell was Jones doing this? She pitched, turned, dove, rose, driving relentlessly toward the enemy. Yet as he watched, the overwhelming sensation of death faded and Ben found himself anticipating her movements. It wasn't so bad, he realized. Small turns, varied thrust, random motion, active avoidance of the closest blasts. As before, his hands itched to get on some controls, but it was easier to trust Jones's flying now. God, that nav bot hack almost got them killed.

Ben corrected himself. The nav bot hack actually had gotten two of them killed. Anger flooded his chest, and he suddenly understood why Lawrence wanted to go on the offensive. It was probably the smart play anyway—they weren't gaining anything by running—but smart or not, he wanted blood.

"Thirty seconds to range," Krista called.

The *Blue Fin* suddenly stopped accelerating, the Raptors evidently realizing the *Rock Badger* had turned. "*Blue Fin* cut thrust, now eighty seconds to range," Krista said.

"Burn at four point three," Captain Lawrence said.

Ben barely registered the increased G as Jones accelerated harder. The *Rock Badger* weaved through the deadly blaze pouring from the enemy, the minute stretching endlessly, until finally Krista announced they were in range.

"Fire at will!" the captain said.

The blaze through the window wall doubled in intensity as the *Rock Badger* opened fire. Christian fired the *Badger*'s four plasma cannons continuously, sending a barrage at their larger, faster enemy. Their weapons were small, but Wenner's aim was true and he struck the Raptors as often as he missed. The *Blue Fin*'s pilot was less skilled than Jones, even with a nav bot, and their evasive maneuvers weren't nearly as successful. Ben cheered with each blast that landed. The loss of his crew members stung. It felt good to hit back.

Jones dialed back the thrust now that they were in weapons range, and Ben could concentrate better with the G at a more manageable level. He kept an eye on the hull and engine readings on his console, but there wasn't much to do unless they got hit again. He decided to run a systems check to see if the hacker had interfered with anything besides the nav bot.

He checked weapons first, cursing himself for not thinking to do it earlier. The targeting AI was similar enough to the nav bot that the hacker could have compromised it with the same ease. Ben breathed a sigh of relief as he checked it and found it clear. That was puzzling, but he didn't dwell on it. They probably hadn't expected it to turn into an all-out fight. He started on power systems next, deciding to work his way from the most to least likely target for a hacker to hit given what he knew. It was hard to concentrate with the *Rock Badger* constantly shifting directions, sometimes dramatically, and the temptation was always there to look at the window and watch the plasma fly. He wanted to shoot, or better yet to fly the ship, but this was the best way for him to help.

He quickly worked through power systems, life support, bridge controls, comms, sensors. Everything checked out. He came to the engine. Ben didn't really expect to find anything when he looked at the engine systems. He only accessed them for the sake of due diligence and to keep from calculating the odds of his own death in the next five minutes. Jones had been adjusting thrust nearly constantly since the outset of the engagement, with no apparent difficulty. Ships' engines were some of the most secure pieces of equipment in the solar system. They had to be—a compromised fusion engine could wreak untold damage when docked at a colony, so manufacturers had built in layers of fail-safes to prevent anyone from accessing them without authorization. That was doubly true, Ben knew, for ships like the *Rock Badger* that had some upgrades courtesy of Titan Intelligence.

Ben ran his console's automated scanner and peeked at each system on its own. The scanner blinked green after a few moments, indicating nothing was amiss. Ben started to close the files, satisfied, but something in the code for thrust control caught his eye. He took a closer look. It seemed off, somehow, but he couldn't pinpoint exactly what. He scanned some more, scrolled up and down through the code, and suddenly it hit him.

"No no no no no!" he said through clenched teeth. He scanned it again quickly, confirmed a familiar recurring line in the code, identical to a small section of the line that had invaded the nav bot. It must have been a Trojan horse, not only compromising the nav bot but introducing a malicious string that would continually try to break into the engine's systems. He didn't know if it had gained access yet, but it had been chipping away this whole time. And this hacker was good…

"Captain!" Ben called. "Malicious code in the engine systems. Repeat, I've identified malicious code in—"

Just then, the engine went silent and Ben felt weightless, the G force pinning him to the wall suddenly gone. He cried out in alarm.

"We've lost thrust!" Jones said. "Trying to reengage."

With no thrust they were helpless, cruising through space at a constant velocity. It didn't matter that they were moving fast. The *Rock Badger* could rotate in place using lateral thrusters, but couldn't change direction or speed. They just flew, quickly but constantly—predictably—on their current course, which was taking them closer to the *Blue Fin*.

"Adams, Mosley, get our engine back," Captain Lawrence yelled. "Weapons, pour on the fire, turn the pressure up on them."

The ship shuddered and an alarm blared as a blast from the *Blue Fin* hit home. "Breach over zero!" Eric yelled. Ben focused on the code in the engine, showing Harriet what was wrong and working with her quickly to try to reengage the thrust.

He glanced up at the window wall and saw that they were slowly rotating end over end. The *Blue Fin* came into view on the bottom of the screen and moved toward the center, a bright speck amid the starfield. Then the screen grew dazzling white, the whole ship shook, and a deafening screech erupted in Ben's comm as a single plasma blast tore through the *Rock Badger*.

Ben looked around, stunned. How was he alive? He thought the blinding light in the window wall would be the last thing he ever saw, yet here he was, dazed but otherwise unharmed. Harriet and Eric were both working frantically, calling out damage reports and working to contain multiple hull breaches.

"— bridge venting atmosphere at —"

"— engine systems at 60 percent and still off-line —"

"— diverting power from —"

"——rence do you copy, over? Captain Lawrence do you copy? Jones, Wenner, please respond, over."

Ben heard Levi's voice distinctly, and thought he made out Krista's alongside Eric and Harriet, but he couldn't detect any transmissions from the others. A glance at the display beside the window wall told Ben what had happened: the entire forward section of the ship on the schematic was lit up in red. The bridge was obliterated. *My God*, he thought. The captain. Jones. Christian. They had to be gone, nobody could have survived a direct blast like that. They most likely had been vaporized immediately; any remains would be floating among the debris in space. Ben closed his eyes tight, tried in vain to hold back tears. The fact that they'd met a swift end was no comfort at all.

He shook his head, opened up his console and started to help where he could. The *Blue Fin* wasn't shooting anymore. Guess they figured the *Rock Badger* was sufficiently blasted to hell. Ben checked the Raptors' velocity, saw they were rapidly approaching at constant speed. Eight minutes away, a little longer by the time they slowed enough to board.

"*Blue Fin* on an intercept course, ETA ten minutes," Krista said, confirming Ben's thoughts.

Ben focused. All he could do was work the problem at hand, then move to the next one. Their options were quickly vanishing, but they had none at all without usable engines.

"Captain Lawrence, do you copy? Over," Krista said. She waited a beat, then, "Captain Lawrence, come in!" Another couple of seconds, then she addressed the remaining crew. "This is Krista Barnes. I'm assuming active command until we reestablish contact with Captain Lawrence or First Mate Wenner. Priority one is to contain hull breaches and stabilize life support in the hab ring. Adams, Wong, seal off the forward compartment. Mosley, you're monitoring sensors, keep us updated on the *Blue Fin*'s approach. They're going to board, and we're going to fight. When they're inside five minutes…"

Ben worked as Krista spoke, momentarily blocking her out as he focused on the malicious code. In seconds he isolated it, started to remove it, but hesitated. He remembered what he'd told the captain earlier about the nav bot hack. The Raptors were broadcasting the code continuously, they'd be foolish not to. Removing it now would only bring them right back to square one. And he couldn't set up any kind of effective firewall—the hacker would get through it in no time. So he could remove the code but had no way of keeping it out.

Unless…

"Wong, when the forward compartment is contained, get over to cargo and bring whatever weapons you can," Krista went on. "Ashley, you go and —"

"I can fix the engine," Ben said.

"No time," she snapped. "They'll be here in nine minutes."

"Sorry, I mean I already—I found the problem with the engine. It's a simple fix, done in seconds. But…"

"But what? Out with it. You can either fix it or you can't."

"I can fix it, but we'll have to shut down all sensors to keep it online," Ben said. He quickly reported the malicious code he'd found. "They're already through our firewall, and I bet you anything they updated the virus already. If I remove it, they'll reload and gain access right away. But we can go dark, shut down all sensors, incoming communications. Anything that would give them access."

"So you can restore the engine, but we'll have to fly by visuals alone?" Eric asked.

"Yes," Ben said. "I don't know if it's better than fighting, but it's another option."

"It's insane, is what it is," Levi said.

"Probably," Ben agreed.

"We'll have to rely on random evasion, no idea how close they are or where, and hope we don't get shot. And who the hell will even fly it?" Levi said.

"We can hit them," Eric said. "Weapons are still online. If we disable them, take out their engines, we give ourselves a chance to get away."

"We'll only get one shot," Harriet said. "Have to bring them in close so we can't miss. If we burn hard, get out of range before they get a chance to turn and target, it could work."

"I say we fight. Let them board and give it to 'em hard," Levi said.

"There's gotta be at least eighty Raptors on that ship," Harriet replied. "If we fight—"

"It's better than running blind and getting blasted to bits."

"Enough!" Krista said. "There's no time for discussion and this isn't a democracy. It's a good plan, Ashley, but I don't like our odds flying blind. We—"

A loud groan cut Krista short, followed by two abrupt bangs. Ben heard what sounded like strained grunting, then a thud. "Captain!" Krista shouted. "Mosley, get her in here! Jones and Captain Lawrence are alive and wounded," she said for the benefit of the others. Mosley is examining them."

"Jones is unconscious but stable," Levi said after a moment. "Captain Lawrence just passed out. He brought Jones over. God, how'd he do it? Looks like a bad wound on his torso, but his suit sealed itself."

"*Blue Fin* ETA five minutes," Eric said.

"Strap them in," Krista said. "We're going to run."

Levi snorted. "I thought you said—"

"I said I didn't like our odds, but injured survivors change things. We can't keep them safe in a zero G fight, and I won't just abandon them here. We run."

"Copy," Levi said. He didn't sound happy, but he knew when to shut it.

"Who's our pilot?" Eric asked. "We can't risk it all on a straight, fast burn. We'll have to evade, and do it smart." "

"Ben can do it," Harriet said.

Ben turned to look at her, eyes wide. "You're not serious."

"You can do it," she said. "It has to be you, there's nobody else. Jones has been training you, and we've all seen you on the sims. You can do this."

"No," Ben said. "That's crazy, you—"

"Give him pilot control on his console," Harriet said to Krista. "He can get us clear, burn it hot. Put as much distance between us and the *Blue Fin* as he can, then go evasive. We'll spot for you."

"Guys, I— I don't know."

"Our pilot is unconscious and her primary backup died already," Krista said, her voice oddly calm as she recalled Mike's death. "If we're running, it's got to be you."

Ben's heart beat faster at the thought of having all their lives in his hands, but he knew deep down she was right. He swallowed and took a breath. "OK."

Chapter 23

Ben sat alone on Deck 3, surrounded by holo displays with visuals from across the *Rock Badger*. The window wall and display with sensor readings had been combined into a single, wide field view out the front of the *Badger*, while the holo on his console had a view out the rear. The other two consoles, which Harriet and Eric had used, showed views out the right and left, and could be toggled to show him other angles. They'd disengaged all sensors, so it was visuals only.

At the moment, the one on the right showed the *Blue Fin* approaching, slowly pivoting to turn one of its hab rings toward the *Badger*. Ben guessed the ring's center held their dock point.

"*Blue Fin* at one kilometer," Levi reported. "ETA one minute, nineteen seconds. Breach Team has visuals on four short-range turrets. Over"

"Copy that, Breach Leader," Krista said. "Maintain visuals, stay out of sight. Stand by to fire on my mark."

Levi, Harriet, and Eric—Breach Team—had taken position in what used to be the Deck 1 gym, where the hull was penetrated early in the engagement. The hull opening was not quite two meters wide, big enough to give them a view of the *Blue Fin* as it drew near. Periscopes on their blaster rifles allowed them to watch its approach without being spotted. Not for the first time, Ben felt grateful that Lawrence's crew hadn't skimped on the rifles and other weapons. Not only were their blasters powerful enough to take out the *Blue Fin*'s small turrets—at least, they hoped—the rifles were equipped with scopes that could give them valuable data about its speed, orientation, and distance. Because they weren't tied to the *Rock Badger*'s systems, Levi and the others could use these sensors without compromising the engines.

"Ashley, we'll need plus rotation of three degrees, then another five point two degrees."

"Copy, Breach Leader," Ben said. "Plus three, then five point two on your go."

"On my go," Levi confirmed.

Endless seconds ticked by. Ben checked and rechecked his visuals. He idly hoped that deleting the hacker's code really had fixed the engine. There was no way to test it, and if it didn't work they'd all be toast.

"*Blue Fin* at four hundred meters. Movement at the docking port. Docking shaft engaging."

Ben watched his own view as the *Blue Fin*'s docking shaft slowly extended toward the *Rock Badger*. He noted that the Raptors hadn't tried to reestablish contact with them. *Either they think we're all dead, or they know we're geared up for a fight.* In any case, no point talking. The Raptors were going to come aboard with guns drawn, prepared to shoot first and ask questions later. Ben wasn't going to let them get that close.

"*Blue Fin* at two hundred meters. Docking shaft at one hundred fifty meters."

"Stand by," Krista said.

Ben was sweating. *Just go already*, he thought. *Let's get into it.*

"*Blue Fin* at one hundred meters. Shaft at forty-seven."

"Stand by for my mark," Krista said. "Three, two, one, mark."

Ben rolled the *Rock Badger* three degrees, bringing the lip of the hull opening into view of the *Blue Fin*. Three quick blasts lanced out from the breach, taking out the nearest of the *Blue Fin*'s small turrets.

"Go!" Levi shouted.

Ben rolled another five point two degrees, bringing more of the breach into view. Now Eric, Harriet, and Levi were clear to fire at will. They each took a turret, bringing down all four small guns in seconds with a hail of rifle fire.

"Turrets down, go!" Levi shouted. They continued firing, concentrating on points of the enemy's hab ring at Levi's command. Their rifles were small by starship standards, but by focusing their fire together they were able to create two breaches in the enemy vessel. It was minimal damage, but enough to throw off the Raptors and buy them precious seconds.

As they fired, Ben spun the *Rock Badger* in place, keeping the Breach Team turned toward the enemy so they could do as much damage as possible. "Thrusting!" he called. He accelerated at two G, a quick burst to take them past the rear of the enemy ship, then cut the thrust and turned back toward the *Blue Fin*.

The *Badger*'s main weapons opened fire, pounding the Raptor's engines. Ben kept the front pointed at the *Blue Fin* as they coasted by, giving Krista a clear opening to fire away.

The Raptor pilot saw what was happening and reacted fast. The *Blue Fin* fired its engines and began to turn, bringing their powerful forward cannons to bear on the *Badger*. Ben kept the ship aimed at the enemy's engines as long as they were in view, then turned again and reengaged the thrust as they rotated out of sight. "Burning!" he called, accelerating once again toward the rear of the *Blue Fin*.

Krista pivoted the blasters and continued firing until she couldn't adjust anymore. "Out of sight!" she called. "Engines still operational." They were even with the *Blue Fin*'s side now, and needed to get back around to hit the engines again. Ben kept burning hard, trying to get behind and turn the weapons back toward the enemy.

Ben's heart pounded, his breathing fast. *This was part of the plan*, he reminded himself. He'd secretly hoped Krista would destroy the engines on the first pass. Then they could fly away safely, no need to evade. Easy. No pressure on Ben. But the *Rock Badger*'s guns were small, and they knew they couldn't knock out the *Blue Fin*'s engines right away. The plan was to take as many passes as necessary. They had to take those engines out. Two passes was easy. Three was a stretch. If they didn't destroy the engines in four, well. Best not to think about that.

The two ships circled each other, Ben trying to stay in view of the *Blue Fin*'s engines and the Raptors trying to line up a kill shot. More of the small turrets on the *Blue Fin*'s other side rolled into view and began firing, landing several blasts against the damaged hab ring of the *Rock Badger*. They didn't penetrate, but they rocked the ship and made it tougher for Ben to focus. Slowly he eased ahead, staying out of sight of the Raptors' main cannons and moving toward the rear of the ship.

With a growl and a short, high burst of G, Ben got around to the engines and turned the ship back toward the *Blue Fin*. As soon as he did, Krista let loose with all four blasters.

"How much longer?" Ben said. "We gotta destroy those engines."

As if to emphasize the point, the *Rock Badger* sustained two turret blasts in quick succession, and the lights above Ben flickered.

"That hull's tough," Krista said. "I can't get through." She growled in frustration as the engines drifted out of sight.

"Burning again, hold on!"

The *Rock Badger* shot forward as Ben upped the thrust, but getting around the enemy was slow going. Now the Raptors had momentum on their side, and they'd increased the distance between them and the *Rock Badger*. Ben had more space to cover as he tried to circle around behind them. He burned three G in a wide arc through a hail of small fire, desperately trying to stay ahead of that main cannon that would blow them apart. He wondered if they'd miscalculated and wouldn't even get a third pass, but it was too late to second-guess themselves now.

They slowly regained their advantage, circling meter by meter back toward the *Blue Fin*'s engines. *Now or never*, Ben thought.

Krista began firing as soon as they came into view, and as they eased past, Ben turned once more, allowing Krista to keep up her attack. Krista yelled as her blasts pummeled away, but with the *Rock Badger*'s thrust cut, the enemy quickly turned the engines out of sight and brought their forward guns around.

"Engines still operational," Krista said. "Get us around again!" Everything hinged on those engines.

Ben turned once more and burned at a crushing six point five G. He struggled against the sheer force of the engines battling his own body's inertia, pushing him into his restraints and pressing him flat. It took every ounce of his strength to work the controls. The damaged *Rock Badger* shook violently under the strain, and small plasma fire flashed past Ben's screen as he maintained the turn. He didn't dare check his side view to see where their main cannons were. There were only his weapons and the *Blue Fin*'s engines. Nothing else mattered.

Again they eased forward, circling too slowly toward the rear of the enemy ship as the *Blue Fin* burned hard trying to thwart their maneuver. Ben couldn't hold on much longer, and he knew this was the last shot they'd get. One more pass had to be enough, right? He felt sick, and wondered absently if vomiting was even possible under so much pressure. He grimaced, hoping he wouldn't find out. There was a distant screech and scrape, and Ben caught a small metallic flash on his right screen. It looked like something had broken off the ship and tumbled into the void. "Everybody OK?" he managed to ask through the strain. It hurt to speak.

"Keep burning," he heard Krista say through gritted teeth. He thought the others murmured their assent as well, but the small turret blasts rocking the ship made it tough to tell.

They'd been above six G for a full minute. It felt longer. Ben forced himself to keep up the thrust as the *Blue Fin*'s engines rotated into view and Krista started shooting. The *Blue Fin*'s hull began to glow, and pieces of debris broke away. Ben kept going. They would only get one more shot, and he had to get far enough ahead to give Krista as much time as possible.

With his chest tight and his vision darkening around the edges, Ben finally cleared the back of the ship. He cut thrust and spun hard toward the engines, the maneuver causing his stomach to lurch. Bile rose in his throat, but he forced it back down. He hoped Jones and Captain Lawrence were OK, to say nothing of his friends staring out into empty space with nothing but webbing to hold them in place.

Krista poured on fire as the *Blue Fin* turned in front of them, hitting the Raptors with blast after blast at full power. More pieces of the big ship's hull broke away and a huge section was glowing red. It wasn't enough. The *Blue Fin*'s engines slowly began to rotate out of view. The hull above the engines visibly fragmented, but held up. Krista kept firing— she knew it was too late, she had to, but she wasn't going to give up.

Ben hung his head, cursing their luck and the *Blue Fin*'s armored hull. They couldn't do another pass. The fourth one at six G had almost killed them without the *Blue Fin* needing to fire a shot. They could burn ten G now and it wouldn't do the job. Ben's mind spun, running through options that weren't there. Run? The other ship would chase them down in minutes. Let the Raptors board after all? Something told him the Raptors wouldn't bother now, they'd just blow the *Badger* to atoms at point-blank range.

The answer came to him in a flash, and he kicked himself for not thinking of it before. "Hang on!" he called.

Ben whipped the *Badger* perpendicular to the *Blue Fin*'s spin and flew beneath it. The maneuver put them full in the line of the enemy's lower turrets, but it took the *Blue Fin*'s momentum out of the equation. He poured on the thrust even as the turrets unleashed their fire.

The Raptor pilot reacted fast to the new tactic, rolling the big ship to continue bringing the main cannons to bear. Ben adjusted course, keeping the *Badger* headed toward the all-important engines. The *Rock Badger* shook and the displays registered damage as the volley of turret fire hit home again and again. Ben prayed the ship would hold together. Harriet and the others were on the opposite side of the hab ring, but it only took one hit to knock out engines or more vital systems.

Ben gritted his teeth and squinted his eyes against the bright streaks of plasma ahead of him, and then suddenly they were clear. The *Blue Fin*'s engines were right beneath them. Ben cut thrust and pivoted toward them.

Krista fired at close range, screaming over the comms with adrenaline and desperation. For a moment Ben thought it didn't work this time either. The *Blue Fin*'s hull cracked, twisted, glowed, but held together. He readied himself to try one more pass. Then something changed. The glow deepened and intensified. A huge swath of the hull buckled outward. It paused, the last tension of the material hanging on for a split second more, then the back of the Raptors' ship erupted.

A blaze of light engulfed the whole rear of the enemy ship. Hull fragments, fuel, and pure white light exploded outward. Ben twisted the *Badger* out of the main blast, hearing only a few bangs and scrapes as smaller bits collided with his ship.

The blast knocked the *Blue Fin* off course and sent it into a slow, tilting spin. Ben registered the rotation and snapped out of his reverie. In moments the spin would bring the enemy's main cannons level with them, and engines or not, Ben wasn't going to risk them getting a shot off. He turned the *Rock Badger* away from the deadly cannons and burned at four

G, keeping an eye on his rear visuals in case the Raptors turned toward them again.

"Nice flying, Ashley," Krista said, her voice tight under the high G. "Breach Team, come in. Do you copy?"

"This is Breach Leader," Levi said after a moment. "Breach Team all present and unharmed."

"Good work, guys. Jones and the captain are with me. Both still unconscious but stable. I'm showing new hull and systems damage for the *Rock Badger*. Mosley, get to a console and check it out. Nothing looks critical but I want it verified."

"On it," Levi said.

"Wong, give us distance to the *Blue Fin*."

"Fourteen kilometers," Eric said. "Estimated four minutes to range limit."

Ben watched as the *Blue Fin*'s spin continued, bringing their main cannons back around toward the *Rock Badger*.

"Hang on," he said. "We're not out of the woods yet." He pulled up, away from the direction of the *Blue Fin*'s turn. The Raptor ship shifted subtly, following his movement a few degrees, but then listed and continued its slow spin.

"Looks like they still have lateral thrust," Ben said. "It's minimal, but we need to avoid those cannons."

"Copy that, Ashley. Keep an eye on them and stay evasive."

Ben's heart pounded. He just had to make it four minutes, eight to be safe. He kept up their thrust. Every minute took them farther from danger, and a small amount of tension eased out of Ben's shoulders. The *Blue Fin*'s spin was slow, and he only had to evade three more times before the *Rock Badger* reached twice the range limit. Both times the *Blue Fin* adjusted its spin marginally to attempt to track them. Somebody on that ship was still paying attention, still hoping to line up a good shot.

On Krista's order, Ben cut thrust to one G after eight minutes. They were well past the known range of the *Blue*

Fin's cannons now. Harriet, Levi, and Krista got to work on the most urgent repairs. The engines were still OK, but much of the lower two decks was open to vacuum and power to the rest of the ship was in the yellow. Eric had begun treating the captain and Jones using the scant medical supplies he could access.

Ben relaxed but stayed at the pilot's console, a wary eye on the *Blue Fin*. Whenever the ship's rotation brought the main cannons almost to bear, Ben adjusted their course.

"Ashley, put it on auto and help us reroute power," Krista said. "We need all hands to keep up life support and seal off the breached areas in Deck 2 so we can restore atmosphere."

Ben hesitated and bit his lip. Something was bugging him. They were out of range, but the *Blue Fin* kept tracking them every time it came around. "With your permission, I'd like to stay at the helm a little longer. I can't say why but I think the *Blue Fin* is still dangerous."

"What are you seeing?"

"Minor adjustments to their spin, like they're tracking us every time they come around."

"We're well past their maximum range," Krista said. "Anything else?"

"No. Just a feeling I have."

Krista waited a moment. "OK. Give it ten more minutes, then put the ship on auto. We need you on repairs."

"Copy that."

Ben kept an eye on the *Blue Fin* for ten more minutes. He felt silly, paranoid. Their long-range visuals kept the Raptors in view. But other than adjusting course to track the *Badger* each time they came around, nothing was changing with the enemy ship. They were probably just trying to keep the *Rock Badger* in view, to plot a course and find out where they were headed.

Ben was still worried when Krista ordered him to put the ship on auto again, but he couldn't put his fears into words and didn't want it to seem like he was unhelpful. He made one last adjustment as the *Blue Fin* came around, then put the ship on auto. He unstrapped himself and stood, arching his back and flexing stiff muscles. It felt like he'd been in the chair for a week.

Ben went to another console and set to work, isolating damaged systems and rerouting power where he could, trying to restore as much of the life support and functionality in Deck 2 as he could. As he worked, Ben's mind went back to the *Blue Fin*. Why was he still worried?

The hack on their engines? Maybe the Raptors were still trying to shut them down. But that wasn't an issue, they still had all their sensors down except visuals. So what, then? They had been out of range for more than a half hour now. Why was Ben still afraid of those two cannons on the front of the *Blue Fin*?

He thought back through the battle. Those cannons had fired relentlessly while Jones was making her offensive run at the Raptors. Ben had followed the fire, anticipating the adjustments Jones was making. He closed his eyes, recalling what it looked like. The turrets were quiet. A single streak of plasma flew past the top of the *Badger*. Then another, which Jones dodged. Another.

That's what was bugging him, Ben realized. He hadn't had the chance to process it in battle, but his eyes had picked up on the incongruity. The plasma had come one shot a time, not two, always from the same spot on the Raptor ship. Only one of the *Blue Fin*'s main cannons had been firing. But why…

The *Rock Badger* shook, an easy shudder that went through the whole ship. An alarm blared overhead as the *Badger* tilted off course. Ben fell down and scrambled to his feet. What hit them? It hadn't felt like one of the plasma blasts from earlier, which rocked the *Badger* with heavy blows.

Suddenly it clicked. Ben's eyes went wide and chills spread across Ben's back as he understood why he was afraid, and how Asher Garrison's crew was mixed up in everything. "Major damage at ring one eighty," Harriet was saying. "What the hell hit us?"

"A Lightbeam," Ben yelled as he raced for the pilot's console. Asher Garrison wasn't helping VESA build a Beam ship. The *Blue Fin was* the Beam ship. The *Rock Badger* was still in range of the most deadly weapon they'd ever seen, and only good luck had kept that first shot from hitting direct. But the *Blue Fin*'s spin was slow, and they could alter it to track the *Badger*.

"A what?" Krista shouted.

"Engaging thrust, hang on!" Ben said as he fired up the controls and whipped the ship around. He reached for the accelerator.

The visuals turned white and then the room itself erupted with light. Searing energy tore through the *Rock Badger*. The ship tumbled through space, trailing vented gasses and debris, life support failing and the pilot unconscious at his incinerated controls.

Chapter 24

Death was hot. And cold.

Death was hot and cold and hot again—the endless cycle of Being and Nonbeing. Vigor and vitality blossomed, then poured itself away into oblivion. Something into nothing, nothing into something. A spark in the formless void, igniting, consuming, blazing with energy and matter and force, then plunging once more to silence and frigid absence. Again and again and again.

The period of oscillation was eons, or nanoseconds.

After a billion rounds, or barely one, he returned. *Let there be Awareness*. It came to him as falling, then searing pain, then purpose and tenacity. Identity. He was everywhere and nowhere, then suddenly he was here, now. He was Ben.

Cold, inky blackness surrounded him, punctured by countless points of light. Consciousness waxed and waned, but never extinguished. Careening through emptiness, he held fast to the pale tether binding him to fellow inhabitants of existence.

Inchoate sensation resolved by degrees into sound, sight, feeling. The usual patterns of meaning offered themselves, proved once again reliable enough. Arm. Echo. Gravity. Bright color. Familiar voices. Words.

"…he moving?"

"I can't tell. Ben?"

Red. Sound. Movement. Pressure. Golden.

Harriet.

"Ben, can you hear me?"

He opened his eyes, saw a bright blur that might have been his friend's face or a supernova. He groaned and tried to sit up, then sank back against…a bed? The ground?

"He's awake. Ben, it's OK. You're all right. Just relax, OK? We're here."

"The fever's returning."

"Get it back on."

"Ben, you're OK. Do you hear me? We're right here."

The pressure diminished. Words became sounds, then silence. Darkness took him again.

He faded in and out. Maybe minutes, maybe days. Flashes of cognizance and recollection briefly illuminated the sea of unconsciousness that surrounded him. Gradually the memories became longer, the blips of perception more frequent. They started to string together, and one minute— hour? day?—he was more awake than asleep. Ben opened his eyes.

Nothing looked familiar. Where was he? How did he get here? How was he still alive? The last thing he remembered was a bright flash of destruction tearing through the *Rock Badger*. His breath caught at the recollection and the certainty in his gut that the others had to be dead. *His fault.*

He wept silently, the tears streaming from the corners of his eyes down to the pillow under his head like tiny, salty rivers. Harriet, Eric, Krista. Captain Lawrence, Jones, Christian. Aaron, Mike, and Levi. Dead. They had to be. All of them. All his fault.

After several minutes of despair, Ben swallowed hard, blinked back the tears. He forced himself to put aside the pain constricting his throat. There would be time for mourning later. However it had happened, he was alive. Right now he needed to stay calm, find out where he was and what he needed to do.

It was hard to focus. Everything felt foggy, clouded. It was probably an aftereffect of the sleep—how long had it been?

His arms felt heavy, but he could move them. Legs too. That was a good sign. His eyes hurt, and his body felt as if he'd been run over by a monorail car. He moved his head and felt an odd sensation of pressure. Lifting a hand, gently, he felt his forehead. A large, thick bandage wrapped around his head.

Ben tried to sit up, and discovered the hard way that moving hurt like hell. He winced and tried again more carefully to look around and get his bearings.

He was on a bed in a small room with rough gray walls. Beside the bed was a shelf with a handful of tools, boxes of various bolts and hardware, and a fresh-looking glass of water. The only light came from a single panel on the ceiling. The wall down past the foot of the bed held an outdated solar system map and a door, closed at the moment. Ben could hear muffled noises in what sounded like a hall outside.

What was this place? A ship must have picked him up. Or did Asher Garrison get them after all? This didn't seem like the inside of the *Blue Fin*, but what did he really know about the man or the ship? He grew cold as he considered the possibility. Whatever Garrison had planned for him couldn't be good.

"Hey."

The voice startled Ben, making him jump. A sharp pain lanced through his abdomen, and he cried out.

"Whoa, whoa! It's just me."

Ben turned to see Harriet sitting on the floor beside his bed. "Harriet? Harriet!" Relief flooded his eyes with fresh tears. "It's really you. You're OK."

"Yeah, I'm OK."

Ben fell back against the pillow and let the tears come, happy ones now. Even if the rest was as bad as he feared, he could bear it knowing his friend was alive.

"Sorry, I didn't mean to scare you. How are you feeling?"

Ben sniffled, then wiped his eyes with the back of a hand. "It's OK. I'm just so glad to see you alive. I thought…"

"It's OK. I'm here. I'm OK. Does anything hurt?"

Ben chuckled, which brought a fresh wave of pain into his stomach. "Everything hurts. And I'm thirsty," he said. He looked around the room again. "Where are we?"

Harriet handed him the glass of water. "The continent of South America. Southern hemisphere, about thirty degrees below the equator."

Ben's eyes went wide as he drained the glass.

Harriet smiled. "Yeah. We made it to Earth."

"How?" Ben asked. "I thought this was a ship. The *Rock Badger*, the Raptors"

Harriet nodded. "They hit us hard, but it wasn't direct. We managed to keep life support online, barely. Engines were in bad shape, but we were able to hold a course. We crashed about twenty klicks west of here." She gestured at the room. "Eric saw this house on the way in. We decided to come here and regroup. Turns out it was abandoned, lucky for us."

Ben swallowed. "Crashed. The ship's done for?" Harriet nodded.

"It was a Lightbeam. The Raptors hit us with a Lightbeam."

"Yeah. You were right about that. Once we got everything under control, we were able to analyze the shots that caught us. It looks like the *Blue Fin* is armed with a Lightbeam weapon."

"That means they're the Beam ship," Ben said. "Asher Garrison is the one who took out Verona."

"Yeah. We think so."

"You think they're alone? Or acting on behalf of VESA?"

"It's likely VESA supplied Garrison with the Lightbeam weapon and the Dorium to power it. Which means Garrison might not be the only one."

Ben blew out a breath as the implications of that possibility sank in. After several moments he closed his eyes and shook his head. "I'm sorry."

"For what?"

"I saw it. Something was bugging me about that whole attack, and the way they were tracking us after we were out of range of their plasma. I realized it too late. If I had put it together sooner, if I hadn't—"

"Don't do that," Harriet said. "You maneuvered the *Badger* out of the direct path of the blast. We'd all be atoms if it weren't for you."

Ben wasn't buying it. "I should have paid attention to my instincts. I knew something was off. I should have fought harder to stay at the pilot's controls. I just couldn't put my finger on what I was afraid of. I realized it too late."

"Don't be so hard on yourself. None of the rest of us saw it either. You kept us alive through a hell of a battle and gave us a chance to take out their engines."

Ben shook his head. He'd put them all in danger by not trusting his gut, not listening to himself when he knew something was dangerous.

"Was anybody else hurt?" he asked. "Did anybody…you know?"

"No," Harriet said. "Minor injuries, no casualties from that last blast. You got the worst of it. Well, you and the ship."

Ben closed his eyes, grateful for that. "What about Jones and Captain Lawrence?"

"They're all right," she said. "Jones had a concussion and a broken arm, nothing bone gel and rest couldn't fix. She came around before we approached Earth orbit. Thank goodness it wasn't worse. The ship's fucked, but Jones managed a decent crash landing. Even at 50 percent she can outfly the rest of us any day."

"I believe it. And the captain?"

"It was worse for him. Four broken ribs and some torn tendons in one leg, plus that gash in his side. It was deep. He lost a lot of blood before his suit sealed over the wound. Eric worked wonders, though. Stabilized him quickly and set the medbots repairing tendons and his ribs. He needs more time to recover fully. Jones does, too, but they're in good shape, all things considered. He left Krista in command through the landing, but now he's taken back over."

"We got lucky," Ben said. "How long was I out?"

"Six days. We've been here for two."

Ben blew out a breath. "Six?"

"I'm just glad you made it. For a while there, it didn't look good." Harriet's voice trailed off, and a shadow crossed her face. She shook her head. "Anyway, you made it. That's what matters."

"What aren't you telling me?" Ben asked.

"You really don't remember? Any of it?"

Ben shook his head.

Harriet hesitated, then spoke quietly. "It happened when the *Blue Fin* hit us. The Lightbeam passed through the room next to yours. You caught a blow to the head, and it killed your link. Your whole implant went off-line, including your regulator. It left your Aurora completely unchecked."

"What do you mean, killed it? Like, all the way?" Harriet nodded. "I don't understand. How could I have survived?"

"You almost didn't," Harriet said. She looked away, took a breath, and continued. "You were fully open to the Aurora. What it did to you, Ben. With your implant gone, energy poured into you, and your body just…just took it. The fever, heart rate, pain, all that stuff you know about was just the beginning. You started *radiating* heat, light. I thought you were going to burn up. Not die of fever, I mean actually ignite. It was bad enough to be dangerous for the rest of us too. We worried the energy coming off of you would damage the ship. I've never seen anything like it."

Ben shuddered at her description. Death was hot. And cold.

"How did you…contain it?" he asked, for lack of a better way to put it.

"We put you outside the ship. Exposed your body to vacuum."

"You did what?!"

"We took you to one of the breached rooms, tethered you, and put you through the hull. We had no idea if it would work, or what it might do to you, but we couldn't think of anything else," Harriet said. "It was certain death for you, or probable death. And like I said, we were all at risk. We were still trying to stabilize the ship. We left you there until you cooled down, then brought you back in. You were still alive, barely. I don't know how."

He recalled cold, inky blackness punctured by countless points of light. A spark in the void, plunging to frigid absence. "I…I thought I dreamed that."

"Ben…"

He reached out, placed his hand on Harriet's. "It's OK. You did what you had to do, and I'm alive." The memory was clearly shaking her, though he couldn't tell if it was from care for him or the thought of triggering her own mutation in a similar way. He smiled, trying to lighten the mood. "Plus now we both know you're in love with me. We can move forward from here. This is big for us."

Harriet looked at his hand, then laughed and shook her head. "Krista was quick thinking," she went on. While you were…exposed, she constructed a crude radiation shield out of some of the damaged hull panels. We got you in there, and it helped. Not much—your body temp and energy levels were still climbing fast—but it blocked out some of the energy coming into you, bought us a little time."

"Time for what?"

"Time for Eric and me to fix your link. He got the device stabilized, and I used my own ability to manipulate it some more. You can regulate the Aurora again, adjust it up and down."

"But…?"

"The repair was temporary. It was the best Eric and I could do. The regulator part of your link is deteriorating. We think maybe it will last a month, but there's a lot of uncertainty. It could be three months or more, or as little as two weeks."

A buzzing rose at the back of Ben's mind, and the room seemed to grow brighter. He closed his eyes tight, clenched his teeth.

"You feel it, don't you?"

Ben kept his eyes closed and nodded.

"That's been happening. The regulator doesn't moderate as well as it did before. When there are energy fluctuations, you're going to feel them. They usually don't last long."

As if on cue, the wave of pain ebbed. Ben leaned his head back against the pillow and took several deep breaths, trying to calm his heart rate and bring his body temperature back to normal.

"No wonder I've been slow to recover, if this has been happening," he said finally. "A month isn't very long. What happens when the regulator gives out completely?"

"With luck, we'll be back on Titan by then. Our surgeons will give you a new, functional implant as soon as we're back. You might even get yourself a much-needed upgrade." Harriet tapped his forehead with a smile.

Ben smiled back at her, then turned serious. "And what if it's two weeks?"

"Then we'll have to do…something else."

"You mean you'll keep healing me."

"If I have to."

"What if you can't? What if it's too much for you?"

Harriet paused. "It won't come to that."

Ben sighed and leaned back again. Another wave of pain and light began to rise, then died down before it overwhelmed him. Ben would never take his regulator for granted again.

"Well it's not good news," he said, "but I'm alive. I survived a Lightbeam attack from Raptors and a crash landing on Earth. I got lucky. We all did."

Harriet nodded. Most of their small weapons and medical stores had made it through the run-in with Garrison, a miracle considering what shape the ship was in. The majority of food rations were still intact after the crash too.

"Did you ever find Christian?" Ben asked.

Harriet shook her head. "We looked all through the forward compartment, or what was left of it. If there were any…" She paused, looked away. "If there were any remains, they were unidentifiable. I don't think there were. That whole section of the ship was a wreck, and the bridge was just gone. Christian was either spaced or vaporized."

They both fell silent, and Ben felt his throat constrict. Christian was their friend and first mate. He'd taught Ben how to shoot, or tried to. He was a good leader. Now he was just gone. Disappeared. Lost in space or reduced to atoms. Ben couldn't decide which was worse. He wondered how close he'd come to the same fate. "It sounds like I almost was too. Thanks for taking care of me."

Harriet was quiet for a long moment. "You're welcome," she said finally.

The door opened and Eric walked in. "Harriet. Krista said you'd be here. We struck out again today. Not even a whisper of another ship within two hundred klicks. Did you—Is that Ben awake? Ah, yes it is. Ben, welcome back. Are you all right?"

"Yeah, I'm all right. I mean, everything hurts, but I'm here."

"Good. Glad to have you back. I'll tell Captain Lawrence and the others."

"He still needs rest," Harriet said. "Don't let them all come in at once."

Eric waved a hand. "No chance of that. They're busy getting ready to clear out. We picked up the *Blue Fin*'s signature. Garrison's crew will be here tomorrow."

"Tomorrow?" Harriet asked. "Our last reading had them a week behind us."

He shrugged. "They must have gotten their engines fully back online. We knew it was possible."

"Right. Well if you haven't found another ship, I guess we'll have to use the *McInnes*. It'll be slow."

"That's actually why I'm here," Eric said. "Did you finish checking it out?"

"As well as I could. It'll fly," Harriet said. "I need to do some final prep to get it ready."

"How long?"

"Two hours. Three, tops. Let me finish up with Ben, and I'll get on it."

"All right, good. I'll let Captain Lawrence know about Ashley here. Good to have you back, kid."

"Thanks," Ben said.

When Eric closed the door behind him, Ben asked, "Garrison's coming here?"

"Yeah. A lot faster than we thought too."

"Coming for us? Or for something else? Does he know we survived, or does he have other business on Earth?"

Harriet shrugged. "No way to know that part. We're clearing out of here just in case. We need to put some distance between us and the crash site, so he won't find out anything about our location if Garrison comes to investigate. Personally, I think he was coming to Earth anyway. Where he ambushed us, it's a long way from anything. He could have taken us closer to the *Tethys*, or on the outside of the asteroid belt. The likeliest scenario is that he was headed to Earth already and attacked us on the way, either on his own initiative or in cooperation with Venus. We were getting too close to figuring out what happened at Verona."

"If he was already coming here, odds are good that it had something to do with his arrangement with VESA. Raptors don't just come to the Interior for kicks, and Liam Higgins hinted that Earth was important."

"I agree, and so does Nichols. We'll keep tabs on Garrison's movement here. With any luck, he'll lead us to our next breakthrough to finding out what he and VESA are up to."

Ben sat up and motioned for more water. "Let's hope that doesn't take two weeks. I feel like I'm on a doomsday countdown here." He changed the subject. "So, what's a McInnes?"

"What?"

"The ship you and Eric were talking about just now. A McInnes?"

"The *McInnes*," Harriet said. "It's the name of a ship we came across here. Well, part of a ship. Just the lander. The *McInnes* is an older model designed primarily for space travel. Its engine and hab ring are docked up in orbit somewhere. We have the lander that operates in atmosphere."

"So what's wrong with it? It sounded like you were hoping to find something better."

"It's old as hell for one thing. The place we found it was all overgrown, the struts were actually sunk into the ground. I don't think anybody's flown it for twenty years, maybe more. And it'll be slow. The only fuel we have are for the lateral thrusters, not the rockets that would take it up to orbit. It's big enough for us and our gear, at least, and in its prime it was a high-end model."

"You don't think anybody will miss it? What about the owner who has the rest of it docked in orbit?"

"Those orbital docks are full of forgotten vessels. Somebody paid for an indefinite berth and just left it up there.

It's been here for two decades. I don't think anybody's going to come for it during our little adventure." Harriet stood up. "I'd better see how it's coming, help them finish checking it out. Get some rest. It sounds like we'll be leaving soon. I'll tell Eric to come sit with you in a little while."

"OK," Ben said. "See you later."

"Later."

Harriet left, shutting the door behind her.

Ben closed his eyes, but couldn't sleep.

Chapter 25

"We're clear, the *Blue Fin* is below the horizon."

"Jones, take us up," Captain Lawrence said into his gem.

"Yes, sir." Jones hit the throttle and the lander's thrusters sputtered to life, bearing its seven passengers and cargo upward in a ponderous four-hundred-meter climb.

The old vessel dipped and swayed more than once on its ascent, drawing concerned glances from everyone but the captain. Even Harriet, who'd inspected and prepped the thing, second-guessed its condition. After several tense minutes, they leveled off and settled into a rocking, bouncing trek northward.

The main hold was small but not cramped. With their supplies stacked neatly in the back half, there was room for the five of them to stretch out and move around easily enough. Krista was in the cockpit with Jones, keeping watch on their course and monitoring signals from the ground and local space. The idea was to head north fast, putting several hundred kilometers between them and the wreckage of the *Rock Badger*.

Fast was a relative term, Ben thought as he watched the treetops pass below them painfully slowly. Relying on the horizon's cover would work only if the Raptors couldn't access Earth's satellite feeds, a shaky assumption given their apparent hacking skills. Still, Ben was grateful for a few extra hours of rest before departing. He was far from fully recovered, and the journey would be as uncomfortable as it was long. Eric had set up a makeshift bed for him to lie down on, but he was feeling good enough now to be up and about. He figured it wouldn't last long.

"What was the final reading on the *Blue Fin*?" the captain asked.

"Just outside Luna's orbit, four hundred thousand kilometers," Levi said. "Current velocity, twenty kilometers per second and dropping. Assuming standard deceleration, they'll enter Earth orbit in fifteen hours. On the ground as early as sixteen point five hours."

"Thank you, Mosley," said Captain Lawerence. "We've got twelve hours before they're back over the horizon. We'll head north and set down in the middle of several thousand acres of forest. That will give us plenty of cover by the time Garrison arrives. We'll plan our next move based on what his crew does. Barnes, you're on watch with Jones up in the cockpit for now. Everybody else, get some rest while you can, I don't need to tell you this will be a long day."

The next couple of hours passed quietly. Ben dozed, suffered through one pretty bad surge of the Aurora and several smaller ones but mostly enjoyed the company of his fellow crew members. He looked out the window, watching the clouds and treetops, managing to enjoy his first glimpses of humanity's home world.

At one point he got restless and wandered up to the cockpit, where Jones and Krista were keeping an eye on the ship and their heading. He winced at the din of the thrusters coming through the side walls. Somehow Jones heard him enter. She turned in the pilot's seat and gave him a nod by way of greeting, her eyes obscured by the visor of the clunky helmet she wore. She looked at Krista and said something Ben couldn't make out in the noisy cockpit. Krista nodded, took off her helmet, and got up to leave. Ben stepped back to let Krista pass, then came back in.

Jones glanced back at him. Her lips moved, but Ben could hear nothing over the roar that filled the small space.

"What?" he shouted, leaning near her to make himself heard.

Jones pointed to Krista's helmet in the seat beside her and indicated he should put it on. Ben put the helmet on his head and immediately the noise dropped to a manageable level. Jones reached up and adjusted something on the back of his helmet.

"Can you hear me now?" she said, her voice clear in his helmet.

"Yeah, thanks."

"Have a seat." Ben sat down slowly, still sore from everything his body had been through.

"Loud, isn't it?" Jones said, looking around the lander's cockpit. "The soundproofing is mostly intact in the main hold, but a lot of it's missing up here. We're lucky the owner or whoever held on to these helmets."

"Tell me about it."

Jones jerked her head back toward the entrance. "It was almost time for Krista's shift to end. I told her to take off early and give us some time up here before Eric arrives. You up for that? If not, I'll call her back."

"No, I'm good. I was getting bored and was hoping to see the ship's controls."

"That's what I figured. No pilot can resist a flying machine. Even newbies like you. Want to fly it a bit?" Ben's eyes brightened as he gestured to the controls. "You're sure I'm not gonna crash us into the treetops?"

Jones grinned. "You'll do fine. We've got clear skies and a direct course for the next three hundred klicks. You mess anything up, just let go. The autopilot will straighten it out. It's a lot better than I expected for such an old bird."

She reviewed how to adjust altitude, speed, and direction, then got up and gestured for him to take her seat. "Your turn."

Ben took the controls and brought them up a hundred meters, then back down. The first time was jerky and way too fast, the controls being more sensitive than he'd expected, but after a few more he was able to do it smoothly. He altered their direction, going west for two klicks, then returned to their heading and reestablished the original course toward the northeast.

"You got it," Jones said. "Like I said, the auto does pretty much everything. It's hard to mess up as long as everything works like it's supposed to."

They sat in silence for a while, watching the view out the front window. Then Jones turned toward him and stared, her visor reflecting a perfect, smooth image of Ben's own helmeted face.

"What?" Ben said. "Is everything OK?"

"You tell me,"

"What do you mean?"

"You went through a lot up there," Jones said, glancing up toward the sky. "And I don't just mean your injuries. How are you doing with all that? You good?"

Ben pressed his lips together in a thin line and turned to face straight ahead. "Yeah," he said. "I guess. I haven't thought about it too much."

"OK," Jones said after a moment. "You haven't had much time to process, I suppose. You did good up there. You know that, right? You found that code the Raptors hit us with on the *Rock Badger*—"

"Not fast enough," Ben said.

"You found it," Jones went on, "fast enough to neutralize it and let us get away."

"Tell that to Mike and Aaron," Ben said, surprising himself by how quickly he answered. "Tell it to Christian." His voice was quiet.

"You didn't kill them."

"I could've done more. Could've worked faster, alerted you or Captain Lawrence or…I don't know. Something."

"You don't know," Jones said, regarding him coolly from behind the visor. "I don't know either. Nobody does. If this, if that. You can't know what could've or would've happened."

"Yeah, but—"

"What I do know is that none of the rest of us sniffed out that bad code. Nobody else neutralized it. If you hadn't done it, we would have lost more than three of us. And nobody else got us clear of the *Blue Fin*."

Ben snorted. "Not exactly clear. I got the *Rock Badger* blasted to bits."

"By a Lightbeam. A superior weapon none of us knew about. And somehow you recognized it just in time to avoid a direct hit. They told me about your flying. Krista said you're the reason we're here."

"I don't know about that," Ben said.

"I do," said Jones. "I was out cold that whole time, but when they told me about it, I didn't doubt it for a second."

Ben sat for several seconds, staring out the windshield as the endless expanse of trees stretched out and passed slowly beneath them. "Thanks," he said finally. "That means something, coming from you."

Jones nodded. "We'll get you somebody to talk to back on Titan. Eric knows a few doctors back home. If you need to talk before then, give me a holler."

"Thanks," Ben said.

"I mean it. We've all been through this, but it hits everybody different. I'm here for you. We all are."

They fell silent again, and Ben watched the treetops pass beneath the ship below. As Jones entered a set of course corrections into the ship's AI, he looked out the front and tried to gauge the distance to the next set of hills.

He couldn't do it. Beyond a few hundred meters, the trees lost all scale. Everything was too big, absurdly vast to his eyes conditioned by life on Ligeia. A flock of birds took to flight a ways off. They might have boasted meter-wide wingspans or fit in the palm of his hand. He fought a sudden sense of vertigo as the ground and trees seemed to fall away from him in every direction. He concentrated on the distant clouds until the feeling passed.

Ben remembered how he'd felt looking at Titan from space, the twin cylinders Ligeia and Kraken spinning like tiny tops above the huge moon. He felt something similar now. For the second time in his life, Ben saw his own life's experience for what it was: small, limited, confined. That it formerly seemed grand or fearsome was a product only of his ignorance. He couldn't decide if the new perspective made him bold or terrified. Both at once, if it was possible.

He couldn't take his eyes off the sky, the damn impossible sky, cloudless and piercing blue.The terrain didn't curve upward to the east or west, like it did on Ligeia, just rolling hills and distant mountains but always the sky far, far beyond them. No Terminus to the north, no discernible arc as one looked south. The horizon was a flat line all around, lifting up and down with the hills and trees but horizontal on average.

Ben's mouth twitched in a half smile as he registered the etymology: horizontal, horizon. A natural connection for those ancestors of his who built their language on this world, under this sky. No wonder the human imagination and ambition had soared. No wonder language and sensation and thought had labored, stretched to find meaning on this unbounded sphere. With limitless views like this, Ben found it incredible that only one of Earth's species had evolved to conceive of infinity.

"What a view, huh?" Jones said, bringing him out of his reverie.

Ben only nodded. How could he put to words what he'd just experienced, taking it all in?

The few minutes in the cockpit took a lot out of Ben, and he was grateful when Eric showed up for his shift in the copilot's seat. Ben nodded his thanks again to Jones, took off his helmet, and returned to the main hold.

The far-off hills grew larger and passed beneath them, replaced by more landmarks also an indeterminate distance away. After three hours, Jones brought the airship down below the jungle canopy in a small clearing.

The sun would set soon, but it had given their vessel plenty of charge while it was up. Harriet inspected the power levels and reassured them they had plenty of juice to get started tomorrow. They would sleep on the ship, so there was no need to set up a camp. Better to leave as little trace of their presence as possible. Krista, Levi, and Harriet did a quick but thorough patrol around the landing site and set up perimeter sensors, then returned for a meal and preparations for tomorrow.

"Our current course keeps us over wilderness for another four hundred kilometers," Captain Lawrence said as he and Levi reviewed a holo globe while they ate. "Venus has the most connections with entities in North America. It's a fair bet that's where Garrison will head eventually. If that's the case, we'll go this way. We'll adjust to keep east of Bogotá, and aim to reach the Caribbean here." He tapped an area near the top of South America and traced a straight line northward.

Levi swallowed a bite of his sandwich and reached forward to zoom in the image. "Lots more cities to navigate in the north." He moved the image back and forth a couple of times, adjusting the scale and overlays. Lawrence watched him patiently. "We'll have to keep low at a few places and wind around more than we'd like, but I can find a path that will keep us away from the major population centers. Once we reach the coast, there will be enough traffic that we shouldn't attract much attention."

"Good. All this assumes Garrison goes to North America. If it's somewhere else, we'll have to adjust." The captain looked up and addressed the rest of the crew. "At the moment, we're to observe them only, not engage. Asher Garrison has a

Lightbeam, and our best evidence is that VESA supplied him with the weapon and the Dorium to fuel it. If that's accurate, he and potentially other Raptors pose a direct, immediate threat to Titan. It's critical that we find out what Garrison is doing here, and how it serves VESA." Lawrence paused here to look around at all six of his team members. "This is not just about Titan Intel and our contract with them. It's about Titan itself and all the Outer Colonies. It's about our whole way of life. We can't afford to fail."

"Yes, sir," they all said.

Lawrence looked at Krista. "How do our jammers look?"

"I'm keeping an eye on them, but so far so good," she said. "Everything is working properly, and I tested every hour we were in flight. We're not getting any active sensor pings, which is a good sign. We don't exist unless someone has us in visuals."

"That's rare enough for now, and anybody who sees us won't bother following up. Do you have the false credentials ready for when we reach the coast?"

Krista nodded. "We're ferrying specialized electrical components to the Tennessee Valley for a research group there. It'll be convincing as long as we don't get boarded."

"If we're boarded we'll have a lot bigger problems on our hands," Lawrence said. "The American Commonwealth is tight with Venus, as are Russia and Japan. Wherever we go, we're in the Interior and people will sympathize with VESA and their allies, not with us. We'll be safer when we reach a specific destination and can operate locally—our cover won't have to hold up to much scrutiny there. Traversing continents is when we'll be the most exposed."

They finished eating and the captain assigned watch duties. Ben and Jones got out of it, since Ben was still recovering and Jones was doing all the flying. Ben wasn't complaining; he was dead tired. He climbed into the lander's main hold and fell asleep almost immediately.

Ben woke to the sound of hushed voices outside the *McInnes*. He bolted upright, confused at first, then remembered where he was. He checked his gem, saw it was just past midnight. The voices outside were quiet, whispered, but familiar, and he didn't see Captain Lawrence, Krista, or Harriet on the floor. Odd, Ben thought. There was only supposed to be one on watch at a given time.

Ben got up and opened the door quietly. He wouldn't be able to sleep until he knew what was going on. Harriet, Krista, and Lawrence were huddled around a gem a few paces away from the ship.

"Everything OK?" Ben asked from the entrance.

They all turned, and Harriet said, "Yes. The Raptors found the *Rock Badger*. Come look."

Ben climbed out of the lander and closed the door, walked over to the holo image hovering over Captain Lawrence's gem. It took a few moments to make out what he was seeing. The camera was placed high in a tree, looking down over the wreckage of their ship. Parts of it were actually scattered across several kilometers, Eric had told him, but the largest intact portion was here—most of the hab ring and what was left of the bridge. It had been enough to get them all to the ground safely. Barely, Ben now saw, looking at what was left of their ship.

"We set up cameras around and above the crash site," Krista explained, "in case the Raptors would want to investigate."

"What's all that…stuff? Some of it looks orange."

Parts of the wreckage were almost filled with a bulbous, almost foamy substance. It looked orange, but that was hard to tell in the low light.

"Crash foam," Krista said. "It deploys in the cockpit and all passenger sections during a crash. Designed to cushion you from the worst of it and provide as much protection as possible. The stuff saved all our lives."

"Look," Harriet said. "Our instincts were right."

At the edge of the image, several figures milled around, their bodies and faces obscured by shadow.

"How do you know it's them?" Ben asked. "Couldn't it be locals?"

"We put a passive sensor in a treetop during our patrol. We caught radar and visuals of the *Blue Fin* entering orbit an hour ago, as well as a dropship coming down to the surface. Earth cleared them to land here." She showed Ben her own gem, which displayed a set of coordinates that meant nothing to him. "It's only two klicks from where we crashed."

"So the *Blue Fin* is still up there?" Ben asked, glancing up instinctively.

"Yes. It's doubtful they can ID us in our dropship, if that's what you're worried about. We took precautions getting away from the crash site, and did the bulk of our flying while still hidden by the Earth itself. Plus the treetops provide a lot of cover."

Lawrence nodded. "Our ship is old, but models like it are pretty common in this area, and we're several hundred kilometers away already."

"How many Raptors landed?" Ben asked.

"The dropship looks rated for sixteen," Harriet said. "But we can't be sure. If they explore the wreckage like we think they will, we'll find out soon."

"Here we go," Lawrence said. In the image, the figures walked by twos and threes into the center near the wreckage. Lawrence worked his gem's controls for several moments.

There were indeed sixteen Raptors, and Ben didn't see any others on the edges of the holo. He was surprised by their appearance. He'd been expecting rough-looking individuals with sleeveless vests, bulging muscles, and tattoos, acting raucous and loud. Instead they were all wearing uniforms, moving with purpose and confidence. Nine men and seven women, each with a small backpack, a blaster rifle over one shoulder, and a sidearm. They looked more like soldiers than murderers and thieves.

Ben was still trying to decide if this was better or worse than tattooed ruffians when Lawrence switched the holo and called up a frozen image of one of the Raptors. "I grabbed stills as they were all coming into view," he said. "Let's see if we can ID any of them. We'll run them all through the database tomorrow. But you two at least should be able to tell if Garrison is among them," he said to Ben and Krista.

"That's not him," Ben said when he got a good look at the first image.

"Nope," Krista said. "No. No."

One by one they went through each image. They were surprisingly clear despite the odd angle and low light.

"That's not him," Ben said at the ninth image. Then, "Wait. Oh, shit."

"What?" Krista snapped.

"I know him," Ben said. "That's Val Minos."

He had a nasty scar down one side of his face that hadn't been there before, but the resemblance was unmistakable. It was the same guy that had nearly killed Ben and his friends back on Titan when the deal with Garrison went south.

"Yeah, you're right," Harriet said. "He got away from us on the raid when we…" she stopped short and looked at Ben.

"When you nabbed me," Ben said. "Relax, we're way past that being awkward. Mostly."

Harriet nodded and gave him half a smile.

"So he joined up with Garrison," Lawrence said.

"Looks that way," said Krista.

"We have to get word back to Special Agent Nichols," Harriet said. "He's been looking for Minos."

"This is interesting," Ben said.

Krista nodded. "Some solid intel for our Intel friends back home. It's about time we caught a break."

"No, I think there's something else going on here," Ben said. The others turned to look at him. "The Dorium my friends and I picked up at Port Ligeia—it was intended for the Minos family. They, uh, didn't take kindly to us stealing it."

"He's right," Harriet said. "We picked up some of Val's guys in our raid at The Occident. They didn't give us much in interrogation, but we were able to link him to the Dorium coming through Titan."

"You think he's got something to do with VESA and the Dorium they're moving?" Lawrence asked. "Minos is a big-time Titan family from what I understand. Plugged into everything on the colony, but we're a long way from home."

"I think it's a good bet," Ben said. "Before you raided us, Garrison took off with the Dorium we brought to the deal. Garrison and Val Minos had a history. They'd worked together before. But Minos never joined Garrison's crew. Why now, all of a sudden? I think it has something to do with the Dorium."

Captain Lawrence thought for a minute. "VESA is smuggling Dorium, using guys like the Minos family as the middleman. Some of it is enriched, but Val Minos doesn't know that. He thinks it's just regular Dorium moving around the black market. Eventually the heavy Dorium gets to Asher Garrison, to supply him with fuel for a Lightbeam."

"In the meantime, Garrison cuts his own deal to buy some Dorium," Harriet said.

"Steal," Ben said. "He never paid for it."

"Asher Garrison steals some Dorium in a black market deal gone south, and it turns out some of it is heavy Dorium. Garrison sniffs out VESA's smuggling trail, gets himself a larger piece of the pie."

Ben nodded. "And Garrison brings Minos onto his crew as insurance, to be sure Val will hold up his end of the bargain."

"Or VESA wants Minos to keep an eye on Garrison, to be sure he'll play by their rules," Harriet said. "Either way, it's plausible. And if it's true, Garrison might be retracing part of the trail for us. I'll get on the Quill and send word back to Special Agent Nichols to get his take. It's a solid lead."

Krista nodded toward the image hovering above Lawrence's gem. "How many guys left to check out?"

"Seven more," Lawrence said. He swiped through a few. "Not Garrison," Krista and Ben said. "Nope. No."

The thirteenth image stopped Ben cold. He couldn't talk, couldn't breathe. "No," Krista said. Lawrence swiped to the fourteenth. Ben gasped.

"What?" Lawrence asked.

Ben didn't answer him. He couldn't think of anything. He could barely see straight. The world began to spin around him, and he had to force himself to breathe.

"Ben?" Harriet said.

"You all right, Ashley?" Captain Lawrence asked.

Ben glanced at them, eyes wide, and said nothing. He looked back at the holo, praying he'd imagined it. But no. He would recognize those faces anywhere. Images thirteen and fourteen were Tiro and Jess. His best friends were here to hunt him down.

Chapter 26

"Ashley?"

Ben stared blankly at the frozen image of Jess as one realization after another cascaded through his mind. Asher Garrison recruited Tiro and Jess. It had to have happened on Titan, right? Tiro had gone after Garrison that day, mad as hell. Tracked him down, no doubt, Tiro was good. They probably cut a deal. God, that meant Jess and Tiro had been with Garrison almost as long as Ben had been with Titan Intel. What about Miles? Had Axel, Tory, and Dom joined up with Garrison too? Or had Tiro and Jess left Titan by the time Ben freed them?

What did Garrison have his friends doing? They had lots of skills between them. Tiro was a solid leader, they were all good in a fight. Theft, hacking…

"Ashley?"

Hacking.

A chill enveloped Ben as he understood. Everything about their space battle with the *Blue Fin* snapped into focus. The hack on the nav bot. The trojan horse that took out their engines. *It was all Jess.* No wonder the code seemed strangely familiar. She'd probably enhanced the *Blue Fin*'s targeting algorithms too. Jess's efforts had killed Christian, Aaron, and Mike. She had nearly killed them all.

Ben's vision swam. A heady, buzzing sensation began in the back of his mind. He shook his head and struggled against it.

Jess and Tiro didn't know Ben was here, right? How could they? For all they knew, he was rotting in a cell in some prison can or pursuing his fortunes with an independent shipping firm. Had they even tried to find him?

"Ben!"

The sound of his first name brought Ben back to the moment. He looked at Harriet, then at Captain Lawrence and Krista. "I'm sorry, I…" He closed his eyes tight, suddenly on the verge of tears. He took a breath and opened them. "I know…"

"What are you trying to say?"

Ben turned away from them and sprinted into the forest.

"Ben!" He barely heard Harriet's voice as he crashed through the brush, away from the small patch of light and into the darkness and leaves. Almost immediately, thorns and roots began tugging at his legs and feet. The sound of others moving behind him soon receded. The moon was out and the trees were thick. He ran as fast as he could, not caring where he was going or why.

Ben grew tired after barely a hundred meters. He began breathing heavily and his heart rate increased. He tripped over his own feet, legs weak, but forced himself to go on, ignoring the protests of his muscles and the low but insistent ringing just under the surface of his consciousness.

On and on he ran, well past his team's tight perimeter, unable to see, unable to say what exactly he was doing. Tiro and Jess. Tiro and Jess. Was he running toward them, or away from them? He didn't know.

More than once he stumbled, fell, got up, and kept going. He tore his hand in a nasty bed of thorns, and nearly sprained his knee when he stepped into a ditch. He bounced off trees, scraping his face and arms on their rough bark. Vines slapped across his chest as he ran past them.

The buzzing in his head continued to grow, and the trees seemed to shine in the darkness. The Aurora was surging in response to an unseen wave of energy. He knew his regulator was failing to hold it back, and he was all alone. If it got too bad he'd be in real trouble. He didn't know where he was or how he'd get back to the others, or if it was too late now. Ben didn't much care, he just kept going as the first wave subsided and was replaced by another. The bright ambient energy of this world crashed through him, barely hindered by his damaged regulator, alternately propelling his body forward with a fresh burst of energy and driving it to a halt from fatigue.

Ben ran until his legs burned and dried blood from a hundred scratches caked his arms, neck, and face. He finally slowed and stopped when the light grew too bright, the heat of his body and his pounding heart became too powerful to ignore. He fell to his knees in a small clearing, barely more than four meters across, where several trees had fallen. The half moon illuminated everything in a faint, gray light, but to Ben it was as bright as the sun. He put his head in his hands, trying in vain to block the piercing energy that overloaded sound, sight, feeling. He shook, vibrated, unsure if it was from his own failing efforts or his body resonating with the energy pouring in. He gave a single rueful laugh at the idea of the universe plucking him like a string.

At last the wave subsided, leaving him gasping for breath on his hands and knees. After a minute of huffing he staggered to his feet.

Something moved on the other side of the clearing. A form came out of the shadows, making no sound, not disturbing a single leaf as it padded into view. A large cat. A very large cat. Nearly a meter tall at the shoulders, thick and muscled, its tawny coat marked all over with dark rosettes.

The animal stood on a fallen trunk and regarded Ben from less than two meters away. It sniffed the air once but made no other movements. The hair on the back of Ben's neck stood up, but he held his ground. Not that he could do much, weak and battered as he was. Even if he did, he realized, the sight of his friends with Asher Garrison's crew had left him indifferent. Let the creature do what it would.

The big cat lifted its head and opened its jaws in a wide yawn, exposing deadly teeth. It took a noiseless step forward, crouched, and sniffed again.

A fresh wave tore through Ben, and he screamed. The cat jumped backward, then turned and leaped back into the cover of the trees, crashing branches and leaves as it ran away.

Ben struggled against the latest attack of the Aurora. The effects were worse this time, bad enough to scare him. The universe screamed and battered him. Light came from everywhere, relentless heat, a violent rattling in his head that he was sure would shake him apart. His heart pounded against his chest, and breathing felt like he was inhaling steam.

He fumbled desperately for his gem, found it in his pocket, and somehow managed to open the regulator program. He glimpsed the gem's display with blurry vision before he dropped it.

Sixty. The regulator was at 60, and falling.

He fell flat on the ground as the tide of pain and fire pulled him under. He was vaguely aware of his hands turning white, then orange. He thought his clothes were smoking, but he may have just been imagining it.

Ben struggled against the onslaught, fought for control. The furnace. Remember the furnace. Don't try to hold it, let it flow. Let it move through you. He channeled the energy outward, down into the tree trunk beneath one hand. It burst into flame. He jerked his hand back and rolled away. Did it matter if you got burned when you were the source of the fire?

The display still hovered above his gem, showing his implant at 55 before flames obscured it from view.

He tried directing the heat upward. A tower of fire shot from his hands and chest, rocketing into the dark sky and washing out the stars above him.

He didn't know how long he could keep it up. Call for help. He had to reach his gem. He'd rolled away from it. Too far away. Too much energy.

"Ben!" The voice came from far away, but the second time was closer. "Ben!"

He grunted as loud as he could, unsure if it could be heard over the pillar of fire that roared above him.

Harriet tore through the last of the brush into the clearing, ran over to him. Her eyes were wide, first with confusion, then with fear as she took in the scene.

"Oh God, Ben! What is going—"

"Gem!" he cried through gritted teeth. "Get the gem!" He looked toward the log, which was still burning.

Harriet lunged forward and reached into the flame. She slapped Ben's gem out of the fire and saw the image somehow still hovering above it, reading 49 percent. She swiped upward through it, taking his implant back to 100, but the effects didn't stop. Ben's heart continued to race, breathing came only with great effort. The air still burned above him, and the shrieking in his mind was as loud as ever.

Harriet knelt beside him and put her hands on his chest, ignoring the flame and the smoke curling upward from the grass around him. His skin was scorching, the air above him shimmering with heat, but she flattened her palms against him and closed her eyes.

The tower of flame narrowed. It became a column of soft light, then smoke, then nothing. Somehow, the excess energy was leaving him. He didn't know how, but Harriet was drawing it out. When he opened his eyes, he saw her whole body glowing, sending shafts of light out into the forest. The leaves and vines on the edge of the clearing shook as if in a breeze. With every breath Ben's body slowed, skin cooled.

The tempest inside him finally quieted, but Harriet kept her hands in place. Ben could feel small tendrils of energy moving inside him. That's the only way he could describe it.

Harriet had her eyes closed, a look of intense concentration on her face. Sweat glistened on her forehead. Finally she stopped and looked at Ben for several seconds, watching, waiting. Nothing happened. Harriet blew out a breath and sank back on her knees, shoulders slumped with fatigue.

Ben blinked and sat up, fighting the pain in his abdomen and arms. Had that really happened? There was no sign of what Harriet had done. The trees and plants were still. The bugs and frogs and other creatures made the same noises as before. No supernatural light bathed their surroundings. He looked at himself. His clothes were smoking but he'd suffered no burns, no injuries at all besides the scratches he'd gotten on his tear through the forest. The only remnant of what happened was the trail of smoke rising from the fallen tree trunk Ben ignited earlier. Harriet had extinguished it, or maybe it had just gone out on its own.

"What the hell?" he said, looking around in astonishment, then back at Harriet. He was impossibly tired and in pain, but breathing came easier now at least. "What did you do?"

"Another skill I can teach you," she said quietly, still kneeling by his side, her hair damp from the effort of saving him. "The Aurora is indiscriminate, it takes in all energy everywhere. But with effort you can pull from a specific source. It's hard, but…" She looked at him with a wry half smile. "It helps if the source is strong, brighter than everything else around."

Ben gave a short laugh, which burned his throat, causing him to cough. "I guess that was me. I don't know what happened. My gem…" he said, looking around.

"Here." Harriet handed it to him.

"The energy fluctuations were more intense. The gem said it was at 60 percent, then 55. It's like my regulator lost all control."

"I think it did," Harriet said. "After I took your energy, I did what I did before with your implant. I reached out with my ability. Your implant deteriorated much more than I expected. A lot faster."

Harriet began looking over his scratches and other injuries. By some miracle he had no serious burns, and the wounds on his arms and neck weren't deep. She pulled out a flask of water and washed away some of the grime on his chest and face.

"I felt the signs of it as I ran," Ben said as she worked. "I ignored them and just kept going."

Harriet nodded. "Your body wasn't ready for that much effort. It's still healing. I think you accelerated your regulator's decline. I was able to fix it again, but it won't last much longer now."

"Two weeks? One?"

"I don't know. Maybe just a couple of days."

Ben sat back against a fallen log and closed his eyes. "I'm sorry."

"It's an injury. It's not your fault. Here."

She handed him the flask, and he took a long drink. The water felt good on his scorched throat. "Thanks," Ben said, and handed the flask back to her. He looked around the clearing, up at the treetops which parted to reveal a small circle of sky overhead.

"Why'd you run, Ben? Was it something you saw in the holo back there?"

Ben closed his eyes. Despite himself, he'd almost forgotten. Almost.

"Tiro and Jess."

"Huh? Your friends on Titan?" Harriet asked.

"Yeah," Ben said. "My friends, Tiro and Jess. My two best friends. There were seven of us that robbed the port, you probably know that. We lived together in the Third Ward. You caught three of them, remember? Axel, Tory, and Dom. I— we—helped them escape. All of us were close. But I was always closest to Tiro and Jess. I've known them for ten years."

"What about them?" Harriet said.

"They're here," Ben said. "They're with Asher Garrison, and they're here on Earth. I saw their faces in the holo back there."

"You're sure it was them?"

Ben looked at her and nodded once, his face strained with the effort keeping his emotions in check.

"Oh, Ben." Harriet put her hand on his forearm.

"I don't know if the others came too," he said quietly, finally just letting the tears come. "I didn't see them. Maybe they're up on the *Blue Fin*."

"Do you know why? How? Do you know if they're aware of you being with us? Do you…" Harriet stopped, shook her head. "No, of course you don't. How could you know any of it? I'm sorry. This has to be killing you."

"Jess is a hacker," Ben said. "She got Tiro and me into the port that night we robbed it, gained access to some loader bots to create a diversion. She's good. Really, really good. I think she's the one who hit the *Rock Badger* with that nav bot attack and the Trojan horse on our engines."

"My God."

A light, misty rain began to fall. Ben felt it on his bare arms, looked up to where the water was dropping from infinity. His mind vaguely registered it as something he'd never experienced before. It didn't rain on Titan's colonies. He'd read about rain on the Interior worlds, of course, but to see and feel actual water coming from the sky was something new. Under different circumstances he would have found it marvelous. Right now his head was elsewhere.

"I don't know what to do, Harriet," he said, watching the rain form spots on his clothes. "They're my friends. I've known them half my life. If I hadn't gotten caught, if you hadn't arrested me, I probably would've been on the *Blue Fin* right there with them, shooting at you."

"You don't know that," she said. "I saw your file. You guys were thieves, not killers. Not Raptors." Even as the words came out, she knew they were half true at best. Ben and his friends robbed the port and cut a deal with Asher Garrison. Maybe they hadn't made the leap to joining the Raptors outright, but they were trending that direction.

Ben shook his head. "Tiro was our leader. Even if I protested, we would have gone with him. I'd be on their side right now. Maybe helping them hunt you down."

"You were the only reason we got away," Harriet said. "If you were on their side, there wouldn't be anybody to hunt down." Ben's words reminded them both that a fragile set of circumstances brought them together.

"Yeah," Ben said. "I guess you're right…" His voice trailed off and more tears blurred his vision.

"What do you want to do, Ben?"

"What do you mean?"

"You're with us, but your friends are here now. They're involved with Asher Garrison. It changes things for you, I get that. What are you going to do?"

"I…I don't know. What is there I can do? It's not like I have much choice in what's going on."

"You always have a choice," Harriet whispered, looking at the ground. "The outcome may be out of your control—it usually is—and the odds of success might be terrible. But you can always choose what course to pursue—where you'll cast your lot when it comes down to it. What you want to fight for."

She picked a long blade of grass and twisted it between her fingers. "You know what we're about and some of what Asher Garrison is up to. If success were guaranteed, what would you want? If you knew, whatever else happens, it will work out somehow, what would you try to accomplish?"

There it was. The reason he ran through the jungle, the reason he'd tried to calm his nerves with his ability and nearly burned himself alive. With a single question she'd cut through the dense knot of confusion, right to the heart of the war going on inside him.

Ben didn't say anything at first. The rain picked up, but neither of them moved to find shelter.

"When I first got to Bradley, all I wanted was out," he said finally. "I knew it was impossible, but I kept looking for opportunities to escape. Go back to my people, the life I knew, provide for my brother like before. If you'd asked me that question then—choose between you and Tiro and Jess, I know what my answer would have been.

"Since joining the *Rock Badger*'s crew, getting to know all of you. I've started to see how much you and the others believe in what you do. How much you give. Lawrence doesn't have to take contracts for Titan Intel. They could make plenty of ether doing less dangerous things. But he cares. He wants to make a difference. I don't think I realized it until tonight. But somewhere between Ligeia and this jungle I started believing in it too. What happened at Verona is awful, and if VESA or Garrison is planning to do even a fraction of that again, I have to help stop it. The Interior has never done right by the Outer Colonies. This is a chance to make a difference, help our people, and save innocent lives. I know I'm just a new crew member or whatever. But the thought of fighting on the other side of this…whatever this is, I can't imagine it now. I…"

He clenched his jaw and thought of Tiro and Jess, Miles, Dom, Axel and Tory. He'd never pass around a bottle of Watson Red with them again, would he? Of all the memories he had with them, it was that damn cheap scotch that he thought about now. He knew it was the right decision, but the loss of it sat heavy and cold in his gut. "You asked me what I would try to do if it would all work out. If success were guaranteed, I would talk to Tiro and Jess and whoever else is with them. I'd get them to join us, fight alongside Titan Intel and Lawrence's crew."

Harriet nodded. "I thought you might say something like that. You're a good friend, Ben. And a good man."

"I know it's not likely I'll even have that chance, or that they'll see things the way I see them. But I'll stay with you," he whispered. "It's not easy, but I'm glad I'm here. I can't go back."

"No, not easy," Harriet said. "They're still your friends."

"Yeah."

She put her arm around him. They sat there quietly in the small clearing, under the half moon, the soft rain wetting their clothes. The water ran down their faces, into their eyes, off their hands and shoes. It gathered on the ground in little puddles and pools. Ben wondered absently where it would all go.

"I'm glad you're on our side, too, Ben," Harriet said. "And not just because we'd all be dead if you weren't."

Ben looked at her then, saw the pale light casting shadows across her eyes and lips, the rainwater beading on her cheeks, her hair that was beginning to cling to her forehead. He still didn't know how she felt about him, whether that night on the *Tethys* was just the circumstances or something more. But suddenly Ben knew exactly how he felt about her. Harriet had saved him—and not just tonight or on the *Rock Badger*. Ben knew exactly where he'd be if she hadn't come into his life, and he wanted to be here. With the *Rock Badger*'s crew. With her.

He leaned toward Harriet, his weakened body straining with the effort. He put his arm around her waist and kissed her. Her lips were cool, soft, wet from the rain. Still at first, but only at first. After a moment's hesitation, or maybe just surprise, she returned the kiss, drawing him closer with her arm now around his neck. They embraced there in the grass and leaves of fallen trees, and time slowed, the world narrowed to a bubble that was only their kiss, their touch, their urgent affection, his fingers in her hair, her hands against his back, their breath mingling in the warm air and the falling droplets of water.

"This has to be against the rules," Ben said when their lips finally parted.

"You're already a criminal and a fugitive," said Harriet, smiling and leaning her forehead against his. "And I'm a spy. I live outside the rules."

"You've been my handler before," Ben said. "Maybe you still are. Is this part of the job?"

Harriet's smile faded and she leaned back. "No, Ben," she said quietly. "It's not." She looked into his eyes, trying to read what was there in the darkness. "But I don't know how I can convince you of that."

Ben put his hand on her cheek. "You don't have to," he said. He kissed her again, and the way she kissed him back was pretty convincing.

Chapter 27

They made love there in the little clearing, with a small patch of stars shining through the canopy above and sounds of the wilderness surrounding them. Afterward, under a makeshift blanket of their own clothes, Ben lay awake while Harriet dozed against him. The rain had stopped and the sky was just beginning to brighten in the hour before dawn. Her breath was soft and warm on his cheek, and her dark hair smelled faintly of citrus, honey, and smoke. His hand rested on the firm skin at the curve of her hip, just above where the weight of her leg lay pleasantly across his own.

Sometime after that Ben fell asleep too. He woke when the first rays of light were coming through the leaves overhead. Harriet was awake already. She'd called the captain and said she found Ben, then gave him the short version of what happened last night. Lawrence said, "OK," and didn't sound too mad about the delay, but Ben figured he was in for an earful when they got back.

"Don't worry about it," Harriet said as they started back into the forest. "The captain will understand when you tell him about Tiro and Jess."

"At the very least, he'll appreciate the good intel," Ben said, following her. "I'm not worried, oddly enough." He really wasn't, he realized. "When you've been shot at and nearly burned to death—"

"Twice," Harriet said.

"—and nearly burned to death twice, a butt-chewing doesn't sound so bad. Even from Captain Lawrence."

"I thought you were going to say last night was worth it," Harriet said, glancing back at him with a grin.

"Well, that too," Ben said.

Harriet led them back to the *McInnes*, following roughly the same path Ben had cut the night before in his wild run through the brush. Ben had run nearly eight klicks through the forest, and he was still weak and sluggish from the events of last night. It was slow going. Most of the time they had to go single file, but occasionally the forest thinned out and they were able to walk side by side.

"Can I ask you something?" Ben said during a short stretch of easy walking.

"I'm not about to tell you how many partners I've had," Harriet said.

Ben gave a short laugh. "No, you're off the hook there. Long as I don't have to tell either."

"Deal. So, what then?"

"Harriet is an unusual name," Ben said. "Where does it come from?" Then, feeling self-conscious, he added, "Sorry if that's prying."

"It's OK; it is a name you don't hear much. At least on Titan—it's more common around the rest of the Colonies."

"Is there any story behind it?"

Harriet shrugged. "I guess you could say that. I was named after a family friend who grew up on Earth and moved out to the Colonies. She was really important to us, especially when I was a kid."

The way she said that last part made Ben pause. "She's the one who taught you how to control the Aurora, isn't she?"

Harriet looked at him sideways, then smiled and shook her head. "How do you do that?"

"Do what?"

"See right through everything. It's a gift, you know. Yeah, she taught me. She had the Aurora too. Her ability to control it was incredible. She showed me how, starting when I was five or six. At the time, she seemed like such a hardass. I hated her during those first few years. But looking back, she was incredibly patient. A very good teacher. I didn't realize it until I was older."

"What happened to her?" Ben asked.

"I don't know," Harriet said. "One day she told my parents it was time for her to move on, and she left. They never told me why or where she went. I'm not sure they even knew. I was fourteen by then and had learned enough to control the Aurora on my own."

"I bet that was hard on you," Ben said.

"It was, but I wouldn't admit it at the time. When you're fourteen you pretend like it's no big deal."

"Tell me about it," Ben said, recalling his own experience of becoming his brother's guardian around the same age.

"OK, my turn," Harriet said, ducking beneath a low-hanging bundle of vines and jumping easily across a deep, narrow ditch. "What happened to your parents?"

"I should have seen that coming," Ben said. He stepped slowly across the ditch and slipped as he got to the other side. He got up and brushed off his hands.

She smiled. "Yeah, you should have."

"My dad owned a small mining company," Ben said. "They had a few ventures on Neptune, but mostly they operated in the Belt. He was progressive, liked the idea of transsystem trade. So he'd take on contracts for the Interior—Earth, Venus, whatever. A lot of his colleagues in the Colonies didn't like that, but dad was a stand-up guy and had their respect. At least from what I could tell. I was young, you know?"

"Sure," Harriet said.

"Anyway, I don't know exactly what happened. But nine years ago, he got into some trouble with a Venus-based company. There was an accident, in the Belt, I think, and he got sued. Under transsystem law he was protected, but the corporation got the Venus government to come up with some bogus criminal charges so they could extradite him. That exposed him and his whole company under Venus law. Dad's company went under, and he had to go stand trial."

"That's awful," Harriet said.

"Yeah. You see why I don't have much love for the Interior. Anyway, my mom went with him to support him in the trial. They disappeared somewhere on this side of the asteroid belt. I guess observations in the area make an asteroid collision most likely. The models say it hit their fusion engines, caused a…chain reaction. There was nothing left, nothing to recover."

"And you and Simon were left alone?"

Ben nodded. "And never got to say goodbye."

Harriet shook her head. "I'm sorry, Ben. That's tough." She slipped her hand into his.

"They knew the trial might take a while, so they left us access to their accounts. We did all right for a while, but we were young and Dad's company was gone. We ran through the ether fast. I had to forgo the Academy. You know the rest."

They walked in silence for the next couple of kilometers, Harriet helping Ben navigate the worst of the terrain. When they got near the *McInnes*, just past the first perimeter marker, Ben said, "So what's the deal with…this? Us?"

"What do you mean?"

"You know what I mean. Last night. What's the deal?"

Harriet raised her eyebrows. "What do you want the deal to be, Ben Ashley?"

"Well, obviously we can't tell the others about…"

"Sure we can," Harriet said. "They're gonna find out."

"What? How?"

She rolled her eyes. "They've been around the block. Lawrence and Krista used to work in intelligence. I might be good enough to hide it from them, but you're definitely not."

Ben opened his mouth to protest, then closed it. Crap, she was right. "So what do you think we should do?" he asked.

Harriet stopped and turned to face him. "I like you. And I liked last night. But I also know it's stupid and dangerous to mix romance and a mission. We owe it to each other, and to the rest of our team, to stay focused on why we're here."

"You're right about that," Ben said. "So, what, we'll tell everyone what happened, put the brakes on it for now, and see where we are when…if we get out of this whole thing alive?"

Harriet nodded. "Assuming you also don't want it to be a one-time thing."

"Nah," Ben said, and kissed her again.

When they got back, Ben told the others about Tiro and Jess, how he knew them and how close they'd all been. Asher Garrison must've signed them on during his time on Titan, Ben said, after Tiro tracked him down when he made off with the Dorium. He told them about Jess's remarkable skill, how she'd almost certainly been the one who hacked the *Rock Badger* during their fight with the Raptors. And he described how smart and tough Tiro was, how his friend was probably already making a name for himself among Garrison's crew.

"It sounds like the three of you were close," Captain Lawrence said.

Ben nodded. "They were my family. Are my family, still, I guess. I don't know. Yeah, we were close."

"I take it you didn't see the rest of your friends from Ligeia among the Raptors," the captain said. "Do you think they're involved?"

"I don't know, sir," Ben said. "It's possible they are, and they're just staying aboard the *Blue Fin*. I don't know for sure, but Tiro was our leader. If Jess went with him, there's a good chance the others did too."

"All right. We should assume they are, for now. And we'll keep your friend's considerable hacking skills under advisement."

Lawrence chastised him for running last night, but didn't light into him as badly as Ben was prepared for. Ben also told them about the episode with his regulator, how he'd nearly burned down the forest, not to mention himself.

"How bad was it?" Lawrence said, looking at Harriet.

"Bad. The events of last night caused our repair of Ben's regulator to deteriorate much faster than it was already. It's going to fail again, keep failing."

"And then what?" Lawrence asked.

"When it fails, if it's bad enough, the Aurora is unchecked. We get a repeat of what happened last night." She saw Ben shudder, then said to the others, "A repeat of what happened to Ben on the *Rock Badger*." She looked at Krista and Eric, and saw from their eyes that they knew the stakes.

The captain didn't miss it either. "Can you keep fixing it?"

"For a while. But not indefinitely. A lot of it hinges on Ben's ability to keep the Aurora in check on his own."

"You'll teach him?"

"Yes."

"All right. Is there anything else we need to know?"

Ben looked to the side, unsure how to mention Harriet.

"They hooked up," Krista said.

Ben whipped his head toward her, his face looking like she'd just described in detail what kind of underwear he had on.

"What? It's all over your face," Krista said. "Hers too."

Ben looked at Harriet, who just tilted her head sideways. "Told you she'd know."

"I, yes, we, uh—" Ben felt his ears and cheeks turning a bright, hot scarlet as everyone looked at him, then at Harriet, then back at him.

Captain Lawrence cleared his throat. "Right. Is this going to become a problem?"

"No, sir," Harriet said. "Ashley and I talked—"

"I wasn't worried about you." The captain fixed his eyes on Ben.

"It won't be a problem, sir," Ben said, his face still a deep red. "Harriet and I talked, and we're both crystal clear that this mission is our focus. Our only focus."

"Good," Lawrence said. "Let's load up and get in the sky."

Chapter 28

They hauled ass north, if the lander's crawl across the treetops could be described that way. Watching through the window, it seemed to Ben that they were floating leisurely beneath the clouds. He was surprised when Krista announced how far they'd actually gone in two hours. He still struggled to make sense of the size and scale of this world.

Garrison's crew hadn't spent much time at the *Rock Badger*'s crash site. They did a cursory investigation and left in their dropship, which Krista tracked to southeastern North America. The captain had been right about that part. The Raptors landed near a small city called Luxor. It would take the *McInnes* the better part of another day to get there.

Ben was looking out the window, catching up on rest, when he glimpsed the end of the vast stretch of forest they'd been flying over. One minute they were surrounded by treetops as far as the eye could see. Then they crested a hill, and the horizon ahead of them suddenly became thick, a cord of deep blue marking the boundary between earth and sky. After another hundred kilometers, Ben realized it was water. Somewhere far ahead, the forest just seemed to stop abruptly.

"The Caribbean Sea," Eric said beside him. "We're almost to the edge of the continent."

Ben glanced over at his friend and pictured the holos he'd seen of Earth. "That's the ocean?"

"Part of it," Eric said. "The shortest route will be straight across. We'll be over it soon."

They'd seen only a handful of other flying vessels so far—two small quadcopters and four or five planes with broad, flat wings—but as they neared the coast the air traffic picked up considerably. Fast-moving jet planes, far slower dirigibles, helicopters, and several slow-moving landers like theirs. To the east, suborbital ships streaked upward at regular intervals, bearing their cargo or passengers up on columns of flame, off to the other side of the globe in an hour or less. "Must be a launch point over there," Eric said.

Minutes later, Jones piloted the old lander across the last of the forest, past a narrow strip of sandy beach, then out over open water. Watching from the window of the main hold, Ben gasped when the sea came into view. He'd seen holos of methane lakes on Titan, courtesy of Novalink's remote miners on the moon's surface, but this was entirely different. There was so much water, endless water, stretching away in every direction. What he could see alone would fill Ligeia and Kraken ten times over. Beneath him, the ocean's surface was torn apart by a million ripples, waves whipped up by the wind before crashing down upon themselves in a foamy spray. Farther from shore, long swells sent huge ocean vessels lurching up and down on the surface like so many bobbling corks. Even from his perch a kilometer high, Ben understood that the sea was an alive thing. The water moved, breathed, seethed with life and energy.

They reached North America six hours later. Ben was in the cockpit with Jones, enjoying the view as they rapidly approached the coast. The *McInnes* flew over a beach and then expansive marshes, the coastal plain crisscrossed by waterways and dotted with small communities, larger towns, and one sprawling metropolis several kilometers to the east. Somehow a section of the ocean kept going, as if it had worked its way onto the continent in a thousand creeping fingers before settling into a wide band stretching away north as far as Ben could see.

"The Mississippi," Jones said through the comm when Ben asked her about it. "Not the ocean. It's a big, big river." She opened her gem and brought up a globe, then spun and zoomed in the holo on North America. With her other hand she traced the dark, squiggly line extending up from the Gulf of Mexico, which cut a winding course from north to south across the lower half of the continent.

"This is a river?" Ben asked, looking from the gem to the water and back again. The holos he'd seen and small, artificial streams on Ligeia had led him to think of rivers as narrow courses. "It's so broad. I always pictured them as smaller."

Jones nodded. "Uh-huh." She pointed out several larger lines leading away from it. "These other rivers all feed into it. Hundreds of them, all told. It's a tremendous amount of water by the time it gets this far."

"All the rivers go into this one?"

"A lot of them. Not all. Just like the lakes and rivers on Titan, except it's water here, not methane. Water on the continent drains through smaller rivers—creeks and streams— into bigger rivers, then bigger ones, until it eventually reaches the ocean." Jones indicated several other rivers that ended in the sea, some to the west and some to the east. "Some of them take other routes. A lot of the central area of the continent drains through the Mississippi to the Gulf."

"Incredible," Ben said. His mind flashed briefly to the rain that fell in the jungle last night. The water pooled on the ground, trickled together into small puddles, spilled away and flowed off…somewhere. The river. Ultimately the sea, he supposed, the living, breathing ocean that wrapped around this world. Was the river alive too? It moved, flowed…

"A lot of trade travels along the Mississippi," Jones said, interrupting his thoughts. "Centuries ago, back before humans could fly, moving goods upriver was an effective way to get them places. A lot of it goes that way, even today. Much of Earth's population still clusters around the old urban centers established more than a thousand years ago. Boats and river barges are slow, but they get things where they need to go."

"Is our destination along the Mississippi?" Ben asked.

"No, it's to the east, a bit north of here."

"But we're sticking to the Mississippi for a while, to blend with the local traffic."

"Bingo," Jones said. She cleared the globe and brought up a map showing their course. "This is what Krista laid in before we left. Looks like we're going north for a couple hundred kilometers, then we'll turn east."

Soon they were on the ground, a few hundred klicks from the edge of the great river. Jones set the lander down in a rural area near another, smaller river flanked on one side by flood plains and on the other by massive rock bluffs. On their way in, Ben saw the remains of an ancient roadway that cut like a faded scar across the ridges and stony hills. Though the highway lay in ruins and hadn't seen traffic for centuries, it had not yet been consumed by the surrounding forest. It seemed to bear witness to an era long gone, when this area, like Earth in general, had been far more heavily populated. To the north lay a fresh incision in the landscape: the monorail system that carried goods and passengers from one urban center to another across this section of the continent.

Garrison's crew had settled in Luxor, a small city to the east. It was vibrant enough judging by the air traffic above its skyscrapers. According to Krista and her gem, it was built on the remains of an earlier city that had once been a booming center of tourism, entertainment, and a particular slice of old American culture. Like so many North American cities it suffered greatly after the fall of the United States. The climate disasters brought on by the Second Cosmic Storm in the 2400s had ravaged it further and led to its abandonment. Luxor was established some three centuries later, on top of the earlier metropolis. The new city's metrics suggested it was on a slow but steady path to prominence since the rise of the American Commonwealth three centuries ago.

Despite Ben's injuries and lingering weakness, the ten-klick hike to Luxor was easy. There were several ridges to cross, which Ben took slowly, but the treetops provided ample shade and the undergrowth wasn't too thick. Compared to the rainforest where he and Harriet had gone on their little adventure, the wilderness of North America was a piece of cake. Ben found himself enjoying it. The forest here was a totally different world than the small game preserves on Ligeia. The experience was intoxicating. He relished the green all around, the crunch of last fall's leaves beneath his feet, and the feel of the warm, heavy spring air with its countless scents that even the best technology couldn't replicate on their colonies. At once he felt a sense of kinship to those who lived here, and a deep resentment toward them for taking it all for granted and looking down on those who dwelled farther from the Sun.

They reached Luxor by midafternoon, first the handful of settlements, shops, and office buildings on the outskirts and then the town itself, a dense metropolis full of life and energy. People walked or rode on two-wheeled vehicles, and several elevated monorails crisscrossed the city. The streets and surfaces were clean and most boasted fresh paint, and the buildings represented a mishmash of architectural styles—gracefully curving arcs, soaring angular structures, and bulbous collections of spheres alongside more modest and traditional geometric designs. Despite the variety, or perhaps because of it, the whole felt oddly harmonious.

There was a slow, broad river to their left, and as they made their way through the winding streets. Ben saw that it curved around the town, bordering it on three sides. Krista got on the Quill and booked them a block of rooms close to the city center.

"All right, that's him," Ben said. "That's Minos."

Ben, Jones, and Lawrence were crowded around a table in the captain's hotel room. They watched a holo of four people talking outside a restaurant. After checking into their rooms, the crew had split up to look for signs of Garrison's people in the city. Krista and Eric tracked down some of the Raptors almost immediately. They were wearing street clothes and trying to blend in, but this was a world of the Interior. Those from the outer areas of the solar system stood out clearly, including Raptors. Krista and Eric followed them to this restaurant and set up surveillance.

"What about the other three?"

The day was warm, and an umbrella above their table shaded two of the Raptors' faces.

"No, I don't recognize them," Ben said. "I can't see the guy's face, but he's too large to be Tiro, and the woman's definitely not Jess." As he spoke, the woman shifted in her seat and her face came more into the light.

"Wait," Ben said. "I have seen her before. She was with Garrison on Titan, when Tiro and I met him. He seemed to trust her, even more than the guy I fought on the *Tethys*. I'd bet anything she's the leader of the landing party." He got goosebumps as he recalled the woman's casual, predatory confidence that day at The Occident. "I don't know her name, but you'll want to keep an eye on her."

"You guys catch that?" Lawrence asked.

"Yes," Levi said.

"Yes," Krista answered in a low voice. A double tap on the comm indicated Eric's affirmative, followed by the same from Harriet.

It was a busy day, and there was a lot of foot traffic among the shops, restaurants, and bars along the popular stretch of Luxor called the New Gulch. Eric was seated across the street at a small coffee shop recording the meeting, while Levi watched from a rooftop bar and Krista and Harriet patrolled the streets looking for signs of the other Raptors. The crowd looked normal for a weekday afternoon.

"Sound incoming," Eric whispered.

A fresh audio feed cut in, and they picked up in the middle of the Raptors' conversation.

"…told you it's behind schedule?" the one on the left said.

"It doesn't matter who told us," Minos said. Ben noted that his voice matched his memory of what Minos sounded like too. "What matters is that we know you're delayed, and that doesn't work for us. We need you to pick up the pace."

"Or?"

"Best not to find out," the woman added. "Trust me, it's better for everyone if you just get it back on track."

A group of pedestrians passed in front of their Raptors, and their conversation blocked whatever they said next.

"…sorry. I don't know what to tell you. We had the shipment ready, but you didn't arrive when you said you would. So we assigned it to another customer and reset our templates. We'll go back to your product as soon as we can, but you'll have to wait until the current run is finished."

"You sold our shipment," Minos said. "Easy fix. Get it back. Tell them there was a mistake."

"I'm afraid that's not possible. They've already left the planet."

"Who'd you sell it to?"

"You know we don't disclose our clients for…that type of business."

"Bullshit," Minos said.

"It's why they come to us. It's why you come to us," the man said. He stood and made an apologetic gesture. "Your shipment will be ready in six days. That's the best I can do, and there's nothing else to say about it. If that bothers you, I suggest arriving on time to pick up your shipments in the future."

Minos started to stand, but the woman put her hand on his arm and he sat back down.

"Perhaps you know someone else we can talk to," the woman said. "One of your associates who might be more interested in the efficient and safe operation of your plant." There was an unmistakable threat in the way she said "safe." Ben had no doubt she would deliver on whatever threat she intended.

"There's no one else to talk to, and nothing to talk about, I'm afraid. Now if you'll excuse me, I must go. You're wasting your time here." The man turned and walked away.

Val Minos got up fast and walked after the guy, caught him by the arm, and spun him around aggressively. When they moved Eric lost the sound, but Val's mouth was moving like he was shouting, and Ben imagined the voice easily carrying far enough for Eric to overhear.

After a heated exchange, the woman approached Minos and intervened, trying to talk to Val. She separated them, and the guy turned again and walked away. Val didn't follow. He said something to the woman, the three Raptors had a short exchange, then they left the restaurant and walked in the opposite direction.

"Garrison's guys are heading south, unknown contact walking north," Levi said.

"I have eyes on the Raptors," Krista said. "Maintain visuals on the unknown contact."

A double tap from Eric acknowledged her instructions, and the holo shifted to follow the person Garrison's crew had been talking to. The man wore a crisp business suit with neatly trimmed blonde hair. They didn't get a good look at his face while he walked away from Eric. He could have been thirty years old, or more than sixty.

"Eyes on the contact," Harriet said. "Approaching from the west."

"I'm on Twelfth Avenue," Krista said, "two blocks east of our friends. Transmitting my location now."

Captain Lawrence cut Eric's holo and brought up a map of the local streets. A red blip appeared and moved slowly south along Twelfth Avenue.

"Copy that," said Lawrence. "I have you. Mosley, get down to street level and support Barnes from the north. Adams, follow the contact but do not engage. Let's see where he's going." He turned to Ben. "What do you think?"

"It sounds like Garrison's people are smuggling. Whatever they were supposed to pick up has been delayed, and they aren't happy about it."

The captain nodded. "They interacted with the other guy like newcomers to the business. New associates, not longtime partners. Both sides trying to feel each other out, gauging how much each can push."

"The unknown contact seemed legit," Jones said. "He mentioned clients 'for that type of business.'"

"You think he has different clients for other types of business?" the captain asked.

Jones nodded.

"I agree," Ben said. "A legitimate business, manufacturer of some kind it sounded like. They make products on the up-and-up for a respectable customer base. But someone deals with smugglers too."

"And now Raptors. Dealing in illegal goods? Or just an illegal pipeline, selling regular stuff to people they shouldn't?"

Ben shook his head. "Could be both. But given what we know, I'd say it involves Dorium."

The captain leaned back, though for a minute, and checked Harriet's location on the holo. She was headed east, but still close by the hotel at the moment. "It's not enough to go on, yet. We need more than just a location, we need to find out what they're up to. Adams needs backup. Are you feeling up to it?"

"Yes, sir," Ben said. He was still sore, but his strength had gradually been returning.

The captain spoke into the gem again. "Adams, I'm sending Ashley to support you. See if the two of you can get close and find out what the contact is providing for Garrison's crew."

Harriet acknowledged with a double tap as Ben left the room.

Chapter 29

Ben crossed a railcar line and continued east. He trailed their contact, keeping the mystery man in sight but staying far enough back to avoid suspicion. Harriet moved parallel to them a couple blocks south, ready for anything unexpected.

They moved slowly east on Broadside Avenue. The contact ducked in and out of shops, pausing now and then and looking over his shoulder. Whoever it was, he'd gone far out of his way to meet with Garrison's crew and was wary of being followed back to his home or business. They were in the heart of downtown Luxor now. Rows of tall office buildings interspersed with low-rise apartments, with retail and nightclubs occupying much of the street level.

"We're getting close to the river," Harriet said. "I think he's going across it. There's a bridge on Broadside."

Ben looked at the road ahead and frowned. "There's a hill in front of me. I can't see the river."

"It's there. I'm going across ahead of him, and I'll pick him up on the other side. Let me know if he turns, and I'll double back."

"Copy," Ben said.

When he crested the hill and began heading down the other side, Ben saw the river more than a kilometer away. A wide suspension bridge led across it with a lot of pedestrian and vehicle traffic.

"He's going over," Ben said to Harriet. "See you on the other side."

A sign beside the bridge said they were crossing the Historic Cumberland River. Ben peered down at the water's surface some thirty meters below, and saw that it was flowing from south to north. The river was far smaller than the Mississippi, but still an inconceivable amount of water, always moving. He paused and craned his neck to the right and to the left, foolishly trying to spot the river's beginning or ending. For several seconds he just stood there, at the near end of the bridge, watching the water, mesmerized by its constant flow. So much water, hundreds of thousands of liters, always on the move. Powerful, dynamic, unrestrained but also, somehow, contained. Directed. Channeled.

Ben snapped out of it and walked on. At the bridge's center, the main support post bore a faded red line three meters above their head. A bronze sign beneath it caught Ben's eye. The metal was badly weathered, but the writing was still legible. "Water Height, June 4, 2411. The Great Flood." Luxor, or whatever city was here before, must've had a hell of a time with the river that high. Ben glanced backward, trying to imagine just how much of the city would have been underwater. The flood and damage must have been devastating. Everyone knew the climate disasters wreaked untold havoc on much of Earth during the early 2400s. Seeing it depicted this way unsettled Ben in a way he hadn't expected.

"You see that sign? About the flood?" Ben said, knowing Harriet had already passed beneath it.

"Yeah."

"Must have been something, huh? All that water. Can you imagine the devastation it must have caused?"

"Those floods unleashed so much power. I read about it on my gem last night. Thousands of people died," Harriet said. "It took them three centuries to begin rebuilding in this part of the city. No, I can't imagine how bad that must have been."

"The river holds a lot of power."

They walked in silence for a bit, then Harriet spoke. "OK, I have our guy. Go two blocks north when you're off the bridge and parallel us. I'll let you know if he moves."

They followed the contact for another ten or fifteen blocks. He had indeed gone a long way to meet with Garrison's people. Harriet tracked him to a small, chic office building on the other side of the river. This time of day there were a lot of people out and about, on their way to work or various appointments around the area or across the river. Ben joined her to scope the building, and they had no problem blending into the crowd as they approached it together.

A sign out front told them this was the Balle Corporation's Luxor headquarters. Ben looked it up on his gem. Balle was an American manufacturing firm owned by VESA. They specialized in custom vehicles and spaceship components.

The office building facing the street was connected by a series of covered walkways to a larger, much more plain metal building that took up the better part of two blocks. Harriet swiped and tapped through a program on her gem, then nodded toward the building. "That's their manufacturing plant. Let's go have a look."

"No way. We'll get caught."

Harriet pointed to her gem. "This has me in their system. It's already cleared us on their security AIs, which are running a fairly standard set of programs."

"What if we see people?"

She gestured at their clothes. "You see the people going in and out? We blend in well enough. Walk right in the front like you belong here, and they won't give us a second thought." She got up and strode toward the front door of the metal building.

Ben went behind her, his heart racing. What if the Raptors were here somehow? What if Tiro and Jess were here? What if this firm that dealt with Outer Colony smugglers had an extra, invisible layer of security that would tip someone off as soon as they were inside?

He thought all these things as his feet moved forward, and then suddenly they were through the door and surrounded by quietly humming machinery. A handful of people were busy in the room, walking here and there or peering intently at a piece of equipment. Several more were walking along second- and third-floor balconies that overlooked the main floor. As Harriet said, nobody gave them even a glance.

"Keep going," Harriet said. She walked straight to the center of the room and began to look around.

Ben followed her lead, trying his hardest to look like he knew what he was doing. They scanned the floor, taking in the array of machines and the products being made. Ben couldn't tell one thing from the next. It all seemed like a jumble of metal and plastic, a collection of grotesque, noisy animated sculptures. The accompanying holo displays showed graphics and streams of text that were equally indecipherable.

"How the hell are we supposed to know what we're looking for?" Ben said through the side of his mouth, facing away from Harriet.

Before she could answer, the main door burst open and the contact they'd been following walked in, letting it slam shut behind him.

"Where's Charles?" he shouted, to no one in particular. Ben and Harriet moved casually toward a machine and turned to face it. He probably hadn't noticed them on the street, but you couldn't be too careful.

"Back there, Z," someone said.

"Charles, we have to stop production…" The contact's voice faded as he moved toward the back of the room.

Ben and Harriet exchanged a look, then moved around the machines to the wall. They worked their way back toward the contact until they were close enough to hear him again.

"…the M Series foils. Come on, Z, we're halfway through the run. We're going to lose five or six days if we have to set it up again."

"I don't care about the M Series," Z said.

Charles lowered his voice. "Is this about the…you know?"

"Yeah. Yeah, it is."

"Jesus. I told you we shouldn't have sold those apertures."

"It's too late for that. We just have to make more. Right now."

"We need more containment tubes too. We're behind on most of the components for Archimedes."

"I know. Just get as much of our equipment on it as you can. Do it today."

"How bad is it, Z?"

"It's all right. I can stall this new guy Garrison and his people a little more. But we need that hardware in three days. Two if you can."

"I'll try, but no promises. We better be getting a damn good cut out of this."

Z laughed. "Don't worry about that. VESA is selling this stuff to civilians."

"Raptors ain't civilians."

"You know what I mean. Nonmilitary. Troublesome civilians, which is even better. These are damn Lightbeam components, man. You know how big that is? It's a shitstorm for everybody if word gets out. They'll pay us good. They have deep pockets, and it's not worth the risk of us telling somebody."

"I hope you're right. Fucking Archimedes. We're in a heap of bad if anybody finds out. Nobody's gonna care if the Beam hardware is empty, you know. Anybody learns about this operation, it's both our asses."

Ben's eyes went wide, and he saw Harriet's did too. Lightbeams? Balle was making Lightbeam weapons?

"Let's check those aperture templates again, be sure we got the bugs out from last time. If we have to redo them, might as well get it right from the start."

"They're in here," Charles said. Their voices receded as they ducked into Charles's office.

"Lightbeams," Harriet whispered. "Archimedes."

"VESA's contractors are making the weapons here, and someone else is sending the heavy Dorium separately," Ben said.

"But why? Why not use their military facilities to make them? Surely they can cook those books, make it look like they're building fewer than they are. Why not use the military supply?"

"Civilians. Z said civilians," Ben whispered. He suddenly understood. "Raptors. Harriet, they aren't building secret warships. They're arming outlaws in the Colonies. That's what Archimedes is. You said the ancient inventor burned ships with focused sunlight. One big mirror—or hundreds of small ones. VESA's contractors are building compact Lightbeams here and sending them to the Raptors like Garrison. He isn't a special VESA conscript. He's just one part of the larger operation. They're turning the Raptors into a navy of mercenaries. All carrying Lightbeams. And all aimed at the Outer Colonies."

"Shit," Harriet said. "They'll kill our shipping, travel, everything. Threaten our Dyson Arrays. One ship with a Beam like that took out a whole colony. Our Militia won't know where to look or who to suspect until it's too late."

"And VESA won't be tied to it at all. Just like Verona. They'll start a war and win it without ever coming into the light."

Harriet shook her head. "They'll just swoop in and pick up the pieces. Assert their control and governance in exchange for bringing peace. God, do they really think they can control the Raptors?"

"This is bad," Ben said.

"Let's go. We've learned enough here. We need to report this now." Harriet started to leave.

Ben took one step, then his world erupted with light.

The wave came at him with no warning, no slow buildup like before. He staggered backward and put his hands on his head, shutting his eyes and shaking his head in vain trying to get away from the light and heat rising within him.

"Ben, hush," Harriet said when he groaned. She turned and saw him. "Ben!" She touched his arm and withdrew her hand immediately, surprised at the way his skin was already burning hot. He took two steps and fell down, writhing, groaning as he fought for control.

"Ben, you have to fight it. The furnace, remember the furnace." She put her hand on him and started to draw the energy away, trying to stay quiet. Ben lay there, tense and shaking, shoes squeaking on the floor and arms bumping against the nearest machines.

Two people leaned around the closest equipment to see what was going on. "It's OK," Harriet said. "He's just had a little fainting episode, happens all the time since his surgery. Give us some space, please." She tried to sound casual, but her voice bore an unmistakable edge of urgency and concern.

She finally drew the energy out of Ben and got him settled, but by then a small crowd had gathered. Ben lay there with his eyes open and unfocused. "Is he OK?" somebody asked.

"I think so. The worst is over, anyway," Harriet said, sitting back on her knees.

"What happened?"

Harriet shrugged. "Nothing. He gets these—"

"What's going on out here?" Z's voice cut her off. "Stop standing around and get back to your equipment. What are you all— Who the hell are you?"

Harriet wiped her hands on her pants and stood up. "We're new employees, sir. This is—"

"Charles hasn't hired anybody new for weeks. Let me see your gem."

"Of course."

Harriet took one step toward Z, then shot her hand forward and punched him in the chest. He staggered backward. Harriet hefted Ben to his feet and ran for the door. Ben stumbled but recovered quickly and ran beside Harriet. Z roared as they neared the center of the room. "Stop!"

They didn't stop, and none of the factory's workers was keen on getting involved in whatever excitement this was. Ben and Harriet reached the door and bolted for the street, just as they heard Z call for security.

Ben staggered and fell as another wave hit him. Harriet helped him up and pushed him forward. "Keep moving," she shouted. Five security guards emerged from the office building, heading for the plant. One of them spotted Harriet and Ben and shouted, pointing at them. The others stopped, exchanged a look, then all five sprinted toward them.

"This way!" Harriet said, jerking Ben sideways as they reached the corner. They had to get out of sight fast.

They ran faster, turning right, then right again, then left. Ben lost count of the turns and any sense of how far they went. At one point he stopped, pitched forward and vomited. Harriet urged him on before he was finished. They had to stay out of sight of the guards, had to keep zigzagging. The minute they were spotted, it was over. Harriet rushed on, half leading and half dragging Ben behind her.

Ben couldn't see where they were going. The world around him swirled and blinked with color as the light poured in, the humming energy rising to a high-pitched wail in his mind. His heart was in overdrive, hands twitching, skin on fire. He staggered on, trying desperately to channel what energy he could into one step after another.

He failed. He fell. Harriet stopped beside him, touched his chest. Drew out some of the energy. Not all of it, but enough.

He got up and kept going, but they made it only two blocks before it hit him again. Either the wave wasn't subsiding or his link was fried for good. Maybe both. They couldn't keep this up.

"Just go," Ben said through gritted teeth.

"Shut up," Harriet said. She looked back behind them, watching for guards turning the corner. She put her hand on his chest and pulled out more energy, sending it outward and down into the ground, which warmed beneath her.

"No. You have to get word to the others. We can't get —"

"I'm not leaving you. So cut the martyr crap and get up. Move!"

Ben got up and stumbled forward. It was better, but he could already feel the tide rising in him again. They turned into an alley and Harriet paused, looking around. Ben was right. They couldn't get away, not with him like this.

On the other end of the alley was an old-looking building. The windows were dark and it looked deserted.

"In there," Harriet said, nodding toward the door. If they could get inside somewhere, off the street she could take time and heal Ben, get his link back online and his Aurora under control.

They crossed the street, reached the door. Still no sign of the guards. "Come on, please," Harriet said. She pulled at the door. It was locked.

"Damn it! Let's try another one."

"Wait," Ben said. His eyes were shut tight against a new surge. "What kind of lock? Mechanical or—"

"Electric. The pad's right there."

"Put my hand on it."

She guided Ben's hand to the pad. With the amount energy careening through his body, it was hard to find the circuitry. Like trying to pick out a whisper in a barrage of shouts and alarms. Ben considered blasting the lock, destroying it. That would be easy enough, but it would also leave evidence that they'd been here.

He tried to concentrate while Harriet kept watch. "Ben, we don't have long. Any minute now."

Just before the tide took him under, Ben felt it. A tiny swirl of electrons standing out from the backdrop. He reached forward, holding back everything but a tendril of force.

"There!" The door opened and they collapsed inside. Harriet slapped the controls and the door slid shut. She thought she saw a guard across the street just before the door closed, but she didn't know if he saw her. She didn't think he had.

A groan from Ben made her turn. He was still fighting but starting to lose. His hands and eyes were growing bright, and his skin was hot enough to blister her finger.

"Come on, Ben, stay with me," Harriet said. She flattened her palm against his chest and began to draw the energy out of Ben. She worried it was too late. She'd expended a lot of effort already, and her own strength was fading. The current rushing through him was enormous, almost as bad as it had been in the jungle. She pulled it out of him as fast as she could, but she couldn't focus enough to repair his link too. She felt her own heart rate beginning to climb, and her cheeks began to get hot.

Ben's breathing grew quieter, less forceful. For a terrifying instant Harriet worried she was losing him, but she glanced at his face and saw him looking calm. He placed his hands on top of hers. Harriet watched him, bewildered but too exhausted to ask questions.

A faint orange light began to glow beneath their palms, illuminating Ben's skin where they touched. Harriet felt the torrent of energy lessen. Barely, at first, then it slowed to a trickle. Ben's eyes were closed in concentration as he helped her control the energy.

"Something is wrong," Ben said.

"Your implant. It's gotten worse. Can you keep the energy back?"

"Yes." His voice was calm and sure.

Free to concentrate, Harriet worked to repair Ben's link. The latest tide had been too strong. It increased the damage to his regulator. She repaired the circuitry as well as she could, but the effort taxed her. She struggled to concentrate and knew she was missing crucial connections in the implant.

Harriet felt a new flow of energy coming into her. She breathed in sharply and fought against it.

"Let me help you," Ben said.

For a moment Harriet didn't understand. Then she realized Ben was sending his energy into her—not a torrent like before, but a controlled stream that restored her strength. He couldn't help with the repair, didn't know what to do, but he could give her the energy she needed. Harriet breathed in again, focused, opened herself to it. It took effect right away. She felt strong and attentive. She allowed the energy to fuel her, illuminating Ben's implant and showing her where to restore the broken connections.

Harriet and Ben worked together in silence, all their attention and effort focused on the repair. At last it was over. They restored the failsafes and power to Ben's implant. Harriet sat back, exhausted. She watched Ben warily for any sign that another surge was starting, but his body stayed calm. The repair was intact, stronger than before.

Ben began to stir and finally opened his eyes.

"We did it," Harriet said.

"It's fixed?"

Harriet nodded. "That was…I don't have the words. The way you helped me. Used the Aurora…"

"Together," Ben said. "We worked together. Sorry I couldn't help more."

Harriet smiled at him and squeezed his hand. "It was enough. I think your implant is fixed all the way now. Everything was so clear with you helping me. I don't think it will be a problem anymore. How do you feel?"

He closed his eyes and took two deep breaths. "OK. Tired, but OK. Thanks for saving me. Again."

Harriet leaned forward and kissed him. "You're welcome." She checked her gem and stood up. "We should go. Those guards will have called for backup, and they'll check this building eventually. We have to get back to the others. Can you walk?"

Ben stood slowly, gauging his strength. "Yeah, I think so."

"Good. It will be better if we split up. The guards saw two of us running together. That's what they'll be looking for. I'll go first. You wait five and then come out after me. Go back to the hotel, but take an indirect route and keep checking that you aren't being tailed." Harriet started to open the door, then Ben stopped her. He kissed her again. She pulled away and smiled, then opened the door. She stepped out cautiously and walked away at a brisk pace when she saw the coast was clear.

Ben waited five or six minutes, grinning stupidly the whole time. He couldn't help it; Harriet was incredible. When it had been long enough, he opened the door and left. He looked around, reassured himself that the guards and anyone else who was looking for him had moved on. Still, he'd have to be careful.

It took him a moment to get his bearings. He spotted one large building he thought he recognized and walked toward it. He got there and found he could see the river straight ahead, and the bridge to the south. It wasn't too far away. He made for the bridge, keeping it in view while making a few turns to throw off anybody who might be following him.

He'd gone five blocks when he saw the man. Fifty meters down and across the street, a tall figure stood out from most others. He was broad-chested but not heavyset, and though he wore the same kinds of clothes as everyone else, he seemed to have an impatience about him. Ben considered him for a moment, then dismissed any oddness by telling himself that everyone must have off days, or maybe the guy was a relative newcomer like Ben himself. He started to pass the man by without a further thought, but then the guy stopped and spoke with someone else. Ben didn't catch what he said, but something about the man's voice and posture seemed vaguely familiar.

His back was to Ben, and Ben crossed the street and walked quickly to try to catch up with him and get a closer look. Maybe it was someone from his hotel, or someone he'd seen at the Balle Corporation's facility earlier. When Ben was half a block away, the guy turned. Ben's blood went cold, and he instinctively turned his head and ducked out of sight against an entryway in the nearest building. He'd only gotten a glimpse, but a glimpse was enough. That face was burned into his memory. Asher Garrison.

It was impossible. Garrison was supposed to be waiting up in orbit, on the *Blue Fin*. What was the Raptor leader doing here? A chilling possibility arose: Had Garrison followed them here? Were some of his crew about to attack Harriet right now? Ben's pulse was racing. He risked a casual peek around the corner, hoping he'd been wrong. No. The guy was turned partially away now, but it was unmistakably Asher Garrison.

Ben's brain screamed a hundred questions, but there was no time to dwell on them. He'd have to sort it out later. Right now he had to get back to their hotel and tell the others, and not get himself caught in the process. He only hoped Harriet had gotten back without any issues.

Ben left the small alcove he'd ducked into and walked away from Garrison, following the street until he'd cleared the nearest building and gotten out of the Raptor captain's line of sight. He looked around, trying to find the most direct route back to his hotel. The last thing he wanted was to round a turn and run straight into Garrison by accident. Then Ben remembered the buildings around him. Most had a series of restaurants and shops on the first couple of floors. If he could cut through several of those, it would keep him off the streets and maybe let him take a straighter, more direct route. He could avoid Garrison and, with a little luck, save himself some time.

The closest building didn't have a public entrance, but the one just beyond it did. Ben went for it, walking as quickly as he dared while still trying to look casual and unhurried. He saw with relief that the first two floors were a restaurant. It would seem perfectly natural for him to use that as an entrance to access the walkways above.

Ben walked inside, reassuring himself that he'd put some distance between himself and Garrison. The restaurant was called the Smiling Goat, and it seemed popular. There was a large crowd by the entrance, which would help him remain anonymous. He made his way inside, gave a confident smile to the hostess and reassured her that he was just passing through, and paused a few steps in to look around for stairs or a lift that would take him up to the walkway.

"Oh my God, Ben? Ben Ashley. Is that you?"

Ben stopped in surprise, recognizing the voice immediately. He swallowed hard and his hands began to sweat. He took a breath before turning toward the voice, praying his face wouldn't show the fear that enveloped his heart in a block of ice. He turned to his right and lifted the corner of his mouth in a wry half-smile.

"No way, I don't believe it! Hi, Jess. It's been a while."

Chapter 30

Jess hugged Ben and he returned it fiercely, surprising himself by how quickly he slid back into old habits. He reminded himself to keep his guard up. Past or not, she was with Garrison now.

"What on earth are you doing here?" Jess asked, stepping back and looking at him. "You look good."

"Thanks," Ben said, looking down at his street clothes. He was glad he blended in halfway with the locals, and that there was little sign of his injuries earlier.

"Holy shit!" a voice said to his left. "Ben? No way."

"Tiro," Ben said, turning to his old friend who had just walked up. "God, it's good to see you two." Ben hugged him, desperately trying to come up with a good reason why he was here. "Are the others here too?" he asked, partly to buy some time and partly because he was genuinely curious. "Axel, Tory, Miles, Dom?"

"Axel, Tory, and Dom got arrested shortly after you did. You didn't know?"

Ben filed that tidbit away. Jess and Tiro left Titan before he helped the others escape Bradley. "I knew. They got away, same as me. I thought they might have hooked up with you. What about Miles?

Tiro and Jess exchanged a glance. "Nah," Tiro said. "He's still on Titan. A lot has happened, man." He shook his head. "Though, clearly you can say the same. How the hell did you get here? Axel told us you got arrested outside The Occident that day."

"I did. It's a long story. Man, I can't tell you how glad I am to see you two."

"Come eat with us and tell us all about it," Jess said. "We were just about to sit down to an early dinner. Unless you were on your way somewhere."

Ben weighed his options. He needed to let Harriet know as soon as possible that Asher Garrison was in Luxor. And, of course, Garrison might well be on his way to join his newest crew members for a meal. On the other hand, bailing on his two best and oldest friends would generate suspicion. Far as they knew, he was unconnected to the Titan Intel contractors the *Blue Fin* shot down in space. Best to keep it that way. Plus, he was genuinely happy to see them in spite of everything.

"Of course I have time," Ben said with a grin. "And you two owe me some answers. How did you get here?"

"First thing's first, let's find a table," Tiro said.

"Anybody else joining us?" Ben asked in a tone he hoped was casual.

Tiro paused. "No. Why?"

"That table should work if it's just the three of us," Ben said, pointing to a small one that was just cleared.

"Good eye," Tiro said. The three of them walked over and sat down. Tiro peppered him with questions before the server even glanced their way. "All right, I gotta hear it. How did you get out of jail? What happened that day? How'd you get to Earth? What are you doing in Luxor?"

"Well, like Axel told you, I got busted. And it wasn't the police."

"Right. Titan Intelligence," Jess said. "And they turned you over to the Militia."

Ben's eyes went wide. "How did you—"

She shrugged. "Titan's Quill security is shit. I got into everybody's records. Started with the police, then went through different agencies till I found something."

Ben laughed. Of course. "Yeah, Titan Intelligence picked me up. But they didn't give me to the Militia." A small dose of truth would help sell the story. "They held me for questioning."

"Makes sense," Tiro said. "They created a bogus file on you in case anybody came snooping. Which we did."

"Anyway, after a few days inside, I was able to use my Aurora ability to leave my cell. I tried to escape, but it was a maze down there where they were keeping me, and I could only last an hour at a time. Eventually I found Axel, Tory, and Dom. I guess they got arrested a day or so after I did."

"Wasn't even a day," Jess said. "They came after us hard and fast. We barely got away."

"I'm glad you did. Anyway, eventually we found a way out of the complex where they were holding us. I helped them escape."

"You didn't get away yourself?"

Ben shook his head. "It was a close thing. I got busted. Again. Just bad luck. But then the Intel guys were mad, and they decided to send me off to a prison colony for 'alternative interrogation.' Next day I'm on my way up to the spaceport with a few other prisoners. It's Titan Intel, so I can only imagine what sort of high-level stuff they were being held for. One of them takes a chance up in the zero G, tries to escape. He took out a guard and almost made it, but they got him with a stunner." Ben paused, hoping the story was plausible. "But that whole thing created a big fuss and the other guards were distracted. I don't even really know how, it all happened so fast, but I was able to get away in the confusion. I managed to get across the link and back down to the A side, and hid out for a while in the Fifth Ward."

"The Fifth Ward?" Tiro said. "You were so close. Why didn't you come find us? We were trying to find you, coming up with all kinds of crazy plans to try to get you out."

"It was too risky," Ben said, shaking his head. "The Intel guys knew all your names. They told me, even had photos of you. I figured they'd be watching you, and if I tried to go anywhere near the Third Ward they'd get me and all of you as accomplices. I told Axel and Tory and Dom to stay away for a while, not to try contacting you too soon. I figured I'd better follow my own advice. I knew I couldn't stay on Ligeia. So I stole a few things in the Fifth Ward, bribed my way onto the first off-world ship I could find. It was headed for Earth."

"That's crazy, man," Tiro said. The server came to offer them water and take their orders. The offerings were simple, and none of them needed more than a glance at the menu.

"Yeah," Ben said. "Obviously I would have rather stayed in the Outer Colonies, but the Interior was better than staying put. Anyway, one of the other passengers was on her way here, to Luxor. She and I got to talking and she learned I needed work. I didn't give her too many details, but I did mention I'd done some mining bot operation. She told me there were opportunities here, how the big farms up north could always use bot overseers and drivers. After we got here, she helped me get set up."

"So you're a bot driver? Legit and everything?" Tiro asked.

Ben nodded "Clean as a whistle, man."

"Come on."

"It's true. I thought I was going away forever. I don't know what they had in mind, but life in a prison can is what I imagined. It got way too real, way too fast. No way I can risk that again. I'm living a simple life, low profile, staying out of trouble."

Jess finished her water and asked the server for a refill. "How long have you been here?"

"Not long, a couple of weeks. But the work is good so far. And the people of Luxor are great."

"For the Interior, you mean," Tiro said. He looked around with an expression of disgust on his face, conveying just how much he admired and trusted the people of Earth, nice or not.

"Yeah," Ben laughed. "Yeah, I guess so."

The server came with their food. A large salad with thin slices of pork for Ben, and hot chicken sandwiches with mixed vegetables for Tiro and Jess.

"I can't tell you how exciting it is to see you," Jess said. She swallowed her first bite of food and looked away for a moment. "We tried to find you right after Titan Intel picked you up, but nothing was going to work. We didn't think we'd ever see you again."

"That's right," Tiro said. "We hated the thought of you in prison, or worse. Well, I don't know if anything is worse than a prison colony."

"Thankfully, I won't ever have to find out," Ben said between bites. "Anyway, that's the short version of my story. What about you? How long have you two been here? And how did you end up on Earth, and in Luxor of all places?"

"Three days," Tiro said. "We've been here for three days. And we came with Asher Garrison."

Ben stared at them both in what he hoped was convincing feigned surprise. He took a slow drink of water. "Asher Garrison," he said after a moment. "The Raptor captain."

"Yeah."

"The guy we met at The Occident? The guy who took our Dorium and set us up?"

Tiro nodded. "It's wild. I told you, a lot has happened."

"Obviously," Ben said. "So tell me about it."

"I went after him after those cops or Intel guys or whoever busted up our meeting behind The Occident, you remember?"

"How could I forget? I thought you were crazy. Axel said to let you go, there was no stopping you anyway."

"Axel was right. It took me a little bit, but I found him. I got past the people who raided our meeting. I grabbed a custodian's jacket on my way out, but mostly it was just luck that I got away without getting stopped. Garrison was on his way to the spaceport, looking to get off-world as soon as he could. He was pretty surprised when I caught up to him just as he reached the monorail station."

"What'd you do?" Ben asked. "You were pretty pissed, but even you wouldn't have attacked him in public like that."

Tiro shook his head. "You know I wanted blood, but I cooled off a little by the time I got to him. And it was three against one, remember? I didn't like those odds." Tiro chuckled to himself. "Turns out that was a good call. Farrah's a bad bitch. I wouldn't have lasted ten seconds."

"Farrah. That's the woman who was with Garrison?" Ben asked. He recalled her indifferent eyes and predatory posture.

"Yeah. The other guy who was with him is Norris. He's a tough dude, but not like Farrah."

"No way," Jess said. Another bit of intel. They didn't know Norris was dead. But they had gotten to know him, which probably meant he was sent to the *Tethys* to find Liam Higgins sometime after they joined Garrison's crew.

Tiro went on. "So, three against one, I figured I needed a different approach. I walked right up behind them and told Garrison if he wanted to keep his Dorium, he needed to come with me right now. Farrah wanted to take me out, but Garrison was curious. I guess getting away from Val Minos took me up a few pegs in his eyes. I told him the meet-up had been raided after he left, and I'd bet anything that whoever it was had eyes on the spaceport. He wouldn't get to the elevators before they arrested him."

"You were probably right about that," Ben said. "I wouldn't have thought of it myself."

"I was right. Garrison made a call and found out from an informant that there was definitely a suspicious police presence at the port. He decided to lie low for a little bit, at a place where he knew the owner and trusted him to keep quiet. I forget the name of it. Garrison told me to join him there, and asked why I helped him and what I wanted in return. I told him I wanted my Dorium back."

By now they'd finished their meal, and the server came to clear their plates and refill their waters.

"Garrison, of course, refused to part with the Dorium, but he did offer to pay me half the amount we agreed on. Or, he said, I could join up with his crew and make a lot more than that in time."

"Wow, just like that?" Ben said.

"Yeah," said Tiro. "Now that I've gotten to know him better, that's sort of his style. He sees an opportunity and goes for it. As far as he was concerned, I got away from Minos and knew better than to attack Garrison directly. It showed him I was the right mix of smart and outlaw, so why not offer me a job?"

"And I guess you must've mentioned Jess?"

"I mentioned our whole gang," Tiro said. "I told Garrison there were seven of us, and wondered if he'd be interested in seven crew members instead of just the one. I didn't know about you getting caught yet. He said he'd consider it, but didn't want to make any promises until he met with everybody. He was going to be on Ligeia for a couple of days lying low, so we had some time to think it over. I went back to our place in the Third Ward. That's when Axel told me you'd been arrested. I didn't even get a chance to tell the others about Garrison's offer."

"That's right. We were already trying to get to you," Jess said.

"It's OK," Ben said. "Really. They had me locked up pretty tight in the Bradley Complex. Even if you'd found me, there's not much you could've done."

"And then the police, or I guess it was Titan Intel, came after us hard and rounded up Axel and Tory and Dom. We didn't know they managed to get away. I'm glad it worked out like that."

"So you and Jess joined Garrison," Ben said.

"It seemed like a good opportunity, especially with Titan Intel on the hunt for us."

"I have to say, I never saw that coming, but it makes sense the way you describe it. But that still doesn't tell me why you're here. I thought Garrison worked the Colonies."

"He does, mostly," Tiro said. He lowered his voice and leaned in close. "At least he used to. But he got a sweet new arrangement that's gonna have him making some trips to the Interior."

"What kind of arrangement?" Ben asked, lowering his voice to match Tiro's.

"I can't tell you specifics. Let's just say the Venus Solar Alliance is looking to make some friends among the Raptors and other, uh…unsavories out in the Colonies. Asher Garrison's setting up to be their middle man."

"And taking a cut at both ends, like a good Raptor?"

"Damn right."

"Why Luxor, though?" Ben asked. "VESA doesn't have a base near here that I've seen. I can't imagine the American Commonwealth would be cool with the Venus military having a presence on its soil."

"Not VESA itself, no. But they work with plenty of contractors on Earth. The whole Interior is one big mixed-up economy," Jess said. "But what are we telling you for? You've been here for a little bit now, you've seen it. Plus there's this big interplanetary research center nearby. Venus has a big stake in that, and a lot of their output is leveraged by VESA down the line."

Ben nodded. "Yeah, I guess that makes sense. How do you feel about working for the man who's working for the Interior?"

Tiro shrugged. "It's better prospects than anything on Titan. I'm all about the Raptor life now."

Jess smiled. "Yeah. Asher Garrison's crew is tight; they take care of each other and live well. Titan wasn't providing that for people like us."

"I guess I'm happy for you then. Never would've figured you two for Raptors, but it looks like it suits you. Still, VESA." Ben paused here, like he was thinking. He had to be careful. "That have anything to do with the Dorium Garrison took from us?"

Tiro eyed Ben suspiciously, then cracked a smile. "You always were too smart for your own good, man. Yeah, something like that."

Ben shrugged. "Seems like a reasonable connection to me. VESA's a logical buyer if he was looking to offload it somewhere. And he seems like the type to turn something like that into a mutually beneficial long-term relationship."

"You'll never guess who brokered the deal," Tiro said.

"I know it wasn't you two."

Tiro shook his head. "Our friend Val Minos."

"What?" Ben said, feigning surprise.

"Yeah, I guess he got away from the raid, too, and he came after Garrison looking for his Dorium or his money. Garrison pressed him, said he knew Val was moving Dorium for somebody. He wanted to know his source and where Val was sending it. Anyway, Garrison liked what Minos described and told him he was taking over the operation. Val was welcome to join the crew if he wanted in on it."

"Was Minos cool with that?"

"Hell no," Tiro laughed. "But it was that or nothing. He wasn't really in a position to refuse. And he's been pretty helpful. Made the connection with VESA, like I said, plus our contacts here."

Ben struggled to keep his mind from racing ahead to more questions and possibilities. If he pressed much more, he'd raise their suspicions. And he already had plenty of things he needed to tell Harriet and the others.

"I can't tell you both how thrilled I am that you're here. This is incredible," he said in what he hoped was an unhurried tone. He made a show of checking the time on his gem. "Shoot, I have to go. I'm supposed to meet someone for dinner, about job prospects. I've got that one gig lined up already, but since I'm so new I'm still putting feelers out there. I don't want to miss out on the right thing."

"Oh yeah, of course." Tiro gave him a huge grin. "Lucky bastard, I'm glad you made it out. You free to get together tomorrow?"

"Most definitely. I can't wait. How long are you here for?" Ben asked.

"We should've been gone already. We got held up, probably gonna be a few more days before it's fixed. Plenty of time for the two of us to get in trouble with you."

"I like the sound of that," Ben said, smiling at his friends.

"Hell yeah," Tiro said. "I'll ping your gem and we'll set something up." They all stood up, and Tiro gave Ben a big bear hug. Jess did the same. "Looking forward to tomorrow."

Ben said good-bye and left. As soon as he was out of sight, he picked up his pace. He practically sprinted the half kilometer back to his hotel.

Chapter 31

"What?" Harriet said, sliding open her door. Ben had been pounding on it for thirty seconds, and now he pushed past her into her room.

"Hey! Jesus, Ben, what's going on? And where have you been, we've all been worried sick."

"Asher Garrison is here," Ben hissed.

"What?" she said, clearly surprised and too loud. She closed the door behind her and lowered her voice. "Garrison is here. You're sure?"

Ben nodded once. He was still flushed from hustling through downtown Luxor. "And Tiro and Jess."

"And you're sure it was them? It wasn't your imagination or someone who looked—"

"I *spoke* with them, Harriet. Yeah, I'm sure."

Harriet sat down on her bed, a confused and uncertain expression on her face. "Tell me everything."

"All right." Ben told how he'd seen Asher Garrison on the street, and had ducked out of sight into a restaurant when Jess and Tiro spotted him.

"I had to talk with them a bit, it would have looked suspicious otherwise. We had a quick meal and made plans to meet tomorrow and catch up some more."

"Sounds like you came up with a good cover story about why you're here," Harriet said. "But they may have been suspicious anyway. You being here at the same time they are is too strange to be a coincidence."

"Maybe," Ben said, "but I've gotten pretty good at reading Tiro. We've been friends for a long time. I feel like he bought it. Jess too. Plus they told me way too much about what Garrison was up to here. I don't think they would have done that if they didn't trust me."

"We'll find out soon enough, I suppose. Garrison will act fast if he thinks you're a threat. We'll keep our guard up. Were you able to learn anything?"

Ben nodded. "We were right about Val Minos smuggling Dorium for VESA, and then Asher Garrison taking over and muscling him out. Tiro didn't come right out and say Garrison's their primary mover, but he made it sound like they have a long-term relationship with VESA. Garrison is a middle man between VESA and the Raptors and other unsavories in the Colonies, as Tiro put it. He didn't come right out and say it was Lightbeams or anything, but it aligns with what we've learned so far."

"Did he say anything about the Balle Corporation? The arrangement Garrison and VESA have with them?"

"Not directly, but he did mention contractors in Luxor that VESA works with. Tiro said there was a delay, and whatever they were here for was supposed to be done already."

"Well that corroborates what we heard from Z and Charles in the plant," Harriet said. She gestured toward the door. "This is good. Come on, the others need to hear this."

"Wait. I learned something else too. Something new."

"What?"

"Tiro mentioned a think tank near here. A research center, I guess. He didn't say how close or anything. He said it's interplanetary and Venus has a sizable stake in it. And that a lot of the research and development coming out of there ultimately benefits VESA down the line."

"You think Garrison's involved with it somehow too?"

Ben nodded once. "I don't think Tiro would have mentioned it otherwise. Whatever this research facility is, odds are good it'll be a part of VESA's Archimedes project. We need to find out what it is and maybe pay it a visit."

Harriet called Captain Lawrence and arranged a quick meeting. She filled the others in on what they'd learned at the Balle Corporation's headquarters, as well as Ben's close call and chance meeting with Tiro and Jess. Ben told them all about the research center and his suspicions that Garrison had business there.

Krista looked it up on her gem. She found it almost immediately. "Ash Mountain Research Institute. Advancing a Bright Future for Humanity," she read. She showed them the holos of the sprawling campus a few hundred kilometers east of Luxor.

"I've heard of it, actually," Harriet said. "AMRI. I didn't realize it was here."

"Says here it's an interplanetary research center in the American Commonwealth. They pioneer a lot of fundamental research here. Biotech. AI. Alternative energy. Next-gen Quantum Line communication."

"Where's Garrison fit in?" Lawrence asked.

"Not sure. I'll poke around on here, and…wait. Look." Krista zoomed in on one sector of the campus, which the display told them was the materials lab. She isolated a building and pulled up the information. "The materials lab at AMRI has a small Astruc reactor. Used to enrich small quantities of Dorium for research purposes, purely academic."

"Officially, that is," Lawrence said, his eyebrows raised.

"Officially. And guess who has an outsized stake in the materials lab, specifically."

"Venus," the captain said.

"Venus."

"They're enriching the Dorium right here on Earth. Small quantities, for small Lightbeam weapons on small ships."

"Archimedes," Ben said.

"And what moon houses Dorium refineries specializing in small crystal output?" Harriet asked.

"Miranda," Eric said. "Verona."

There it was. The reason VESA targeted Verona. Not just to expand the influence of Venus in the outer solar system or to boost its Dorium trade with a sudden vacuum in the supply. All that was just the icing. The real reason was to gain control of its Dorium, which was mined and processed in smaller crystals than most anywhere else in the solar system. The mines and refineries were situated on the surface of Miranda and were protected from the attack on the colony itself.

Ben paced the hotel room as he talked it all out. "Project Archimedes. VESA creates a navy of mercenaries in the Outer Colonies by equipping Raptors with small Lightbeams. They enrich the Dorium here, at AMRI, disguising it as business-as-usual research and development. But they can only keep that quiet for so long. They need a reliable, steady supply of small Dorium that won't call attention. So they take out Verona using Asher Garrison, one of the early beneficiaries of their program. Now they have a steady source of Dorium, a facility to enrich it, and damn good Raptors to move it wherever it needs to go."

The room fell silent as Ben finished, the weight of the situation sinking in.

"If I were VESA," Jones said, "I'd be setting up an enrichment facility on Miranda. Energize their Dorium right at the source."

"That has to be in the cards," Lawrence said.

Harriet stood, an excited look in her eyes. "But they haven't done it yet. They can't have. There's too much scrutiny out at Verona right now. They're putting the lock on who comes in and out, but they can't make big moves beyond salvage and investigation without attracting a lot of attention."

Ben was following her. "Then that means—"

"It means all the enrichment is happening at AMRI. Hopefully it means they haven't equipped a lot of Raptors yet."

"Right," the captain said. "AMRI is the bottleneck. That's where we have to strike. We can't do anything about the heavy Dorium that's already gone out. But we can stop that pipeline right here and get word back out to Titan Intel back home. Let's recon AMRI and come up with a plan for messing things up.

"Yes, sir," they all said.

Harriet caught up to Ben as they left. "How are you? You just ran into your friends, and they dropped some big intelligence on you. I know it must be strange."

Ben nodded. "Yeah, it is. But you asked me in the jungle whose side I'd be on. I told you that night, and it hasn't changed."

Early the next morning, Harriet woke Ben and took him to a small park beside the river. It was a public garden, close to their hotel, but surrounded by a dense patch of trees that gave the place a secluded feel. This early, before sunrise, they were the only ones there.

"We need to get back to your Aurora lessons," she said when Ben asked her what they were doing. "We've had plenty of reasons to hold off, but with your implant getting worse I don't think that's an option anymore. If you can learn more control, maybe it will help."

Ben nodded. As wary as he was of turning his link down again, he knew she was right. He had to try.

They took up positions in the cool, humid morning air. Harriet led him through body movements designed to help him harness the residual energy moving through him. "Find the furnace," she said. They practiced over and over, more than two hours, until the sun was bright and hot peeking through the branches.

However hard he tried, Ben couldn't sense anything, much less control it. Maybe he was still weak from the injuries he'd suffered. Or maybe he was distracted by Harriet and their night in the jungle. He'd be lying if he said he didn't think about it every time he saw her. Or maybe he was afraid.

"Again," Harriet said.

Ben's head was pounding from the effort of concentration. Sweat dripped from his nose and chin. But he tried again. And failed again. He punched the trunk of a tree in frustration, then immediately wished he hadn't. His hand erupted in pain. He flexed his fingers, reassuring himself that he hadn't broken anything. His knuckles were cut and bleeding, and there was a small smear of blood against the tree's bark.

"Again."

He was definitely afraid. They'd dialed his regulator back to 98 for training, but Ben insisted they not take it down any further. He'd lost control before, but now he saw how truly dangerous his unchecked Aurora could be. He'd nearly killed himself and others. What if his regulator failed again and he unleashed that kind of power in Luxor? What would stop him then? He was definitely afraid. Maybe it was this fear unconsciously holding him back. Something was. Whenever he tried to find the furnace, it eluded him. It seemed always at the edge of his consciousness, always just beyond the periphery of his senses.

Still, he tried. He moved his body mimicking Harriet exactly. She led him through a longer routine this time, silently, leaving him space to concentrate.

"OK," she said finally. "That's enough for today. We'll try again tomorrow."

Ben shook his head. "I can keep going. Tomorrow is too late."

Harriet placed her hand on his shoulder. "We need you at your best when we get to AMRI, and that means rest. It's good if you can learn to control your ability, but we'll make it if you can't. Your implant will hold."

"I hope you're right."

Tiro reached out about getting lunch, but Ben put him off. He made up something about a rescheduled training session for his new job. He'd have to think of something else soon—Tiro would ask again and evading too much would look suspicious. It was hard, though. As dangerous as he knew it was, he really wanted to see them. Once his shock at seeing Jess the other day had worn off, catching up with her and Tiro had hit him like a breath of fresh air.

Later that morning, Ben and Harriet joined the whole team to hatch a plan for infiltrating AMRI. Krista managed to get into the institute's databases through the Quill, which was no easy feat with state-of-the-art encryption and highly secure facilities. Even when she was in, her access to anything important was restricted. Luckily there were enough unencrypted maps and floor plans to give them a good view of the overall campus and many of its buildings.

The *Rock Badger*'s crew—Ben still thought of them like that even though the *Badger* was a heap of debris in South America—worked every possible angle. What at first seemed to Ben like a dearth of useful intel turned out to reveal a number of insights and opportunities for them to exploit. It was amazing what human minds working together could wring from even a little information when they combined painstaking analysis with intuitive leaps.

By evening they had an overall strategy and a multiphase plan. Now it was time to drill down into each phase, work through the steps, identify weak points, and make necessary adjustments. Much was unknown and flexibility was crucial. There would be no time for fact-finding or second-guessing once they got into the facility.

"All right, what do you see? What are the pitfalls? Where will things go wrong?" the captain asked after outlining their second phase.

"A lot of this hinges on hacking their security AI. It's no walk in the park. They have multiple levels of passive defense as well as state-of-the-art active monitoring." Krista's infiltration of AMRI's database had given her a chance to probe the network's security. The places and means by which they shut down her mild attacks gave her insight into the nature of their Quill defenses. It was extremely high level, but they expected as much.

"Is it a deal breaker?"

"Maybe. It'll take time to develop and test my algorithms and make the necessary adjustments."

"How much time do you need?"

"A day. Maybe two. I'll still need to switch up my approach on the fly once we're in and I see what last-line defenses look like. It's doable with preparation, but not guaranteed."

"What's your confidence level?"

"Seventy percent."

"All right. Let us know if that changes, up or down, as you keep working on it. What else?"

Jones worried about driving the loader with enough precision. She felt OK about her and Ben's abilities, but what if one of them got hurt or compromised? Levi was concerned about the number of guards they'd encounter—manageable if it went as planned, but they could multiply quickly if things went wrong.

"The part where we leave the tour worries me most," Harriet said. "Not only do we have to impersonate official Helia inspectors. We have to obtain Quill credentials to back that up. Whoever we talk to in there is going to take a good, hard look at us. We'll have to be flawless."

"You're a secret agent," the captain said. "I have all confidence in your ability to pass as whoever you need to be. Are you worried about me?"

"No, I suppose not. It's the credentials. That's a huge weak point, and by the time we get there we're fully committed to the op. I don't trust the programs we have with us."

"Isn't that something Nichols can help us with? Surely Titan Intel has the ability to fabricate what we need quickly," Jones said.

"Normally yes, but Helia is a Venus-based company. Nichols just pulled a lot of strings to get us on that salvage operation at Verona. That was Venus and VESA, too, remember. He compromised several of his assets and put a lot more at risk to get that done. He's spent years cultivating them. Decades, in a few cases. He won't put that kind of pressure on his network again so soon."

"Not even for something this important?" Eric asked. "We're talking about exposing and stopping a potential widespread attack on the Outer Colonies."

"Not if it means going dark on intel from VESA for the next five years. That's the kind of risk he'd be looking at."

"All right, I hear you," Captain Lawrence said. "Who do we have besides Titan Intel? Who can we reach out to?"

The room was quiet. "Aaron could've gotten it done," Jones said after a minute, giving voice to what they were all thinking. "He would have been our guy, and he knew a few people who could help. Everybody I know, for this, the trust isn't there. VESA's got their hands in too much that we don't know about. I don't have anybody I'd go to for something like this."

"Me either," Levi said. Krista nodded.

"I might know somebody," Ben said finally. "Back on Titan. Her name is Tory. She's good with Quill credentials. Got us everywhere we needed to go on Titan, even when there was heat and added scrutiny. And managed to successfully impersonate a Solacore research director." He left out the part about Asher Garrison seeing through it all. He was pretty sure that wasn't Tory's fault. "She might not be able to do it. But it's worth a try."

"Do you trust her?" the captain asked.

Ben didn't hesitate. "Hell yes."

Axel called ten minutes after Ben messaged him on the Quill. Ben advised his friends to lie low when they parted, but thankfully they'd stayed on the Quill and were at least monitoring messages. Ben sent one to Tory, Axel, and Dom in hopes that at least one of them would see it quickly. When Ben opened his gem, all three of them were looking back at him.

Axel was happy and mildly surprised to see his friend. "Ben! It really is you. I worried it was a setup or something. Tory told me she vetted the message and it was legit, but you know me."

"Careful, it might still be a setup," said Tory, teasing Axel with a barely hidden smile. She looked at Ben and whispered, "Blink twice if it's a setup."

Ben laughed. "God, it's good to see you three."

"We missed you," Dom said. "How have you been?"

"It's a long story. Are you still on Titan? Did you ever hook up with Tiro, Jess, and Miles?" Ben hoped his question would seem natural. He had no idea whether Tiro or Jess had contacted them, and the fact that Miles wasn't with the others right now made him pause. Despite what he told the captain, reaching out to them was a risk. If they were in touch with Tiro and Jess and leaked any part of what Ben was going to ask them, it would doom their mission and very likely lead to Ben's capture. Still, Ben had set his friends free from prison. That had to count for something. If he couldn't trust them, who in the whole solar system could he trust?

Axel shook his head, and the look on Tory's face told Ben they were in the dark about their other friends. "We haven't seen or heard anything from them. We reached out several times, but none of them have responded. Nobody's heard a peep from them on Ligeia. We think they've left the colony. Honestly we're worried the Militia or somebody picked them up."

"They shouldn't have," Ben said. "My deal with Titan Intel was supposed to cover them too. They're probably fine, lying low somewhere else around Saturn for a while."

Tory nodded and her face brightened. "Speaking of this mystery deal, is there anything you can tell us now? Where are you? Somewhere exotic? Or shitty? I bet it's somewhere shitty, isn't it?"

"Depends on your perspective, I think. I can tell you a little bit now about what I've been up to. Actually that's why I reached out. I need your help."

"Done," Axel said. "All three of us are able to talk now because you got us out of Bradley. We kind of owe you. And you know we'd help you even if we didn't. Tell us what's up."

Ben took a deep breath and laid it out for them. All of it, from the trip to Verona to the *Tethys* to nearly dying in a space battle. He protected the identity of the *Rock Badger* and its crew, but held nothing else back. He told his friends everything they'd uncovered about Archimedes, and VESA's plans to arm the Raptors, and how Asher Garrison was caught up with it all. He told them about AMRI and how they planned to stop the Dorium enrichment operation there. Ben couldn't have talked for more than a few minutes, but summing it all up left him drained. Reliving it all showed him just how much he'd experienced and endured over the last couple of weeks.

"Damn," Dom whispered when he finished.

"Yeah," Ben said.

"I hope this crew you're with appreciates you," Axel said.

"Thanks, man. They do. I appreciate them too. They've saved my life more than once. They're a good group."

"Yeah, yeah. Almost your favorite. Second-best all time. We hear you," Tory said.

Ben smiled, grateful for his friend's levity. "That's right. Second-best crew I've ever worked with. And now we need help from the number one. Titan Intel can't leverage their assets to get us the credentials we need to get into AMRI. I'm hoping you can hook us up, Tory."

"Probably."

"That's what I thought. We need to look like undercover inspectors acting on behalf of the Helia Group. You know them?"

"Interplanetary conglomerate with their hands in everything from security to manufacturing? Never heard of them," Tory said.

"Cute. Yeah, that's them. They support the work of AMRI in a lot of ways, including the materials lab. We need to look like undercover official inspectors conducting a surprise evaluation. Can you get us credentials? They'll get a good bit of scrutiny."

"You have specifics on what you need?"

"Yeah, I'm sending them now." Ben sent her the details Krista and the captain had put together based on their knowledge of Helia and AMRI.

Tory scanned them, then nodded. "Yeah, I can do this. It'll take time."

"How long?"

"A day."

Ben grinned. "That's perfect. Just shout when you have them ready."

"We're happy to help," Axel said.

"You just say that 'cause Tory's doing all the work."

"Yeah right. We have to live with her after she helps save the Colonies. That's a full-time job."

"I can't argue with you there. Thanks, guys. You are the best. I can't begin to think of how to repay you."

"We're repaying you," Dom said.

"Yeah, OK," Ben said. He frowned and hesitated, knowing he needed to say more but unsure how to start. "One more thing before I go."

"What is it?"

He closed his eyes and gathered himself before speaking again. "Look, my companions here said I should keep this from you. But I can't. Tiro and Jess, I know where they are. They're here on Earth. They're Raptors. They joined Asher Garrison's crew."

Dom's eyes went wide at the news. "So you're…working against them?"

"Yeah," Ben said. "It doesn't feel good."

"How do you know they're with him?" Axel asked.

"I saw them. And talked to them."

"And what do they think about all this?"

"I don't know. I couldn't exactly come right out and ask them, you know? But it's Raptors. Partnering with the Interior to threaten Titan. I don't know how they're justifying it."

"Maybe they don't know," Tory said.

"They seemed to know plenty when I spoke with them."

"Yeah but maybe they don't know…all of it. Not everything you know, anyway. Maybe they don't see how bad it is."

"I'm not sure what to think. I want to believe you. It's Tiro and Jess. But I don't know."

"You said you spoke with them?" Axel asked.

Ben nodded.

"Can you do it again? Find a way to talk to them about all this? Show them what you know, get them away from the Raptors?"

"I don't know. I don't think…God, it's risky. We're talking about protecting all of Titan. All the Colonies. If we fail, it jeopardizes everything."

"Ben, you have to try," Tory said. "It's Tiro and Jess."

Dom nodded beside her.

"What would you do?" Ben said, looking at Axel.

The big guy shook his head. "I can't say. It's a hard decision, and you're the one who has to make it, because you're the one who has to do it. Whatever you do, we're with you."

"Thanks," Ben said. "I'll try. I can't promise it'll work. But I'll try."

Chapter 32

It was late when Ben finished up with Tory, Axel, and Dom, but Harriet was still awake.

Ben found her down in the hotel lobby. "They're going to help."

She sat back and looked at him with a weary smile. "That's great news."

"What are you still doing up? It's nearly midnight."

"I thought I'd go back over the monorail schematics Krista got, be sure there aren't any surprises."

"We've all been through it a few times. Finding anything?"

She chuckled. "No. The truth is I'm just too wired to sleep. This stuff VESA's got in motion. I'm with Titan Intel. I'm used to dealing with bad, important stuff. But the stakes now are higher than I've gone up against."

"Well, you're making me feel better at least. I'm scared out of my mind."

"Too scared to sleep?"

Ben thought about his talk with Axel and the others, how he promised to talk to Tiro and Jess. "Something like that."

"OK. That's it. Come with me. We'll work on the Aurora a little bit. It'll put both our minds at ease, or at least give us a distraction."

"I'll take either one," Ben said.

They walked back to the park in the warm night air. Few people were still out on the streets, and by the time they reached the copse of trees with its semiprivate garden, they were the only people around.

"How does the Aurora feel? How's your link?" Harriet asked as they found the spot they'd used before, with about ten meters cleared between three wide, tall trees.

"Better. Stronger," Ben said. "I think. It's hard to tell."

"It's OK if you progress slowly. That's why we're practicing. We worked at 98 percent last time. Tonight I want you to go down to 95."

Ben took an involuntary step backward. "What about 97?"

"Don't worry, you got this. Take it to 95. You've handled way worse than that."

Ben sighed and adjusted his gem, the air seeming to hum around him as his light Aurora activated and began to absorb and detect energy.

"OK?" Harriet asked.

"I think so. I'm definitely sensing things, so that's an improvement over yesterday."

"Well then, let's see if you can use some of it." Harriet took up a relaxed but ready posture, with feet spread, knees bent, and hands loosely posed in front of her.

Ben faced Harriet and mirrored her stance, then began to copy her as she moved her arms and legs in a simple but elegant pattern. Soon he found her rhythm, matching his movements to hers in a slow, steady sequence. He focused on his center, the source of his body's energy, pictured the fire there and the breath that fed it. Images of his friends back home kept coming into his mind, and he fought to get rid of them.

"Focus on your breathing," Harriet said. "The Furnace. Feel the energy as it comes in. Feel it as it goes out with each movement."

Ben concentrated, pushing his friends out of his mind. He focused his thoughts on following the movements as he tried to picture their power. A source of light and heat, dancing around within him: in with each breath, out with each slow punch, kick, or block.

Once he almost had it. The power coalesced into a ball at his core, bright and tangible in his mind, but as soon as he became aware of it the thing dissipated and bled away, replaced by a recollection of Tiro and Jess laughing. His movement faltered as he registered his frustration, and he stumbled and fell just as Harriet was beginning a new sequence.

"I'm sorry." Ben slapped the ground beneath his hand, leaving a shallow divot of broken grass and sunken earth.

"It's OK," Harriet said. "You were nearly there, I saw it. We'll practice again tomorrow."

"Yeah."

"We worked with your implant dialed back further. That counts for something."

"Yeah," Ben said. He wished he was as confident as Harriet was. He turned his gem back to 100, already dreading the next session where she would push him to drop it down even more.

As they walked back, Harriet asked, "How's it going with your friends, Tiro and Jess? Do they think something is up?"

"I don't think so. I've only been in touch with them once, to push our meeting by a day or two. I was noncommittal, and they didn't press it."

"That's good. They may get suspicious, but seeing them is too risky even if you're careful."

"Yeah."

Harriet caught the way it was bothering him. "With luck we'll be out of here soon, and the operation at AMRI will go quickly. We can be out of here before they realize something is wrong."

"Hopefully," Ben said.

The next day, Ben woke to a message from Tiro asking if they could get together for lunch. He tapped out a quick reply saying he was too busy today but tomorrow was wide open. His finger hovered over the holo, ready to press *Send*. He hesitated. This might be his last chance to see his friends, his last chance to talk to them and try to offer them a way out. He knew all the risks, but he told Tory and the others he would try. He had to try. He *wanted* to try. They were his friends. Tiro and Jess.

Ben deleted the reply and tapped out a new message.

Lunch today sounds great. Pick a place and let me know where to meet you.

He hit *Send* before he could change his mind again.

Ben and the others worked through the morning to refine their plan for making a run at AMRI. He told them he wanted to review some notes over lunch, so he was going to eat on his own. Nobody batted an eye. He left the hotel and took a winding path toward the river.

He'd agreed to meet Jess and Tiro at a park on the eastern edge of town, about three kilometers from where he was staying. It was a breezy, warm day and Luxor had a pleasant atmosphere, with its people out and about in the city and its buildings reflecting the midday sun.

As he walked, Ben wondered how far he would have to go to convince Tiro and Jess that Garrison was bad news. Maybe he'd made a mistake agreeing to meet them. How much would he have to tell them? How much was he willing to tell? Ben would try everything he could to convince them to leave the Raptors without revealing anything, but he had an uneasy suspicion that wouldn't be enough. Asher Garrison was almost certainly keeping them in the dark about the worst of what he was up to. If Ben could lay it all out for them, tell Tiro and Jess about Archimedes and the danger it posed to Titan and all the

Colonies, surely that would change their minds if other arguments failed. Could Ben risk going that far in an effort to save his friends?

He reached the river and turned left, following a path that went alongside the riverbank. There were fewer people by the river, and Ben could let his mind wander as he walked. Up ahead the path curved, tracing an arc around the heart of Luxor. If he kept to it, the path would take him all the way around the city almost back to where he started. The sun was warm on his skin. It made dancing sparkles across the river's surface, stirred into easy ripples by the breeze.

Ben's insides felt just as agitated as the river below, as he wrestled with the weight of everything bearing down on him. His old friends. His new friends. Simon. Archimedes. Titan. With each step he took toward the park, the questions became more urgent. What would he do? How far would he go?

The decision is yours, Ben. Harriet had told him that back in the jungle, or something close to it. Ben wanted to do everything he could to save his friends. But what if it meant exposing the *Rock Badger*'s crew and the valuable intel they'd gathered? What if it meant jeopardizing his mission and risking his own life and future? *If you knew that, somehow, it was all going to work out, what would you choose?* Harriet's question echoed in his mind. He would choose it all, that's what he would choose. Stop Asher Garrison and VESA and still find a way to rescue his friends. But what about the achievable? If he couldn't accomplish both, which would he put first?

Ben reached the park with no clear answers. Low walls bounded it on three sides, and the area overall had a contemplative feel. It was spacious and open like much of Luxor. An expanse of soft but hardy grass covered the area, and natural-looking boulders were scattered sparsely throughout, rising like islands in a green sea. On the far end were tables for playing games, taking a rest, or congregating around simple meals.

Tiro and Jess were already there when Ben arrived, and they waved him over to the table they'd claimed. Two large bags were on the ground beside them, and Tiro was stacking their contents onto the tabletop.

"Nice timing. We just got here with the food," Jess said as Ben walked up. A man sat alone five tables away from them, and a young couple at another table farther down, but otherwise this area of the park was empty.

Tiro paused after setting a dish down. "I hope you're hungry. We brought a lot."

"I'm starving," Ben said. His mouth was dry and he hoped his friends wouldn't read the agitation on his face. He moved to help with the last of the food, but Tiro waved him off as he set the last two platters down.

"You're a busy man. I was worried you forgot about us," Tiro said. He took a plate and began putting food on it. Ben and Jess did the same, passing the dishes in an efficient circle among the three of them.

"Sorry about that," Ben said. "This new job has a lot of training, and they keep changing up my schedule. I'm glad I was able to get some time for a long lunch today. I haven't had more than a minute to myself before this morning." He paused as he took a bite of a vegetable dish, savoring the taste and letting it bring him some calm. It was earthy, rich, and slightly bitter. "God, this is good."

"We picked it up at a restaurant back that way," Tiro said, gesturing behind him. "What was the name of it?"

"I didn't catch the name, but I remember where it was. At the corner of Twelfth and Jade. Ever been there?" Jess said.

Ben shook his head. "I haven't eaten out much here. I'm sorry it's taken a couple of days to meet back up with you. I'm glad today worked out." He grinned at both of them and shook his head. "You have no idea how incredible it was to see you two the other day." The smile and the words were genuine, unforced. He couldn't forget the situation, but their affiliation with Asher Garrison didn't affect their past history together, the joy and laughter and trust they'd cultivated over ten years of friendship.

"It's good to see you too," Tiro said. "I just wish we could celebrate with some Watson."

Ben closed his eyes and sighed. "Watson Red. Remember the last time we had some back home?"

"It was the night we robbed the port, wasn't it?" Jess said.

"Yeah. But by the time I got home it was morning."

"We're all pretty far from home now, aren't we?" Tiro said.

Ben looked around. "Got that right. Look at us. On Earth."

Tiro started to raise his glass, paused when he saw it was just water, then raised it anyway. "Fuck it. To new adventures and the same old friends."

They touched their cups together and drank, tasting the water that came to Luxor from somewhere deep in the Earth. It occurred to Ben that billions of friendships had formed, dissolved, or simply carried on over gestures just like that. The exchange of words, the clinking of glasses, the truth and the lies, the liquid that bound them to the Earth and to one another. A lump formed in his throat at the thought, and he swallowed it before either of his friends could notice.

Tiro cracked some joke then, which made Ben laugh and Jess roll her eyes. The three friends settled into comfortable reminiscence and conversation as they ate. They were in no hurry, and for an hour or more the fraught circumstances that brought them back together were far from Ben's mind. He was simply here, in this foreign and wonderful place, with Tiro and Jess, the friends who'd had his back in scores of street fights and near misses with the police in Ligeia. The friends who'd been there for him and Simon when their parents left and Ben got word, sooner than he should have, that they weren't coming back. The companions he'd celebrated holidays and birthdays with, gotten drunk with, fought and argued with, committed crimes with. Tiro and Jess who, with Axel and Tory and the others, had been the most important people in Ben's world for the last ten years. A pit formed in his stomach as the thought crept in that they were now on opposite sides, and he forced the unpleasant idea down, shut his mind to it, and kept the remembering and ribbing and good mood going. God, what he wouldn't give for a glass of Watson Red right now.

"We were thinking," Tiro said after a lull in the conversation. "Jess and I were talking last night."

"You should join us, Ben," Jess said.

"Join you? What do you mean?"

"Join Garrison's crew. Become a Raptor."

"Are you serious?"

Tiro shrugged. "Yeah, why not? It's a good setup, and the crew's tight. They're tough, but nothing you can't handle. You'd fit right in, and I'm sure Garrison would love to have you on board."

"I'm not so sure about that," Ben said. "My criminal career hasn't exactly taken off. Something tells me I wouldn't be as valuable to Garrison as you think."

Jess smiled. "Actually, we spoke with Garrison about you last night. We know for a fact he wants you on board."

"You told him about me?"

"Yeah. Told him he'd met you before, same day he met me," Tiro said. "Said you'd been the one who stole the Dorium and lost the cops at Port Ligeia, and it was your idea to contact him about selling it. He liked the sound of all that."

Ben searched their faces for any sign of deception. This was dangerous territory. Not entirely out of the blue; he'd expected Tiro or Jess to ask him about joining them. In fact, he was a little surprised they hadn't done it the first day he saw them again. But he didn't like the idea of Tiro going into that much detail about how Garrison had met Ben before. Even if his friends weren't suspicious, Garrison might be. He had to be careful.

"I can't, guys," he said finally. "I'm making a new life here. It's not easy, but it's a way for me to keep supporting Simon back home, and—"

"Raptor life's better," Tiro said. "Asher will take care of Simon and still pay you. Pay you well, way better than you're getting here."

"You don't know what I make here."

"I know Asher will beat it."

Ben saw his opening and went for it. "He's a Raptor, Tiro. I can't get mixed up with him and honestly I don't see how you two can do it either. Those guys made it hard on us out in the Colonies. You know that, right? Them robbing the big cargo ships curtailed supply of just about everything and drove up prices. Not to mention the blackmail and protection rackets they had going on. We were poor, had to claw to get by, and Raptors are a big reason for it."

Jess shook her head and smiled. "We used to think that, too, but it's not like that. If Garrison and the other Raptors weren't doing their thing, do you think prices would have been lower? No way. Stuff would still be expensive. We still would've been scraping. The government and businesses would just be lining their pockets with more of the profits, that's all. Garrison doesn't take from the people, he takes from the wealthy. That's what all the Raptors are about."

"I don't believe that. It's probably what Garrison and the others tell themselves to keep their consciences clear, but I don't buy it and you shouldn't either. He probably does hurt the business owners most, but you can't pretend we all don't feel it out there when the Raptors are feeding."

"Just come give it a try," Tiro said. "Come meet him. Talk to him. Talk to the rest of the crew. See what you think."

"Even if I bought it, Garrison's in business with VESA now. I don't know what he's doing, and I don't need to. I don't want to. But I know what VESA does. I know whose interests they pursue, and it's not the Titan's or any of the Colonies. If Garrison is helping VESA, he's helping the Interior. I can't be part of that."

"Ben—"

"Honestly, it's killing me that you two are a part of it. It kept me up the past two nights. Think about what you're doing, who you're helping. What you're giving your talent and energy to."

"We're happy, Ben," Jess said. "It's a good life, free, not attached to all this BS." She gestured at the park around her, as if it were a symbol of all that was wrong with human society.

"You're not free. Guys like Asher Garrison will always come to collect in the end, even if it's just your conscience. You'll see it. I'm just afraid it'll be too late." Ben spoke with an urgency that he didn't have to fake. He wanted Tiro and Jess out of there. He wanted his friends back. "You can leave. It might be too late soon, but it's not too late now. Get out of that life. You can stay here, with me, or go anywhere."

Tiro actually laughed, and Jess gave him a sad smile. Ben knew he hadn't gotten through. "Here we are trying to get you a piece of our action, and you're giving us the hard sell to leave it behind."

"Tiro, I—"

"It's OK, man, I'm not mad. Just…sad, I guess. Disappointed. It would've been great to have you running with us again. And you're missing out on a lot of opportunity. But if you say it's not for you, that's all right. We're still cool."

Ben felt a tightness in his chest, and for a moment he worried the Aurora was attacking him. But no, it was just the recognition that the moment was here. He'd done his best to convince Tiro and Jess to leave the Raptors, and it hadn't worked. The only thing left to try was to come clean to them about all of it. He could tell them about joining the *Rock*

Badger's crew, what they found at Verona, and what they learned on the *Tethys*.

Ben closed his eyes as he rehearsed the arguments Tiro and Jess mustered in Garrison's defense. *Come with us. Join Asher Garrison's crew.* He'd known the invitation was coming, but still it rocked him. Did they really believe all that about how the Raptors didn't harm everyday people? Was there some truth to the idea that Ben wasn't allowing himself to see? Could Asher Garrison really be that bad if two of his best friends chose to join him?

Ben knew, deep down, that the arguments and justifications Tiro and Jess offered were just that. The Raptors were bad news, not least because they were willing to aid VESA if the price was right. Which, for Garrison at least, it was. His friends were misguided, on the wrong side, and he'd failed to convince them of the truth that was obvious to him. *It's obvious because you can see the full picture*, he thought. Could he risk showing them that same picture? Was saving his friends worth jeopardizing the whole mission the *Badger*'s crew was on now?

"There's something you need to know," Tiro said before Ben made up his mind.

Ben tensed ever so slightly at the new tone in his voice, and the way Jess glanced at him anxiously, as if she knew what subject he was about to bring up.

"What is it?" Ben asked with a nervous smile. "You sound serious all of a sudden."

"It is serious, man. I don't know a good way to tell you this. Miles is dead."

Ben sat back as if he'd been slammed in the chest with a hammer. "What?" He prayed he'd heard it wrong.

"Miles is dead. I'm sorry, Ben. We should've told you the other day, but we hadn't expected to see you, and we weren't sure how to say it, you know?"

Ben didn't say anything. Tears pricked his eyes and a sudden void opened in his heart. Miles was gone. Miles was dead. Goofy, crazy, fun-loving Miles. Dude would do anything, and he'd do anything for you. He'd always been so happy, and now… Miles was dead.

"When? How?" Ben asked finally.

"A couple of weeks ago," Jess said. "We had a run-in with a ship…"

Ben snapped his head up. "Miles was with you? I thought you said he and the others didn't join Garrison's crew?"

"That was only partly true. Like Tiro said, you caught us by surprise and we didn't know how to break it to you. Tory, Axel, and Dom were still locked up when we left. But Miles came with us. He was all-in with Garrison. You know how much he liked Tiro. He was a good crew member, and the others liked him right away."

"I'm sure," Ben said. "Miles is…was…a likable guy."

"Yeah."

"So what happened?"

"On our way to Earth, we had a run-in with another ship."

"What do you mean a run-in?" Ben asked.

"A fight. In space, about a week out from Earth. Garrison wanted to capture the ship and board it, but they ran. We chased them, and it turned into a battle."

Ben felt like a ball of plasma went through his chest. His heart beat faster and sweat began to break out on his forehead. Hearing Jess describe the fight that had nearly killed him was surreal. He worried that he might throw up.

"They were fast and put up a good fight, but we had them outgunned, and I was able to hack their nav system and engines," Jess said. "We shot them up, disabled their engines, and were approaching to board. But then—"

"But the fuckers surprised us," Tiro said, his voice dark. "They caught onto Jess's program, I guess, and got their engines back up and running. They flew around to our rear when we were too close to evade. They took out our engines and left us drifting."

"Miles was back there," Jess said, her voice barely above a whisper. "There were eight crew members in the engine room, and one of them was Miles. All of them died. It took us three days to repair our fusion drive."

Ben let out a breath he hadn't realized he was holding. He let the tears fall in silence. "What'd you do with his body?"

Jess shook her head. "We never recovered it. He was either spaced or vaporized."

"Hey, we got those bastards, though," Tiro said with a smile, though his own voice was choked with emotion too. "Our main cannon managed to hit them solid with a blast before they got out of range."

Ben noticed he didn't mention anything about the Lightbeam weapon Garrison boasted. Did they know? Or did Garrison have them in the dark about that too? "You destroyed their ship?" he asked.

"Our sensors showed them getting to Earth at least partly intact. We hit them hard, though. I'm sure it killed a handful of them. Their ship crash landed in South America, and it looks like some of them at least survived. We think they were coming here, actually," Tiro said.

"To Luxor?" Ben asked. How the hell had Tiro figured this out?

Tiro shook his head. "To North America. Maybe Luxor, I guess. VESA's dropped some hints to Garrison about what those guys might be up to here. Nothing concrete, that I can tell." He shrugged. "We'll find out. As soon as we get ahold of this shipment we're waiting on and take care of some other business, we're gonna track them down. We'll get the rest of those fuckers, don't worry." The ice in his voice made Ben shudder. Did Tiro suspect that Ben was on the *Rock Badger* after all? Or was this just his anger rising to the surface.

"I was there," Ben said. The words came out before he realized what he was doing. "I was on the *Rock Badger*. The ship that you fought in space, I…I was on it. Piloting it at the end, actually."

"What?" Tiro's tone was a dangerous mix of rage and confusion. Ben plunged ahead anyway, determined to get it all out now that the floodgates were open.

"The ship you fought in space was called the *Rock Badger*. I was part of the crew. It's how I got away from Titan Intel. What I told you before, about how I escaped, it wasn't true. This crew does contract work for TI. The authorities at Bradley told me I could go free if I joined them, worked with them on behalf of Titan Intelligence. We went to investigate the wreckage of Verona. Your ship, the *Blue Fin*, attacked us after on our way to Earth, and we fought back." Ben couldn't believe he was revealing so much, but what else could he do now that he'd started?

"Why are you telling us this?" Jess asked.

"Because of what we found out there," Ben said. "At Verona, and what we learned later on a big luxury liner called the *Tethys*. Asher Garrison destroyed Verona. That's what he's doing on behalf of VESA. They gave him a Lightbeam, and he blew up a colony with it. Now he's helping them equip more Raptors with the same weapons to attack the Outer Colonies."

"You're lying," Tiro said.

"Why would I lie about this? You just told me Miles is dead." Ben paused as the words caught in his throat. "What kind of sick fuck do you think I am, that I would make up something about being responsible for it?"

"Who else is on this crew of yours? Why are you here, in Luxor?"

"I can't tell you who I'm with. But we're in Luxor because we're trying to stop Asher Garrison and the people he's working for. VESA. The people you're working for. They're amassing a mercenary navy to attack Titan and the rest of the colonies. We're doing what we can to keep that from happening. I didn't know about Miles. I didn't know you'd joined up with Asher Garrison until you told me about it the other day. I don't want to have to fight you. Again. I couldn't anyway, but now…after Miles… I can't fight you again. Please leave the Raptors before it's too late."

Tiro and Jess sat in silence, their expressions unreadable. Ben looked from one to the other, desperate for some sign of what they were thinking and feeling.

"Can you prove any of this?" Tiro said finally. His voice was barely above a whisper.

"Nothing concrete," Ben said. "Firsthand examination of Verona's wreckage. Statements from witnesses who are dead now. A few bits of—"

"But you believe it."

Ben nodded. "I do."

"I don't know anybody smarter than you. If you put it together that way, I believe you. We can't be a part of something like that." Tiro looked at Jess, who closed her eyes and nodded her agreement. "We'll get away from Garrison as soon as we can," Tiro went on. "It'll take some time to avoid drawing suspicion, but we'll figure it out."

Ben's heart soared. Even as he was telling them about Verona, he was expecting it not to work. "Sooner is better. Today. The crew I'm with, we can help you get away. There's got to be a way to—"

"It's too risky," Tiro said. "Asher and his crew know us. You didn't tell us how you're working against them, exactly, and I don't want to know. The more we know, the closer we are to you, the more likely we'll be to draw his attention and tip him off."

Ben saw the wisdom in that, but he didn't like it. "You have to get away soon."

"We will. Don't worry. Thanks for telling us. About everything. I know it wasn't easy."

Ben felt the corners of his eyes getting wet. "I'm sorry about Miles."

"We are too," Jess said.

Chapter 33

True to her word, Tory came through with credentials for Harriet and the captain. The *Rock Badger*'s crew did everything they could to refine the plan for infiltrating AMRI, rehearsing each step from countless angles. The Helia credentials were the last piece to fall into place, less than a day after Ben reached out to his friends back home. It was go time.

Just after sunrise they checked out of the hotel in Luxor and made their way back to the *McInnes*, which they'd left in the woods to the west. Krista and Jones inspected it closely and verified it was undisturbed. They loaded the old ship and took off east, flying over Luxor on their way to the Ash Mountain Research Institute with its Astruc reactor and supply of heavy Dorium.

Ben checked his gem at least five times on the short flight. He'd been hoping for a message from Tiro or Jess saying they were out of Garrison's crew. So far they hadn't reached out. It made Ben nervous. He knew they had to be careful, but every hour they delayed made it more likely Garrison would draw them in deeper.

The AMRI campus had a high level of security, unsurprising for a state-of-the-art research institute that housed everything from top-secret government projects to highly regulated experimental substances. Hundreds of AIs monitored activity across the grounds and within each facility, identifying faces, tracking heart rates and body temperatures, and observing the behavior of each individual and the crowd as a whole. Anything out of the ordinary was flagged for a closer inspection by the Coordinating AI and clearance by human security professionals. Security was airtight at the various entrances to the campus itself, ensuring that only authorized personnel were allowed to enter.

Early in the crew's planning, Krista had identified the monorail leading to the campus as a vulnerable point they could exploit with unique skills contributed by Ben and Harriet.

Jones set the *McInnes* down in a wooded area five klicks from the monorail line. She and Levi stayed behind while the others hiked to the rail. It was still midmorning, and the early spring air was cool and humid.

Ben and the others reached the line without incident. The thick support posts rose forty meters to the track above, which just cleared the highest treetops. Krista approached the nearest support warily, watching her gem as she stepped closer. When she was satisfied that she hadn't triggered any sensors or alerts, she waved the others forward.

A set of rungs was embedded into the side of the support, and Krista climbed up while the others waited below. She stepped off onto a small platform below the main track, just big enough for her move around on. The underside of the track was perfectly smooth and white, except for a half-meter groove that ran along its center.

Krista found an access panel in the support, opened it, and plugged her gem into a hardline port. In seconds she was staring at a schematic of the controls and electrical wiring that governed power, traffic, weight distribution, and other critical features of the monorail line, which carried people and goods across a huge swath of southern North America. She used a multitool to pry up the control panel and reveal a tangle of wires behind it. She checked the schematic again, then shrugged and pulled a wire loose.

The schematic flashed red, and above them a yellow light in the side of the monorail track began to blink. Krista quickly tugged the loose wire apart, snapping it cleanly, then rubbed the severed ends against her multitool to fray them. She plugged the free end back into its port and checked her gem. The display still flashed red, and the light above continued to wink on and off. Krista reattached the control panel, unplugged her gem, and set the access panel back in place. She climbed down the rungs quickly and joined the others.

"What now?" Eric asked.

"We wait," Krista said. She nodded to a small copse of trees a few meters from the post. "Let's get behind these in case the bot has eyes on the ground."

Less than five minutes later a high-pitched whine sounded in the distance. It grew louder, and a minute later a large bot came into view traveling briskly on the underside of the monorail, suspended from the groove cut into the track's bottom. The bot had come from AMRI, or so they hoped. It came from the right direction at least.

The bot slid to a stop at the post Krista had just sabotaged, the yellow light reflecting off its chrome and faded white hull. An arm extended from the bot and removed the access panel with mechanical precision, then the bot went to work diagnosing the problem that had brought it out of the city.

"You're up," Krista whispered to Ben.

Ben crouched forward, just outside the cover of the trees, and extended one hand in the direction of the bot. He closed his eyes, visualized the machine, and stretched out his mind to its electrical innards. He could feel the hum of energy moving through each circuit: from the power it drew from the monorail line above down to the scurrying of information across its processor. Visualizing the bot's inner workings, he reached out with his mind and sent a gentle nudge of energy toward the bot's main power. It whined and clicked twice overhead, then the thing fell silent.

"Is that it?" Krista asked.

"I think so," Ben said. "It felt right."

"Neat trick," said Eric. "Good job, Ashley."

"It's not done yet," Lawrence said. "Let's go." He sprinted forward and leapt onto the rungs set into the support, climbing quickly toward the dormant bot up above. The others followed. By the time they got to the platform, Captain Lawrence had opened the bot's small crew door and climbed inside.

Their plan took advantage of a longstanding practice throughout the solar system: most large, industrial bots were required to have a compartment for human control. That was the case for the monorail repair bots. Most of the time these rail bots could fix any problems that arose along the line, but occasionally one or two human mechanics needed to assist. Judging from the stuffy, stale air inside the compartment, this bot hadn't needed crew assistance in several years.

Harriet, Ben, Krista, and Eric climbed into the close space after Captain Lawrence. Lawrence and Ben sat in the compartment's only two chairs. Eric closed the door behind him and crouched on the floor beside Harriet and Krista, their shoulders pressed together and legs folded uncomfortably. They leaned away from Ben to give him room to work.

Ben plugged his gem into the bot's controls and uploaded a variant of the program Jess had given him back on Ligeia, which prevented the loader at the port from registering the presence of a human occupant. This one had required only slight modifications to achieve the same thing with the monorail repair bot. That was the hope anyway.

With the program running, Ben powered the bot up again so it could finish fixing the electrical program that had summoned it. They all held their breath as the bot turned on, worried that the program wouldn't work and the bot would signal an alert to its Coordinator back at AMRI. But nothing out of the ordinary happened, and the readings on Krista's gem showed the bot behaving as if it were empty.

"Ben two, bot zero," Eric said with a grin. "You're good."

"Indeed," said Krista.

The bot replaced the damaged wire quickly, ran a diagnostic to verify all was in order, and returned to the monorail station at AMRI. As expected, it bypassed the main cargo and passenger stations and headed for its berth in the maintenance hangar. The trip barely took fifteen minutes, but the crew space was cramped and the air hot and thick. When the bot coasted to a stop and Ben verified it was safe to exit, the five of them piled out with little ceremony, grateful to have room to move and cool, dry air to breathe.

Now they were on the clock. Undoubtedly one of the security AIs had picked them up, and someone would be there in minutes to investigate.

Ben closed the bot's access door behind him and used his gem's program to remove all evidence of tampering. The others fanned out throughout the hangar, looking for the small transports that carried equipment and supplies across AMRI. Thanks to the schematics Krista had acquired, they knew all the bots shared a common facility for storage and charging.

"Here!" Harriet called, her voice echoing through the narrow corridors. Ben cringed at the noise, but they'd surely been detected already. Nothing to do now but move fast. He and the others converged on Harriet's location, where seventeen bots waited in silence. There were berths for twenty-five, but the eight on the far end were unoccupied. Evidently those bots had already left to begin their day's work. It was still early; most of the others would no doubt be leaving soon.

Ben approached the bot nearest the last empty spot, reasoning it would be deployed first. He put his hand on the bot's access port, closed his eyes, and reached. A soft orange glow emanated from the hull beneath his hand. Just as he did with the monorail bot, Ben stretched out his mind toward the network of wires and eddies of electromagnetic force around them, homed in on the right pathway, and gently directed the energy toward the lock. The bot's access port slid silently open.

Harriet did the same with the bot beside his, then moved to a third one while Ben scrambled up through the access panel and into the transport bot. He worked quickly, installing the program that would give Jones remote access to the transport—again, a modified version of what Jess had developed for their robbery of Port Ligeia. He crawled out of the bot, dusted off the knees of his jumpsuit, and activated his gem once more. An image sprang to life in the air above it: a schematic of the loader on the left and lines of code on the right. He touched and swiped the image in the air above his wrist, verifying that he had remote control.

He nodded to Captain Lawrence, who spoke into his gem. "Verify remote access."

"I have remote access," Jones's voice said. "Testing now."

The bot's access panel slid shut. "Remote access successful," the captain said. "It worked."

Ben let out a breath, relieved, then moved on to the next one. "You're sure it won't have a record of tampering?" Eric asked as he worked.

"No," Ben said.

Eric shrugged. "Guess this'll be a quick op if it doesn't work."

They installed the programs and tested remote access on the remaining two bots, then Ben climbed inside the third one. Harriet leaned in after him. "Good luck," she said.

"You too," Ben said. "See you on the other side."

Harriet gave him a quick smile and ducked back out, then Ben slid the door shut after her. He set about installing the last program, which would keep the bot from sensing that he was inside. Harriet and the others moved quickly toward the exit.

It had been less than three minutes since the monorail car brought them in.

As soon as Ben and the others exited the monorail repair bot, their presence in the maintenance hangar was observed by sensors and registered by AMRI's Coordinator. The powerful AI ran an elaborate calculation and sent an alert to one of the security officers on duty. *Unauthorized personnel in Maintenance Room C. Five individuals. Confidence level 71 percent.*

The officer read the alert at his desk and raised an eyebrow. Maintenance Room C was an odd place for somebody to go. He opened the alert and scanned the data. There were no cameras inside, so the intruders hadn't been directly observed. But the Coordinator was powerful and its algorithms had been thoroughly tested and vetted. If it said there were people inside Maintenance Room C, there were people inside.

The officer called one of the patrol leaders and sent them to check it out. The leader protested, something about being sent on a wild goose chase two days before vacation, but that wasn't the officer's problem. True, these things were almost always nothing. That's probably what it was now too. But protocol said to follow up any alerts with a security inspection, and that's what he intended to do. If this was something wrong, it wasn't going to go uninvestigated on his watch.

Harriet, Eric, Krista, and Captain Lawrence exited the maintenance hangar and found themselves in a short hallway with a single heavy door at the end. Krista pushed it open and led them into another, longer hall with several doors opening off of it. She stopped to consult her gem when one of the doors opened behind them.

"Hey," a deep voice said. "Who are you? Are you authorized to be back here?"

Harriet turned and saw a man in his midfifties, wearing the slacks, tucked-in shirt, close cropped hair, and surly expression of a security guard who didn't put up with a lot of bull crap. Six other guards stood behind him, all standing alert with hands close to their sidearms.

Harriet flashed an easy, apologetic smile and said, "Probably not. Sorry. We got turned around. We're here with the tour from Memphis?"

The leader nodded to the guard on his left, who opened his gem and pulled up a document. "Wait right there, please. Don't move."

"Checks out," the second guard said. He showed the gem to the leader.

"OK, this says the Coordinator recognizes you and you are authorized to be here for the tour." The leader pointed to the end of the hall. "Through those doors and up the stairs to your right. That'll let you out on the east end of AMRI's main avenue. Looks like the tour is just arriving at the Aquatics Lab."

He paused and looked at them. "You aren't anywhere close to the tour. This is a restricted area. How the hell did you get down here?"

Harriet laughed. "I have no idea. We really got lost."

"Wiggins will escort you to the tour."

"That won't be necessary, I'm sure we can find our way now that we know where to go," Harriet said.

"Wiggins will escort you," the man said again, in a tone that told them this wasn't up for discussion. He nodded to the guard on his right, who stepped forward. "This way, please," Wiggins said. He walked briskly toward the doors without bothering to look back.

"Thanks! And sorry!" Harriet said with a wave. She and the others followed Wiggins through the doors, up some stairs, and out one more door. They emerged onto the sprawling campus of AMRI, which was bright in the midmorning sunshine. They were in.

When Wiggins led the intruders away, the patrol leader took the rest of his men into the maintenance hangar for a visual inspection. The alert mentioned five individuals, and they'd only seen four in that little tour group. They did a thorough pass through the whole hangar, followed by another. The whole thing was annoying, but if he had to do a job, he intended to do it the right way.

Nothing seemed out of the ordinary—it was the same old, musty, rarely-seen-by-a-human space it had always been. He called the security officer. "We caught four individuals exiting Maintenance Room C. They were registered with the tour and had gotten lost. I sent one of my team to escort them back to the tour."

"Roger that. Please confirm, you said four individuals? The alert from the Coordinator showed five."

"Confirm, four individuals. We made two passes in the maintenance hangar and found nothing out of the ordinary. If you'd like, we can look again." The patrol team groaned at the offer, but the leader silenced them with a look.

"Negative," the security officer said. "The Coordinator assigned it a confidence level of 71 percent. That's a big enough error margin that I'm not worried. I'll feed the actual number back to it so it can adjust its algorithms. Continuous improvement and all that."

"Roger that," the patrol leader said. "We're returning to patrol."

They left the hangar, and Ben blew out a breath. He'd heard their voices and seen glimpses of the patrol from his view screens inside the transport bot. Nobody had any idea Ben was inside. He sat back in the cramped chair, letting his mind wander. All he had to do now was wait.

Chapter 34

The tour was nearly finished when Captain Lawrence and Harriet walked away from it.

For the past hour they'd dutifully paid attention, captured holos on their gems when appropriate, and refrained from doing so when signs or tour guides told them not to. They'd seen the most interesting facilities that were open to the public, among them the Aquatics Lab, the Center for Alternative Propulsion Technology, and the Extreme Biome Simulator. More than half of the buildings were restricted from the tour, and the guides were not permitted even to discuss them, underscoring the classified nature of much of AMRI's research. One large facility they could discuss was the Astruc Reactor, which housed the intricate and high-energy processes used to enrich Dorium, ostensibly in small quantities and for research purposes only.

The final stop on the tour was the administrative complex, which was thoroughly mundane but which housed the gift shop and cafeteria as well as a holo theater where groups could learn more about the history of AMRI. It was here that Captain Lawrence and Harriet underwent a subtle transformation from eager tourists to businesslike administrators who had a bone to pick with whoever was in charge.

"I'm sorry, sir, ma'am, but you aren't authorized to enter this area," a guard said as they approached a set of double doors leading deeper into the complex.

Lawrence said nothing. Instead, he opened his gem and pulled up a document, which he showed to the guard. The guard gave it a quick scan, then looked wide-eyed at the captain and Harriet before reading it again, more closely.

"I apologize, I had no idea we'd be getting a visit from you today," the guard said. "If you'll just allow me to authenticate this letter, I'll take you right in."

Captain Lawrence nodded while the guard transferred the file to his own gem, then verified its authenticity with VESA. In moments the gem told him the letter was genuine, the guard apologized again to Lawrence and Harriet, and he led them through the double doors.

The tour guide was puzzled by the departure of two of his guests and even more perplexed by their exchange with the security guard. He considered it a moment, then dismissed it. Whatever was going on was clearly above his pay grade, and security was obviously OK with it. He had other guests to look after. Only Krista, Christian, and Eric knew what was happening.

The captain's gem had a file, expertly counterfeited by Ben's friend Tory, that designated them as covert inspectors for the Helia Group. This is what he showed to the guard. It authorized them to observe all processes and facilities at AMRI in which Helia had a vested interest, to interrogate computer programs and AIs, and to discuss protocols with administrators. Helia Group was infamous for surprise top-to-bottom inspections throughout their operations, and both the manner of observation and the identity of their agents were closely guarded secrets.

Captain Lawrence informed the guard that he'd like to speak first with the director of the materials lab, then entered the director's office with no announcement or preamble. "I need to inspect your Astruc Reactor right away."

"Who the hell do you think you are?" the man said, rising from his chair as Lawrence approached the desk.

"We're inspectors for Helia, who's funding your operation." He flashed the gem in front of the director's eyes, which widened slightly before he regained his composure. "They've had some issues with quality control in the samples they've received and sent us to observe the process from end to end."

The director glanced at the guard. "The credentials are authentic?" The guard nodded.

"Forgive me. I was unaware that Helia had sent you or that Helia was unhappy with our operations or their results. Every communication I've received has—"

"Spare me. Our job is to observe, and that's what we intend to do. We've already inspected your facilities and processes as a part of the tour."

The director blanched, clearly flustered at the thought of an unscheduled and unprepared inspection. Lawrence caught the man's look and pressed his advantage. "We find that surprise inspections offer a more insightful look at operations. We see things as they are, not as you wish us to see them. But for obvious reasons, the workings of the Astruc Reactor aren't a part of your tour. That's what we need to see next."

"But you can't just observe the reactor at work. There is a schedule and a predetermined—"

"There's an enrichment procedure taking place in ten minutes, yes? That's what I have on my schedule. Or have there been changes?"

"Well no, the procedure is still scheduled. But the area is necessarily restricted, and only a certain number of observers are allowed at a given time."

"Kick out whoever you need to, and take us there now. This authorization comes from Helia Group. I'm sure you don't want next year's budget to reflect a lack of confidence on their part."

The man pressed his lips together. "Of course not. Come with me."

It took nearly the full ten minutes to walk to the reactor, the director shouting orders into his gem the whole time. He brought Captain Lawrence and Harriet to the facility's main floor, helped them don the requisite protective gear, and situated them behind a thick, heavily tinted glass.

The Astruc Reactor was little more than a large room, about ten meters square and half as high, with a narrow pillar in the center of it. A series of openings were embedded in the walls at half-meter intervals. "Laser apertures," the director said. He led them through the room, giving the walls and the pillar an appraising look before nodding his approval and continuing on. The wall on the far side of the room slid open, revealing a bustling observation room. Flat panels and holo tables covered every available surface, the chaos managed efficiently by the engineer in charge.

The director mumbled an apology at the last-minute visitors, but the engineer to his credit gave Harriet and Lawrence a smile and told them he was glad to have them. He toggled one of the flat panels, which activated to reveal a view of the main reaction chamber. Harriet pointed to the pillar, which now bore a single sphere of Dorium resting on its top.

At ten o'clock, right on schedule, the reactor engaged. There was a low whirring sound in the room, and the various technicians suddenly paid close attention to their holo images and monitors. Lawrence and Harriet watched the screen with interest, but apart from those changes in the operating room, nothing appeared to be happening. There was no movement or lights. The Dorium looked unaltered. Suddenly the little sphere dimmed, as if someone had cast a shadow on it.

Harriet and Lawrence exchanged uneasy glances. From what they understood about the process, huge quantities of energy should be pouring into the Dorium right now, presumably from the hundreds of apertures in the walls. A series of lasers, at very specific frequencies, should "open" the Dorium, activating what little understood quantum processes made it receptive to energy, but apart from that there was supposed to be a torrent of light and heat bombarding it throughout the process. Now it looked like someone had turned off a spotlight. What had gone wrong?

The director caught the look on their faces. "You're wondering if it's doing anything, aren't you? I assure you, it is. Every bit of energy in the reactor is focused at the exact point in the center of the Dorium. You're seeing nothing because it's all going there, and it's all being absorbed. Even the ambient light in the room is being absorbed, that's why it appears shadowed. You won't see any effects until the Dorium is saturated, that is, fully enriched to its practical limit. Actually, you won't see anything at all. At the first blip of excess energy, the reactor will stop. Ah, there we go!"

The whirring suddenly ceased, and the sphere of Dorium snapped back into clarity, as if someone had turned the spotlight back on. The technicians looked at their monitors, verified all remained well and safe in the reactor, and nodded one by one. The director smiled. "I don't get to observe this process much anymore. As disruptive as it is to my day, I'm glad for the chance to see it this morning. An amazing sight."

The door to the reaction chamber opened, and a technician walked inside. "May I?" Captain Lawrence asked, gesturing toward the door.

"By all means, the reactor is off and the Dorium is quite safe to handle," the director said.

Lawrence and Harriet entered the chamber and began an inspection of each component of the reactor, recording the pillar as well as each surface and its apertures from all possible angles. Feigning the idle curiosity of someone who'd never given it much thought, Harriet picked up the sphere and gave it a cursory once-over, turning it this way and that in her fingers. "Amazing that something so small and unremarkable can store and supply so much energy," she said.

"Indeed," said the director, regarding her nervously. Harriet caught the man's expression, smiled, and returned the sphere to its pillar. "What happens to it now?" she asked.

"Now it will go into storage with the rest of the enriched Dorium we produce here. From there it will be sent to those who request it." The director said that last part with a cryptic tone that made Harriet wonder just how much he knew about the Dorium moving through here. Surely he'd noticed that they were producing heavy Dorium at a much faster rate than they'd ever done before, and that their quantities were leaving the facility just as quickly. Did he know where it went, and what VESA was doing with it?

"Where do you source your Dorium? These are smaller quantities than the big Dyson Arrays use, correct?"

"Oh, yes, much smaller. We enrich it for research purposes only, not industrial use. As you might imagine, we have several sources. Would you like to see a nonenriched sample?"

"Perhaps later. For the moment, I have some more questions for you. Is there somewhere we can talk?"

The director forced a smile and gestured toward a small office on the other side of the reactor. "Of course, right this way."

As they walked away, a technician loaded the newly enriched Dorium into a transport bot, which turned to carry it to storage.

"Got it," Levi said. He sat in the main hold of the *McInnes* with an expansive holo schematic of AMRI in front of him. A small blip near the Astruc Reactor's exit moved slowly across the screen.

When Harriet picked up the enriched Dorium, she had attached a microscopic sensor to one side. In moments the bug began transmitting its location to Levi's gem. He tracked it on the schematic until it came to rest. After waiting a few moments to be sure it wouldn't move again, Levi nodded to Jones.

"We've located the storage facility for the enriched Dorium," Jones said. "Transmitting location now."

"Got it," Ben's whispered voice said from her gem. "Us too," said Eric.

Levi looked at Jones. "Looks like our bots are close. You're up."

It took just a small thing to trigger a wholesale reboot of AMRI's bots. Jones overrode one of the compromised machines and drove it remotely across the path of another. The second bot adjusted its course to avoid a collision, but the Coordinating AI had little tolerance for deviation in a place as highly sensitive as AMRI. It immediately registered an anomaly in two of its bots, calculated an unacceptable likelihood that others were breached as well, and shut them all down.

The reboot took three minutes, not fifteen like at Port Ligeia, and the rest of the system remained online. The Coordinator blasted the affected bots with an override code that wiped everything but a simple instruction to drive to maintenance. It scanned the other bots, confirmed that all was normal, and set them back to work. At no point did the security system lose sight of the heavy Dorium, the various entrances and exits across campus, or any of the people within its boundaries.

What the Coordinator failed to register was the human occupant sitting inside one of the bots it allowed to continue working. By a combination of luck and Ben's careful arrangement, it assigned this bot to the sector that included the Astruc Reactor and adjacent Dorium storage facility. It also failed to detect the hidden, persistent program burrowing its way into the complex network of sensors and monitors. The surgical Trojan horse was a modified version of the one the

Raptors used against the *Rock Badger*'s engines. Krista managed to lift the code from their ship's wreckage in a moment of impressive foresight and skill. Now she was running it from her gem inside the administrative complex while Eric kept lookout.

"Barnes, how we doing?" Captain Lawrence asked.

"She's had to make adjustments," Eric whispered. "These sensors were locked up tight and it slowed her down. Give us a couple of—"

"I'm in," Krista said.

"Scratch that. We're back on track here," Eric said. "In and ready for Phase Two."

"Good work. Stand by." The captain knocked on the door where Harriet was questioning the director. "Are you almost finished?" he asked, catching her eye.

"Just wrapped up."

"Good." Lawrence turned to the director. "Can you show us the Dorium storage facility? We'd like to see some additional samples of your heavy Dorium. Representative of the full scope of your operations."

The director cleared his throat. "Our storage facility is difficult to access. That's part of what makes it so secure. We use bots to transport the Dorium in and out. I can have one of them bring up some samples for you. I can also show you real-time holo footage of the storage unit."

"That will be fine," Harriet said.

The director tapped out some instructions on his gem. A hundred meters away, the bot with Ben inside entered the storage facility and arranged a sample. Ben watched carefully through the bot's displays, noting the size and arrangement of the storage room. When the time came, he would have to move fast.

His bot brought up the samples for Harriet and the captain to examine. They made a show of looking over each piece and asking pointed questions, taking their time. Then they asked to see the holo footage. When they finished, the director sent Ben's bot to return the valuable mineral to storage.

Harriet excused herself and stepped aside. "No surprises. Estimated eighty to one hundred samples of enriched Dorium, all neatly stored and labeled."

"That's what I saw too. Thanks for confirming," Ben said.

Harriet returned to the director and captain Lawrence. "I think we've seen all we need to see here."

"I agree," Lawrence said. "Let's return to the administrative complex to finish up."

"Of course, right this way," said the director.

Ben's bot was carrying him and the Dorium sample inside the storage facility.

"Here we go," Ben said. "Approaching the storage unit in three, two…"

Jones took control of a second bot and drove it erratically, triggering yet another reboot. All bots stopped in place for three crucial minutes. The lights and displays surrounding Ben went dark as his bot initiated the reboot. He was alone inside the storage unit.

"Ready," he said.

Krista activated the program she'd been running and took control of the storage facility's sensors. She kept them online, but interrupted their data feed and sent nominal responses to the AI monitors. They wouldn't register any anomalies inside their Dorium storage unit.

"You're clear, Ashley," she said. "Two minutes."

Ben exited the bot and got to work. In the end there were ninety-five small samples of enriched Dorium. He loaded them efficiently into five boxes and stacked them in the bot's interior. He crawled in behind and found there was too little room for him get all the way in. He reemerged and started rearranging the boxes.

"Thirty seconds," Krista said.

Ben settled the boxes and managed to get all the way inside. He tried to close the hatch, but one of the boxes blocked it from sealing. "Dammit."

He leapt back out and tried one final arrangement, turning the last box at an angle.

"Ten seconds."

Ben leapt into the bot and slid the hatch closed behind him just as Krista said "one." The bot's interior lit up and returned to full functionality.

"I'm in," he said.

"Cutting it close," said Krista.

"Still counts."

When the bot exited the storage facility, Krista gave the Coordinator an electronic nudge. Effectively she suggested that the bot may have been compromised in the latest anomaly. It was safest to remove it from operation until maintenance could check it out. That response fell within the usual protocols. The Coordinator heeded her nudge and sent Ben's bot back to the maintenance hangar with five boxes of Dorium inside.

Krista stayed in the system long enough to disable the sensors inside the hangar, giving Ben a chance to move the Dorium from the AMRI bot to the one servicing the monorail. The monorail bot's interior was larger, and he had little difficulty fitting the Dorium and himself inside it. He closed the hatch, sent a message to Krista, and settled in to wait for the bot to give him a ride out, the same way it brought him in.

Inside AMRI's administrative complex, Harriet and Lawrence finished up with the director and rejoined the tour, which was about to conclude. They would leave campus with Eric and Krista and the oblivious tourists.

Chapter 35

"I'm clear of AMRI," Ben said into his gem.

There was no response, so he tried again. "I'm clear of AMRI."

He kept his voice low, which was silly. The program he'd installed would prevent the bot from registering his presence. And if it failed, the bot would pick him up before he made a sound. Still, he couldn't shake the urge to whisper. He was nervous. The op had gone too smoothly, and it gave him an uneasy feeling that everything might go sideways at the slightest mistake.

The five boxes of enriched Dorium resting beside him didn't help either.

He frowned when his second attempt was met by silence too. The lack of response increased his anxiety. Maybe Jones and Levi were both occupied, but that was doubtful. At the very least he should have gotten a double tap to acknowledge his message.

He was just about to try a third time when Jones's voice piped through. "Copy that, Ashley. See you shortly."

Ben breathed a sigh of relief. Everything was OK. Her voice sounded strained, but that was probably just nerves. They were all on edge, so close to the finish line. He hoped Harriet and the others had gotten out of AMRI as easily as he had. With luck, they'd be on the *McInnes* back to Luxor in less than an hour, and making their way off-world a few hours after that.

Minutes later the bot slid to a stop at the same support post they'd sabotaged earlier. Ben idly wondered if Levi had frayed a wire like Krista had done, or if he'd opted for something different. It didn't matter, really. The local transit authority would get suspicious either way, but by then AMRI would know they'd been robbed and Ben's team would be long gone, hopefully on a ship back to Titan.

Ben dialed back his implant. He reached forward with the Aurora and killed the bot's power, surprising himself with how easy it was now. He really had learned a little something from Harriet, despite his many failures at mastering his ability. He carefully removed all trace of his activity, then slid open the door.

Ben blinked. Jess was standing there, aiming a blaster at his chest.

"Sorry, Ben," she said.

Ben swallowed, immediately understanding that everything had gone wrong. "I'm sorry too."

Jess had a small, open-top vehicle with a flat platform on the back. She made Ben load the five boxes of Dorium onto it, then tied his hands and feet before strapping him tight into the passenger seat. She climbed back up to the bot, went inside, and came back out after several minutes.

"You modified my program," she said as she sat beside him.

"Yeah," Ben said.

"Not bad, but not the way I would've done it. Vulnerable to third parties who might want to use it for their own purposes." She opened her gem and brought up a display, which she tapped and swiped through several times. Above them the bot sprang back to life. Jess then remotely deleted the program and all evidence of her presence in the AI. "See? My way is better."

"Yeah," Ben said.

Jess began driving through the woods, heading north. "You're mad."

Ben looked at her but didn't say anything.

"We gave you a chance to join us," Jess said. She gestured at his bound hands. "It didn't have to come to this."

"No, it didn't. I told you everything and you chose to betray me. You chose to remain with Garrison. God, Jess. Why? After everything you learned about the Raptors and VESA—"

"We already knew."

"What?"

"The stuff you told us. Tiro and I knew about all of it already. Well, not about your involvement. That part was new but not surprising. It was a bit suspicious, you showing up on Earth, exactly where we're operating, you know? But the other stuff, about Verona and moving those Lightbeams for VESA."

"You knew?"

Jess shrugged. "Of course. Asher Garrison is open with the whole crew about what we're doing. People buy in. He's a good leader."

Ben couldn't believe what he was hearing. "He's a good *leader*? Look at where he's leading you! How the hell did you and Tiro 'buy in' to more attacks like Verona? That's what you're working toward."

"That all depends on how the Colonies respond. VESA thinks they'll do anything to avoid another disaster like Verona. We tend to agree with them."

"This isn't a bluff, Jess. Garrison destroyed Verona. He'll do it again."

"That will be up to the Colonies. They'll have a choice in how things play out.

"You're risking millions of lives. Turning against the Colonies. Against Titan. For what?"

Jess glanced over at him, her expression hard. "Do you really think it matters for most people whether they're governed by VESA or by Titan or by some independent federation of glommed-together Colonies? Things won't change when VESA comes to power. For the business owners and elites, maybe. Not for people like us. Not for the Raptors. Just a changeover at the top. And we get a cut for making it happen. Worth it if you ask me."

Ben clenched his jaw and said nothing. There was no arguing with that logic, flawed as it was. Jess had swallowed the standard Raptor justifications whole. How could she and Tiro not see the harm Garrison and those like him caused? The ways VESA would inevitably exploit the Colonies if they were in power?

Jess drove through the woods in silence until they reached a large road. Jess turned right onto it, heading for AMRI.

"How'd you find me?" he asked finally. "How did you know I would be at AMRI?"

"Your gem."

"What do you—" Ben stopped short as he realized what she meant. "You hacked my gem?"

"I told you, Tiro was suspicious. I was too. You being here was too much of a coincidence. We got to talking, and I remembered I still had your gem's image from when I helped you install that program for your light mutation thing. Speaking of…" she reached over and took Ben's gem. "Better if I hold onto this for a little bit. Anyway, we decided to prepare a tracer program. I installed it remotely after you told us…what you told us."

"So I bare my soul to you, my best friends, trying to get you away from Asher Garrison. And you respond by putting a tracer on me. Dammit Jess, do you even care about me at all?"

"In my defense, the tracer was necessary. You didn't tell us about your plans at AMRI."

"Yeah, well. You killed three of my friends up in space, and almost killed me. Self-preservation took over."

"And you killed Miles," Jess said, her voice hard.

Ben ignored that part. He was sorry about Miles, but he wasn't about to feel guilty when he'd been fighting for his life. Instead he asked, "How'd you know what we were up to here?"

Jess glanced at him. "VESA suspected your team was after the Dorium enrichment facility. They tipped Asher off to be on alert, that it was a possible target. Once we saw where you were headed, we knew for sure."

Ben raced through his options. He could try to fight Jess. She'd taken his gem, but he'd learned a lot and she'd always been more of a hacker than a fighter. He dismissed the idea. Ben didn't want to hurt Jess if he could avoid it. And there was no way to know how many of Garrison's crew awaited him at the *McInnes* or where they were holding Harriet and the others. That is, assuming they'd been captured too. Maybe one or two of them had gotten away. No, there were too many unknowns right now. Fighting was an option, but better to wait until he knew what he was up against. And if he could do it without putting Tiro and Jess in danger, so much the better.

Could he get on the Raptors' good side? Jess was playing it cool now, but he was pretty sure she didn't like the idea of capturing him. They'd been friends for years. Unless she was completely heartless, killing him or torturing him or whatever Garrison had in mind would tear her up. Tiro too. Maybe he could use that. Pretend he'd had a change of heart, he wanted to join them after all. Would Tiro and Jess buy it? Would Garrison go for it, even if they did?

After a few kilometers Jess turned off the large road to a narrower access road. Signage at the entrance let Ben know this was a maintenance and cargo entrance for AMRI. It also cautioned that the area was secure and trespassers would be arrested on sight.

"For what it's worth, I don't like this," Jess said, breaking into his thoughts. "I wanted you on our side."

"You could let me go. Say I put up a good fight or ran too fast."

"If I thought you'd leave, I might do that. Would you just leave?"

Ben didn't say anything.

"I thought so. Those Intel contractors have gotten to you, Ben."

"They're good people," he said. "And they fight for a good cause. We're trying to stop VESA, not just Asher Garrison. Trying to prevent another attack like Verona. We're trying to protect Titan. Protecting all the Colonies. We're trying to protect—"

"You're protecting the wealthy, the elites. Or have you forgotten that? Those of us on the underbelly of Titan—"

"Are still citizens of Titan. Yeah, Titan has its ugly side. I know that more than anybody. But is the solution really to steal what you can, to rob and thieve from Titan and any other colony or ship you come across? Is the solution to hand it all over to VESA on a silver platter? Is Garrison improving things for the little people of Titan?

"They really have fed you a load of crap, haven't they? And you've just believed every word."

"He's working for VESA, Jess. You're working for VESA."

"You picked the wrong side," Jess whispered.

They rode in silence the rest of the way.

The back entrance to AMRI was formidable. A five-meter wall of concrete and steel stretched into the woods in both directions with a heavy gate across the road and a guard tower on either side. A guard stopped them as soon as they were within twenty meters. He began to question Jess aggressively—she had somebody tied up in the seat beside her—but a buzz on his gem interrupted him. He read the message, then motioned for someone to open the gate. He waved Jess and Ben through.

Jess drove them through the rear sector of AMRI to a sprawling open area, where a handful of aircraft and dropships waited. Four of the dropships looked similar to the ones that had landed with the Raptors in South America. More of Garrison's crew had come down to the surface.

To one side of the clearing were several hangars, evidently for craft operated out of AMRI. Jess drove to the nearest of these and maneuvered her vehicle inside. Tiro and Asher Garrison waited in there with at least fifteen other Raptors. The rest of the *Rock Badger*'s crew sat in a line along one wall, their hands tied behind their backs. Ben swallowed and looked away when he saw them. Jess drove to the Raptors and gestured for Ben to get out.

"This your guy?" Garrison asked Tiro.

Ben's friend nodded. "That's him."

Garrison stepped closer and looked at Ben, squinting. The Raptor captain stood a few centimeters taller, dressed casually as he had been when Ben first met him on Titan. "Ben, right? Yeah, I remember you. Silent and trying to look tough, like a bodyguard for that other fellow." Garrison turned and spoke to someone over his shoulder. "You remember him?"

"Yeah. Yeah, I do."

Ben turned toward the new voice and saw Val Minos standing there. The Kraken smuggler-turned-Raptor punched him in the stomach.

Ben exhaled sharply and doubled over, his stomach muscles clenching as he fought the sudden urge to vomit.

"Easy, easy," Garrison said, pushing Val back. He looked at Jess. "Is this all of them?"

"He was alone, sir. There were five boxes of Dorium with him." She gestured to the back of her vehicle where they sat. "That matches AMRI's records of what they had in storage."

So if we missed somebody, they aren't bugging out with our heavy Dorium. That works for me." Garrison pointed at four Raptors, then to the boxes on the back of Jess's vehicle.

"Load that on one of the dropships, then put these prisoners in a room somewhere. I'll have Farrah get on the Quill to Titan Intel and see if they're worth anything. If not, well…" He looked at Val and shrugged. "No need for us to haul them around, right?"

Val grinned.

Ben swallowed. Garrison's meaning was clear enough.

"The rest of you, go wait for that shipment coming out of Luxor. It's supposed to be here in an hour. I want to assemble a few of the parts before we clear out, be sure it all works. Not the monorail, it's coming in the back on that access road. Get going."

The Raptors fanned out and got to work. Two of them shoved Ben roughly over to Captain Lawrence and the others, while two more grabbed the heavy Dorium and carried it out to one of Garrison's ships. The two guards escorted the *Rock Badger*'s crew to an empty room off the main hangar area. Ben sat in the floor beside Harriet. "Ashley, are you OK?" the captain asked.

"Yeah. Stomach hurts like hell, but I'll survive."

"Good. Glad they didn't hurt you worse," Eric said.

"We really missed something," Harriet said. "I have no idea how they found us. We knew they would come pick up the Dorium, but no way could they have known what we planned or when."

Ben closed his eyes and took a breath. "Guys, I—"

"He took us right to you."

Ben looked up and saw Tiro standing over them.

Harriet saw Tiro, then glanced at Ben, confused. "What's he mean?"

Tiro smiled. "I don't think we've met. I'm Tiro. Ashley here's best friend, right?" He kicked Ben playfully on the knee. "We put a tracer on his gem when he met us for lunch. We figured he and whoever he was with were up to something that would mess with our plans. When we caught him heading east at a good clip, the *Blue Fin* was able to ID your ship from orbit and get a look at his associates."

"How the hell did you have a tracer ready for Ben's gem?" Krista asked. "Those aren't plug and play, they have to be customized. You just had one of those in your pocket on the off chance you'd run into him here?"

"Nah, Jess is good but she's not that good. We didn't have the tracer when we met Ben the first time. Jess put it in when we met him the second time."

"Second time?" Harriet said. She snapped her eyes to Tiro, then back at Ben.

"Oh damn, she didn't know?" Tiro looked at Ben and started laughing. "Sounds like you two need to catch up a little bit."

"What's he talking about, Ben? What second time?"

Ben ignored Harriet, staring daggers at Tiro. "Why? Everything I told you. I was trying to get you out of this life, man. Why'd you come after me?"

Tiro snorted. "You're always trying to save everybody. Bailing on the Academy to look after little brother. Giving yourself up for Axel and Tory and Dom. Even that guard back at Port Ligeia you didn't want to hurt, and your hesitation got you stuck inside. Nobody's asking you to do that, you know."

"Why, Tiro?" Ben said through gritted teeth.

Tiro shrugged. "Money. Power. Influence. All of the above. Raptors have it going on, and Asher Garrison is about to be the kingmaker out in the Colonies. Why would I miss a chance to get on the right side of that action? You had that chance, too, man. Jess and I gave you the opportunity. Don't forget it was your choice that landed you here. He kicked Ben again."

Asher Garrison called for Tiro. "Sounds like I gotta run. I really am sorry it ended this way. But, you know. At the end of the day we gotta get it done for ourselves, right? You never did figure that out." He turned and left the room, jogging toward Garrison.

"Tiro. Tiro!" Ben called. His friend didn't answer. One of the guards outside peeked into the room, then closed the door with an amused grin.

"Dammit," Ben hissed and kicked the floor.

"What did he mean, Ben?" Eric asked. "He said you met him and Jess a second time. What does that mean?"

Ben looked at the floor. "I had lunch with them yesterday. When I told you all I wanted to go over some notes on my own. I left the hotel and had lunch with them."

"Why?" Harriet asked.

"I couldn't just let them stay with the Raptors. I had to try to show them what Garrison was up to, make them see what a danger he is to Titan and the Colonies. He and Jess are my best friends. When I talked to Axel and Tory and Dom about our credentials, that drove it home. I knew I'd never be able to face them again unless I did everything I could to get Tiro and Jess away."

"I don't understand," Levi said. "How did you going to meet with them tip them off about us?"

Harriet got it. She was always fast. "What did you tell them?"

Ben didn't say anything.

"What did you tell them?" Harriet's voice had a hard, unforgiving edge to it.

"I told them what we found, OK? I told them I was on the crew of the ship they fought out in space and that earlier we'd discovered Asher Garrison was behind the attack on Verona. I told them we knew he was acting on behalf of VESA and helping them build a mercenary navy out of the Raptors."

"You betrayed us," Harriet said. Even now she didn't want to believe it was true. "After everything we've done together, all we went through, you sold us out and told them everything."

"I didn't tell them everything," Ben said. "I didn't say a word about your identity, any of you. I didn't—"

"Oh come on, Ashley," the captain said. "You were giving them enough to go on. It was plenty for them to put it all together. I refuse to believe you're stupid enough to think they wouldn't get the full picture and know exactly what our next play was."

"Dammit, Ben," Harriet whispered.

"Harriet…"

"Don't talk to me."

"Harriet—"

"I said don't talk to me!" she yelled. She leaned forward and stood up, hands still behind her back. She walked across the room and sat down by Eric. The others shifted their posture—some slid away from Ben, others just turned. It all sent the same message.

"I'm sorry, guys. I'm sorry."

Chapter 36

An hour passed slowly, then a second. The others talked among themselves but not to Ben. He tried to make out what they were saying, but they were keeping their voices down and the sounds of the hangar outside drowned out most of it. He tried apologizing, too, several times, but they weren't having it. He supposed he didn't blame them. It's how he would have felt if he were in their shoes.

Judging from the voices and noise outside, something happened toward the end of the second hour. Ben guessed it was the shipment arriving from Luxor, carrying the components of the Lightbeams. He could picture the flurry of activity as the Raptors unloaded the equipment and began piecing a few samples together so Garrison could check things out. He wondered who on Garrison's crew was engineer enough to assemble and check everything. Ben also guessed that if the materials had arrived, the Raptors wouldn't hang around much longer down here on the surface.

Sure enough, less than ten minutes later the door opened and four Raptors walked in with blasters drawn. Their faces were cold and their posture held a tense air of malice. Ben saw right away that they were here to dispose of their hostages, not move them.

Ben looked around for something to do, but it was all happening so fast. He was leaned back against the wall, and getting to his feet would be far too slow. He was in no position even for something as desperate as a bull rush with his hands tied. Ben breathed faster, his throat grew dry as the Raptors filed into the room and lined up in front of the *Rock Badger*'s crew.

The attack happened fast and without warning.

One moment the Raptors were preparing to fire, the next one of them had fallen, crashing to the ground with a thud. Harriet whipped her leg sideways, catching a second Raptor in the leg before the others registered what was happening. He dropped his blaster and fell to the floor clutching his knee.

Lawrence and Levi rushed the other two, using their shoulders to knock the guards to the ground. They pressed their advantage while the Raptors were down. Krista kicked one in the temple as soon as he hit the floor. Eric stomped down hard on another's throat. Harriet kept her feet moving, knocking a third out cold with a vicious twisting kick. Levi slammed his head into the final Raptor's nose, hitting him again and again until the guard stopped moving.

It was over in a matter of seconds.

Ben watched in fascination and amazement as his friends took stock of their carnage. Harriet already had her hands free and was working to cut the ties of the others. She'd moved so quickly in the fight, almost too fast for his eyes to track. He looked at her wrist ties and saw they'd been pulled apart, not cut. Harriet had used the Aurora. God, it made her strong. No wonder the fight hadn't lasted long.

She and the others tied the fallen Raptors quickly and took their weapons. They managed to find their gems in the guards' pockets too. Then they started to leave.

"Harriet!" Ben was still tied up on the floor.

She stopped at the door as the others ran ahead. "Cut me loose," Ben said.

Harriet looked at him sadly and shook her head.

"What are you doing? Come on, cut me loose."

"You're not coming with us, Ben."

Her words hit him like a hammer blow. "What?"

"We're going after Garrison. There's a chance he hasn't sent the Dorium up to orbit yet, and even if he has we'll find some way to stop him."

"Yeah, that's what I thought. I'll come too. I'll—"

"We can't trust you anymore, Ben. You have to stay here."

"They'll kill me. Are you really just going to let them kill me?"

"We don't think they will. We talked about that. Me and the others. Your friends Tiro and Jess, they still care about you. There's a better than fair chance they'll let you go, maybe even let you join them. Especially when they see we've left you behind."

"I don't want to be left behind, Harriet. I want to go with you. To fight."

She looked over her shoulder, torn between the need to be fast and the desire to explain it to him, some part of her still caring that he understood. "I believe you had your reasons for telling your friends about what Garrison was up to. I believe you really did want to save them, and you thought that was the best way. Maybe the only way."

"Yeah, I did. But now I know they won't leave, and I'm ready to fight for Titan. I can't let VESA or Garrison get away with what they're doing. We—"

"There is no 'we' anymore. You let us down. You betrayed us. We needed you, and you turned against us. Put the whole mission in jeopardy. You can't go with us now."

"I—"

"Do you have any fucking idea how much this hurts? We needed you, Ben. We still need you. The people around you need you at your best, and you managed to take yourself out of the equation."

"Harriet—"

"I have to go. We have to stop Garrison." She turned and left before Ben could say another word.

"Harriet! Harriet!"

Ben cursed. He had to go after them. Even if they didn't want his help, he had to go do whatever he could. He couldn't just let them fight alone. He set his mind to work. The Raptors here would be out for a while, but somebody might come looking for them any minute. Job number one was to get away from here as fast as he could.

Ben managed to get to his feet. He squatted beside one of the Raptors, trying to find a knife or something sharp. He tried turning backward and feeling about with his hands, but that didn't do much besides painfully twisting his shoulder and elbow. Then he turned around and tried using his nose and teeth to get at the Raptors pockets. That was even less useful. After a few minutes Ben gave up and left the room. At least his legs were free and he could move somewhat quickly. He'd find something in a better hiding spot.

Ben excited the room and ran along the wall. This hangar was mostly empty, but he could hear a lot of noise from the next one over. He thought it sounded like blaster fire. Ben crossed the open space quickly, eyes swiveling to be sure nobody was around, and out the back of the hangar. He crossed to the next one, found its back door, and ducked inside.

It was blaster fire, all right. The *Rock Badger*'s crew was shooting their way toward one of the Raptors' dropships. Harriet and Eric were concentrating their fire at the ship itself, trying to take out whoever was holed up inside. The other four were keeping the rest of Garrison's crew at bay with suppressing fire to the side and back toward the hangar.

Harriet closed the distance and got to the ship first. She ducked inside and a Raptor fell to the ground behind her, then Jones was at the ramp and running in to take the controls. Seconds after she entered, the ship lifted off and swiveled, sending a barrage of small fire toward wherever the Raptors were shooting from. The return fire stopped, and she swiveled back to allow the captain and the others on board. She fired the dropship's thrusters and sped away from AMRI before the ramp was all the way up.

"Dammit, that's our Dorium!" a familiar voice shouted.

"After them!" Val Minos said, then ran toward one of the other ships.

"Wait! They have a head start and a damn good pilot." Asher Garrison swatted at his gem. "Lieutenant Austin, send somebody up there and chase down my dropship. It's been stolen and they have VESA's heavy Dorium on board." He turned to Jess. "See if you can get control of their engines."

"Yes, sir." Jess ducked inside the hangar and opened her gem. She spread out a wide array of holos and started swiping through them. Somewhere nearby, loud engines began to fire. Ben guessed it was the ships Lieutenant Austin, whoever that was, had ordered to give chase.

Garrison continued shouting orders at his Raptors and into his gem, but the sound receded as the captain moved out into the open area for a better view of the action. Ben suddenly realized he was alone in the hangar with Jess. She was about fifty meters away and trying to bring down the dropship his friends were flying. And she still had Ben's gem.

He moved closer, quietly at first, ducking behind small bots or supports at regular intervals. His hands were still tied but he closed the distance quickly. Jess had her attention fully on her holos, and as Ben got closer he started to run. She finally looked up when he was three meters away. She didn't have time to react.

Ben lowered his shoulder and knocked Jess down. With his hands tied, his angle and leverage weren't the best, and he tripped over her as she fell. Ben scrambled to his knees in time to see Jess swinging a fist at him. He ducked under the blow and leapt forward, leading with his head. His forehead collided with hers, and Ben's vision erupted with light. He rolled onto his back, shook his head and closed his eyes. When he opened them he was still seeing stars. He sat up slowly and saw Jess sprawled on the ground, unconscious. She had gotten the worst of it, barely.

Ben slid and shimmied until he was right next to her, then rolled so his back was against her hip. He felt around her pants, finally located her pocket, and reached inside. It was empty.

Dammit, why can't it be easy for once?

Ben rolled and slid to Jess's other side, contorted himself to reach her other pocket, and finally managed to grasp his gem. He flicked it away from her, rolled onto his stomach, and used his nose to activate the Aurora program. He swiped down and took his implant to 85 percent.

The Aurora hit him hard. Eighty-five was lower than he'd intended, but he didn't exactly have the best control using his nose. Still, his training with Harriet had paid off, and he weathered the storm of light that set his heart rate and body temperature soaring. Ben felt the energy move through him, gathered it to his center, and sent it out toward his arms. He gritted his teeth as the restraints dug into his skin, then pushed harder. The restraints finally snapped.

Ben scooped up his gem and sprinted for Garrison's second dropship. One guard and the pilot both saw him coming and called out to the other Raptors. The guard tried to cut him off, but the Aurora gave Ben incredible speed. He knocked the guy aside, raced up the ramp, and tossed the pilot out behind him. He slapped the button to close the ramp before they could get back inside. Ben took the ship into the air, riding its atmospheric thrusters while an angry Tiro and astonished Asher Garrison watched him fly away.

Ben struggled to focus as the ship rose. His heart beat fast and the view ahead was a confusing blur of light. He panicked for a split second, then remembered the Aurora. His implant was still at 85. Ben turned it back to 100 and things calmed down. He could see and think clearly now. Up ahead, three small, nimble ships were chasing the other dropship. Ben looked around the cockpit, taking in the controls. There was the acceleration, the display toggles, guns, altitude. Orbital rockets to the left. Radar, scopes, and holo to the right. He called up the holo and focused it on the four ships ahead of him. The dropship was moving fast, but he could see at a glance that the others were gaining on it. The closest one had started to shoot. Jones was taking the dropship through evasive maneuvers that it wasn't designed for. Ben isolated one of the enemy ships in the display and brought up the AI's analysis. It was a standard VESA atmospheric fighter, which VESA often deployed to provide security operations where it had interests to preserve. So, VESA was providing security here at AMRI. Ben guessed more fighters or ground personnel were on their way. He had to end this quickly.

Ben pulled up the dropship's guns. They weren't much, but the range was pretty good—they had to be if you needed to fire on something from orbit or beyond. Ben targeted one of the VESA ships and fired, catching it near the rear. Its thrusters sputtered and it lost altitude, slowly at first then plunging toward the treetops below.

One down, two to go.

The first was a lucky shot that took them by surprise. The others wouldn't be nearly so easy. One of the remaining ships maintained pursuit of Jones and the others, while the second broke off to confront Ben. The little VESA fighter came at him fast, jinking and juking and not allowing a clear shot as it chewed up the distance. Ben spun away as it reached its gun range and began to fire, looping the cumbersome dropship through a long bank and roll. It wasn't sexy, but it got the job done. Ben tried to come back and get a bead on the enemy before he could turn, but the thing hit its accelerator and got in behind him before Ben could turn.

Stupid dropship. He couldn't win a dogfight in this thing no matter how good a pilot he was. The VESA fighter was designed for atmospheric confrontation, while Ben's vessel was meant primarily to move from orbit to the surface and back. Up and down.

Well, if that's what it was designed for…

Ben angled the dropship toward the sky and fired its orbital rockets. The dropship leaped upward on a column of flame just as the VESA ship's blaster cut through empty air behind it. The thrust pressed Ben into his seat at more than three G. He cut the burn almost immediately and turned back toward the surface, surprised at how much altitude he'd gained. He had the high ground now, literally, and Ben hit the thrusters to hover above the VESA ship down below. The other pilot saw his peril and tried to run, but Ben was an excellent shot. He fired three blasts in a rapid burst, anticipating the other ship's evasive action. The last shot clipped the ship's right side and sent it spiraling.

Ben turned to the final ship, which was firing relentlessly at Jones and the others. Jones was evading, but it was only a matter of time before she messed up or the other pilot got lucky. Ben accelerated toward the VESA ship and fired. The guy saw him coming, too late, and Ben's blasts cut through the fighter as Ben drew even with their altitude.

Chapter 37

"Yeah!" Ben whooped and pumped his fist as the last VESA ship fell from the sky, breaking apart on its way down. Beyond it his friends continued to accelerate. Their vessel was venting smoke and tilted oddly in the sky, but they were finally clear of AMRI and no other fighters were launching.

Ben allowed himself a smile as he hit the throttle to catch up. The others would probably still be mad at him, and maybe they'd still refuse to let him join them again. But he'd helped them. He'd done his part. That counted for something. Ben figured they were probably headed for the *McInnes*. He reached for his gem to get its location and follow them.

That's when the sky fell.

The grin was still pasted to Ben's face when a column of blue flame erupted in front of him, lighting up the world in a brilliant flash. The lance demolished his friends' ship, cleaving it in two and slamming it to the ground with devastating force.

"Ahhhh!" a hiss escaped Ben's lips as he tried to process what was happening.

Superheated air radiated outward from the blast, leveling trees in an expanding ring of destruction. The sonic boom arrived a moment later, a roar that reverberated through the ship and rattled Ben's body with a sickening vibration. The shockwaves tossed his ship around like a pebble in a hurricane, sweeping it backward and sideways before casting it up toward the clouds.

Ben endured the disorienting spin and roll as he fought to regain control. In seconds he righted the ship and got his bearings. He looked west where his friends had been. There was a deep crater at the epicenter of the blast, with a pillar of smoke rising from it. There was no sign of life, and little chance any of them had survived. Still, he aimed his ship toward it and pushed the acceleration as high as he could.

"What the hell was that?" he said through gritted teeth. He raced toward his friends, eyes sweeping the horizon from left to right. The blast was immense. It looked like it came from space, but even an orbital strike didn't pack that kind of a punch. It was almost like they'd been hit by a…

Lightbeam. The truth hit Ben like a jolt of electricity. They'd been hit by a Lightbeam from orbit. The *Blue Fin* was in the game, and Garrison was playing dirty.

Ben's eyes went wide as he recognized the danger he was in. If Garrison was willing to fire once…

He jerked the ship sideways just as the second beam tore the air apart right where he'd been. The expanding, superheated air caught up with him in an instant and threw the ship forward, adding to his own momentum and propelling him toward the crater. Several Gs of force crushed him back into his seat, and he struggled to keep the ship upright under the acceleration of the first shockwave and sonic boom that followed.

He kept control for a moment, but the blast was relentless. The shockwave pitched the tail of Ben's ship to the left, tipped it onto its side, and sent him into a roll. It flew through the air, a small bit of metal twisted and turned and shoved forward by an invisible, malicious hand. Just before he crashed, Ben caught site of the crater and guessed he was going to hit within a kilometer of it. Small comfort that he'd die close to his friends. He told himself he'd be brave, that he'd watch the ground as it rose up to kill him, but everything was spinning and the whole world was a blur. He shut his eyes to spare himself the indignity of vomiting in his final moments.

There was a crunch, a hiss, and an impact that wasn't nearly as forceful as it should have been. A rough, grinding vibration filled the cockpit, followed by a wrenching screech. It sounded as if the ship's hull were being torn apart and twisted back together in some grotesque parody of itself. The noise reminded him of that music Harriet listened to. Between the screeching roll and series of lurches, Ben couldn't tell which way was up or how fast he was moving.

Finally the loudest sounds died away and the sensation of movement vanished. Ben tensed, expecting the worst, but it didn't come. He was alive. By some miracle, he wasn't even injured. In fact, he felt no pain at all. Ben opened his eyes and tried to unstrap himself, but found he couldn't move. He couldn't see anything either. The world was pitch black. His heart beat faster and panic began to set in. He was paralyzed and blind. Injured after all, in the worst way possible. No, wait. He still had feeling in his limbs. There was a vague sense of pressure all around him. So he couldn't be paralyzed, right?

He was…immobilized. Trapped under or within something that was remarkably consistent in its pressure and texture. A firm, spongy substance surrounded him, pressing him heavily, perfectly contouring to his body on all sides.

Crash foam, he realized. It deployed on impact, surrounding him in an instant to cushion his body against the tremendous force of the ship slamming into the earth. That also explained the inability to see. He breathed a sigh of relief. He was alive after all, and he'd just endured a roller coaster of emotion to go with his wild ride back to earth. Well, he'd take it if it meant he survived and had a chance to help his friends. Assuming they'd survived too. Crash foam may have helped them. God, he hoped so. But they'd gotten a direct hit from the *Blue Fin*'s beam.

Ben struggled against the thick, gel-like layer surrounding him. How did crash foam work, again? Did it just keep you still until rescue teams arrived? That seemed silly. What if they were hours away? There had to be a way to get out on your own.

He pushed with one hand, then the other, then both. He tried pulling. Arching his back. Kicking. Nothing worked. He strained all his muscles, this way then that way, but the stuff held fast. Ben growled in frustration as he struggled, expending tons of energy but not moving so much as a centimeter.

"Let me out!" he yelled.

An even voice replied, "Site is safe. No injuries detected." A seam appeared in front of Ben's face, and the crash foam began to split apart.

Ben blinked, then snorted at himself. Of course it was voice activated.

He climbed out of the foam and stood in the center of what used to be his ship. It was barely recognizable as a human-made thing now, just a lump of crushed and fused metal. The crash foam stood out as a bright orange blob filling what had been the cockpit. He looked around quickly, determined that nothing useful could have possibly survived the crash, and found the edge of the crater from the other ship. It was less than half a kilometer away. He sprinted for it, praying that his friends were OK.

He was nearly there when an engine sounded above him, and he looked up to see another dropship high overhead. Ben stopped and hid behind a fallen tree. The ship moved out over the center of the wreckage and hovered, then slowly descended.

The crater was wide, more than a hundred meters across. The vessel dropped below the edge and its engines lowered in pitch as it landed. Ben crept toward the scene, staying low, and dropped to his belly as he reached the lip. He crawled forward the last couple of meters and raised his head just enough to see down into the depression.

The wreckage of his friends' ship was in the center, with several small fires and smoking debris radiating outward. Somehow the ship was still recognizable. It helped that Ben knew what to look for since he'd just flown an identical ship himself. The remains of the cargo area were on the left side of the wreckage, separated cleanly from the cockpit, which was more than ten meters away. Garrison's Lightbeam had cut the ship in half.

The cockpit was cracked open at three places and badly dented, but a glimpse of orange gave Ben hope. Crash foam had deployed there too. With luck it would have kept his friends alive through the violent blast and crash that followed.

The second dropship had landed at the far side of the wreckage. Tiro jumped out first, followed by twelve others. Thirteen against seven, assuming Harriet and the others were all OK. He didn't like those odds even if the Titan team came out shooting.

Tiro and the others fanned out, searching the site. They had to be looking for the Dorium.

Ben watched the crash foam for any sign of movement, but nothing happened. Why weren't the others reacting? Maybe they were injured after all? Or maybe the foam was detecting a threat and wouldn't let them out? Whatever it was, they were sitting ducks just lying there immobile in the cockpit. Surely Tiro and his companions knew what crash foam was.

He had to do something. He didn't know what, but he couldn't just let the Raptors take the Dorium they'd worked so hard to get. Maybe he could cause a distraction or something, long enough for his friends to get clear and start fighting Garrison's crew.

Ben made up his mind. He waited until nobody was looking his way, then leapt over the edge of the crater. He ran toward the first bit of debris he saw, a section of hull panel that had lodged itself upright in the ground. He dove behind it, peeked out to be sure he hadn't been spotted, then ran another several meters to a dip in the earth that was deep enough for him to hide in. He worked his way closer until he was less than ten meters from the crash site.

"Here!" one of the Raptors called. Tiro and three others followed the voice to a spot well away from the cargo hold's remnants.

"You found something?" Tiro asked.

"Three of them," the guy said, then pointed. "And one more over there."

"Good work, that means just one left. Load these up and keep looking for it."

The first Raptor grabbed two of the boxes, and two of the others took one each. Ben got a good look and recognized them immediately as the enriched Dorium they'd stolen from AMRI. Just like he'd thought. He was running out of time. *Come on, Harriet, help me out here!* he thought.

Ben raced ahead another five meters, bringing him painfully close to the nearest Raptor. He bumped into a piece of hull as he ducked behind it, making a noise. Ben winced. He thought he saw the guy's head turn just as he fell out of sight. He held his breath as he heard what sounded like footsteps coming closer.

"You spot it?" a voice called.

"Nah, thought I saw something move over here," came the reply. It sounded like it was just on the other side of the hull plate. Ben tensed, ready to strike if the guy saw him. He wouldn't win a fight against all thirteen, but maybe that would provide just the distraction the others needed.

He heard another footstep as the guy came closer, then another.

"I got it!" another voice called.

The footsteps stopped, then retreated as everyone ran toward the voice.

"Hell yeah," Tiro said. "Put it on the ship."

Ben eased his head around the piece of hull and watched as the last of the Dorium was loaded. He watched for any chance to strike, to make his way toward the dropship, but there were too many eyes in the area. He'd never make it. He'd have to wait and regroup with the others, come up with a plan to go after it again. He cursed to himself. This had all gone sideways in a hurry.

"All right, let's take care of these fools," Tiro said. "The captain wanted us to bring them in, but he didn't say they had to be alive."

Tiro drew his blaster and strode over to the cockpit, followed by six others. They all took aim at the orange stuff visible in the cockpit, then shot.

Thunder and fire erupted from the weapons, lighting up the wall of crash foam.

Ben watched in horror as blast after blast tore through the gel encasing his friends. He had no idea how crash foam worked or whether it could withstand plasma at point-blank range, but the pieces of foam that fell away and the sickening burnt smell that reached his nostrils told him it wasn't good.

A sob escaped Ben's lips as the first shots were fired, but it was drowned by the roar of blaster fire and the Raptors didn't hear. He bit his fist and his stomach clenched, anger and sorrow crushing him in an icy, heavy grip. The Raptors fired mercilessly for twenty seconds before Tiro put a stop to it.

Ben couldn't breathe. His vision blurred, shoulders shaking as despair pressed in on him. He felt as if he would burst or simply die from the heartbreak of watching his companions murdered. Watching Harriet die.

Something snapped him out of it. Maybe the end of the plasma fire or the movement of the Raptors toward the ship or a word from Tiro he registered only subconsciously. Whatever it was, the hopelessness that rendered him incapable of thought or action vanished. In its place arose a desire for blood. Ben jumped from behind the hull panel that hid him, wide-eyed and full of fury. He cried out as he rushed toward Tiro.

The Raptors turned as he closed the distance. The two closest to him still had their blasters drawn. Ben hit the first one before he could fire, a vicious punch that knocked the guy out cold. The second got off a hasty shot, but it sailed past Ben's head and then Ben was on him. He grabbed the weapon, wrenched it away, and slammed him with an elbow. He turned the blaster and shot the man in the chest. The weapon was heavy and unfamiliar, but Ben was too close now to miss. He fired once, twice, three times, each shot taking out a Raptor.

The others had found cover and drawn their guns now. They looked frantically for more attackers, not believing Ben had come at them alone. Ben killed another enemy before they realized what was happening and focused their fire on him. A blast tore through his left shoulder and knocked him off balance. He recovered, unfeeling and fueled by rage, and killed the shooter with a blast to the face.

Somewhere in the back of Ben's mind, he realized he couldn't win. The initial rush had taken them by surprise, but they'd recovered and he was surrounded, out in the open. It had been less than ten seconds since he attacked. He wouldn't last five more if he kept at it like this. But fuck it, Harriet was dead and their mission a failure. For the first time in his life, he plunged ahead not caring if he won or lost.

Somebody tackled him, and he fell. The back of Ben's head struck a bit of metal. His vision swam. Someone was on top of him grasping for his blaster. He was vaguely aware that the Raptors' fire had stopped. Whoever it was jerked the blaster from his hand and thrust a knee downward, knocking Ben's breath out of him. When his vision cleared, he saw it was Tiro, a triumphant expression on his face as he turned the blaster in his hands.

Ben slapped at the barrel of the weapon, knocking it aside. He balled a fist and caught Tiro with a backhand strike across the cheek. Tiro fell sideways and the two of them scrambled to their feet. Ben was quicker. Ben kicked the weapon out of Tiro's hands. Tiro swung a fist at Ben's head instead of going for the blaster. Ben blocked it, struck, missed, took a knee to the stomach, retaliated with another punch that connected.

Ben and Tiro exchanged blows, circling one another, neither gaining the upper hand. They swung, missed, struck again with a fury of attacks and dodges. They knew each other well, had sparred playfully plenty of times in the backyard of their place in the Third Ward. Tiro was always better, but Ben had learned some things from the *Rock Badger*'s crew and he fought now with rage and urgency he'd never shown before. His shoulder was on fire with pain from the shot he'd taken. He gritted his teeth and ignored his body's protests, pushing himself on.

Ben became vaguely aware of the other Raptors standing, watching, weapons drawn but unwilling to fire with Tiro in the way. Ben grew tired. Each breath didn't bring him enough air. Still Tiro came, looking as fresh as ever, but Ben knew his strength was flagging too. Tiro was always a good actor.

Just when Ben thought he couldn't throw another punch, Tiro disengaged. His friend backed away, out of Ben's reach, and dropped his guard. Ben didn't follow, either out of fatigue or bewilderment.

"I see you picked up some new moves," Tiro said. He smiled and his voice was even, but a strained undercurrent to his speech betrayed how tired he was.

Ben said nothing, afraid that if he spoke he'd lose hold of whatever adrenaline was keeping him upright. Already the uneasy feeling of five blasters trained on him was causing him to lose his resolve.

Tiro looked around at the Raptors Ben had killed. He shook his head. "Why'd you have to come after us, man? Look at this shit. I don't want to have to kill you. You could've just stayed put. Are you mad about us shooting up your Titan Intel contractors? Nothing but spies, I don't care what you call them. You're better off with them dead. We all are."

"They were my friends," Ben said.

"We're your friends!" Tiro shouted, his face red and spit flying from his mouth. He pounded his chest. "I'm your friend! Jess is. Miles," he said through gritted teeth. "You killed him for those Intel clowns. I should have ended you when I first put it together."

"You attacked us, Tiro. Remember? Asher Garrison ambushed the *Rock Badger*. You made the choice to sign on with him and bring Miles along. That's on you, not me."

Ben struck a nerve. Quick as lightning, Tiro rushed at him, swinging a fist too quick for Ben to dodge. The blow connected and sent Ben to the ground. He rolled as he landed, got to his feet quickly, but Tiro was on him again and Ben couldn't find enough space to defend himself. His friend landed a series of heavy blows to the head and stomach. Ben took an elbow that bloodied his nose, then a shot to the chin that left him seeing stars.

Ben fell to his knees, then forward onto his hands. Tiro kicked him in the ribs, and Ben's chest erupted in pain. He wheezed as he drew in a breath, shuddered when he exhaled. He'd awoken Tiro's blind rage by laying the blame for Miles on him, and there was no more chance of mercy or reason. Tiro was going to kill him, one fist or knee or boot at a time. Ben scrambled away, trying desperately to get to his feet, but Tiro kicked him in the back and knocked him flat on his stomach.

Ben coughed, a fine red spray erupting from his mouth and painting the ground in front of his face. His view of it blurred as he struggled to focus his vision. Tiro stood over him, saying something about being more disappointed than anything else, how with everything they'd been through together he couldn't believe it was coming to this. Ben was only halfway hearing it. His mind was on Simon. He was sad to be leaving his kid brother behind. Would he even know what had happened? Or would Titan Intel just tell him he'd been killed in some sort of accident?

His mind was on Harriet too. He forced himself to remember her, not those last terrible moments where Tiro had killed her, but the way she'd been before. Her laugh, her focus, her fierce love for Titan and everything it stood for. He thought about all they'd been through together, her willingness to teach him everything she knew about the Aurora and how to channel it. She'd saved him when his injuries and lack of ability allowed it to overwhelm him. She'd showed him its power, opened doors for him he never knew existed. He'd failed her and the others miserably, never had learned to do much with the Aurora, but that hadn't been Harriet's fault.

Ben's eyes snapped open. His strength was failing, but he clung to the thought of his gem and the Aurora. It was the one hope he had. Even now Harriet was saving him, thoughts of her showing him the one advantage that still remained.

He reached into his pocket, fumbled for his gem between Tiro's blows. His friend was still ranting about something, but Ben's focus was single-minded now. He got hold of the gem; it slipped from his fingers. He grabbed again, managed to hang on this time, and pulled it from his pocket. With a surge of energy he didn't know he had, he got up and ran from Tiro, buying himself precious distance and a split second to act. He opened the gem, found the program, and pulled his implant back to 90.

The world brightened. Tiro stood out like a living chrome statue coming for him. He was no longer his friend, no longer even an enemy, just a human-shaped flow of energy lashing out at him with power and intention. Ben saw it and countered with his own energy, precise and focused. He dodged Tiro's attack as easily as water moving past the body of a swimmer, then directed a powerful blow to Tiro's center. He was aware of his friend's cry, not as a sound coming to his ears but as ripples of energy, his friend's loss of balance and focus. Ben struck again, feeling the world's energy coming into him now, not exactly restoring his strength but allowing him to act with more force than he could muster on his own. Sunlight fueled his muscles, drove his fists and his legs, carried him a power that could counter his friend and more.

A blaze of light flew past him, far more than he could absorb or channel safely. There was another, and another, they were coming faster now. The Raptors were shooting at him, bursts of plasma that carried more light and heat than he could handle.

Ben ran. He used the blaze of energy coming to him to get away, his feet carrying him so fast he was nearly flying. He put distance between himself and the Raptors, leaving Tiro behind angry but too injured from Ben's attack to follow.

Ben ran until he could run no more. The mad dash took him through a swath of the forest west of AMRI. Underbrush tangled his legs and tripped him more than once. Thorns and the rough bark of trees tore at his skin. It reminded him of the time he ran in the jungle, just a few days ago, when he'd first realized Tiro and Jess were part of this conflict. His throat constricted as he remembered how Harriet had come to save him, knowing that this time she wouldn't be coming.

He finally stopped running, his energy spent. He didn't know if he'd run one kilometer or thirty. Ben hoped he'd gotten far enough away. He was too tired to run anymore. He decided to hide, just in case the Raptors had pursued him. He concealed himself below the root ball of a fallen tree, in a hollow spot in the ground that was surrounded by leaves.

When he was well hidden, he turned his implant back to 100. The world dimmed to normal as the last of the energy coursing through him began to subside. Ben relaxed, only now really feeling the pain in his shoulder and chest from a blaster shot, a broken rib, and who knew how many other injuries. He was so tired.

"Ben." Tiro's voice startled him. It was way too close, almost right beside him. Ben jumped, instinctively shrinking back into the little shallow in the ground.

"I know you're out there, Ben." Ben breathed a little easier when he realized the voice was coming from his gem. Tiro was broadcasting it, hoping to send him a message. "I know you can hear me. We're not going to look for you. Your team is dead. You lost. I'm sorry it's come to this, but you had more than your fair share of chances. You could have joined us or left us alone. This is your last one. No more. Leave. Go do something else with your life. If I see you, I'll kill you."

A roar sounded from far off as something blinked a bright reflection off to the east. Tiro's dropship raised up into the sky and took off, leaving the destruction of his friends' ship behind.

Ben laid his head against the dirt and closed his eyes. His hands and legs began to shake in the aftermath of what he'd just witnessed and done. He'd taken life. Killed not just one person but six or seven. Damn, he really didn't even know how many, did he? He'd seen his friends murdered and nearly met the same fate himself. It was all too much. He wanted to sleep, but all he could do was shake and weep and try to breathe.

Chapter 38

Ben groaned as he woke, his side feeling like someone had plunged a hot knife between his ribs. He sat up slowly, wincing with every wrong move that sent a fresh wave of pain radiating outward. He peeked out from the hole he'd been hiding in, through the stringy tree roots and clumps of dirt hanging from them. The ground beyond was damp, the sky still bright outside. It looked like midafternoon. Ben must've fallen asleep after all, but he couldn't have been out for more than an hour.

What was he going to do? For the first time in months, he was truly alone. Free. Nobody was keeping track of his whereabouts. Nobody would be coming to rouse him and tell him to get on with the mission, they had work to do. Nobody would point to the deal he'd cut with Nichols, remind him of his responsibility and calling as a citizen of Titan, challenge himself to be the best. Anybody who would have done that was dead.

The bitter thought crashed over him and pulled him under. Dead. Harriet was dead. So were Eric, Jones, Captain Lawrence. Krista, and Levi too. As if that weren't enough, his mind turned to Mike and Christian and Aaron, remembering the crushing finality of his first taste of friends dying in the heat of battle.

At least Mike and the others who died on the *Rock Badger* had the dignity of going down fighting. The rest had been murdered, held still by the foam that was supposed to keep them safe while Raptors burned their lives away.

Ben cried again, racking his body and weeping until no more tears would come. The salty water dripped from his cheeks and made splashes on the ground before soaking into the earth and disappearing. His body shook with sobs, each convulsion sending a lance of pain into his ribs. Ben welcomed the agony. Suffering it kept him grounded, prevented him from dwelling on the pressure mounting in his chest, the icy weight in his stomach, the tangible regret over what Tiro had done and what Ben could have done, should have done, to stop it.

Why hadn't he attacked Tiro sooner? Why hadn't he flown just a little better, maintained control of his ship so he could reach his friends faster and rescue them before Garrison's team arrived? Why hadn't he thought about the *Blue Fin* using a Lightbeam from orbit and warned the others? Why, why, why, why, why?

He wanted to dig deeper into his hole, bury himself under the tree, shut out the world. Somewhere deep down, he knew that path led nowhere. He'd never been the type to feel sorry for himself. Nobody would know if he gave up now or indulged a few moments wallowing in self-pity. Nobody would see. But what good would it do? It wouldn't bring his friends back. Wouldn't bring Harriet back. He had to find a way to keep going. For them. For her.

Keep going. Just put one foot in front of the other. But where? His companions were gone and their mission a failure. Asher Garrison would leave Earth today, if he hadn't already, to take the heavy Dorium out to the Raptors. How soon after that would VESA set them loose on the Colonies? Months? Weeks?

But really, what did it matter? Jess was right, the Raptors were bad news mostly for the wealthy of Titan. How much did their actions harm people like Ben, who lived in the Third Ward and scrapped or stole for every advantage? Would being governed by VESA, in the end, be so much worse than an independent Titan? How much of Titan would really be upended by a change of leadership?

So Ben would return to a changed Titan. But what else was there? He sure as hell couldn't make a life for himself in the Interior, for all he'd tried to make such a choice sound plausible to Tiro and Jess. His friends would still be on Titan, he hoped. Axel and Tory and Dom. Simon too. Ben crawled out of his hole and stood up. He wiped the mud from his hands and opened his gem. He pulled up a local map. Luxor was to the west. The big river that ran through it was to the north. It looked like the most straightforward route would be to get to the river and follow it to the city. It would be longer, sure, but why hurry? Ben sighed and started walking north.

The huge pile of metal and foam thudded to the ground behind the dropship, swirling dust. It rolled a couple of meters before settling to a stop. The lumpy thing was as wide as the whole ship, and almost half as tall. Asher Garrison watched with a mixture of curiosity and disdain.

"What the hell is this?" he said as Tiro exited the transport. "And where are the rest of you?"

"Ben Ashley put up a hell of a fight. Caught us by surprise and killed the others."

Garrison took in the survivors and did some math. "Seven? He killed fucking seven? One guy?"

"I told you he was a badass. That's why I wanted to get him on our crew. Too late for that now."

"So you got him?"

Tiro nodded. He flicked his eyes to Jess, who was standing nearby and listening. Her face paled and fell with a flash of regret, but she quickly masked the reaction.

"Well I guess that's something." Garrison lifted his eyes and spoke to the others. "We'll talk about you idiots getting caught by surprise later. You all will be responsible for your fallen crew members' work for the foreseeable future. If you can't kill one fucking guy before he did that much damage, you'll have to make yourselves useful in other ways." He turned to the heap they'd towed here from the crash site. "Now tell me what this is. It better not be my Dorium."

"No, sir," Tiro said. "We recovered the Dorium intact. All five boxes, all full. All accounted for." He gestured to the boxes, which were stacked haphazardly beside the transport. He turned to the big mess in question. "This is…our enemies. Or what's left of them. That orange material is crash foam. It deployed just before impact."

"They're alive in there?"

"Probably not. We lit them up with plasma. Figured they'd be less trouble if they were dead on arrival. Is that a problem, sir?"

Garrison narrowed his eyes and thought. "You made the right call. Shoot first, ask questions later. Even one guy can cause problems." He glared at Tiro. "Too bad you found that out the hard way."

"It won't happen again, sir," Tiro said.

"Damn right it won't. Tag!"

A young man who was busy by the second dropship looked up, stopped what he was doing, and jogged over. "Sir?"

"This stuff is supposed to have medical diagnostics, right?" Garrison gestured toward the crash foam. "There's an unknown number of occupants inside, maybe alive, likely dead. Can your instruments interface with it, tell us who's in there and their status?"

Tag gave a curt nod. He wasn't the *Blue Fin*'s primary doctor, but he had a lot of medical training and was a quick study. He was competent and confident. Garrison liked him.

The young man ran back to the dropship, retrieved a bag full of medical tools and sensors, and quickly found a small device with a sharp probe at the end of a cord. He turned on the device and shoved the probe a few centimeters into the crash foam.

Garrison watched with fascination. "That's it?"

"The foam contains several thousand nanobots, which are deployed to detect and treat injuries after a crash. When they sense the probe, they upload all the data they've collected. There we go."

Tag's device cast a holo display in the air above it, with six different columns of data. He took in the report quickly, scrolled through two of the columns, then shut down the display. "They're all dead. Two of the bodies have injuries consistent with a crash—they were bad but survivable. All the mortal wounds look like plasma fire."

Garrison nodded as Tag disconnected the probe and packed the device back up.

"All right. These guys caused a hell of a mess. The American Commonwealth and several other Earth authorities are shitting their pants over military action at AMRI. They've got eyes on the sky and local space, so we're not going anywhere for a while. VESA tells me they can smooth things over. In the meantime, our delivery boys from the Balle Corporation are still here. Get them to walk a few of you through assembling those Lightbeam weapons. I want a lot of us fluent in these weapons, it'll give us leverage when we're dealing with our fellow Raptors."

Tag and several other Raptors turned to follow the command. Tiro started to go with them, but Garrison called him back. "Not you, Washburn. Hook this back up to the dropship and return it to the crash site."

Tiro blinked. "We're going to leave them here?"

"Not here. At the crash site."

"But what about information? Ransom?"

"We already accessed their gems, we won't learn anything else from these guys. And nobody's gonna pay ransom. They're contractors working for spies. Titan doesn't want the bodies. They don't want them to exist at all. Leaving them here for Earth's authorities to find and ID will cause Titan Intel a lot of trouble, keep the heat off us, and make VESA happy. Win, win, win."

Tiro nodded. That made a lot of sense, and he'd just as soon not have to deal with six bodies. "Yes, sir."

The river wound along to Ben's right, broad, swift, and muddy. From up here at the top of its steep southern bank, the current seemed slow, almost casual. Ben had been walking for a few hours now, stopping to rest whenever the pain in his side grew too unbearable. His gem told him he had hundreds more kilometers to go before he'd reach Luxor. At this rate it would take him many days to reach it. What did it matter? There was no urgency.

The air had cooled and grown humid since his last stop. A breeze was blowing from the west and had picked up noticeably in the last hour or so. The clouds overhead were growing thicker.

In his mind Ben saw the flashes of blaster fire, over and over again. He saw the sky split with flame cutting through the dropship carrying his friends. He shook his head, tried to think of something else. He saw Harriet turn away from him at the end. Heard her words. *You betrayed us. We needed you at your best, and you took yourself out of the equation.*

Ben replayed the scenes of his friends' demise, rehearsed his decisions that led to it. Why had he told Tiro and Jess about the *Rock Badger*'s crew? What was he thinking, trying to save his friends? They'd made their choice to join Garrison and apparently had no problem leaving him in jail on Titan. Why was he always trying to do too much? Save his friends. Save Titan. How could he do any of that when time and time again, he hadn't even been able to save himself? Well, he wasn't going to try to do too much now. Save himself, if he could. Find a way back to Titan. Just focus on the road in front of him, one foot in front of another. Pick up the pieces and move on as best he could.

A sense of unease began to gnaw at him, growing more insistent with each step. Despite the pain in his chest and soreness in his muscles, Ben tensed with nervous energy. He flexed his fingers, felt his breathing pick up. Adrenaline. Part of Ben wanted to act, to fight, to do something other than just lick his wounds and regroup. He pushed the feeling down. What good would it do to go back and die, if Garrison and his Raptors were even still around? It was just sadness and regret messing with him, the desire to change the past that was too late to undo. He breathed deep and kept walking.

A low rumble sounded in the distance ahead of Ben. He looked up, saw flashes of light in the sky. For a terrifying second he thought the *Blue Fin* was attacking again, raining down hellfire in the form of another Lightbeam. But it didn't look the same as before, and the devastation never came. He decided it must be something else. The clouds brightened and dimmed as if illuminated from within, and bright jagged streaks appeared at the horizon. The wind grew stronger and the sky darker. A dot of water appeared on his sleeve.

What was it Harriet had told him? *The outcome may be out of your control—it usually is—and the odds of success might be terrible. But you can always choose what course to pursue.…If you knew, whatever else happens, it will work out somehow, what would you try to accomplish?*

He'd answered that question before. He wanted it all. Save Tiro and Jess and Titan. Well, he knew where that kind of thinking would take him. Ben had made a mess of everything. Betrayed the crew of the *Rock Badger* just as he was beginning to feel like he belonged. Sabotaged their mission and gotten them all killed.

Ben shivered and shuddered, feeling afresh the absence of his friends and that it was his fault. He choked out a sob and clenched his teeth. Ben had lost so much, had so many people taken from him. He thought back over his life, not just the last couple of months but the last couple of years. How many of his own mistakes had been to save somebody else? He got a future for Simon at the expense of his own. He got Axel away at The Occident the day he was arrested, and he managed to help Axel and Tory and Dom escape Bradley. He'd tried to save Tiro and Jess. Look where it had all gotten him.

The lights continued in the sky ahead, and the distant rumbling grew closer and more frequent. More dots of water appeared on Ben's shirt, and a couple of drops splashed his face. He looked over to the river but couldn't see anything flinging water all the way up the bank. The wind was making agitated ripples on the surface, but there was no other movement.

Ben started running. He had to get away. From what? From the past. From the future. From the damn present that was so full of sorrow and anguish. He wanted to outrun the moment, the now, with its harvest of yesterday's failures and seeds of tomorrow that promised only bitterness.

Running again. The words came to him in a voice he didn't quite recognize. Maybe Harriet's. Maybe his own. Maybe some combination of the two. *Running again.* Ben was running again. But what else was there to do? *Stay here. Now. fight. You always have a choice.*

Despair nearly got the better of him, then. He stopped, looked around, suddenly feeling like no direction was the right one. Running was fruitless, and he was so tired of it. It was too much, as if a balloon were inflating in his stomach and would burst any minute. His past and future were colliding in this single, electric moment that was too small to hold them both. Back to Luxor. Back to AMRI. Up. Down. No course seemed worthwhile. There was no way to escape his pain, no way to undo all that had happened. Ben stopped and closed his eyes tight.

He was lost, unsure of where he was going and unsure, really, of where he had even been. All the potential he once saw for himself stood in relief against the path he'd actually taken in the end. How was it that he'd ended up here? Part of him wanted to just dive in the river and swim downstream, forget it all and make his own way somewhere else, start over totally disconnected from the fraught past he couldn't reconcile with the road in front of him.

Once again he felt that tightness in his chest, longing and frustration building inside him, overshadowing the pain of his broken rib. He growled at himself. He wanted everything to be different, but he couldn't undo it. So why was he feeling this urge to go find Garrison, to find Tiro, to fight? There were God knows how many Raptors, all armed, and Ben was injured and alone. What good would it do to throw his life away? There was no choice to be made here. The world left him only one path, guiding him back to Luxor, back to Titan eventually. Yes, his mistakes were part of that equation, but weren't they always? He couldn't go back and undo those any more than he could change anything else. It didn't matter what he wanted. This was the only way.

No. It wasn't. *You always have a choice.*

Ben stopped, raised his eyes to the sky as the truth of Harriet's words filled him. She was right, as usual. He couldn't keep going, not this way. He'd spent his whole life running. He wasn't going to run anymore.

A certainty took hold of him then, a recognition of his ability and the responsibility he had to use it. The road ahead was the hard road, and he had to be the one to walk it. Nobody but Ben could answer for what he did, which meant nobody else could claim it for themselves. His life belonged to him, not to Harriet or Tiro or Jess or Titan. Not even to his little brother, Simon, as much as he loved the kid. It was for Ben and Ben alone to choose, to decide how to direct the energy he'd been given, his life, to assert his claim over it if anybody else tried to choose for him.

He turned and began walking back toward AMRI. *This is stupid*, he thought. Some small remainder of fear and self-preservation trying to reason with him. *You're walking forward into certain death. What good is this going to do?* Even so, he felt strangely at peace with his decision. He would fight. He would die. What else was there?

The sky erupted. A lance of electricity streaked through the clouds, and the air shook with a terrible boom as if the heavens were tearing in two. Torrents of water began to fall from above, drenching Ben before he knew what was happening. Thousands of raindrops slapping the river bank created a roar that drowned out all other sound, except for the crackling explosions in the sky that Ben now knew must be thunder. He ducked his head and looked around for shelter but saw none. He kicked himself. *Stupid offworlder*. He'd been too distracted with his own struggle to think about his surroundings, and he hadn't understood what it was until the rain was right on top of him.

There were trees a couple hundred meters to the south. Ben ran for them, then slowed again to a walk after a few dozen meters. His clothes were already soaked through, and tiny streams were running down his hair and face. The thunder and lightning were probably dangerous, but running or walking wouldn't make much of a difference. He'd already run from so much. He'd determined not to run away from Tiro and Jess and Asher Garrison now. Why bother running away from this? The thought was oddly reassuring. Sometimes all it took to be strong was to choose strength. Here he was, wet and uncomfortable, cold despite the hot, humid day, but here. Surviving. Existing in the storm. Defying nature itself by his refusal to run. That was something. After every defeat he'd suffered, that was something.

Ben stepped in a puddle. His boots splashed some of the water into another, larger puddle beside it. Something about that caught his eye, and he stopped. The rain pounded his back right through his clothes, as if he weren't wearing a shirt at all. He looked down at the two little pools of water, ignoring the rain streaming into his eyes. There. It was hard to see with the raindrops splashing and making ripples, but there it was. A narrow stream connected the smaller puddle with the larger one. And from the larger puddle, another stream led away to one more, back toward the river.

A chill ran down Ben's back, not just from the rain falling on him. He turned away from the trees and back toward the river. He followed the water from one puddle to the next, then to another. Closer to the river they all ran together, connecting and dividing and crisscrossing like exposed capillaries of the Earth itself. Ben walked right up to the river bank, and looked out at the rain falling on the water's surface. To his left a stream was already rushing down the slope, crashing over rocks and sending ripples outward where it met the river.

It's all one.

The realization hit him like one of those great lightning strikes in the air overhead. The river, the ocean, the rain. His tears, even. It was all one. The clouds dumped water from high above. It gathered in trenches, puddles, ponds, underground aquifers, and great lakes. Then they sprung up, or flowed out and down, over the land and into a creek, a stream, a tributary, one of the great arteries like the expansive Mississippi. All the way to the sea. But it didn't end there. Carried by currents, the water swirled, moved, heated and cooled, nourished life, froze, thawed. Sooner or later it rose to the surface and then back up, away, carried in the warm air to the clouds, where it would swirl, bob, coalesce, and fall once more. Land, sea, sky. A single great river, always on the move.

It was the same with this world's energy, Ben saw. With every world's energy. With the universe's energy. Just as there was one river of water, there was one way of energy. Carried in the exchange of photons and the curving of space-time, energy flows, always moving, always connected. From the outside to the center, down, down, then heated and stirred and back out, away, spinning, moving, flowing. It resides in matter for a time, in life for a time, then back to space. Back to the flow. Back to the in-and-out. Back to the universe.

The River is one. The flow of water on this world, the great Mississippi and the world-ocean it feeds, is a small tributary of the one River. Warmed by the flow from the Sun, pulled toward the lake and the ocean by the pooled energy held for a time in the dense gathered matter called Earth. The Sun's flow feeds other suns, just as other suns, long dead, have fed our Sun. The River is one. It flows from the Beginning, toward all things, away from all things, through all times and belonging to no time. One flow. One River.

These thoughts captured Ben's mind as he stood there, enveloped by the falling rain, seeing it drip past his eyes, feeling it flow into his mouth and ears, watching it stream off his fingertips and down, down to the ground where it gathered in a puddle and began making its way inevitably toward the river.

The universe was a River, and he was part of it.

In that flash of awareness he attained mastery of the Aurora that had eluded him for so long. There was no furnace burning inside Ben. He was not the source of energy within himself any more than the river was the source of water that flowed through it. He could hold energy for time, but it was never his. Never his.

Without thinking he brought out his gem and took his implant down to 80. He opened himself to the energy of the world, imagining it as a great flow that neither began nor ended with himself. It was easy, effortless. He felt the energy move through his body, gathered it in his center, moved it out to his hands or feet as naturally as a cook stirring water in a pot. He reveled in the sensation, feeling the connection with every creature of the universe, mediated by the ageless photons swirling from them to him and back.

Ben closed his eyes and felt the energy course through his body, swirl around and through his broken rib, and leave it whole and strong.

He reached out his hand and fingers, felt the energy move with him.

He opened his palm and cast the energy from him like a child splashing in a bathtub and watched in delight as a spray of mud shot up from the ground, leaving a wide divot that soon filled with rainwater. He held out both hands and formed a bright orb of light in each one, flung them both out into the river where they made twin geysers of hissing spray. He laughed and took off running through the rain.

He must have looked like a madman sprinting back and forth in great strides, heedless of the thunder or lightning or the fact that he was soaked to the bone. Ben felt for the first time the energy of the universe, heard its song, and felt alive and powerful like he never had before.

He stopped going back and forth and ran straight ahead, back east toward AMRI, sprinting with the energy of the world as his fuel. His blood pumped and the rain poured down. Asher Garrison and his crew were probably long gone from AMRI by now, but that was OK. Ben would find a ship and chase them down if he had to.

Chapter 39

By the time Ben got to the crater, the downpour had stopped. The dark clouds sat to the east, flashes of lightning still showing among them. Overhead and to the west it was bright, with broken clouds cluttering the blue sky. The late afternoon sun beamed down and made the air hot and sticky, doing little to dry up the puddles and droplets of water that covered everything.

He'd decided to return to the crash site before pursuing Garrison. It wasn't much of a detour, and there was a chance Tiro had left something useful in the cargo hold. He'd been interested only in the Dorium, and the Raptors had taken off quickly after Ben escaped them. Jones had stolen the ship in a hurry, and there was no telling what else was inside. Maybe weapons or food or at the very least a dry set of clothes.

Ben reached the crater and looked around cautiously. The Raptors were almost certainly long gone, but he didn't want any surprises. As he took in the scene, something bugged him. It didn't look right, but he couldn't put his finger on it. He focused on the idea, tried to assess what was bothering him. Danger? No, that didn't seem likely. The place was quiet, but not that eerie kind of quiet where you feel like you're being watched.

He closed his eyes, pictured the scene from earlier. It looked just like he'd pictured it before. Nothing had been distrubed. Even the bodies of the Raptors he'd killed had been taken away. Tiro must have taken them back to Garrison's drop ship. He opened his eyes and looked again. Yes, there. The bodies had been close to the cockpit, but now they were gone. Then it hit him. The cockpit.

Tiro had told his team to load up the cockpit, but it was still here. Maybe Tiro hadn't taken it after all. It was different—in the same place as before but turned on its side. Or maybe its back, it was hard to tell given the shape it was in. Tiro must have tried to load it up, found it was too heavy to transport, and left it here. Ben wondered if the Raptors had taken his friends' bodies too. He decided to go investigate.

The crash foam looked undisturbed. Charred and full of holes and otherwise shot to hell, but no visible seams where the stuff had opened.

Ben placed his hands against the orange foam, closed his eyes, and let out a breath. Harriet was in here. Krista and Eric and the others too. It didn't feel right to just leave them. He bowed his head and whispered their names, slowly, one by one, picturing each of their faces. When he finished, he decided to bury them. Somebody would come to investigate the crash sooner or later, and he knew they wouldn't honor them as he would. He would bury them, together, and say goodbye in his own way. It wasn't much, but it was the best he could do.

Ben took a breath, steeled himself for the sight of his friends dead, afraid of how they would look after plasma tore through them in countless places. He tried to make himself ready, then realized it wasn't the kind of thing he could prepare himself for. Better to just get on with it.

He placed a hand once more, reverently, on the foam. "Open," he said.

The voice caught him by surprise. "Cockpit and occupants have been displaced from impact location. Assessing new site and condition of occupants. Stand by."

Odd, Ben thought. The cockpit had definitely shifted, but it was still in pretty much the same place as before. It was hardly at a new crash site. Whatever detectors the thing had must be especially sensitive.

"Site is secure. Six subjects detected," the calm voice said. "Three subjects unresponsive with critical injuries to vital organs. Three subjects stable with serious but noncritical injuries. Releasing stable subjects."

Ben blinked. Had he heard that right? Nobody deceased? Three subjects stable and responsive? He gasped as his heart soared with hope, which he refused to entertain until he saw for himself.

Three seams appeared in the crash foam and slowly began to widen. Ben was nervous, confused, hopeful. The crash foam's sensors must be damaged. Nobody could have survived those blasts, right? But it was functional enough to speak to him and open on command. As the seams opened wider, a ray of light crept into his mind. What if they had survived after all? What if Harriet was alive?

Spurred by the idea, Ben reached into the first seam and pulled with both hands, trying in vain to make it part faster.

"Jones!" he said when the seam had widened far enough to let him look inside. Her eyes were open and focused on him. "Are you all right?"

"Yeah," she groaned. "I was hit but it's not bad."

There was a large, jagged hole in the foam to her right, where no seams appeared. "Who was beside you?" Ben asked.

"Lawrence," she said.

"Damn." Ben closed his eyes tight, then opened them and spoke to Jones. "I think he's critically injured. This stuff is opening slow but you'll be able to move soon. I'll be right back." He rushed over to the next seam and looked inside. Eric was there, a pained expression on his face, but he seemed alert.

"Eric, are you injured?"

"Arm. Hurts like hell." He coughed, and a line of thick, red liquid dripped from his mouth. Eric licked his lips and gave a bitter smile. "Lungs, too, I guess." There was a slash through the foam where Ben guessed Eric's abdomen was.

"You've been shot," Ben said, "but I don't think this stuff would release you if injuries were critical."

Eric shook his head as much as he could in the foam. "It's got some basic diagnostics and medicine, nanobots, enough to stabilize most wounds. If it's letting me out, I'll be all right."

"Jones is conscious, too, but hurt. Is there a med kit?"

"Back of cargo hold, if it survived."

Ben nodded. "I'll find it."

"What about the others?" Eric asked. He coughed again.

"The foam said three are unresponsive with critical injuries. I don't know who. Let me go check on Jones and find that med kit. Sit tight."

He jumped back to check on Jones, who assured him that she was still OK, then darted off to find the med kit.

He ran to what was left of the cargo hold and tore through bits of twisted metal where he guessed the back of the ship was. It was hard to tell. He'd almost given up when he spotted a heavy white box with a red cross on it, a universally recognized sign of medical aid. It was badly dented and scratched but looked intact. These things were built to survive a lot.

The box was mostly buried under outer hull panels, and one of the ship's girders was pinning it to the floor. Sweat dripped from Ben's face as he struggled to move the thick panels. The first two came off OK after some effort, the third after he used the first one as a lever. The girder didn't budge right away, but he finally managed to roll it off and get the med kit clear.

Ben dragged it back to the crash foam, where Eric was almost fully released. His friend lay back, eyes closed and breathing through pain. His left arm was badly swollen, and there was a round, black spot on his lower abdomen that Ben guessed was a plasma blast.

Ben opened the box and looked in, totally clueless as to what anything was for or how to use it. He picked up a large package. Maybe these were bandages?

"Bring that here," Eric said. He gestured with his good arm toward the box, waving frantically for Ben to grab something. Ben held out the bandages. "Not that. The other one." Ben tried again. "Jesus, kid. That one!"

Ben finally found what Eric was after and brought it to him. He started to open the package, but Eric slapped him on the hand. "I got it."

Ben sat back and looked over to Jones, who was now free of the crash foam and sitting up. Her right shoulder had a nasty gash across it and she winced as she moved her arm back and forth, but she seemed to be all right.

"Nothing broken," Jones said. She pointed to her shoulder. "Whatever this was just grazed me. Doesn't hurt as bad right now."

"Tiro and the Raptors were here after you crashed. They fired into the foam, I guess trying to take out any survivors."

"Bastards," Jones said.

"Yeah."

The third seam was open wide enough now. Ben raced over to it, praying it was Harriet. He saw Levi already trying to sit up, and his heart sank. "Levi, are you hurt?" he asked, trying to hide the disappointment in his voice.

"I don't think so. I felt somebody shoot me in the leg but it's not hurting now. Don't know what that's about."

"Painkillers," Eric said, still working on himself. He was applying some sort of gel to the hole in his torso, grimacing with each touch. "The crash foam has painkillers. Probably treated your wound with that. It's why you aren't hurting too bad."

"Makes sense. You all right?"

Eric finished up and nodded. "I'll get some bone gel for my arm in a minute, but the bleeding down here has stopped and the painkillers are working now. Let's see about the others." He lifted a small, circular machine out of the med kit and began unspooling a cable from the underside of it, but it was awkward with just one good arm.

"Let me help," Ben said. He took the cable from Eric. "Just tell me what to do."

"Pull out a little more slack. Little more. There, that should be good. Find the free end and twist off that cap."

Ben turned the cap and slid it off. It was about four centimeters long, and underneath it was a pointed metal tip that made up the end of the cable. "Push that into the crash foam. Doesn't matter where," Eric said.

Ben hesitated, then found a spot and stuck the tip of the cable into it. "That's good?"

"Yeah." Eric tapped a few spots on the machine, and a holo display sprang to life in the air above it. "This lets me pull all the data from the crash foam. A lot faster than asking it a bunch of questions."

Eric's eyes darted back and forth, increasing concern showing on his face. "Captain Lawrence has a bad head injury, likely a concussion. He's unconscious. Shot through the arm and both legs too."

"Jesus," Jones whispered.

"What about Harriet?"

"Krista has a bad wound in her abdomen, lots of blood. She's in critical condition. Looks like one of the blasts caught her right through the stomach. It's fifty-fifty whether she'll make it."

"What about Harriet?" Ben asked again.

"Adams is…hmmm." Eric said.

"What?"

"Wound to the head. Looks like a blast just grazed her. Brain looks fine, but…"

"But what?"

"Her vitals are off the charts. Extreme heart rate, body temp high and rising. I don't…"

"It's the Aurora," Ben said. "Blast to the head, right? It probably damaged her implant, same as mine did before."

"We don't know that," Eric said, but Ben wasn't listening. He was reaching down toward the crash foam, eyes closed, concentrating.

"What are you doing?" Eric's voice sounded like it was muffled by a blanket, as Ben blocked out everything but the energy beneath him. He still had his implant down at 80, and now he opened himself, just like he'd done in the rain. It was effortless, the energy pulsing beneath him waiting to be listened to. The world came to him like a bright swirl, which resolved after a moment into familiar shapes, strange colors, and otherworldly movements. The brightest thing of all was an orb of light beneath his palms, right where Harriet was supposed to be.

Ben reached out toward it. He'd never tried to pull energy from a specific place before, but he knew it was possible. It was how Harriet saved him in the jungle and then again in Luxor. He remembered the River, imagined Harriet as a deep pool into which a torrent of energy was surging, overflowing her banks. He touched the pool, pictured it opening, pictured it flowing into the pool that represented himself.

The flow started right away. Harriet's energy subsided as Ben's began to increase. He didn't hold it, just let it move through him and out, away into the destroyed forest and down into the ground beneath them. He pulled the energy from Harriet until it felt right, until her glow matched that of Eric and Jones beside him.

The two watched him wide-eyed as he glowed, faint rays of light extending from him in all directions.

Ben kept his hand on the foam. He stretched himself outward toward the circuitry of her implant.

It was a small flaw. A single circuit was dark amid a tiny boiling sea of electric energy that sparked and flared around the problem spot. Ben reached out, touched the broken place, nudged it with his own energy, made one tiny adjustment after another until the flow was restored. The boil subsided, returned to a swirling simmer, and Ben let go.

Ben took his implant back to 100. He blinked as the world returned to normal. "What did you do?" Eric asked.

"Did it work?"

"You were glowing," Jones said. "These weird rays of light…"

"Did it work?" Ben asked again.

"Yeah," Eric said, watching the display. "Yeah, I think it did. Heart rate is decreasing, still stressed but now within limits, temperature is in the range of a high fever but falling slowly. She looks OK."

"Bring her out. Can you open it?"

"We should wait. Be sure she's stabilized. The foam needs to run a lot more tests to find out what was going on."

"I know what happened. Bring her out," Ben said.

Eric hesitated, looked at the display once more, looking for any reason to doubt what Ben had done. He found none, so he shrugged. He swiped through the gem, gave it a few commands and overrides, and sat back.

A seam opened in the foam and began to expand. Ben sat back, giving it some room. He looked inside, half expecting Harriet to be dead or to find that it had been Krista beneath him all along. He was fearful and hopeful at the same time.

Ben's shoulders slumped when he saw her. Harriet. A wave of relief coursed through him, then guilt at the idea that he seemed to value her life more than the others. He shook his head. No time for thoughts like that right now.

Her eyes were open, staring straight ahead. Her breathing was shallow and skin pale, but it was improving even as Ben watched.

"Are you OK?" Ben asked.

Her eyes tracked over to him and brightened with recognition. Her mouth turned up in a weak smile. "I'll live."

"What hurts?"

"Just about all of it."

"It should get better soon," Eric said. "I'm pumping you full of painkillers as we speak."

"What happened?" Harriet asked.

"The *Blue Fin* hit your ship from space. Lightbeam. Crash foam deployed, but then the Raptors came to get our Dorium. They shot up the foam."

"I know." She tapped her head. "I felt the shots coming and did my best to redirect the energy so it wouldn't hurt us. Garrison's crew took us to his dropship and I think they ran some diagnostics. I tried to convince their sensors we were dead."

"You must've succeeded. They brought you back here," Ben said.

"Smart move," Levi said. "It'd cause a lot of trouble for Titan if we were found here."

Harriet looked around at Ben, Jones, Eric, and Levi. "What about the others? Are they…"

Eric swallowed. "Krista and the captain are in bad shape. The foam is keeping them alive, but it's serious. Either of them might not make it."

Harriet closed her eyes and a tear flowed across her cheek. "So I didn't…" The words died on her lips.

Eric put his hand on hers. "You saved yourself and us. That's what you did."

Harriet nodded, keeping her eyes closed. She took several breaths, then opened her eyes suddenly. "What about me? What happened to me? My Aurora. I felt the energy growing, getting hot." She locked her eyes on Ben's.

"They damaged your implant. Bad luck. It let your Aurora run wild. The fever, heart rate, everything."

"And?"

Ben shrugged. "I fixed it."

Harriet looked at him skeptically. "You can do that now?"

"Yeah." He told them about fighting Tiro, then about the rain and the river, how he'd unlocked his abilities in the storm.

"So all it took was a shift in perspective?" Harriet asked. "Thinking of energy as a river instead of a furnace?"

Ben smiled. "I think it was more than that. It was…everything. What you've taught me, the pain when I thought it was all over. Wrestling with whether to abandon our mission or go back to Garrison to die. It was all of it. I felt not just an understanding of the way energy works but an awareness of my own place in it."

"And what now?" Harriet asked.

"Now we go finish what we started. If you all will have me again. I don't blame you if you don't want to work with me again. But I'm going back to fight, and if you want to do the same we should coordinate our efforts. If you still don't trust me, then stay out of my way."

"You fought Tiro and lost, then came back for more," Levi said. "And you stole a ship and shot down those VESA fighters that were chasing us. I think you've earned a little trust back."

"Yeah," said Jones. "I'm with you."

"Me too," said Eric.

Harriet reached out and took Ben's hand. "Let's go finish this."

Chapter 40

Eric stabilized Krista and Captain Lawrence through some medical genius Ben didn't understand. The *Blue Fin*'s dropship was as light on medical supplies as it was on everything else. They'd managed to find a single blaster rifle and some old food rations. Not exactly what they needed to storm AMRI. At least they'd make good time traveling light.

Harriet checked her gem. "Let's move out. The *Blue Fin* is still in orbit according to this. I don't know why and it could change at any minute. But that gives me hope at least that Garrison and his people are still at AMRI."

"Shouldn't one of us stay with them?" Ben asked, gesturing to the crash foam that still held Krista and the captain. "Eric, you're the doctor and you're hurt anyway. Stay here. You'll do more good keeping an eye on them."

Eric shook his head. "I got them stabilized. There's nothing I can do for them that the crash foam's nanobots aren't already doing. We need to get them to a hospital, but they're all right for now. No way I'm sitting this fight out."

"Ben's got a point. What if we don't make it back? That crash foam can't keep them alive forever," Jones said.

Eric looked around. "This is a crater, guys. Somebody is going to come search the wreckage. That's why Garrison wanted to leave us here, remember? So local authorities would find our bodies and link us with Titan Intel. It's a matter of hours before somebody comes. In fact, I bet Garrison and VESA are the reason they haven't come already. He fired from orbit with a Lightbeam. That's got to be a shitstorm, and he can't stave it off forever. If none of us makes it back, whoever comes will find and treat the captain and Krista."

"That's our captain and our first mate," Harriet said. "Think about both of them. What would they order us to do?"

"Leave them here and go kick ass," Levi said.

"All right then. Let's go."

The dropship had crashed not too far from the main road connecting AMRI and Luxor. The plan was to follow the road to AMRI's rear entrance with Ben and Harriet using their Aurora abilities to disable any sensors that might alert any guards or AI monitors. With a bit of care and luck they could take the guards by surprise and get inside before they contacted anyone.

Luck was on their side for once. About halfway down the access road, Harriet motioned for them to stop. "Listen," she whispered.

"A vehicle?" Eric asked.

"Sounds like it. I hear it too," Ben said. He listened for a few seconds. "It's up ahead. It's gotta be coming from AMRI, right?"

Jones nodded. "And it sounds like it's alone."

They came up with a plan and got in place just as the truck rounded the bend. Eric lay in the road pretending to be injured. Harriet stood beside him waving for the truck to stop. "Please help," she said as the driver slowed and rolled his window down. It was a large truck, with a driver and passenger up front and a closed-off box for goods in the back. The truck had the Balle Corporation logo on the side. It was probably the same one that brought the Lightbeam components to Garrison earlier.

"Get out of the road," the driver called.

"My friend's hurt," she said.

"So call somebody. We're not allowed to stop. Move it."

Harriet stepped toward the window. The guy leaned out, watching Eric. "He's conscious. What's the problem? Get him up and off the road, lady. This is a restricted area."

Harriet smiled. "I thought it might be. I'm sorry. I just—" she reached forward and jerked the man through the window. He hit the ground hard and reached behind his back. Harriet hit him again before he could grab whatever he was going for.

"Alice!" he yelled.

"She's a little busy at the moment," Jones said from the other side of the truck. "Move slow, Alice." The passenger scooted across the seat and out the driver's side, with Jones's blaster trained on her the whole time.

"There are more of us, you know," she said.

"Thanks for the heads-up, but I think we're good," Harriet said. She looked toward the back of the truck. "Are we good, boys?"

Levi and Ben jumped out. "Yeah, we're good. Four of them inside, but I only had to fight three. Ashley's all right when he gets the drop on somebody," Levi said. Ben rolled his eyes.

Harriet relieved the driver and five passengers of their gems and weapons. They didn't get much, but the driver was carrying a sidearm and one of the passengers had a rifle in the back. With Jones's blaster, that upped their gun count to three.

Harriet tied their prisoners' hands behind them, then made them stand back-to-back. She tied their hands together tightly so they made a big, awkward circle, and made them kick their shoes off. She threw their shoes into the woods. Then she tied everyone's legs together at the knees and ankles. They would probably find a way to get free, eventually, but it would take awhile. In the meantime they wouldn't go far or have a way to call anybody.

"Thanks for the truck, guys, Don't go anywhere," Harriet said as she climbed into the driver's seat.

The driver yelled some kind of curse that Ben didn't catch. Levi jumped out of the back and walked over to them. He glared down at the driver for a moment, then gave him a light shove sideways. The driver lost his balance and fell to the ground, taking his companions down with him. They fell in a tangle of tied-together arms and hands and bodies. Levi smirked and walked back to the truck, leaving them cursing behind him.

"Was that really necessary?" Harriet asked as he passed.

Levi shrugged. "It was fun."

Harriet drove them to AMRI's back entrance. She and Eric were up front, with Ben, Jones, and Levi in the back.

They got to the gate and slowed to a stop.

"You guys forget something?" the first guard said as he approached.

Harriet put her gun in his face and ordered him not to move. Eric and Jones jumped out and moved to either side of the gate, with Ben and Levi following them. In a matter of seconds they had subdued all four guards without anyone raising the alarm.

They took gems and tied the guards together in the same way as the others, back-to-back and leg-to-leg. This time Harriet and Ben tied them to a tree about fifteen meters into the woods, out of sight. She made them take their shoes off, too, and threw them away on the other side of the road.

"Why the shoes thing?" Ben asked as they walked back.

"It's uncomfortable and makes it hard to run," Harriet said. "But mostly it reminds them who's in charge."

Ben blinked.

"What?" Harriet asked.

"Nothing, just…Damn."

They got back in the truck and Jones opened the gate. Harriet drove them inside, making their way toward the hangars and the Raptors. She parked them beside a handful of other trucks. They got out and scanned the open area where ships landed. There were a few more VESA fighters and several local transports in the vicinity, but the *Blue Fin*'s dropships weren't visible.

"Where are they?" Ben asked.

Harriet growled in frustration. "Did they take off? Please tell me they didn't take off."

Jones had a holo open on her gem. "The *Blue Fin*'s still up there. I'm not showing anything on an orbital trajectory from AMRI."

"Must be in one of the hangars," Levi said.

"Let's go see."

They checked the first hangar, but it was empty except for local transports and cargo fresh off the monorail. The second hangar looked much the same, and Harriet motioned them on to the third.

"Wait," Eric said. "Listen."

Ben heard it too—the unmistakable sound of Asher Garrison's voice. They crept farther inside, past several stacks of containers and a few ships. About fifteen Raptors had cleared some space on the floor. Ben saw Jess and Tiro among them, alongside the Raptor captain. Several smaller containers lay open with various metal and carbon components strewn about.

"Lightbeams," Ben whispered. One of the devices was fully assembled. It was a thick metal cylinder, about two meters long, attached to a boxy housing on one end and surrounded by a tight collection of hoses and protrusions. The Raptors with Garrison were disassembling and repacking everything while Garrison barked orders.

"Looks like they're packing up to leave," Eric said. "We got here just in time."

"Over there," Levi said. He pointed to the far end of the area the Raptors had cleared. There were the five boxes of heavy Dorium, neatly stacked.

"All right," Harriet said. "Give me the pistol. Ben, you and I will go around to the Dorium. The rest of you, take the blasters and cover us. If we can get the Dorium without being noticed, we'll do that. If not, I'll signal for a diversion. Use the blasters and light them up."

"We'll shoot and move, make it feel like there's twenty of us," Jones said.

Harriet nodded. "Here we go."

"Hey!"

Ben turned and saw Val Minos staring at them. The smuggler grinned. "We have company, boss!"

"Shit!" Harriet fired at Minos and missed. Then a barrage of fire erupted from the Raptors.

Ben and the others ducked behind a container as hell flew around them.

"OK, plan B," Harriet said. She put her blaster around the corner and fired off a couple of shots. "Direct assault. Take them out and get the Dorium."

Eric started to fire, but a fresh volley sent him cringing back to cover before he could shoot. "Is there a plan C?" he asked. "Cause Plan B sucks."

Ben looked around for some way to help. They were pinned down, and there were too many enemies. The Raptors would flank them soon and then it would be over. They only had three blasters among them. Levi was crouching below Harriet as if he had a reckless bull rush in mind. Brave and certainly Mosley's style, but more likely to get him killed than accomplish anything.

More fire came from the next container over. For a terrifying second Ben thought they'd been flanked already, but it was Jones lighting up the Raptors from a new position. Somehow she'd crossed the gap to new cover. Spreading out would protect their flank, and it sounded like she actually managed to hit a couple of them. Ben grimaced. Jones was tough as hell, but she could only buy them a few extra moments.

He could think of only one thing. Get the Dorium. Ben opened his gem and dropped his implant to 80. He shuddered briefly as the Aurora's familiar effects overtook him, the energy of the room brightening his vision and sending his heart rate soaring with adrenaline. He could see shots from the Raptors' plasma guns like thin trails of light, could read the balance of the fight in the room's energy.

Ben leaped from cover and made straight for the Dorium. Immediately he drew fire from at least five different directions. Ben's heightened awareness and Aurora-boosted speed allowed him to dodge and keep moving forward. His path took him close to a Raptor who was too slow to react. Ben knocked him out and kept going.

Harriet and the others upped their rate of fire and fanned out, taking out a handful of the Raptors. Levi tackled an enemy from behind and took his blaster. He leaped behind a crate and started shooting.

Ben almost made it to the Dorium. He was less than five meters away when Tiro and two others closed up around it. They drew together and fired at Ben, forcing him to alter course and dive to cover. Ben cursed as he hunkered down. He hadn't even managed to get himself a blaster.

His distraction allowed the others to move closer and establish a better position. They'd managed to pick off a few more of Garrison's crew. Ben hadn't made it, but he bought them time and space. They might actually be able to get the Dorium after all.

Just as he had the thought, more Raptors came running from the hangar next door.

"Load this shit up and get to the dropships," Garrison shouted between shots. "VESA can go to hell, we're getting out of here."

He and the first Raptors kept firing while the others finished repacking the boxes and carrying everything to the next hangar. The *Badger*'s crew tried to move in, but the Raptors kept up a steady barrage of plasma. In minutes, Garrison's crew had cleared out, risking a few stray shots from the next hangar over before sprinting away.

Ben swore. They'd managed to survive and actually had the Raptors on the run, but Garrison was about to bug out. Restrictions or not, he wasn't one to just sit idle while somebody came at him. He'd blow off VESA and their efforts at quiet diplomacy, shoot his way out of here if he had to. They had to get that Dorium now, before Garrison got to the dropships.

Harriet and the others emerged cautiously as the enemy fire stopped. They swept the area. The Raptors were gone and hadn't left a single piece of equipment behind.

"Come on!" Harriet shouted. She sprinted toward the door leading to the next hangar. Eric, Jones, and Levi followed close behind. Ben recovered a gun from one of the fallen enemies, determined not to be without a weapon this time. He chased after them, his Aurora still humming at 80 percent.

Ben caught up to the others just as Eric and Jones were ducking inside, with Levi and Harriet giving cover from the door. Ben skidded to a stop beside Harriet.

"Take the left," she said. "Mosley, go!"

Ben turned his blaster into the hangar and started firing. Levi ran in and took up cover behind an information console. Eric and Jones almost five meters were farther in, behind a low wall.

In the brief glimpses he got between shots, Ben took in as many details as he could. This hangar was larger than the other. Evidently it was used for receiving and storing incoming cargo. Much of it was full of shipping containers and loader bots. There were even several lines of containers suspended from the ceiling. Empty ones, maybe, or medium-term storage of things that couldn't ship out right away. A set of control consoles lined the far wall, where a lot of the fire was coming from. A group of the Raptors had set up over there to cover their companions. The rest were in position around the two dropships, about halfway to the large exit doors.

Plasma flew, and the best Ben could do was squeeze off return shots of his own. This was another direct attack through a pinch point against more Raptors than they'd encountered before. Ben took a deep breath and kept firing, desperately trying to work out how to get to the ships.

Chapter 41

A handful of VESA guards entered the hangar from the opposite door and began firing. Shit, VESA was sending in troops now too? So much for keeping their hands clean and letting the Raptors do all the shady stuff. Evidently VESA had decided the Dorium and Lightbeams were too important to leave to contractors. Ben grimaced. He wished Titan Intel hadn't left this job to contractors.

He ducked back into the hallway as the plasma intensified. They were facing at least ten enemies before. How many were there now? Fifteen? Twenty?

Harriet pointed toward the dropships. "They're clearing out! We have to get in there before Garrison takes off with the Dorium."

Ben peeked around the edge and saw the ships' engines heating up. The Raptors were still loading everything into the ships, but the stacks were dwindling. He wondered if Garrison would leave some of his crew behind. Probably not under usual circumstances, but with heavy Dorium on the line, who knew? And with VESA's guards providing cover, it wouldn't take much to get the last Raptors on board.

Eric and Jones were still pinned down behind a low wall five meters farther in. They'd made good progress getting here, but hadn't advanced much against the guards and Raptors. Garrison had picked a hell of a spot to make a stand.

More plasma fire started coming from above. "They're on the second floor now!" Jones yelled. She and Eric turned their attention to the new threat, while Harriet and Ben concentrated on the enemies at the far side of the hangar. Every now and then Harriet squeezed off a shot at the dropships, but they were having no effect. The ships weren't completely loaded yet, but it couldn't be much longer.

Harriet leaned around the corner and fired three quick blasts into the room, taking out one Raptor and wounding another. She ducked back to safety just as return fire poured through the doorway.

Ben put his blaster around the door frame and fired blind, then risked a look. Jones was by herself at the low wall. For a sickening moment Ben thought Eric had been hit, but then he spotted him behind some containers, firing at the VESA guards on the opposite wall. Ben had no idea how he'd gotten that far. He was under cover for now, but the enemy was pouring on the fire so Eric couldn't risk a run at the ship. The guards and Raptors were overwhelming them. Even if they held position it wouldn't do any good. Garrison was going to leave AMRI and take the precious Dorium with him.

"We're cut off here," Harriet yelled over the din of blaster fire. "Let's try to get around the hangar, come at them from the other side."

"No time!" Ben yelled. At least one ship's engines had started. The other couldn't be far behind. He blew out a breath. Now or never. He jumped through the door and fired at the nearest Raptors, then ran along the wall to the right. He got to cover behind some equipment but didn't plan on staying there. He had to keep moving.

"Dammit Ben, what are you doing?" Harriet yelled behind him.

Ben kept going along the wall, moving from cover to cover, staying just ahead of the plasma fire each time. He didn't see any way of getting any closer to the ship, still a good hundred meters away. It was out in the open, no cover within thirty meters. He'd be gunned down before he even made it ten steps. What had he been thinking?

He fired blind again, jumped across five meters of space to more cover. He couldn't keep this up for long. Maybe he'd create a distraction and allow one of the others to head for the ship. He looked back toward the door, saw them still in position. Even with his risky move, they couldn't get clear. There was just too much opposition.

Ben risked another glance toward the ship to get his bearings then noticed his cover was a small cargo loader—not too different from Novalink's miner bots he'd driven back on Titan. They weren't exactly built for speed but had a lot of power to haul large, heavy cuts of ore. Ben smiled at the memory of racing them with his coworkers on slow days. Not a bad way to go out, he thought. Definitely better than just sitting there getting shot at.

Ben put a palm against the loader and toggled the hatch open with ease. He peeked around, squeezed off a handful of blasts toward the heaviest enemy fire, then jumped into the loader. He sealed the door, got his bearings, and activated the controls. Then he floored it.

Plasma fire lit up his world as soon as he was inside, but he was safe for now. These cargo bots weren't blast-proof, but they were built tough, with thick hulls, and would resist more than a few shots. He turned toward the ship. The fire fight outside was making it hard to see.

He found the windshield controls right where he expected them, and dialed up the window tinting until they blocked the worst of the blasters' light. Much better. The closest ship was just fifty meters away now, and he was heading straight for it. He didn't know how much cargo the Raptors had loaded already, but the ramp was still down so he had some time.

With Ben drawing so much attention, Harriet was suddenly in the clear. All the Raptors and VESA guards were blasting the hell out of that cargo loader and the idiot inside it, driving like a madman toward the ship.

"Come on!" Harriet yelled to Eric and Jones. They ran after the cargo loader, darting from cover to cover and shooting everything they saw. A few Raptors returned fire, but most stayed focused on the immediate danger to the ships. Apparently their orders were to get the Dorium off-planet at all costs.

Harriet noticed a VESA guard on the second level pulling the pin on a grenade. She gunned him down, and the grenade clattered to the floor and dropped to the level below, exploding and taking out two Raptors.

That guy wasn't the only one bringing out the big weapons, though. Harriet glanced around as they ran and saw several VESA guards throw grenades. She fired at a few and hit at least one. Jones saw the threat, too, and took out two more. There was no way to get them all. A volley of grenades joined the plasma fire converging on the loader. Most missed, but two exploded right beside the loader and rocked it off course. It skidded and spun, stopping just forty meters from the ship's loading ramp, the left side caved in and smoking.

"Stop!" Harriet cried to the others. "Cover me and keep those grenades off the loader!"

Jones took up position behind a wall of containers and started firing. Eric advanced three more meters and ducked behind a second loader. He threw a grenade of his own at the nearest VESAs on the second floor, then they both concentrated their blasters on the far wall. They'd made a dent in their enemies' numbers, and suppressed the worst of the hostile fire for now.

Harriet kept going, trusting her teammates and their skills. She sprinted across the open area toward the ship, hoping she was quick enough—and lucky enough—to make it.

Inside the loader, Ben's head was swimming, ears ringing. He was on the floor. Seatbelt next time, he thought. He shook his head to clear it. Had to get to the ship.

He pulled himself up and looked out the windshield, which was thankfully still intact. No ship. No no no no no, too late! Then he realized his loader was facing the near wall, not the hangar exit. He must've spun when the blast—grenade? bomb?—when the whatever-it-was hit him and rocked his world. He looked left, then right. There it was, less than forty meters away out his right window. Ramp still down, engine still powering up. It couldn't be long.

Ben got into his seat, pushed the starter. The loader was in bad shape and half the indicator lights were out or blinking, but its engine fired up. He saw a figure out his window, running toward him. Harriet! She'd come to help but was crossing a totally clear area with enemies all around. A blast hit her in the leg and she went down. She struggled up, fired at her attacker and gunned him down. She shot two more then fell back down.

Ben slammed the pedal to the floor and crossed the twenty-five meters between them. He stopped beside her just as several plasma blasts crashed against the loader's side. With the loader blocking the bulk of the enemy fire, Ben had a few seconds to get to his friend. He opened the door, jumped out, and helped her up. Harriet dropped her blaster as he shoved her into the loader. He put a foot in then felt a searing pain tear through his left arm. The damn Raptors had already repositioned. He screamed and tumbled forward into the loader as more fire lit up the door frame.

Harriet grabbed Ben's blaster and fired twice, dropping the guy who had hit him, then sealed the door. "You OK?"

"Arm," Ben grunted. "Got me in the arm."

"Let me see," Harriet said.

"No time. Ships." Ben said. He waved her off then sat up. It hurt like hell, but he was still clearheaded. Plasma burned like a mother but usually did its damage right away. The heat cauterized wounds, so you wouldn't bleed out. If a shot didn't kill or maim you right away, you'd probably be OK. At least that's what they said in the holos. He hoped it was true. It seemed like he could still move his arm. Harriet looked OK too—that blast must've just grazed her leg. He looked at her and she confirmed it, then shouted "Let's go!" Time to get to the dropships and get what they came for.

Ben called up the reverse camera then floored it. They accelerated backward toward the ship. The ramp was still down. They were going to make it. Almost there…

BAM!

Another grenade blast rocked the vehicle. Not a direct hit but enough to knock them off course. They shot past both ships as Ben struggled to straighten them out.

"You missed!" Harriet yelled.

Ben kept the pedal down, following their new course, still concentrating on the reverse camera.

"Ben, what are you—"

Harriet's question was cut off as the loader slammed a wall of monitors that the VESA guards had been using for cover. They tried to jump clear, but Ben and Harriet came too fast. A small explosion shook the loader as the wall of monitors crashed and debris flew in every direction.

Ben recovered quickly and opened the door. One guard stumbled away from the crash, close enough that even Ben couldn't miss. He took the guy out with a point-blank shot then jumped out and swept his blaster from side to side. It looked like the loader or explosion had got the rest of the enemies in the immediate area.

Harriet tackled him as plasma fire from the second floor tore through the air. They ducked behind the loader, and just before they reached safety Ben glimpsed Eric and Jones advancing toward the dropships slowly under heavy fire. The Raptors were making them work for it, but they were making progress. Maybe Ben's stunt helped after all. He hadn't seen any other guards enter the hangar, and the enemy fire was a little less intense now. A little. Maybe. Not that it mattered if they couldn't get to the ship soon.

Harriet leapt out toward one of the fallen VESA guards nearby, risking exposure to get herself a new blaster. Ben saw what she was doing and fired off a few shots, trying to keep the enemies pinned down.

"I'm making nine enemies left," Harriet said as she returned. She winced as she adjusted position behind the loader, the wound in her leg giving her some pain. "Just two guards left up on the second floor, and seven down here. Three VESA guys by that wall," she pointed right, "and four Raptors holding position around the ship."

Ben peeked around the loader. The four by the ships were staying put, content to hold position rather than maneuvering to try to take them out. Not good.

Harriet read his mind. "They're almost ready to bail," she said. "We have to move now."

Ben peeked into the loader. "Looks like this still works," he said.

"That move was crazy before, no way it works a second time," Harriet said. "They'll see it coming a mile away."

"I'm counting on it," Ben said, as he leaned forward into the cabin. "Cover me!" He stretched all the way across the seat with legs sticking out the side. Plasma crashed against the opposite window as he worked the controls, this time turning off the manual override and giving control back to the AI. Harriet didn't know what he was up to, but she gave him cover fire. What else could she do?

Ben set parameters as well as he could, knowing the bot would be programmed to avoid collision with the ships. He worked fast, then slid back out as the loader lurched forward and accelerated to a moderate speed optimized by the AI for a flat, obstacle-strewn surface.

"What the hell—" Harriet started to ask, but Ben waved off her question and pointed down along the wall, past the ruined monitors to a line of containers, small craft, and off-line bots that would give them a bit of cover. "Let's go!" he whispered.

Harriet darted forward as she realized his plan. Ben quickly followed. Fire from the Raptors pummeled the loader as Harriet and Ben repositioned, advancing quickly along the wall parallel to the ship. Harriet signaled for Ben to continue, while she paused behind a crate and focused her blaster up toward the second floor. She had a clear shot at the guards up top, and she was going to take it while they were distracted. Three quick blasts brought both the guards down, leaving just the seven enemies on this floor. Eric and Jones poured on heavy fire from their position, pinning the Raptors in place beside the ship.

Just when it looked like they might make it, the Raptors shot a final volley of plasma, then jumped aboard the first ship. The ramp retracted and the door closed. The engines on both ships brightened. They began to hover, and first one then the other moved toward the main hangar doors and the air outside.

"No!" Ben shouted.

He ran after the ships, ignoring the fire from the handful of VESA guards still occupying the hangar. He saw the bank of controls by the hangar door and began firing desperately at them, to what end he didn't know. The first dropship left the hangar and accelerated upward, climbing at a quick clip and tearing a course toward the atmosphere and space beyond.

In a moment of clarity, Ben remembered his implant. It had been down at 80 all this time. He'd been battling in the bright, unphased by the energy boost and increased sensitivity of the Aurora. And if the implant was still down…

Ben stopped and gathered himself, taking only a split second to focus and harness what power he could find. He gathered it in, down, at his center. He pushed his hand toward the hangar controls and sent energy outward.

Light erupted from his palm. It ignited the air in front of him in a thin trail of blue fire. Across the hangar, the door's controls burst apart in a small explosion. The heavy doors, held aloft by electromagnets, released and crashed to the floor just before the second dropship could get clear. The ship slammed into it with a head-jarring scrape, then tilted sideways as the pilot fought for control.

Ben blinked. He couldn't believe it had actually worked.

Two blasts cut across his vision, causing him to stumble backward. Right, he'd forgot about the VESA guards. Before he could turn, several more shots rang out behind him. He ducked instinctively, then saw it was Harriet and the others leaping to his defense. In moments they'd dispatched the remaining guards.

"How'd you do that?" Harriet asked, eyes wide.

Ben shook his head. "I don't know. I just decided to try it. My implant was still lowered, and I guess it—"

More shots rang out, this time from the ship. Garrison or whoever was at the helm was trying to blast the hangar doors open. They fired several times, but did little more than blacken a few patches of metal. Those doors were made to withstand tornadoes and tank fire, and the dropship was armed only with small guns.

The ship flew backward, and Ben and the others hit the deck just in time to avoid it. It backed up almost to the rear wall, then accelerated forward. Ben held his breath as it flew, hoping like crazy the doors would hold.

The ship hit the doors with a violent crash, smashing them outward. They bent and dented, the whole hangar shook, but they held. The ship lay on the ground, venting smoke and skewed at an odd angle. Even if it had gotten through, Ben wasn't sure it was space worthy anymore.

That wasn't stopping the pilot, who was apparently relentless. The ship righted itself and hovered once more, then backed up again. They were going to take another crack at it, and Ben felt like this time the ship would win. The doors looked bad and had to be terribly weakened by the last collision.

Ben looked around. They couldn't let it get away. Maybe it wouldn't get to space, but it didn't have to. All they had to do was get away from here, away from Ben and the other TI agents. Maybe the Dorium was on the other ship, already on its way up to the *Blue Fin*, but there was nothing else to do. He had to hope it was on this one, and do everything he could to stop it from leaving.

Just as the ship readied for its second try at the doors, Ben spotted them. Shipping containers. Dozens of them, suspended from the ceiling in stacks at least three high. They went right up to the front of the hangar, right above the doors.

Ben gathered his energy and stretched out a hand again, this time aiming up. He released enough energy to burn through the cables that held up the large, heavy cubes. He swept his hand across the whole hangar in a line, left to right, then back, then once more.

The containers fell like a giant's dominoes, one by one in rapid sequence, hitting the ground and spinning, toppling, smashing the floor and one another in a dusty, smoky heap. The dropship had begun to head for the door but stopped just short, this time managing to avoid a crash. Maybe they would have blasted through the doors, but no amount of forceful, stubborn ramming would carry them through three rows of shipping cubes.

"Hell yeah!" Jones said. Ben grinned, a bit out of breath with the effort of channeling so much energy. Harriet clapped Ben on the back. "Way to go. You're gonna have to show me how to do that. Let's hope they're the ones with the Dorium on board."

"Uh, guys…" Eric said.

They all looked at him, then at the ship. It was turning, bringing its small blasters level with them. They leapt away just as the ship began to fire.

Chapter 42

Plasma fire from the dropship cut through the air, sweeping across the hangar. Ben ran from cover to cover, following Harriet. Eric, Jones, and Levi were doing the same on the other side of the hangar, moving parallel to them. The dropship's weapons were powerful, but there was little room for it to maneuver. Ben and the others worked their way closer, counting on cover and the pilot's inability to line up an accurate shot.

Suddenly the ship stopped firing. A metallic scraping echoed through the hangar as it set down, then a hiss and thud when the door opened and the ramp dropped to the floor. Five Raptors poured out, blasters drawn and already firing at anything that moved. Ben and Harriet hunkered down behind a crate, hoping they hadn't been spotted.

"You motherfuckers!" Ben recognized Garrison's deep voice, bellowing his anger. "This is my Dorium. I dare you to come fucking take it."

Then another voice Ben also recognized. "Fan out! You two that way, you to the right. Ben, I told you I would kill you. You think I was joking, man?" Tiro.

Explosions sounded behind Ben as the Raptors fired, trying to draw them out. They didn't know where Ben and Harriet were, but it was only a matter of time.

"We can't sit here," Harriet said, keeping her voice low.

"We're close to the ship. If we can draw them away from the Dorium…" Ben said.

Harriet nodded, then spoke into her gem. "Draw their fire and lead them toward the far end of the hangar. Ben and I are going to make a run on the ship."

Eric and the others didn't respond, but several more blaster shots rang out. They were followed by shouts from the Raptors. The noise moved away from them.

"Go," Harriet said, then leapt out and sprinted toward the ship. Ben ran after her, sweeping his blaster side to side as he ran. Garrison and one of his crew stood outside the dropship. Garrison was opening a crate at the bottom of the ramp while the crew member stood guard.

The guy's eyes went wide as Harriet ran toward him. He managed to get off a single shot. It sailed wide and Harriet fired back, taking him down. Garrison drew his blaster, but Harriet reached him before he could shoot. She barrelled into him and knocked him down. His blaster clattered to the floor. Harriet kicked it out of reach and stood over him, aiming her blaster at his chest.

Ben ran up beside her and took in the scene. Asher Garrison lay on the ground, looking calm and collected. He didn't doubt that Harriet would shoot him, but this wasn't the first time he'd stared at the business end of a blaster. The crate Garrison had been working on lay open. At first Ben didn't recognize what was inside. Metal cylinder, square housing, random-looking hoses and connectors. Where had he seen it before? He stared at it, puzzled, until he saw the box of heavy Dorium on the ground beside it.

It clicked. Garrison had gotten out one of the Lightbeam weapons and was in the process of arming it.

Ben's eyes went wide as he realized what Garrison was up to, and he looked at the Raptor captain with a mixture of shock and horror. Garrison saw the expression on his face and smiled to himself.

"What is it, Ben?" Harriet asked, keeping her gun trained on Garrison.

"A Lightbeam. He was about to mount it on the dropship and blast his way out of here."

Harriet looked at him, and he pointed to the weapon inside the crate. Then he showed her the left blaster at the front of the dropship, which Garrison had begun to detach.

Ben was actually impressed by the idea. He was rigging up the main blaster controls to fire the Lightbeam. He probably planned to just quick-weld it in place. It didn't have to hold up, just stay attached long enough for one shot to blast their way out of there.

"Asher Garrison, you're under arrest," Harriet said, returning her full attention to him.

"You don't have any jurisdiction here," the Raptor said.

"You let me worry about that," Harriet replied through clenched teeth. Before she could say another word, a shot of plasma flew through the air, not five centimeters from her head. She ducked instinctively and turned to see where it had come from.

Ben turned, too, and saw Tiro racing toward them with another Raptor right behind. Ben shot twice, took out the Raptor but missed Tiro. He ducked behind the Lightbeam crate as Tiro returned fire. Ben cursed as he dropped his blaster. It slid out into the open, too far out of reach.

With the split second's distraction, Asher Garrison kicked Harriet in the knee and knocked her sideways. He rolled away and got to his feet before she could recover. He picked up the box of heavy Dorium and swung it at her head. She turned and caught the blow across her shoulder, avoiding the worst of it, but the impact knocked her blaster loose. Garrison pressed his advantage, moving toward her and swinging the box with all his might.

Tiro kept firing, blast after blast, so that Ben wondered if he was trying to shoot right through the crate. All Ben could do was stay down and hope he wouldn't risk shooting Harriet while she was engaged with Garrison.

All at once the shots stopped, and Ben got up cautiously in time to see Tiro swinging his blaster at Harriet's head. She dodged it and took a swing at Tiro. Garrison used the opening to throw a shoulder and force her off balance.

Ben ran in and caught hold of Tiro's blaster before he could swing it again. He tried to wrestle the weapon out of his friend's grip, but Tiro was strong and Ben's arm still hurt from getting shot earlier. Tiro thrust the butt of the gun into Ben's stomach, then brought his elbow across Ben's face.

Ben's vision flashed white as his cheek exploded with pain and heat. He rolled sideways just as Tiro fired his blaster, the plasma searing a deep hole in the floor where he'd been a moment earlier. Ben leaped forward and tackled Tiro before he could get off a second shot, throwing a punch that caught his friend in the eye. They both went down. Tiro dropped the blaster and Ben scrambled on top of him, trying to grab it. Tiro caught his foot and pulled him backward, twisting his knee in the process. Tiro tried to get to the gun, but Ben recovered and tackled him again, taking them both to the ground once more. They rolled several times, taking them farther from the dropship, each man trying to gain an advantage on his opponent.

Meanwhile Harriet battled Garrison. Neither of them was armed, a situation where Harriet normally had a clear advantage. She'd pegged the Raptor captain as more of a leader than a fighter but saw now that she was mistaken. Though in his forties, he was wicked strong. Fueled by her Aurora, Harriet was stronger, but Garrison was fast and savvy enough to keep her from engaging him directly. He wielded the box of Dorium like a shield, parrying her strikes and swinging it in wide arcs to keep her off balance.

Harriet feinted to the right, then pivoted and slipped inside his guard. She caught him with a hard uppercut that knocked him backward. She kept after him, pressing close, trying to get inside his reach. Garrison left her an opening and she went for it but saw too late that he was drawing her in. He stepped backward and grabbed her arm then jerked sideways to pull her off balance. With his left hand he thrust the box into her ribs with crushing force, knocking her into the crate with the Lightbeam weapon. She stumbled, fell to one knee. Garrison struck again, bringing the box backward across her face.

She fell onto her back, then rolled toward Garrison as he followed up the attack. She caught him by both legs and swept her left leg up and around his waist, then twisted the other way and brought him down across her body. He crashed to the floor, face down. Harriet maintained the roll, letting their momentum carry her around, rising to her knees with Garrison's leg still held in her arms. She gripped his lower leg with both hands and bent his knee at a terrible angle. Garrison groaned as she turned and pressed, straining his knee and hip. She leaned in, hard to the right, twisting, feeling Garrison's sinews growing taught against her.

Garrison twisted his body and kicked, jerking Harriet sideways. The sudden motion destroyed his knee, tearing his ligaments with a sickening pop. The move was unexpected. It caught Harriet by surprise and broke her grip on his leg. Garrison whipped the box of Dorium toward her face, fueled by rage and pain. It caught Harriet across the bridge of her nose. She fell backward, nose pouring blood, and smacked her head against the floor. Her vision went fuzzy. She shook her head to clear it, but then Garrison was on her, swinging the box again. He brought it down onto her forehead, then hit her once more for his ruined knee.

Garrison screamed in rage, tears streaming from both eyes as he stood. His knee was hot, burning, tight already with swelling, and his lower leg was numb. He stood on one foot, unable to put any weight on his left leg. He did what he had to do, gave up his knee to win. Knees could be repaired, he'd be back to normal in a few days. But it still fucking hurt. He spat on Harriet's body. She messed his knee up. He picked up the blaster she'd dropped, staggered up into the dropship, and found the med kit just inside the door. He put two shots of painkillers into his knee. In seconds the pain subsided, and he limped back down the ramp. It was time to finish this shit.

With his implant down at 80, Ben's Aurora hummed, fueling him with energy and focus. It was the only thing keeping him in the fight. Between getting shot and the energy he'd already expended in the firefight, and the ass-kicking Tiro had handed him yesterday, he was nearly spent. Ben wished he'd turned the thing down more, but Tiro wasn't giving him any openings.

Their fight had carried him and Tiro away from the dropship. Twice Tiro had taken Ben down—he'd always been the better grappler—but both times Ben had eluded him and gotten back to his feet. Blood trickled down Ben's left cheek, warm and thick, where Tiro had caught him with the elbow. His eye was nearly swollen shut. Tiro was favoring his ribs on his left side. Ben didn't remember where Tiro's blaster was, and he hoped Tiro didn't either. In any case they were fighting too furiously for either of them to stop and think about it.

Ben took a punch from Tiro, rolled with it, and stepped forward. The move brought him inside Tiro's guard, and Ben struck fast, catching Tiro in the chest. His friend staggered backward, and Ben followed with a lightning-quick combo of punches, left-right-left. The first two connected, but Tiro ducked under the last one and landed an uppercut right to Ben's chin.

Ben staggered backward, vision swimming, but Tiro closed the distance and pressed his advantage. He punched Ben in the stomach then kicked him again in the ribs. He kept coming, stomped the inside of Ben's knee, dropping him to the ground, then swung a left hand and landed a blow to Ben's temple. He followed that with a knee to Ben's face that toppled him backward. Ben sprawled onto the floor, staring up at the ceiling.

"I told you I'd kill you, Ben." Tiro stood over him and kicked him in the ribs. Ben grunted as the blow knocked the wind out of him and delivered a sharp, sudden pain to his side. His next breath wheezed and brought pain so intense he nearly passed out. He heard Tiro walk away. Ben rolled over and got to his hands and knees. Tiro returned, holding the blaster he'd dropped.

"I gave you every chance to leave this alone. Every fucking chance. Now I have to shoot you. And look. Look around." He gestured to the hangar, which was shot to hell, smoking in a dozen places, and strewn with broken shipping cubes. "All this and we're still gonna get away. You could've joined us. You could've left us alone and gone to live somewhere else. Anything. But you came back. All you did was throw your life away." He jerked his head backward, toward the dropship. "For what? For that Intel bitch?"

Ben gritted his teeth and glared at Tiro. "For Titan. For me."

He jumped forward and slapped Tiro's blaster away. He caught his friend by surprise and brought his fist backward across Tiro's nose, feeling the crunch of cartilage as he broke it. He punched with his other hand and drove Tiro backward into the ground. Ben leapt on top of him, straddled his chest, every movement agony as his cracked ribs twisted and bounced and made breathing like inhaling fire. He struck once, twice, poured all his energy and more into the attack, drawing and channeling the ambient energy of the room and his own focused rage.

The third hit knocked Tiro unconscious, and Ben stood, doubled over with the pain in his side. He picked up the blaster and ran toward the dropship. The fighting there had stopped. There was no movement. Ben gasped as he saw Harriet lying on the floor, motionless on her back. "Harriet!" He ran faster, ignoring the protests of his abdomen. His only thought was his friend. He had to get to her. She had to be alive.

Asher Garrison shuffled down the ramp, intent on the crate with the Lightbeam weapon. When Ben yelled he looked up. Ben saw him too late to react.

Garrison lifted the blaster casually and shot Ben in the chest.

Ben jolted upright as a dart of light and pain tore through his abdomen. He took two faltering steps forward and fell on his face. He rolled over, back against the floor, already growing pale and cold. He struggled to remain conscious as Asher Garrison set to work on the Lightbeam.

The Raptor captain worked efficiently, prepping the weapon and attaching it in minutes to the dropship's left gun mount. He paused to check his work. The ship's small plasma cannon lay beside him trailing loose wires. The Lightbeam was too big and he'd done the welds quickly, but everything looked solid enough. Maybe it would hold for ten shots, maybe two. All they needed was one. He triple checked the wiring, even though he was plenty confident in that part. Garrison gave it another once-over, then nodded to himself. It would do.

He hobbled past Ben over to Tiro and swatted the younger man a couple of times. Tiro came to, then sat up. "You got your ass kicked, kid," Garrison said. "Let's go."

Tiro followed him to the dropship, glancing at Ben on the ground. Ben was still alive, it looked like. Maybe. He couldn't tell. Ben's eyes were glassy and unfocused, and it was hard to tell if he was breathing. There wasn't much blood. Anyway, he wasn't getting up. Neither was that Intel lady, whoever she was. Garrison knocked her out cold. She lay on the floor in an odd, twisted position.

Garrison sent Tiro into the dropship to fire up the engines. He paused beside the Lightbeam and opened a compartment. He chose a sphere of heavy Dorium from the box still at his feet, put it into the weapon, and closed it up. A green light on the weapon's inner lining told him it was armed. Garrison shrugged. Guess there wasn't much else to it. He grinned to himself. This was going to be fun. Garrison closed the box with the remaining Dorium and shuffled aboard his ship, half-dragging his injured leg. In minutes the engines were humming, running up to full power.

Eric and Jones ran up to Ben just as the dropship's ramp closed. They saw the gaping wound in his chest. Levi was right behind them, hand clutched to his side against a bleeding wound. "Damn. Poor kid was a hell of a fighter," he said.

Ben was alive for now, but had minutes left, if that. They went to see if Harriet was any better. They'd lost. Eric swore. They'd eliminated the other Raptors, given Harriet and Ben a clean path to the Dorium, but it still hadn't been enough. Garrison was getting away.

All they could do now was save Harriet, Ben, too, if they could, but it didn't look likely. Regroup and try again. Live to fight another day.

Eric assessed Harriet. She was unconscious and her forehead was badly swollen on one side, but her breathing was normal. She had no other obvious wounds. Her pulse was faint but steady. Eric looked up warily at the dropship, at the incongruous weapon fixed to its side. They couldn't see inside the cockpit, but the ramp was staying up. If Garrison had seen them, he'd decided he didn't care.

Still, better to get Harriet out of sight. Just in case.

Eric and Jones lifted her, careful to support her head. Eric winced with the effort and the pain from an injury to his arm. They carried her the ten meters or so to the loader bot Ben had crashed earlier, which was on its side but somehow still intact despite taking heavy fire and more than one grenade blast. Eric stumbled the last few steps, quads and calves burning, but they managed to set Harriet down gently on the floor. Levi was right behind him, dragging Ben by his arms. He wasn't going to make it, but they weren't about to leave him behind.

They laid Ben beside Harriet then sat down beside them behind the downed loader bot. Eric leaned back against the thing and closed his eyes. He heard and felt the low rumble from the dropship as its engines engaged.

Chapter 43

Life was hot. And cold.

Life was hot and cold and hot again—blood and love and purpose fighting the tug of emptiness, the hole seared into him, the creeping impulse to surrender. Desire, determination, ambition stood firm against the tide of dying, of resignation and regret. The stalemate endured for eons, or nanoseconds. Everything burned and chilled together. Then slowly turned. Life was hot and cold. Hold on. Just hold on. Win, damn it.

Ben moved. Slow, not exactly steady. A centimeter at a time. He reached into his pocket. Fumbled, grasped, came up empty. Failed. Tried again. His fingers closed around his gem.

Asher Garrison's dropship lifted off the floor, tilting with the added weight of the Lightbeam. It hovered in the air, pivoted to face the hangar doors and the heap of debris blocking it. Garrison pointed the ship in the right general direction, gripped the hastily rigged controls, and fired.

The Lightbeam erupted in a flash of heat and light. A roar filled the hangar as the blast incinerated the air and sent it rushing outward. Inside the dropship, Garrison and Tiro shielded their eyes against the white blaze in front of them. Behind the overturned loader bot, Eric and Jones and Levi winced and huddled close as hot air swept past them in a violent swirl. They did what they could to shield Ben and Harriet beside them.

The light stopped abruptly. The whoosh of air faded after a few seconds. There was a gaping round hole where the center of the hangar doors had been, its edges defined by distorted, molten metal. It was more than large enough for the dropship to pass through. What was left of the fallen shipping cubes lay in cooling lumps of material to either side of where the beam had passed. Nothing remained in the wake of the beam.

The same was true of the landscape beyond the hangar doors. Trees, buildings, rocks, everything ahead of the doors had all been pierced through. A neat little hole had been punched in the horizon itself. Beyond the horizon even. Frantic, squawking voices on the comms told Garrison and Tiro that the blast had gone into low orbit and beyond. Ships in the vicinity were yelling about a dangerous near-miss from Earth and wanted to know what the hell was that?

Asher Garrison grinned and nudged the ship forward, through the opening and into the field beyond the hangar and the wide open sky above. He was out, the hard way. He'd been carving his own path his whole life, and now he had done it literally with the baddest weapon around. On his own ship. Hell, on his own *dropship*. Nobody could mess with him, and anybody who tried got what was coming to them.

That last thought made him pause. Better make sure.

Garrison slowed the ship to a hover a few hundred meters off the ground. He'd seen those last three idiots trying to recover their friends' bodies. He didn't have to do anything, they weren't going to follow him. But he didn't like leaving loose ends. You never knew when something could come back to bite you. Plus his knee was swollen and was gonna hurt like a mother when those pain meds wore off. He was still pretty pissed about that.

Garrison swung the ship back toward the hangar.

"What are you doing?" Tiro asked.

"Making sure we aren't followed," Garrison said, teeth gritted and a hard edge to his voice. "Better not to leave loose ends." He picked a spot on the roof, angling down toward where he thought the dropship had been sitting. This wasn't going to be precise, it might take a few tries. It would be fun.

"You got the stomach for it?"

Tiro pressed his mouth into a line, narrowed his eyes. He felt bad about Ben, he really did. But he'd given his friend enough chances, and it was already done. Tiro nodded.

"Good. I've been saying you're a tough SOB." Asher Garrison pulled the trigger.

A bright lance bisected the hangar from floor to ceiling, less than fifty meters from Eric and Jones and Levi. They turned, shielded their eyes against the flash, and put their backs to the heated air rushing over them. The Lightbeam cut downward at a steep angle, tearing through a stack of shipping cubes and melting a five-meter hole in the floor.

"What the hell?" Eric asked. He looked at Jones with wide eyes, then up. "Shit!"

Above them a clean, broad, perfectly round hole in the ceiling revealed the dropship. "He's trying to take us out," Jones said.

A second blast tore through the hangar, this time a bit farther away.

"We have to—"

There was a loud groan and Jones looked down. "Ben!"

Ben was awake somehow, pale and taking shallow, quick breaths. He was struggling to sit up.

Eric reached out for him, pressed him back down. "Easy man, easy. How are you alive? Sit still, Garrison's firing at us with a Lightbeam."

Ben shook his head and slapped Eric's hand away. "Stop…him….I…can…stop…him."

Levi put a hand on Ben's shoulder and pressed down. "What the hell are you talking about? We can't let him know where we are?"

"I can stop him," Ben said. His voice was stronger this time. He coughed. A trickle of blood fell from the corner of his mouth.

"Stay down. Hide," Eric said.

"You think that'll keep us safe?" Jones asked. "He's trying to kill us. He'll blow this whole place apart before he lets us go—"

A third blast ripped away the west side of the hangar, exposing a wide swath of the building to the empty flat land beyond. Part of the roof fell in without the wall's support, and another huge section sagged precariously.

"We can't stay here," Levi said. "He'll keep shooting till he gets us."

"You got a better idea?" Eric asked. "Anywhere we go, we'll be slow with these two." He pointed to Ben and to Harriet, who was still unconscious. Ben had his gem out and had activated a program.

"I can…stop him," Ben said again, each word coming with effort and punctuated with several short breaths.

"Ben, it's all right, we'll figure something out," Jones said. "We'll hide or stay beneath cover or…"

Ben shook his head, eyes shut tight, as a fourth blast traced a slow arc around the floor. Much of the hangar's southeast quadrant was on fire now, and pieces of the roof were beginning to fall to the floor.

The floor shook beneath them. Harriet stirred and woke. "What happened?" She shut her eyes tight and shook her head.

Eric gave her the quick version, including how Ben had been shot. Harriet placed a hand on his shoulder. Ben turned, put his hand on top of hers, and gave it a weak squeeze.

"We have to get out of here," she said.

"You can barely move, and we're not leaving Ashley behind," Eric said. "The minute we move, Garrison sees us and turns us to atoms. Our best bet is to hunker down and hide."

Harriet glanced up. "I don't like those odds."

"The odds of making it running are worse."

Ben gritted his teeth and leaned forward. He sat up and got a hand on the ground.

"Ben!" Harriet hissed, "stay down."

"It's OK. I can stop them."

Ben got to his knees, then his feet. Jones pulled at his arm, and he jerked it away. The effort made him fall forward, dropping to one knee, but he regained his balance before going all the way down. That was good. Getting up at all had been a tremendous effort. He wasn't sure if he could do it again. Levi reached out, but Ben slapped his hand away too. "Let me up!" he roared. "I can stop him."

"Let him go," Harriet said.

Ben put a hand on the floor and rose to both feet, slowly, balancing against the overturned loader bot that was still behind them. In his other hand he held his gem, with the implant regulator program opened and the familiar image hovering above it. It showed the implant still holding at 80 percent.

He'd lost some blood and had a hole burned right through his chest. It must've missed his heart, but no way were his lungs working properly. How was he even conscious, much less thinking, standing? It must be the Aurora, Ben realized. With the implant down at 80, it would have been channeling energy into him. Not an overwhelming amount, but apparently enough. What usually came as pain and disorientation was now supplying his body with the energy to keep fighting, to keep striving. He didn't know how much longer he'd have control over it, but time had to be short.

He looked up and saw Asher Garrison's dropship hovering above the hangar. He knew what he had to do. There was only one way, after all. Maybe this was all it had ever been, in the end.

Ben gritted his teeth, ignored the protests from the others, which were already fading as a rush of white noise filled his consciousness. His vision narrowed, everything seemed to move in slow motion. Was he dying? Or just hyperfocused on what had to be done? Either way, best do it now.

Win, damn it.

Ben lifted his gem, touched the holo image, and dropped his implant to zero.

Light exploded into his consciousness. Bright white, all colors at once, from every direction. It burst from within him, a rising pool of heat and light. It was searing and beautiful and altogether too much. A shrieking tempest consumed his mind, drove out all thought or feeling. There was only energy, overwhelming energy that would tear atom from atom, a crushing dynamic tide that burned and drove him down, down, down.

Hold on. Just hold on.

Ben fought, struggled with everything he had. Everything hinged on his ability to hold it, to contain and control the vast energy pouring in. It was the only way. Hold on. Just hold on.

He couldn't hold it. The energy burned, tore, consumed. In seconds it overwhelmed him, wave after wave tossing him about and eating away at his mind and body. The world around him had gone supernova, and Ben was trying in vain to survive. Dimly he became aware that he was ablaze, his limbs and eyes and hair radiating energy in all directions. He'd become part of the chain reaction, and nothing would stop it now. It was too much. His conscious mind began to dissolve. Feeling and thought faded. He was energy, and energy was…

The River.

Don't hold it, a voice told him. It was Harriet's, but sounded far away. *Channel, direct. Don't hold it. Remember the River.*

Ben stopped fighting as Harriet brought him back to himself. He relaxed. Let it come. The light poured in, then through, then streamed out. Down, down to the center, spinning, collapsing, accelerating, then back out, away, on down the River. The blaze washed through unhindered, blurring the lines between himself and the world with its relentless energy. Blurring the lines, but still he was here. He was Ben. He didn't have to hold, fight, conquer the light. He only needed to endure it, to stay in it and remain himself. Let it flow through you. You flow through it. Swim in the deep.

The energy moved in him, following the natural paths established by thousands of generations of human evolution. It came to broken places in his center, dry places where the flow had stopped, and cared nothing for them. The River was not so easily resisted. It leapt the severed connections and knit them back together in its wake. Moving. Restoring. Healing.

In that moment Ben could swim and see. He perceived his surroundings like a bright tapestry, balls of light and racing photons, streaks and crackles and looping arcs. Eric and Jones and Levi and Harriet behind him, his friends, his love for them somehow amplifying their presence. The fallen VESA guards and Raptors still giving off faint light. The bright points of plasma weapons, hot cores visible to Ben like a constellation of deep red stars. Beyond was the machinery of the hangar and the rest of AMRI, each device or system with its own signature of energy, and beyond that the Earth itself, its cities like Luxor, its rivers and forests and jungles, the ships in orbit above, the Dyson Stations beaming energy to receivers on the ground, energy racing from point to point in the Array, all the way back to the Sun.

In a flash Ben glimpsed the web of humanity throughout the solar system, world bound to world by frail filaments of energy, the Dyson Arrays and the endless entanglements that made up the Quill. It was so fragile, so powerful and sure, all at once. He saw Titan, *felt* Titan, grasped its place in the web and his own place too. A place that was threatened now by the huge darkness looking down on him and his friends from three hundred meters up.

The Lightbeam weapon on the dropship stood out not like a blaze of energy but a void. A black hole, a boulder in the River, resolute and impenetrable. When it opened it would unleash hell, but now it was the darkest, quietest entity in the universe.

Asher Garrison fired again, the Lightbeam jumping to life, dazzling white destruction filling the whole right side of Ben's vision. The black hole was a white emitter now, outshining the Sun. Ben was vaguely aware of hot wind whipping at his clothes, rushing over his skin, and the sound of Harriet shouting something to him as the light went out again. He was aware, too, of the ship pivoting overhead, of the void turning toward him. He'd been seen. Somehow he was aware of the malicious intention of the people inside, Garrison and his friend Tiro, directing their focus and energy toward him with the grim goal of obliteration.

But Ben was in the River. The River was in him. He turned his face toward the void up above, felt the energy swirl inside him. Channeling, directing, gently guiding. Down, down to the center, spinning, churning, then back out.

Ben reached out his hands, opened his eyes, and unleashed it all.

A blast of light raced from his palms and slammed through the dropship with incredible force. The energy accelerated the ship backward and up even as it stripped away its hull and incinerated the components within. The torrent of energy was nearly as powerful as the Lightbeam itself. The dropship cleaved in two, and its remains fell in two smoking arcs several kilometers away.

Roaring filled Ben's ears, buzzing in his brain, heat against his face, and light, always light, the world a bright star and Ben at its center. The River. Ben found his gem and turned down the flow, brought his implant back up to 100.

The effect was immediate and jarring. After the godlike perception he'd just experienced, Ben now felt deprived viewing the world through normal eyes. Everything seemed eerily quiet, though if he listened he could hear plenty of sound in the ruined hangar. His eyesight was dim, as if he were viewing things through a heavy screen. He shook his head to try to clear it. Already the memory of the Aurora's intense sensory input was fading, and normal began to reassert itself.

"What the hell was that?" Eric was asking.

"Are you—Oh my God," Harriet said at the same time, putting her hand to her mouth. She was looking wide-eyed right at Ben's chest.

"I'm OK," Ben said. "I used the Aurora. What?"

He put a hand to his chest and looked down where Harriet was looking, then drew back in surprise. Beneath the tear in his shirt, the charred hole in his chest was gone. In its place was new skin, firm and bright. He put his hand back slowly, ran his fingers over the pale, pink flesh. The pressure of his fingertips felt normal against his chest. "Oh wow. The energy…I guess the energy healed me."

"You were almost dead. You're telling me you healed yourself?" Eric asked.

"I don't think so. Not consciously, at least. But the energy that came in, it must have done something. The same thing Harriet did when she fixed my implant, just on a bigger scale."

"I'll say. Your other wounds are gone too." Eric gestured to Ben's cheek, which had been puffy and scarred before. Ben touched his face. It wasn't tender. Smears of dried blood remained, but the skin was unbroken and his face was no longer swollen.

"You shot Garrison's dropship," Jones said. "I didn't see a weapon, but the blast was bright and incredibly powerful. Was that…?"

"Yeah. That was the Aurora too. I turned my implant all the way off. Took it down to zero. There was…a lot of energy."

"I thought doing that would kill you."

"It almost did. I had to control it. Direct it. Which was really learning to move in it, to coexist with it."

"How'd you know you could do it?" Eric asked.

Ben shrugged. "I didn't. But there was no other way. I had to try."

Chapter 44

Asher Garrison's Lightbeam attack leveled AMRI's hangar and several of the nearby facilities. All hands were called to assist with cleanup and putting out fires—literal, in the case of burning structures and equipment, or figurative, in the case of the newly tense relationship between AMRI and the American Commonwealth. Nobody noticed the five survivors of the attack moving west into the forest. If they had noticed, few would have cared.

Ben, Harriet, Eric, Levi, and Jones hiked to the wreckage of the dropship, moving with the deliberate urgency of injured people navigating a life-or-death crisis. Which, in fact, they were. Harriet battled nausea and dizziness the whole way, sure signs of a concussion, while Eric gritted his teeth against the pain in his back that got worse with every step. Jones tried not to show she was limping. Levi was pale and favored his left side. Only Ben traveled without visible difficulty, though he was bone tired after the day's events.

They found the rear section of Garrison's ship five kilometers from the northwest edge of AMRI. It was barely recognizable. Most of the metal and ceramic structures had been melted and fused together in odd, amorphous combinations, or vaporized entirely. The engines were obliterated. Almost nothing within it was salvageable. The exception was five boxes, each built to withstand intense lasers, plasma bombardment, and other high-energy encounters. Even so, they were badly dented and burned.

Inside them were ninety-nine spheres of enriched Dorium without so much as a scratch. Everyone carried a box.

The forward portion of the ship was two klicks to the south. Precious little was left of the cockpit. The powerful Lightbeam weapon lay in a twisted heap, its aperture folded upon itself, the rest of it torn apart or badly dented or just plain gone. The Dorium housing had broken open, and the heavy Dorium that had powered the device rolled away. It took them an hour to locate it. They found it more than ten meters away, at the edge of a thick patch of blackberry bushes. All hundred samples of heavy Dorium were accounted for.

There was no sign of Asher Garrison or Tiro at either site.

"Vaporized," Eric said. "That was a hell of a blast."

Ben nodded and looked away, his throat tight and stomach cold and hollow. Something warm brushed against his hand. He looked down as Harriet's fingers gripped his own, lacing them together, squeezing, reassuring, understanding. Ben gave her a weak smile and was surprised to see tears welling in her eyes too.

"You didn't have a choice," she said. Ben nodded. He knew. It still hurt.

By a stroke of luck, the front third of Garrison's dropship crashed less than a kilometer from where Jones had set the *McInnes* yesterday. Her gem told them it was still there, and sure enough they found it right where it was supposed to be. Ben and the others all wore huge grins when they spotted the faded black hull through the foliage. It had served them well, carrying them across a huge swath of two continents. More importantly, it meant they could stop and rest. They stowed the Dorium and took the bird up to retrieve Krista and Captain Lawrence.

The huge crater was still undisturbed. Eric checked on Krista and the captain while the others stood guard. With Ben's help he released them from the crash foam and got them aboard the *McInnes*. Jones hightailed them out of there before any local authorities came by. They decided to fly north for a couple of hours then stop to rest and regroup. Eric checked on Krista and Captain Lawrence frequently during the flight. Their injured, unconscious companions had a long road to recovery, but they were stable.

Jones landed them in a lonely patch of forest east of Lake Michigan, where they stretched their legs and prepared a hasty meal. As night fell, the five of them relaxed, alternately dozing and eating and recalling the events of the past two days. More than once Ben looked up instinctively, and each time he chuckled at himself.

There was nothing to fear up there anymore. The *Blue Fin* left Earth's orbit shortly after he blasted Garrison's dropship. Evidently the local authorities didn't take kindly to a ship that fired a Lightbeam toward the surface, especially when that ship was IDed as a Raptor vessel. Harriet had managed to hack all the surface-to-space communications in the area, and judging from the audio recordings and transcripts, someone on the *Blue Fin* had managed to stall the American Commonwealth and other nations who were demanding that they consent to boarding. When Garrison went down, though, the Raptors didn't hesitate. They bugged out fast on an untraceable course. Someone had assumed command of the *Blue Fin*. Ben's money was on Val Minos or the first mate, the one Tiro called Farrah. He wondered if Jess would do OK under their leadership. Probably so, with her skills. The hollow pit returned to Ben's stomach as he thought of her. Miles and Tiro, too.

Early next morning, Harriet sent word to Special Agent Nichols via the Quill: *Mission accomplished.* Mostly.

"Well done, Agent Adams. How'd Ben Ashley do?"

Harriet looked at Ben as she answered. "All right, sir. He did all right." Nichols nodded and signed off, no doubt ready to respond to what they'd uncovered and find a way to hold VESA accountable.

They still needed transport back to Titan. "I don't think Nichols will be much help there," Harriet said. "He's gonna have his hands full for the next couple of months.

"I'll call Tory," Ben said. He got on the Quill and explained what they needed.

"I'll take care of it," Tory told him. "Stay put for now."

An hour later she got back to them. True to her word, Tory had taken care of everything. There was a private direct-launch point waiting on them in the Caribbean. The *McInnes* was now formally registered in Jones's name. Tory got them new IDs to load on their gems as well as exact coordinates for the launch point. She also, somehow, arranged for local officials to look the other way and not ask too many questions about the ship that had been earthbound for five decades or more and was now jetting offworld. Ben just shook his head when she mentioned that part.

"Thanks, Tory. You're the best," Ben said.

"Yeah, I know," she said.

"She really does," said Axel beside her. "She's going to be insufferable now."

"More insufferable, he means," Dom said.

Ben laughed. "Thank you. All of you. I mean it."

"You're welcome, man. Come see us when you get home."

"I will….Listen, guys. There's something you need to know. Tiro and Miles are dead. Jess is still with Asher Garrison. I tried to talk to them, but I couldn't… They didn't…" Ben choked back a sob, took a breath, and let the words and tears flow. He told them all about Tiro and Jess and Miles, the events since they met the *Blue Fin* in space tumbling out of his mouth in a more-or-less coherent sequence.

The three of them listened in silence. Tory looked away when Ben got to the part at the end, about killing Tiro, and Axel's eyes welled with tears.

"You did what you had to do, man," Dom said. "Can't ask for more than that."

Axel and Tory nodded. "It's hard, I won't pretend like it isn't. But they made their choice. Can't say that I understand it," Axel said. "But it was their choice to stay with Garrison, not yours. And I don't care what they say, I'm not cool being governed by VESA and Raptors."

"How are you?" Tory asked.

"I'm…OK," Ben said. "I'm OK. How about all of you? I've had a day or two to process this already."

"You'll need more than a few days," Axel said. "We will too. We'll get through it though. Hopefully together." His voice was clipped, but Ben detected no hint of anger or malice. Only grief.

Tory sniffled and wiped her eyes. "Well now you have to come back and visit. We lost three friends today. Well, before today, but…you know. We can't lose you too."

"You won't," Ben said. "I promise. I'm heading back to Titan. I'll see you soon."

"See you," Dom said. He terminated the connection. Ben hoped they would be OK.

By midafternoon, the *Rock Badger*'s crew were aboard the *McInnes* and making way for their launch point. The ship's hab ring and engine were parked in orbit. Ben hoped they'd reach it soon. With their replenished supplies and the various medical equipment needed to treat Krista and Captain Lawrence, the small hold was cramped. Ben didn't like the idea of spending even a few hours in such a tight space. Then again, judging by the age of the lander and how long it had been on Earth, Ben didn't have high hopes for the rest of the ship either. He had a feeling they'd be working nonstop to keep a hunk of junk together all the way back to Titan. At least they were going home.

The crushing acceleration of launch was followed by several hours of zero G on their way up to the orbital parking facility. Jones found their ship's hab ring amid the thousands of others docked there and linked up with it as efficiently and quickly as only she could. She pressurized the hab ring and spun it up to one G. The whole process was remarkably smooth. Then they went in to explore.

Ben was pleasantly surprised, as were the others. The *McInnes* was evidently a luxury ship, the hab ring built for comfort and the engine for speed. The exterior of the hab ring practically gleamed in the cold starlight. The interior was nicely appointed and well kept up. It was obviously old, a half century at least, but there were few signs of wear and tear and the space was clean. There were three decks, like the *Badger*, with a well-appointed galley and common areas built for entertainment and business.

"This will do," Jones said, looking around with appreciation.

"Yes it will. The *McInnes*. I like it. A few upgrades— weapons, larger hold—and I think we have ourselves a new flagship. Think the captain will let us keep it?"

Jones smiled. "If he doesn't, he'll have to find himself a new pilot."

The new crew of the *McInnes* strapped into their seats, which were quite secure and comfortable. Jones navigated them to the requisite minimum distance for main engines, then engaged the thrust.

Less than twenty-four hours after Ben killed his friend, and nearly died himself, he stood at the window wall watching the blue-white disc of Earth recede. They were going home.

Ben stared transfixed by the awesome planet, the birthplace of the human race—such a big world with its expansive skies and infusion of life—reduced now to a precious ball suspended in inky darkness. The view would be boring soon, he knew. Right now it was marvelous.

The trip home passed leisurely and without incident. Most of it was indeed boring, but Ben didn't mind boredom after what he'd seen and endured on Earth. He figured Harriet didn't mind it either. They got to know the *McInnes* and took stock of what they might upgrade. They played cards, recovered from their wounds, and caught up on sleep. Jones let Ben fly a few times as they passed through the asteroid belt, swinging close to a few of the rocks to get a feel for the gravity.

"Remember the last time we did this?" Ben asked, glancing up at her from the pilot's seat as they crested the end of a kilometer-wide asteroid.

"Yup." Jones was scanning the sensors, paying close attention to the larger asteroids in the vicinity that might hide an enemy. Nothing happened, but nobody really relaxed until they left the last of the belt behind.

They stayed abreast of the situation back home through daily updates from Special Agent Nichols. Six days into the trip, Captain Lawrence came out of his coma, a bit weakened and confused but otherwise OK. Krista came to three days later. They were grateful for the successful completion of their mission. Lawrence looked over the ship and gave it his approval. They needed a ship anyway, and the money they'd get from Nichols would more than cover the necessary modifications.

Three days after that, Harriet found Ben by the window wall. Their path was taking them past Jupiter, inside Europa's orbit, and he was enjoying the spectacular view of the solar system's largest planet.

"Not boring today, is it?" Harriet said.

"No," Ben said with a half smile. "You can say whatever you want, I'll never get tired of a view like this."

"I'd be sad if you did."

"What's next for you after we get home?" Ben asked. "A little time to recover and relax, I hope."

Harriet laughed. "If you call weeks of debriefing and paperwork relaxing, then sure."

"Ah. Fun."

"You'll find out. They're gonna put you through the ringer too. Especially after what you did with the Aurora."

"That's the beauty of being an independent contractor. They can't fire me. I only have to endure bullshit if I feel like it."

"That's what you think. Nichols is up to his neck in it, denying his ass off about any hint of TI involvement in what went down at AMRI, but of course nobody believes it. He's catching hell from every direction. He'll find a way to pass it on to you guys, believe me."

"I do believe you. What about after the debriefing and all that? It has to end sometime. Any idea where Nichols will send you next?"

Harriet shook her head. "Not really. The needs and missions are always changing. I wouldn't be surprised, though, if he has me trying to track down the *Blue Fin*. There's still a lot of loose ends to tie up, and they're at the center of a lot of it."

"Right. They're still going to have a lot of contacts among the Raptors, and I bet they'll stay on VESA's payroll."

"They'll be in it deeper than ever after the shitstorm they caused on Earth. VESA's having to answer for a lot. They'll find a way to keep Garrison's crew on the hook."

"Yeah. Plus they still have a Lightbeam."

"That's why I think Nichols will put a lot of energy into locating them. He'll want to leverage our prior experience to bring them out into the open as soon as possible."

"They might make it easy on you. If Val Minos is in charge, something tells me he won't be able to lie low for long with such a powerful weapon."

"That's what I'm afraid of. This might turn into an open war, before it's all over."

They were silent for a long moment, then Ben said, "Well if you do catch them, go easy on Jess for me. I don't want to lose any more friends."

"Is she still a friend?" Harriet asked. "After she betrayed you?"

Ben nodded. "She'll always be a friend. Friends hurt each other sometimes. Betray each other, even. I wish…" He had to stop as the next words caught in his throat. He closed his eyes, balled his hands into fists, took two breaths before continuing. "I can forgive her. Ask for her forgiveness too. We ended up on opposite sides, that's all. It could have gone a different way, you know? She'd be here, or I'd be with Garrison. It's nobody's fault."

"She's not innocent, Ben. It was her tech that killed Aaron and Christian and Mike."

"I know, but that doesn't mean she's a bad person. Tiro either. They did wrong. Tiro was trying to kill me in the end. But I can forgive them. I think. I hope I get the chance to tell her that. Or at least try to. It kills me that I won't have that chance with Tiro."

Harriet reached out and took his hand. "They made their choices, and you made yours."

"Yeah. I'd make the same choice again too. But ten years of friendship and memories don't just go away."

"No," Harriet said. "No, I guess they don't."

They stood in silence for a long while, watching Jupiter out the window wall. Wide rusty bands alternated with strips of hazy, bluish white. At this distance some of the larger swirls were barely visible, and of course the great red spot, more than a millennium old and counting. From here the gas giant looked static, unchanging. Eternal. But Ben knew it was ever changing. Swirling. Turning. Seething. Violent convection currents and Coriolis forces churning its gases and clouds endlessly. The River, pooling for a time in this god of a planet, then up, out, and away again. Always moving. Always flowing. The River was eternal, nothing else.

"Speaking of your friends," Harriet said after several minutes, "I overheard Captain Lawrence ask you about them joining his crew. Is that right?"

Ben smiled. "Yeah, it is. He was pretty impressed with Tory getting those credentials for us and helping us get off Earth. I assured him that Dom and Axel could more than pull their weight too. They'll be an asset to Lawrence's team. Assuming they'll go for it. I think they will. It's a good crew. I'm anxious to reconnect with them. I guess it's only been a couple of months, but it feels like a lifetime. There's so much to tell them."

"I know what you mean. What about Simon?"

"Simon…I'm excited to see my brother, but I don't know where I'll start with him. He wasn't aware of everything our crowd was doing. The robberies and things. I'm sure he knows some of it—he isn't stupid, and he saw a little of that before he went off to Harlow. But the port robbery, the Dorium, my arrest…" Ben paused and shook his head. "I don't want him to join us. I want a better life for him. I'm going to come clean with him about everything though. He deserves to know the truth." Ben paused. "I'm nervous about that part, I won't lie."

"Well. If it helps, you saved Titan. That's how the story ends." Harriet turned and took one of Ben's hands in hers. "He'll be proud of you. You were somebody to be proud of even before you got mixed up in all this."

"Thanks. I hope you're right."

Harriet smiled. "I always am. How's it going with the Aurora? I know you've been training on your own. I'm sorry I haven't been able to join you."

Ben waved a hand. "You've been super busy. We all have. It's going well. I'm keeping the regulator back at 90 percent most of the time," Ben said. "I'm working my way toward 80 percent, like you."

"Ninety already? That's impressive. How does it feel?"

"Normal for the most part. Odd at times. The ultrasensitivity comes back now and then, and all the pain that brings, but that's getting less and less. It's the strength that's hard to get used to."

"That will come," Harriet said.

"I know. I still think I'm going to need a new implant when we get home, but it'll be good not to have to rely on it to use my abilities. To be able to draw on the Aurora at will, like you do."

"Don't let it make you cocky. I wouldn't want to have to beat you just to keep you humble."

"I blasted a ship apart. Bring it on."

"A dropship," Harriet said. "Hardly counts."

"You wanna go now?"

"And risk damaging the ship when we're a week out from home? I don't think so."

"That's what I thought," Ben said. He elbowed Harriet playfully in the arm. She slipped her hand into his and leaned against his shoulder. They stood in silence, watching Jupiter slowly pass by.

Eight days later the *McInnes* approached their dock point on Titan, right in the center of the Spine. Ben watched the two spinning cylinders grow larger as they drew near. Ligeia to the left, Kraken to the right.

Acknowledgments

I began writing Archimedes in the summer of 2020, but the ideas behind it began to percolate in the 1990s. Like a lot of teenagers I enjoyed Star Wars, Dragonball Z, and superheroes, and I started dreaming up stories of my own. I never thought of myself as a writer—I was always better at math and hated papers—so the stories just sort of rattled around in my head.

Fast forward twenty-plus years and a couple of career changes. All of a sudden I was a book editor with a master's degree and Ph.D. in religion. Somehow I'd ended up writing a lot over the past two decades, and I'd gotten pretty good at it. I finally decided to write one of those old stories down and see what happened. I made some notes and wrote my first words in August 2020.

Like most books, Archimedes was a labor of love that required substantial persistence to complete. And as with most books, I had plenty of help along the way. I'm grateful for Mary and Zack Rinehart, Amanda Moyer, Chet Sigmon, and Andrew Weitze, who read drafts of all or part of this book. Their helpful suggestions made the book better, and more importantly they encouraged me that the story was worth telling.

Thanks also to Brian Murphy, Abby Mathews, and the whole HappyWriter community. An early class they offered on outlining got me past my first major writing hurdle. It went a long way toward developing the story, filling it with action, and bringing it to life. The support, encouragement, and great advice from my fellow writers in the community has been invaluable.

A huge thank-you to my friend and editor, Susan Cornell. She cleaned up my writing and asked lots of helpful questions, drawing attention to many details and inconsistencies that needed to be resolved. Any errors that remain are my own, but this is a far better book because of Susan's talent and effort.

I'm fortunate to be part of a large and close extended family, and every single one of them played a role in shaping who I am and the stories I tell. I can't begin to acknowledge them individually, but I would like to say thank you to my parents, Judy and David, for instilling in me a love of learning, hard work, and creativity, and to my brothers, Joe and Chet, for years of fun and adventure that have doubtless inspired parts of this story.

Thank you to my three wonderful children, Caleb, June, and Molly, who constantly amaze me with their joy, energy, kindness, inventiveness, and ceaseless questions. I love you, and I'm so proud of you.

Most of all, thank you to my wife Amy. She has always believed in me and encouraged me. She was my first reader, and watching her read and enjoy my book gave me the courage to release it into the world. I love you, Amy. Always.

About the Author

Brian Sigmon is a space adventure daydreamer who decided to start writing his stories down. He loves to read and write fast-paced, entertaining sci-fi that grips you from the first page and doesn't let up. Brian has a Ph.D. in religion and serves on the advisory board of AI Theology, a group dedicated to exploring the intersection of science, technology, and spirituality. He used to write articles on religion until he admitted to himself that fiction is just way more fun. Brian is a book editor, woodworker, sports fan, armchair futurist, and half-decent kids soccer coach. He grew up in North Carolina, spent some wonderful years in Wisconsin, and now lives in Nashville, Tennessee. Connect with Brian and learn about his latest books at briansigmon.com.